WYVERN
AND STAR

WYVERN AND STAR

Sophy Boyle

Published by Palestrina
164 Burbage Road
London SE21 7AG

ISBN: 978-0-9956066-0-9

Book design: Dean Fetzer, GunBoss Books, www.gunboss.com.
Cover design: Mark Ecob, Mecob Design Ltd, www.mecob.co.uk
Cover image © DEA PICTURE LIBRARY / Getty Images © Shutterstock.com

For my mother

And my friends Elisabeth, Paula, Maria and Gwilym.

CONTENTS

PROLOGUE

SQUIRE FOR ME

A lice. That night, his mind astir, Robert prayed for another vision of Alice. Instead he beheld, again, the old adversary: Edmund of Rutland. In all these years, the boy had made his regular appearances at the bedside. Sometimes the dreams were disjointed and horrifying; now fewer and farther between, as if the spectre were grown weary.

Yet he'd chosen this – of all nights – to return, when Robert Clifford's thoughts were filled with marriage and the retaking of his lands in England and the past seemed at its most irrelevant, the phantom heralding a nostalgic and word-perfect re-enactment of that dread December day ten years ago. Accurate, even in the flooding emotion: triumph.

As he slumbered, Robert found himself once more beside John on Wakefield's wintry killing ground. The Clifford brothers were swaggering, cock-a-hoop at their victory over the vainglorious Duke of York. They'd wallowed in hot bloodshed. The day was closing; they thought the war was, too.

As the dream opened, the two brothers were heading from the field of battle towards Wakefield town in pursuit of fugitives, when – by a stroke of appalling good luck – they happened upon Edward of York's brother, young Edmund of Rutland, as the youth was hastened away over Wakefield Bridge by his master-at-arms, a knight who'd seen better days.

The two renegades – Rutland and his veteran escort – were swiftly brought to bay and separated, and then began the fair fight: Robert, a steadier soldier than John, stepping up, sword drawn, slowly circling the master-at-arms. John stood at his ease, his arm heavy across Rutland's shoulders, now and then passing comment on the encounter for the boy's benefit, pointing and gesturing. Robert did not expect the youth to profit much from the lesson. Not at this late stage.

Robert measured his opponent. The old knight had lost his sword on the field, though he'd acquired a flail in its place: a superb weapon against a heavy-armoured man if you were well-assured with it, which apparently he wasn't. He had the principles right enough: dagger in the left hand to exploit his adversary's weak points as they came exposed, trying to move in hard and fast. He must have expected Robert to be hampered by his sword, not the weapon of choice against a man in full harness; or at least, not some men's choice. But Robert was massive enough to use his sword as a crushing weapon to deadly effect, and for now he played along, ducking or swaying to avoid the flail's heavy swings.

Robert heard his elder brother, away to the side, call down censure on their adversary; for the knight was not wielding the flail as he should – as if it were a mace – but allowing the weapon's wicked tail to slow him. Turning, Robert could see a few of the men laughing, silently, at John's expression, so sincerely vexed. Rutland, too, was concentrating hard, an intense frown upon his handsome face, twitching reflexively, and rocking with the blows.

In the dream, Robert Clifford watched himself taunt the older man, buffeting him with the flat of the sword and joking with the watching soldiers while he parried the weapon, idly, even while his eyes were off his man. And then, abruptly, and before the spectators could lose interest, he stopped playing with the fellow and killed him, ending it quick and clean. The knight didn't make a sound.

Then it was Edmund of Rutland to whom they turned.

By now, the light was waning and some of the men-at-arms had melted away, perhaps to continue the chase, or because the quick dispatch didn't promise much sport. Perhaps those who remained were rewarded for their curiosity. Or they may have regretted it – he never knew. Smirking now, John was folding his arms; he was leaning upon the frost-bound bridge; he was waiting.

Rutland was a tall lad, barely short of John's height; at seventeen, he may still have been growing. He was at that point coolly composed, remarkably unshaken, expecting to fight Robert Clifford as his master-at-arms had done; probably expecting to die, bravely. John had something different in mind.

"Squire for me, Brother."

And so, at John's direction, Robert acted the squire, stripping the youth of his beautifully wrought armour, plate by plate, sending each one spinning over the stone parapet into the river, banked by snow and in full and noisy spate, the colour of old ale. In the dream he heard again the protests of the watching men: the boy's armour was useful, and expensive; they should be keeping it by. But the gesture was satisfying.

As the dream sped on its dark way, Robert cried aloud and groaned, restless, trembling. Beside him, Loic half-stirred from slumber and reached with gentle fingers, murmuring his drowsy comforts. Even as he slept, Robert pushed aside the hand. There was to be no peace. From afar, John was summoning him. Reluctant now, he returned to the figments who waited, patient and immobile, for his presence to animate them once more.

And so it resumed.

Robert took Rutland into his arms and strove to hold him still while John commenced. At an early stage, the boy's composure deserted him and he started to plead. A little more, and he was shaking uncontrollably. And soon enough, screaming. John was using his sword as it should be used: against an unarmoured man. He was slicing, not smashing as Robert had done earlier, small pockets of flesh detaching and flying with vigorous ease.

At one stage, while the boy was still able to struggle forcefully, he managed to spin his captor just as John's sword was descending, and the blade struck Robert's armoured shoulder, hard enough to jar, badly, and he staggered and cursed in surprise. John pinned the point of his sword in the icy ground and leaned on the pommel, just as they were always taught not to. After a moment, Robert rolled his shoulder and laughed, and they could commence again. The screaming went on far longer than one might have expected, but eventually the sound lapsed to low grunts.

Finally, all was done, and then they walked away and left it there, heaped, an ignominious pile, steaming into the crisp air. It was said that someone took the skull after and sent it to the city of York to be mounted on the gates beside the head of the lad's father, the old Duke, but it wasn't them.

There was a perfect little chapel upon the bridge, overhanging the water, and naturally, in they went, breaking down the door, for the priest had fled. It was pledged to St Mary the Virgin, a wondrous sign, for Robert venerated the Virgin most particularly, even then, and ever after. The Clifford brothers prayed awhile, and embraced, and then headed on into Wakefield in the gathering dusk, probably with more to do, but the dream ended there, and he couldn't, in fact, remember how they'd finished the day.

PART I

THE END OF EXILE

By morning, the nightmare had faded. Nothing was said.

Loic stumbled his way through their dawn devotions, great yawns bumping against clamped lips, nostrils like bells, shivering. At his side sagged Robert Clifford, heavy at the prayer rail, steady-breathing. His mind had slipped its anchor and drifted, untethered, away.

All that day, while the city hubbub stirred to life and echoed in, the little house had a pensive air, as if missing its strident master. Clifford had not left the modest bedchamber. Ankles crossed, he leaned, motionless, in the window nook.

"Rather than simply stare at it, Monseigneur, we'll go down to the Grote Markt, shall we? There's a new woodcarver from Bremen. You should take a look at his work; I've never seen the like. Madame Babette spared a little money for you to buy a gift for your son."

"You go. Take a toy to the lad and tell Babette I won't dine with her after all, for I must wait here at the house. She may come to me later. Much later."

"Wait at the house?" A frown fretted Loic's weathervane face. "If you're brooding still on that dream, Monseigneur, you should thrust it from you. Edmund of Rutland was a rebel and a traitor to King Henry. England is well rid of him; let your conscience rest easy." The French accent clotted the words, as ever, when Loic was deeply in earnest.

"My conscience?" Clifford laughed, showing broad teeth. "My conscience is in rude health. So I dreamed his death again? Ah – that scantling fellow is dust in the wind. It means nothing to me." This was poor stuff; woeful and stilted. A man so practised should dazzle with his skills.

"Then why skulk here all the day?" Loic settled, uninvited, on the bed.

Clifford reached to tug a gilded curl. "Ah – but can't you guess?

Loic closed his eyes. "It's Jack de Vere, isn't it?"

"Listen: so the day has come at last: the day promised by the Lord. Today, in this very house, we begin the invasion of England and the recapture of my lands. You remember the vision? The vision, sent by God himself, foretelling the arrival of de Vere? Well then: here he is."

"For sure. But then everyone knows Jack de Vere is in Bruges. Everyone."

"And I'm the cause of his coming. This is the day he and I seal the alliance to reconquer England. This is the day he offers his sister, the Lady Alice, to be my bride. Pledged by God. As you well know."

Loic knew; he knew all too well. The promise – or menace – was front and central in his mind; beckoning Monseigneur into danger; whispering his heart's desire: *England.* A scarred land, blighted by feuds and bloodletting; a place of Old Testament savagery. But Loic had never set foot in England, and such views were less than welcome.

Overmastered by despair, Loic ground his face with his palms. *England is a snare; it will be the death of you.* He longed to say it. *And you don't need a wife. Not yet. And not this one.* Instead he trod the usual, pricklish path. "Oh! Is it today, do you suppose, Monseigneur? Well, as I say, the news is all over Bruges: de Vere's arrival from France; doing the rounds. He's already seen the others, of course. And come away empty-handed. But yes, I expect you're on his list. At the bottom of the list, after all the rest, for if de Vere's visiting the exiles in order of importance, we must assume that you'll be last."

Clifford returned to the vista and the window steamed with his bull's breath. "Go to my son. Take your impertinence with you."

Loic bowed, gathered a few of the loafing household and left the house. Ensconced in a favourite tavern behind the market, he shared his fears; fears that were swiftly shrugged off and shouted down. Stamping their feet, crowing, the men raised toast after boisterous toast: to the invasion; to England; to home. Ten long years they'd waited for this. Had they glimpsed the future, they might have tempered their joy, for if the road hitherto was rough, it was as nothing to the perils ahead.

Loic was barely one hour gone when the fabled Jack de Vere did, indeed, come calling, a handsome stranger: viridian eyes and locks all silver and tawny. If he and Robert Clifford had ever met, neither could recall it, and de Vere was somewhat surprised to be welcomed as a beloved, crushed, violently, against the chest of an ox. When he'd recovered his breath, the visitor made the long-awaited offer of alliance.

Loic's prediction was also correct: Robert Clifford was, in fact, the last in line, though not the less precious for that, when the other exiles had made Jack so dusty an answer, as if their lost king and their lost lands were jealous treasures, to be burnished in secret.

"My God, but this is a breath of fresh air!" Jack de Vere dropped his voice, though he and Clifford were quite alone. "Your friends are a sorry lot. Anyone would think the loyal lords were resigned to die in Flanders. I'm offering the only chance to reclaim their lands and destroy the house of York."

Clifford filled his guest's cup and leaned back, regarding him. "It's not the prospect of England: it's the means to achieve it. None of the loyal lords has a quarrel with you; the de Veres were always strong for Lancaster. But the company you keep! Now there's a horse of a different colour."

"You mean the Earl of Warwick? No, no. He has turned his back on the house of York; he burned those bridges, believe me. And Warwick's the only man rich enough and mighty enough to ensure triumph in the cause of Lancaster." It sounded rehearsed – and it was: this eager young man had been cap-in-hand all over the city.

"I know that well enough. Restoring King Henry and retaking my lands are all that count with me. Once I'm home in the North Country, Warwick can proclaim himself Archbishop of Canterbury for all I care. Does he know you're offering me your sister?"

Jack de Vere flushed; the barest signal.

That night, when Madame Babette had rejoiced sufficiently in the glad news, she knelt in silence by her lover's bed, below the burnished window; the fading trace of vermilion cloud. Babette was gazing far off, far over the narrow sea, out west, toward England – mind brimming and ears closed. At her side, Robert Clifford prayed, aloud and fervent, for another vision of Alice de Vere; the woman whose form he'd conjectured into being; the bride he'd never seen.

*　*　*

While his new friend was picturing a maiden with emerald eyes and resplendent hair, Jack de Vere had already started back to France, rising early, late to bed, exhausting his horses in the heady rush.

Not so many days later, Jack's trumpet tones rang in the wide yard at Angers, proclaiming his return. At once, Alice was halfway to her brother's borrowed quarters, flanked by her gentlewomen. Angers was a strange castle in a strange land, and in Jack's absence they'd taken to convoying; a little fleet. No sooner had the women glided in than he wafted them back, jumbling the formation, and his sister slipped out to throw herself on his neck.

"How was your visit to Flanders? Do we leave soon for home?" The door closed quietly on the departing women.

"Oh, child! Why did we leave England?" Jack held her at arm's length.

"To join our Queen and gather the exiles."

"To gather them, why?"

"So we may return to England, turn out the pretender and restore King Henry." Alice repeated the dutiful lesson, a child at her catechism. "And the exiles have accompanied you back to Angers?"

"Have I the lords of Lancaster about me? Do you spy them peeping out from under my arm?" The words were jovial; already the tone was turning impatient.

"Oh. Could you not persuade them to join you? I am sorry, Jack. Why would the loyal lords not come? They are gone so long they've forgotten England, perhaps."

8

"An exile does not forget his home." Jack flung himself down, fine features tilted to the light, and gestured her into the chair opposite. Between them, a table of oppressive heaviness, warding her off, cramming her to a corner. "Lord Clifford, at least, will join the alliance; he should be here within the week."

Something was mustering; she stilled.

"Well – I'd hoped for more." The bitterness burst out. "I won't deny it. Christ, but they're a wretched lot! Down-at-heel and down on their luck. And yet God himself has ordained this. So Clifford tells me."

"Ordained what?" But it was a whisper, beneath his notice.

"All that matters," Jack was now hectoring his hands, "is that he brings to our enterprise his...reputation. And his men, what's left of them; those Wyverns were the finest soldiers in England, once." A little shrug, negating the accolade; dismissing an aging and bellicose remnant of the last war. Then he raised his head and skewered her. "You'll wed him before we begin the assault on England."

There was silence – an ill-befitting rejoinder. When it had stretched on too long she said, "He is the one they call *Black Clifford?*"

A little forbearance was in order, no doubt, but the supply was finite and Jack was not a thrifty man. "You'd do well to hold that tongue, Alice. Show no distaste. If Robert Clifford is all we can muster, then so be it. A price well worth paying to regain a kingdom, wouldn't you say?"

He was rattling, at his most brittle, and she was nodding, trying not to provoke; casting about amid the low murmurs of her mind; amid the dark and distant tales. But only the man's name sounded in her consciousness, an echo of some ancient wickedness.

* * *

It was unthinkable not to share the tidings, motley as they were. Alice gathered Anne Neville, her dearest friend, and together they burst in upon her gentlewomen. The girls pulled the scanty communication about and shook it until it rattled, but nothing fell out.

With half her attention on the chatter, Alice caught the exchange of glances between her senior attendants. Shuffling between Blanche and Lady Ullerton on the window seat, too young to stifle so rash an impulse, she begged them to tell all they knew.

Lady Ullerton was pinch-lipped, more so than usual. "The Clifford boys – John and Robert Clifford, that is – had an evil name in the North when we were young. Those two were accused of all sorts of crimes. For certain, they slaughtered Edmund of Rutland on Wakefield Bridge – he was Edward of York's young brother – and time has not washed away that stain. Worse, John Clifford's son and heir, little Henry, vanished after his father's death, and was never seen again, though this Robert Clifford now calls himself *Lord* Clifford, as though the child had never existed. It's better you learn this from me, Lady Alice, for you'll certainly hear it from others."

Dismay flooded her, chill and dispiriting. Elizabeth Ullerton would seldom speak well of anyone, yet here the woman was clipping the tale; Alice could sense it. There were words shearing off, unsaid.

She started up, tremulous. "I feel the need of air. Blanche, will you walk with me in the gardens?" A summer storm threatened, deterring the others from joining them, as they otherwise would.

"Oh, Blanche!" cried Alice, when they were alone among the herb-beds. She had halted and turned about, green eyes wide and wild, the myriad soft shades of hair whipping and tumbling about her brow. "Tell me quickly: does this chime with your knowledge of the man?" The backs of her fingers covered her lips.

Blanche reached to pin the tousled locks, fastening her mistress with a steady regard. "I have never met Robert Clifford, and neither has Elizabeth Ullerton. It is his enemies who spread those tales. And they tell of deeds some ten or fifteen years past, when he was a young man. The most unruly grow tame with age." Beneath the folds of fluttering linen, her periwinkle eyes were candid; they seemed candid. "By now he'll be a grey and toothless lion, wishing only to lay his head in a young girl's lap and be petted."

Alice wrinkled her nose at the image, and Blanche laughed.

It was blustering, and the ladies turned back from the garden. As they passed beneath the castle walls, they fell in with Sir Hugh Dacre, one of the Earl of Warwick's household knights, and a suitor of Blanche – after a fashion.

Before the gentlewoman could prevent it, Alice was rifling him on the subject. "Sir Hugh – you can assist us! Blanche was telling me of Robert, Lord Clifford. We hear he's travelling here to Angers to join the Earl of Warwick's alliance. What do you know of the man?"

Over Alice's shoulder, a furious signalling.

"Oh, Lady Alice." Sir Hugh's mouth drooped like a dog's. "We must be in dire straits if we're forced to seek such friends as he. Yes, I do know this *Lord* Robert, as he now likes to be known. *Lord* Robert! He's no more a baron than I am, and murdered his nephew, little Henry Clifford, for the title. His mother was born a Dacre, so he's a cousin of mine, though I'm ashamed to own it. Black Clifford is as huge as a bear, with the appetites of a beast. Ten years ago he sliced up young Edmund of Rutland, favourite brother of King Edward – no, no, not *King* – oh Jesu! Certainly not *King*. I didn't mean to say that; please disregard it at once. Edward *of York*, rather. Anyway, he diced up young Rutland; butchered him into little collops on Wakefield Bridge while the lad pleaded for his life…"

Blanche was rolling her eyes in disbelief, but he was unstoppable, and speeding up.

"What else? It was Black Clifford who led the sack of Ludlow and Stamford – and those are English towns, mind you, not Moorish citadels for the slaughter. Through all my youth, he and his elder brother were notorious; they terrorised the North Country, first as squires at Alnwick, then back home in Westmorland. No woman was safe from them. They slaughtered at will, robbed gentlefolk and burned houses…"

"Sir Hugh!" shouted Blanche, interrupting the vehement catalogue. "Sir Hugh! Good God! Remember to whom you speak."

He tailed off. "Forgive me, Lady Alice." He was a little shamefaced; not nearly enough. "Perhaps I should not have spoken of such things. I meant only to warn you to keep your distance; that fiend is no fit company for a noble maiden."

11

When Blanche had managed to make the man go away, she was unable to undo the damage. Nor was that the end of the matter: the less discreet among the household had obliged Alice's younger attendants with fervid details, and a day later the girls repeated Sir Hugh's grim chronicle, charge for charge.

* * *

They first saw each other in chapel.

As the ladies settled themselves, Jack pinched her elbow. "Look there! It's the exiles! Or some of them, at least; those with any spirit left."

Alice followed his eyes across the nave. There she saw a group of strangers, talking amongst themselves and looking about them. Amid the men stood one taller and better dressed than those around him, one to whom the others were turning with deference. Catching sight of Jack, the newcomer bowed. His eyes lighted on Alice. He bowed again and slowly he smiled.

She knew then that it was he, the one whose arrival she'd dreaded, but amongst those evil tales, no one had thought to mention how very beautiful he was: lofty, dark and well-formed. She could not catch her fluttering breath. As she smiled shyly in return, he nudged a man who was kneeling at his side and murmured a few words, nodding in her direction. The kneeling man turned from his prayers and glanced across.

Jack was watching too. "So Clifford brought Devon along; he said he would. Good fellow. They're fast friends, of course. Where *is* Robert? Oh, there – look."

The second man unfolded, pushing to his feet, staring across. This one was built along massive lines, unsightly and lumpen, a black eyepatch across his face.

Alice grasped the prayer rail. "Which one is Lord Clifford?"

"The giant, of course! Look there! He's just stood up beside the Earl of Devon." The tone was impatient, but it was his nerves she could hear.

As she leaned, trembling, against the rail, cruel disappointment compounded the disgust. Alice lowered herself on to her knees as if to pray, grasping at her shredding composure.

Blanche was craning around her. "Which one? Which one is Lord Clifford?"

Wordless, Alice turned to her gentlewomen, awash with wretchedness. Beyond Blanche was Joanna's brown and freckled face, and behind her, Constance and Elyn. Four faces, stricken.

Constance digested the news. "Sweet Jesu! No one mentioned he'd lost an eye…as well." And was tactless enough to shudder.

The whispers rustled away among the crowd like wind through grass, eddying round Alice's half-sister, Elyn – over-loud as usual – and spreading onward in waves, beyond the hushing of Lady Ullerton. Lord Clifford had not moved; still he stood, motionless, shameless, staring, chin up and arms folded. The handsome man – the man who could only be the Earl of Devon – clapped a hand on Clifford's shoulder, mouth to his ear.

Alice dropped her eyes. She lost the mass in its entirety, her mind on lower things. Lord Clifford was the very template of a North Country boor. She knew all too well how he would be: the stink of sweat and dogs; the rotten teeth; the scorn for music and dancing. What a bitter fate.

When the mass concluded, Jack gathered the party and crossed the yard. He had not warned her, and in the short time remaining, Alice dared to reproach him.

"Warn you of what?" He knew full well.

"Lord Clifford," she whispered, and when his mulish look told her he would brazen it out, she chided him in her wretchedness. "I always do as you bid, Brother, but it would be easier if I'd known how he was."

"Robert Clifford may not be your idea of perfect beauty, but don't act like a spoiled child. And I did warn you. I told you not to show your distaste."

This was what the directive meant; she saw it now. Unable to give vent, she trembled within; a tiny sparkle of unruly rage. Here was the paradigm Jack, riding roughshod over her natural delicacy. Yet even he, so utterly careless as he was, even he knew that she must be disgusted.

When the party gathered in the great hall, Jack, all charm, presented his sister to the Earl of Devon. With his chestnut locks and languid blue eyes, the man was, if anything, more attractive than he'd appeared at a distance. She kissed him briefly in greeting, regret souring her smile. He seemed to be biting back laughter. And then a dread grew up, lest she had betrayed her thoughts.

Next in rank, Robert Clifford would follow. As he towered over her, Alice was all but wringing her hands, her chest rumbling with the depth of his voice. She managed a brief upward glance, her eyes sliding sideways under the intensity of his gaze. With dark, lank, overlong hair receding on either side of a widow's peak, the heavy face was marked by deep furrows at brow and mouth; hills and ruts, a very memento of the North Country. And worst of all: that leather eyepatch, concealing God-knows-what ghastly ruin of flesh. And yet the man brimmed with assurance; an air almost offensively swaggering. One who looked as he did should not glory in it. Then Sir Hugh's words tumbled and scurried across her mind like vermin.

At last Jack dismissed her and she stumbled up the stairs after her women. Closing the chamber door, Alice pressed her face against the cool of the wood. When she turned, it was to an unnatural quiet. Even Elyn was shy in the face of such public discomfiture. They took up their stitching, and the silence stretched on. One hour, then another: unalloyed misery, so that the summons was almost a relief.

As they descended, Lady Ullerton took her hand. "Hold up your head. If you are disappointed, Lord Clifford and the world should not guess it."

Elizabeth Ullerton – who'd had her share of disillusionment and pain – was a stronger support in adversity than triumph. A desirable bridegroom would have been a serpent's tooth, but she would pet and soothe her mistress through this trial.

Alice was grateful for the timely reproof. The hardest part is over, she thought.

Into the castle grounds strolled Alice, Jack and Robert Clifford. Beneath them lay the town of Angers with its wide and muddy river. The men made idle talk. The gentlewomen followed in a mute and watchful muster. Little by little, Jack slowed until he partnered Lady Ullerton. Lord Clifford took Alice by the hand and led her from the path. She feared the others wouldn't follow, and listened as they fell away. Now the pair were enclosed in a peaceful bower, roses crowding to the sun. Halting, he turned her to face him – or to face his chest; his gaze fixed on her again, staring openly.

With a sharp finger he tilted her chin. His features had vanished against the light. "You wish to wed me – so your brother says."

What an odd way of putting it, as if she'd been begging for his hand.

"You will be my wife?"

She'd thought she was ready, but this was dreadful. She was as breathless as when the Earl of Devon smiled, but hardly for the same reason. The tiny murmur of assent was, apparently, insufficient.

"Do you promise this? *Say* it."

He was entirely in control, pressing his advantage. It was her place to follow, not to take the man within the hour. She would make a clean breast of this to her brother. Uneasy and fretful, she barely nodded, then forced herself to it. "I will be your wife, my lord."

Another silence. Her eyes flicked to his face and back down. Now there was a smile of sorts, the large, even teeth clenched and bared like something feral.

"You thought Devon was me, didn't you? And then your disappointment was plain for all to see. The fool laughed so much he near did himself a mischief."

"Oh!" She looked him full in the face then, wretched and remorseful, and encountered with force the consciousness of failure. This was her calling; her purpose. Yet at the very first test she'd gone awry. She was scalding with blame.

He interrupted the confused protestations. "You fear me now; you'll love me when I'm your husband. God wills it."

Again, the unfathomable self-assurance. At last, his gaze dropped from her. Lord Clifford tugged and twisted from his finger a heavy gold ring of curious design: a beast, devouring its serpentine tail. Large as it was, the circlet was dwarfed by its stone, a gargantuan pink ruby, cloudy and flawed. Removing it was taking a deal of effort. She watched his hands; good hands: the fingers long and sallow, the nails clean and straight, with delicate blue veins over sharp knuckles. Lifting the ring, he revealed, engraved within the band, the

Clifford motto *Desormais*. The inscription was scoured by wear.

"This belonged to my father. Then to my brother. Now you'll wear it as a token of your binding vow."

He took her hand. The ring, which could have encircled three of her fingers, slid straight off. Rifling at his belt, Lord Clifford drew one of the leather thongs that tied his purse, and bound the jewel against her wrist. Her hand remained within his grasp.

She frowned again over the setting until something glinted in the hinterland of her memory: this was not a serpent, nor yet a dragon.

"A wyvern! Is it the Clifford badge?" She rushed in to puncture the bloating silence. "It is! Now I understand: that's why they call your men the Wyverns." The warmth was spreading up her arm. "In point of fact, I was born at a place called Wivenhoe. The *ridge of the wyvern*, it means. There was a nest of these monsters, so they say, on a hill above the Colne. In olden times." The heat had reached her throat. "The badge of the Earls of Oxford is the Star with Streams. A comet. The Star of de Vere."

"I know that. Your brother flits about like a comet, doesn't he? Excitable." Again, he tilted her chin with a finger. The eyepatch obscured the expression, rendering him unreadable.

Ducking his head, Lord Clifford pressed a kiss on her surprised mouth, his lips dry and warm. The kiss was quickly done, acceptable, unexceptionable. But overwhelming the sense of his brief touch was the scent of his skin – particular, clean and agreeable.

* * *

Away in his chamber, Robert Clifford sprawled in the chair, examining his left hand: naked, diminished and weightless. He rubbed the pinched and swelling flesh. Since the day they'd slid that ring from John's finger, it had never left him. He would go on twitching at its absence.

Loic – chamberlain and little French shadow – lounged upon the bed, lute in his lap, as ever. He, too, was studying the master's hands, shaped for killing.

Clifford tilted the chair and regarded his man. "What do you think of her, then?" He didn't want an answer. "When I saw her…well. It was all I could do not to cry my thanks to God, then and there, before a crowd of strangers. Our Lord has given me this maiden for a wife and sent the vision of her to point the way. No doubt you've noticed that I'm favoured in exactly the way as He favoured the Holy Mother of Christ, and St Joseph, and the Three Wise Men? It is a particular privilege, of course. How many others does God honour in this way, nowadays? No one. No one I know."

"So she is the girl of the vision?"

"Did I not say so?"

"Oh. I had the impression, Monseigneur, that the woman in your vision was possessed of a perfect beauty. So when I finally saw the Lady Alice, I wasn't sure it was the same one."

"What can you mean by that?"

"She's very small, Monseigneur. And thin. Her chin is too pointed. I think she should smile more. But I expect her teeth are bad."

"Her teeth? Her teeth are perfect."

Spots of high colour had appeared in Loic's cheeks. He was recalling the unedifying scene in the chapel. The wretched girl had confused Monseigneur with the Earl of Devon and then done a poor job concealing her dismay. And, of course, Devon had pounced on her mistake, soon doubled up with laughter, drawing all eyes to Monseigneur's discomfiture until Loic had itched to strike the fool in his stupid mouth. "The Earl of Devon behaved himself very ill, I thought."

Clifford had regained his composure after his friend's mischief-making. "Devon? Ah – it's his calling in life."

"And the lady didn't do much better." But that was a mutter.

"She showed a most maidenly reserve. She'll love me when we're married and so I assured her."

Loic had stopped listening, engaged in a stern attempt to detach himself; to view the burgeoning infatuation as interesting rather than ominous. It proved beyond him. He nudged his master back to the plotting. "What now? Did you follow the plan?"

Yes, it appeared that part had gone rather well. She had promised herself to him. She was wearing his ring. He had taken a kiss. She hadn't a notion how to stop him.

"And the next step, Monseigneur?"

"You shall approach her gentlewoman, Blanche Carbery. Do it at once. I need her help. Buy her gifts, spend at will. Tell her you're sick with love for her. I shall ride in the hunt on Thursday coming. Mistress Carbery will accompany Lady Alice and you'll divert the gentlewoman so I have long enough for my purpose." He raised a cautionary finger. "And you know I like to take my time."

"Is the lady ready for this? I'd say she's timid."

"Of course she's not ready. But the task is only half-done. Alice has promised to be mine, but once I make her mine in body, we shall be married in the eyes of God, and then not Jack de Vere, nor the Queen, nor Edmond of Somerset can divide us."

"The Duke of Somerset? Why concern yourself with him? Duke Edmond vowed, from the first, that he'll not set foot in France; he'll not join the alliance. Not with the Earl of Warwick as leader, Monseigneur; I've heard him say so on several occasions. Edmond of Somerset has no wish nor reason to wed the girl himself. In fact, I doubt he'll ever leave Bruges. He'll live out the rest of his days there, I shouldn't wonder; and then his bones will moulder, alone, in the Vrouwkerk."

"What do you think Jack de Vere was selling in Bruges? He was touting his sister to all comers. If de Vere can haul Somerset aboard, he won't scruple to throw me over; he won't remember my name if there's a royal duke in the offing for his sister. So, yes, for sure I'd rather wait and say my vows in church as a good Christian, not roll her under a hedge like a churl. But the Queen is here, and where the Queen goes, Somerset is sure to follow. He may already be on his way from Flanders. There's no time to lose. Here – you'll need this."

Clifford tossed his purse to the youth on the bed, who raised a hand. Missing one of its thongs, the leather unfurled in mid-air, deluging Loic with coins.

"Ah – my fault." Clifford grinned. "Mend it for me, mon petit."

* * *

18

Blanche was made happy over the next days by the attentions of Loic Moncler.

She'd spied him at once in the chapel, kneeling to the side of Lord Clifford. An arrogant young pup, a little below middling height; lithe and slender, with good shoulders. Intentionally, or otherwise, the chamberlain aped his master's mannerisms: the same erect bearing and brazen stare. Lacking Lord Clifford's massive and menacing presence, the effect was rather droll. Nonetheless, Loic was a handsome young man, glib and confident. Six years a widow, Blanche was eagerly disposed.

Despite his nonsense, she thought him honest on the subject of his master's feelings. Blanche had been watching Lord Clifford; all was as it should be. It would be acceptable – advisable, even – for Alice to unbend a little to please her bridegroom. And so the woman's help was easily won, without the string of fine garnets that hung from Loic's fingers.

"Make your master understand that he must proceed gently."

Loic moved to loop the gems about her neck. She was taller then he and evaded the entanglement.

"He should not attempt too much. Lady Alice has never been touched. She's easily frightened and Lord Clifford has a grisly reputation."

The young man bridled at that. It was rather endearing to watch as he warmed to his theme. Surely those ears and eyes must be fused shut, to defend his lord so trenchantly in the face of such proofs; the overwhelming evidence of iniquity.

"Do give him my advice," she prompted, eventually. "I'm sure he'll have need of it."

The garnets were not her object. They dangled, still, from the young man's hand; when he left he would have to conceal them from his master. Of greater interest was the stimulus the Frenchman's pursuit was giving to the courtship of Hugh Dacre. For years he'd been circling her, that tall, spare, plain knight with his untidy hair. More than the sum of his parts: intelligent and idle, candidly dishonest, cheerfully lecherous, frankly weak. She wasn't sure she'd accept if he asked, and yet – despite his marked and enduring preference for her company, his attentions and his compliments – he had never asked.

Now that Sir Hugh was giving Master Loic those looks that presage murder, Blanche experienced a nasty spike of joy.

* * *

The next day, Lord Clifford sought out Alice for himself. The younger girls attended them into the gardens: quiet, homely Joanna; beside her, Alice's half-sister, the giddy and excitable Elyn, chattering away, as though the fashions of French ladies were Lord Clifford's particular delight. To their other side, Constance, copper-haired, sharp-tongued and flinty – baseborn daughter of Alice's late brother Aubrey. The three followers fell some way behind the couple, eventually, inevitably, vanishing away.

Alice had a tight hold on herself. After a wordless while, the pair found themselves once more in the secluded arbour with its stone bench. Lord Clifford watched her arrange her skirts before seating himself. Still there was silence. He began, absently, to roll his ankles; great ropes of muscle heaved and rippled beneath the threadbare hose. Her glance sprang away. He could hear her breathing.

"God granted me a vision of you."

She'd resolved to speak warmly, soothing the hurt of yesterday. But now Alice could only stare.

"Your brother came to me in a prophecy; it was before we knew of his arrival in Flanders. Jack told me you wanted me as your husband, and then you entered. Though I'd never seen you in the flesh, I saw you then in the vision. You were wearing your grey silk," he added, as if no further proof were wanting.

Alice was oddly touched. She'd not expected this from him – Black Clifford. He seemed to be awaiting an answer.

"It was me?" This, all she could manage.

He took her hand, holding it in both of his own, turning it over, studying it, touching the ring bound at her wrist. He had half-turned to her. She could sense what was probably coming – an avowal; a demand. Her gown itched like the cheapest wool. Did all maidens find it thus, or was she particularly inept?

20

On he went, rhythmic strokes at her palm, so that the change in tone took her by surprise.

"Does Warwick approve our marriage? I wager not. That man may have suffered a sudden and vehement conversion to the house of Lancaster, but it doubt it extends to me. We've been butchering each other's kin for as long as anyone can remember."

Now came exhilaration: it always sparkled when a man spoke with her as an equal. She was silent a moment, considering with care. "When my father and Aubrey were executed, I was only a little maiden. I was sent to live with the Earl of Warwick in the North Country, and the King granted him control over my marriage. But now that he and my brother have sworn an alliance against King Edward, I suppose my lord of Warwick has relinquished the matter to Jack."

Lord Clifford leaned in. "York is not our king. Don't call him *King Edward*."

"Oh – your pardon, my lord! Your pardon. Edward of York, rather." He was grinning, so she dared a little more. "I think the Earl of Warwick had some trouble convincing Queen Margaret that he truly intends to put King Henry back on the throne. It must stand to his credit if his ward is married among the loyal lords of Lancaster."

She hazarded a swift glance, to test if she'd said the right thing. There was the tail end of a look, swiftly bridled; she couldn't read it. By now the man's thigh was pressed against her own. He was moving in, filled with intention.

The sky had drooped and darkened, and a few fat raindrops gusted against her cheek. "Alas," she said happily, and stood, gently drawing her hand from his grasp. Her good gentlewomen had reappeared.

* * *

That evening, the nobles were invited to the Queen's apartments and Alice found she had been seated beside her suitor – an unwelcome draught of reality.

Lord Clifford served her and cut the fish very small, as if she were an infant. Every movement of his sleeves wafted his scent about her. Around them, others were animated. He did not seem much inclined to conversation.

"Why don't you eat?" His address, when he spoke was as abrupt as she'd come to expect, verging on surly.

The food was making her nauseous. "I do not like fish, my lord; not at all."

He'd scooped a morsel with his spoon and it was hovering beside her mouth. "What do you like to eat?"

"I like sage dumplings. I hope…"

He'd slipped in the spoon before she could close her lips.

She swallowed and hesitated, and then: "I hope, when I'm mistress of my own household, to keep the number of fish days to the fewest permissible."

There was strong reproof in his voice: "This is not right! You should not wish to challenge the teachings of the Church."

She'd not expected to interest, let alone displease, him. She risked a glance at his face, in the hope that he was teasing. He was not.

"Forgive me, my lord. My brother's chaplain says the Holy Book makes no mention of this; men follow their neighbours in their practices." Her voice had dropped to a mutter.

"That may be, but the Church Fathers and his Holiness the Pope have plenty to say on the matter, do they not? In my household, you'll find the chaplain, Reginald Grey, is better informed. He regulates our conduct, as he will regulate yours."

She brooded at the sullen fish. *What else did this Reginald Grey regulate? Torture; murder; rape?* She could not take another bite. Lord Clifford was gulping without chewing; not enjoying it either. He coughed and hawked and brought up a bone. Her eyes wandered as far as they could. Then he tapped her hand with his finger.

"I have it: certain persons are exempted from these strictures, are they not?"

She managed another rapid, sidelong glance. The expression had changed.

"Pregnant women may eat as they please. There is your answer: I will get you with child directly, and ensure that you remain that way."

22

Her belly squirmed. A man as coarse as he was ugly. No lady should be forced to endure this. But it was a petty rebellion that led nowhere, not even in her imagining. She gnawed the skin around her fingernail, eyes downcast.

"Stop that." He clasped her fingers with warm hands. "It's not mannerly."

* * *

The horses reached a fork in the path. Robert Clifford, who'd been entirely mute since they left the castle of Angers, now hailed the party and announced, too loudly and to no one in particular, "I shall show Lady Alice and Mistress Carbery the dell nearby, with its wildflowers. We'll rejoin you in a while."

Alice looked up in consternation. Blanche's complacent eyes travelled to hers, then slid away, gazing around – everywhere but where she was needed.

The company milled about as the smaller group unravelled itself. Who had approved this impropriety? It seemed incredible: there were the good folk of the court, arrayed before her: nodding and smiling, smiling and nodding. The Countess of Warwick would be appalled. Alice tilted her chin at them, puzzled and hurt, but no one came to her aid.

And then Loic led off, a hand hovering against Blanche's thigh. Lord Clifford turned after him, tailed by the groom. They rode once more in silence, some way behind the other two. Murmurs of laughter floated back. Loic seemed to have the plan. When they came upon a little glade, the groom slipped down and lifted Alice, then Blanche, spreading blankets and cushions, food and wine, and leading the horses away to water. Alice picked a little at the food. The wine was too strong. She saw she'd drained her cup already and pushed it away. Lord Clifford, who'd said not a word since they dismounted, was lounging at her side, apparently near sleep. What had dawned as the most limpid of days was now turning oppressive, the breeze failing, moist warmth pressing in. Soft light filtered through tall trunks, and the air was heavy and humming with floating motes and tiny beating wings.

Blanche was sly and blushing, the young Frenchman murmuring in her ear, inaudible to Alice and uncomfortable to witness, with the ogre sprawled beside her. Head lowered, Alice examined Loic's mobile, expressive face; his hair, a

23

dark golden; the thick-lashed eyes, a brilliant blue. This was a cherished youth, and well he knew it. More favoured son than foreign servant.

Taking up his lute, Loic strummed a few notes. Lord Clifford roused himself, a smile of honest pleasure across his swarthy face. With a nod to his master, Loic began to play, and Lord Clifford picked up the song in a voice most deep and profound, but sweeter, more graceful, more refined than she could have imagined. Alice listened: relieved, intrigued, gratified.

In the lull that followed, Lord Clifford asked her to name her favourite. Honesty was not required nor, indeed, much deliberation. But why – at this of all moments – must her mind fill with the verses of *Long Lankin* – a nasty ballad with a beguiling tune; the tale of a cold-blooded child-killer?

"Oh – *Tamlin*! It is *Tamlin of Carterhaugh*!" Good sense intervened, just in time. Fairy-folk and faithful love: a pretty, proper confection. He began at once and Alice joined in the wistfully familiar northern ballad. At times, their lyrics diverged; his version consistently – predictably – more lewd. After a few of these mishaps, each discrepancy pricked her to a scandalised hiccough of laughter. He smiled and held the melody.

Blanche and Loic were regarding each other with an unreadable look. When the ballad was done, there was a perfunctory clapping and then, to her surprise, the pair stood as one. Trailing his cloak, Loic called over his shoulder, "Mistress Blanche wishes to gather the flowers, Monseigneur. We'll be a short spell."

Alice started to scramble to her feet, glad of the prospect. But Lord Clifford had caught her wrist. "There are no flowers," he murmured and, taking up the strings, he began once more to sing.

Nerves soothed, she heard him out with pleasure while the music lasted. His good eye had closed and his fingers strummed on, languorous. In the slightest stir of breeze, Alice caught again the man's enticing perfume: leather, bay, camphor and pine needles. He was less than terrifying, lounging there – the extravagant stature foreshortened. In spite of herself she leaned in, breath tickling his lips, daring to study his features: the weather-beaten skin, the dimples that were furrows instead of points, adding to the impression of ruggedness, of a landscape. The eyepatch repelled her the more with its

24

proximity. She wondered if he wore it at night, in bed, then backed away from that dark alley. As the notes faded, she averted her eyes and turned about, straining for a hint of Blanche.

"*Tamlin of Carterhaugh*. An interesting choice. A young virgin taken in the woods."

In her panic to name a favourite, she'd forgotten the seduction at the heart of the song. "*Tamlin* is just a love song, like all ballads." It was barely above a whisper.

He laughed. "That's far from true! Think of *Long Lankin*. As many do, when they look at me – or so I'm told."

Alice reeled with sharp dismay. He was much closer now, smiling down on her – composed and certain. Despite her feeble efforts, they had strayed to the rim of the precipice. Resting on an elbow, Lord Clifford eased her back until she touched the cloth and lay beneath his shadow, nape cradled in his palm. His face was dark against the sun. She caught her breath. Beneath her line of sight he was drawing back the hem of her gown. Up her stockings trailed the unhurried hand. There was nothing furtive in his movements: they were gentle and deliberate and very slow.

A desperate flush bloomed in her cheeks. Alice swallowed and stared at the rippling treetops, unblinking, until her eyes swam. How many crows; how many crows there were, circling and crying: she tried to count them. But they swung round too quickly to number and the wine had left her dizzy. Now he was murmuring such mortifying promises. She clasped her eyes tightly as his lips brushed hers. The guilty hand made its way. Breathing ceased while the voiceless scream started to build, until she thrummed with it, barely choking the impulse to thrash her legs in panic. He must have discerned it: she felt him withdraw his hand; she sensed him retreat.

All was still. After a moment, with timorous caution, Alice opened her eyes. But there he was: lying over her, blocking the light, his fingers in his mouth. Her stomach roiled. She made a sudden, involuntarily twist to the side and retched. He snatched away. Dark and clotted wine seeped through the dry grass. As the heaving and gasping subsided, she raised her head. He was gone.

Alice gritted her teeth, warring the stinging tears that brimmed and quivered. The man had leaped to his feet in his haste to be apart from her, radiating aversion. Creeping up behind the shame was the resentment. No one had warned what to expect. No one had warned her how to act.

* * *

Clifford strode through the dry undergrowth toward Loic, his thoughts skittering around. Time: he had so little time. In his mind's eye he was carrying Alice off, fleeing with the girl in his arms; Edmond of Somerset was gaining on him; Queen Margaret and Jack de Vere conspiring to wrench the maiden from him and deliver her up to a more splendid bridegroom. He'd felt quite certain of his accomplice, when, with ruinous ill-timing, she had rebelled.

He crashed on, making plenty of noise to warn the pair of his approach, but their attention was elsewhere. Clifford halted at the edge of the clearing. Folding his arms, he leaned against a shady trunk, observing the figures move against each other, clammy and shameful. Loic opened his eyes, favouring his master with the broadest grin, displaying those little, wide-spaced teeth that lent his looks such appealing innocence. After a long and pleasurable moment, he stilled himself and patted at Blanche to alert her. She started in surprise, untangling her limbs from his, briskly, with a poor attempt at nonchalance. Clifford continued to inspect her.

"You weren't long, Monseigneur," remarked Loic. He was deftly repairing his attire.

Clifford shook his head.

Blanche raised her eyes, almost to his face. "I did try to warn you, my lord."

"That you did."

Retracing their steps, they found Alice seated, rigid and red of eye, amid the tidy panniers. Blanche approached with caution, smoothing her dress, but Alice had thoughts only for her private misery. The ride back was interminable. In the depths of the forest, horns were sounding. No one suggested seeking them out.

As soon as they'd clattered into the castle yard, Clifford bowed to the ladies and strode away. The chamberlain paused to speak with the groom, then followed his lord to the chamber. He found Monseigneur just as expected: seated at the table, cheek in one hand, the other scrubbing at his hair.

Loic gave his master's shoulder a slight, impudent squeeze. "You've frightened her, Monseigneur. Let her alone now."

"You are not treating this matter with the gravity it deserves." Clifford turned face-on, and unclenched his teeth. "God Himself conferred that maiden on me. If Somerset does appear – and I don't doubt he will, he's just slower than the rest of us – I'll be out in the cold. You *know* I must put her beyond doubt by then."

Loic shrugged. "Well then, Monseigneur, you should have carried on regardless." He watched the shudder, and turned away to hide a smile. The Queen was with them in Angers: if Edmond of Somerset, their stiff, quiet, courageous leader, was, indeed, drawn, inexorably, to her presence, then the little de Vere girl would be Duchess of Somerset within the month; Robert Clifford would trail home to his mistress in Bruges. All would be well.

* * *

At their release, Alice fled. Flinging wide the chamber door, she hurled herself on the bed like a little girl, flushed and panting, screwing her hot face into the linen. Sighing, the gentlewoman knelt at her side.

"Tell me," directed Blanche.

Alice rocked about.

"Did he kiss you?"

"I don't know." To the quizzical silence she added, voice muffled by pillows, "He did something *worse*. It made me ill."

Blanche thought she could stifle the laughter, but it swelled and burst from her, rending the heavy stillness of the room.

Alice rolled on to her back. "Truly, Blanche!"

"You poor little fool! You'll endure more than that. And enjoy it, too, or you've a long and lonely road ahead of you."

Alas, it was the truth she feared: he'd done no more than a man was bound to do. The ready tears swelled and spilled.

"Stop that," said Blanche. "You've behaved like a child, yes. But all's not lost. Keep to your room tonight. Tomorrow we'll seek him out, and you can apologise for this silliness. All will be well. He'll forgive you – you'll see."

Alice managed a smile, tremulous and brave. Blanche squeezed the girl's shoulder and pulled off her shoes. Then she went in search of Loic.

* * *

Alice had a happy knack of evading any evil not immediately before her. The slumber was peaceful. The next morning, during matins, she repeated to herself the words she'd practised, and envisaged how it would be. When Lady Ullerton was distracted, Blanche slipped her charge away.

She led Alice straight to the yard, where Lord Clifford was training against a burly Frenchman. Quite a crowd had gathered, Jack among them. Lord Clifford wasn't so much defeating his opponent as annihilating him. His strength was a given; what surprised her was the rapidity of the blows; his energy and stamina.

But then it seemed that French honour must be restored, and the ladies were forced to linger while the violence escalated and a queue began to form. Alice was hopping from foot to foot when the Earl of Devon appeared behind them.

"They'll not get the better of our Robert." He was grinning at her again, knowing and insolent. "I'll take his place so you may carry him off, Lady Alice. Give him something after the disappointment of yesterday – there's a good girl."

Alice recoiled. Unsavoury as Robert Clifford might be, she preferred him to this loose fish.

When Devon had chosen a safe moment to attract his friend's attention, Lord Clifford came, unsmiling, to meet them. Alice stammered out her suggestion.

"Walk with you? Not as I am." He scrubbed at his face with a cloth. "Allow me a moment and I will find you." He strode away.

Holding tight to her courage, Alice slid off before Jack seized the chance to speak to her. Since that succession of terrible promises on the first day, she'd done everything she could to avoid making a clean breast of it.

As Alice and Blanche strolled in the grounds, Lord Clifford's chamberlain appeared between them. Monseigneur would be with them shortly, Loic promised; he was having a wound stitched. Blanche rolled her eyes.

"Did you see how he thrashed them, every one?" cried Loic.

"Indeed sir," agreed Blanche, sweet as honey. "We're lucky to have witnessed such a performance. Lord Clifford must be the strongest man I ever saw."

"Aye," agreed Loic. "He is justly famous."

Alice was ambushed by a thrill of pride. When she turned to watch the distant approach, it was he who didn't meet her eyes.

"Were you hurt just now, my lord?" she ventured.

"Nothing to speak of."

"But my lord! So wonderfully brave!" exclaimed Blanche. "Truly, we could not have wished for a more exciting display – and *just* as we happened by."

His mouth twitched and he turned his back on Blanche. With a hand in the small of the girl's back, he propelled Alice on, away from the other two. "You wish to speak to me?"

Inevitably her self-possession was slipping, leaving her stranded with the image of yesterday's mortification. It was – apparently – easier to imagine these moments than to live them. Her voice dropped away and it was hard for him to hear. "I'm very sorry if I offended you, my lord. It must have been the wine that made me ill."

He almost laughed. His hands were heavy at her shoulders, thumbs sliding along the collarbones.

"Did you tell the Earl of Devon?" That was lower still.

"Tell Devon? Not I! Yesterday was nothing to boast of." Now his face was level with hers, for he had sunk to one knee and was leaning in, confidential. "Listen, sweetheart. If you knew how deeply I regret the discomfort I caused, you would surely forgive me. I was confounded – for you said that you are mine, when it seems you did not mean it."

29

She did, of course, mean it. She forgave him. There was nothing to forgive. And blamed herself, repeatedly, repetitively, eventually offering what amounted to an incoherent invitation. He rose to his feet, watching awhile as she floundered in the net, a trapped bird.

"So you *are* mine?" He interrupted her softly, and reached to stroke her chin, running his thumb across her lips, parting them with the pressure.

"Yes, my lord," she answered, relieved, humbled and lost.

On the next day – the very next day – everything was turned on its head.

* * *

Up the great stairs swept Lord Clifford, making his way to wait upon the exiled Queen. Towed in his wake were his senior men. Urgent whispers diverted them: Alice and Lady Ullerton, approaching from the direction of Jack's chamber. Clifford halted. His marshal, Bellingham, paused on the steps below and Nield, the steward, craning around to stare at Alice, stumbled into him. By now Clifford was well used to the girl's inability to meet his gaze; on this occasion though, something was clearly amiss. As she passed, she nodded, eyes sliding about to avoid him.

"Lady Alice!" She had already hastened on as he rose from his bow. His voice caught her retreating back. "The Queen hunts this week. You will accompany me? I promise to water your wine this time!"

Elizabeth Ullerton had withdrawn to the window and was examining the view. Cuthbert Bellingham and Patrick Nield were not so well-mannered.

Alice halted but did not turn. "I cannot give you an answer, Lord Clifford," said she. So entirely typical of Jack, to have triggered this: the abrupt abandonment of his plans for Clifford; warning her off with never a word to her suitor. "Please speak to my brother."

Clifford strode after her. "What's this?" A possessive hand caressed her arm, in marked contrast to the truculent tone. "What has de Vere to say on the matter?"

She turned, shoulders sinking, and glanced in the general direction of his face. "Please, Lord Clifford – speak to Jack."

30

"Forgive us, my lord," interjected Lady Ullerton. "We're expected elsewhere."

Lord Clifford was breathing heavily as the two ladies hastened away and then, abandoning the original plan, he descended the stairs two at a time towards Jack de Vere's chamber.

* * *

"Robert!" Jack sprang to his feet with a broad grin and walloped his guest's back. "You've heard the news?"

There sat a group of men, gaming together. Clifford nodded at William, Lord Beaumont, Jack's faithful comrade; a peaceful fellow, paternal, some years his elder. Their knights rose together like a cloud of gnats. He couldn't match names to faces or tell who belonged where; the households of Beaumont and de Vere were well-nigh communal.

Clifford turned on Jack. "I've heard that there is news." He readied himself, mopping his palms on the back of his hose, producing a run of tiny rents. This garment, like the greater part of his wardrobe, his harness and his weaponry, was giving out on him.

Jack threw himself back in the chair. "The Duke of Somerset is on his way from Flanders, God be praised! The Duke of Exeter, too. You'll be as relieved as I. The stars are aligning, no?" Up he jumped and bounced about the room in some excitement.

William Beaumont grasped for his friend and missed by some margin. "Jack…"

De Vere reseated himself. "Excellent! When I saw you in Flanders I mentioned I was sounding out Somerset on the subject of my sister? You remember. He wasn't keen at the time, but it seems the Queen has summoned him and he's changed his mind, which is grand news. When we're back in England you'll have your pick of noble maidens, of course, so no harm done. One is much like another, after all."

Loic, Bellingham, Nield: frozen, all three of them, eyeing their master. He took the blow manfully, face impassive – forewarned and forearmed.

31

"Oh – one more thing, before I forget: the Queen has asked that you give up your rooms to Somerset and find lodgings in the town. But don't trouble yourself for now, Robert. The Duke can share my chamber until his marriage to Alice."

* * *

The household men bore away their broken-hearted lord. Broken-hearted, but not surprised, for there was a dreadful inevitability in all this.

Clifford's head was cradled in his hands. "I *knew* he would come; did I not always say it? She was given by God, but she's broken faith. How am I to live through this?"

Later that day, the witnesses to the heartbreak made an escape to a tavern below the walls, probing the interesting topic of their master's grief.

"That little girl had a lucky escape; he would have eaten her alive." Cuthbert Bellingham could not reconcile his libertine master with this lovesick swain. "He'll take no lesson from this though. You've heard what he's saying of Somerset? He thinks God will strike the Duke down."

Patrick Nield gave his peculiar laugh: a great shout followed by a high-pitched chuckle. "He always thinks God's itching to smite his enemies. If only that were true, Bell: we'd all be living it up in England now, rich and happy."

"Raise a toast, gentlemen, for it has all turned out for the best. England is a tinderbox; it would have been the death of Monseigneur. We are well out of it."

"You're way off course there, Loic. Lord Robert will never give up on his lands. Nor will the girl's marriage stop him pursuing her. Poor Somerset. He's a decent fellow; he doesn't deserve to be persecuted by a fiend in the form of Lord Robert. This will bring down all manner of trouble on our heads." Patrick Nield had known Robert Clifford a very long time.

A general, mumbling assent and they sipped their drinks. Reginald Grey, the lean and granite-faced chaplain, had approached unseen, laying a cold hand on Nield's shoulder. At once the men shuffled up, leaving more space than was needed.

"What's that, Patrick? Somerset is a fiend? Indeed. Indeed he is. A wolf in sheep's clothing, but the theft of Alice de Vere will cost him dear. Lord Robert must not sit idly by while God's purpose is thwarted."

* * *

Together, Robert Clifford and Jack de Vere climbed the broad and shallow stairs. This moment had to come. Better the old adversaries should meet in private than display twenty years' rancour before the world.

At the door to the great chamber, Jack paused, searching Clifford's face, but the man's expression was as inscrutable as ever. Jack opened the door. There at the centre of the long table sat Richard Neville, Earl of Warwick, papers spread before him, scanning with a finger.

In the old days, Clifford would not have marked Warwick as a handsome man, but the years had been kind; that grey face had grown dignified. And though Edward of York had abandoned the man who made him king – slipped his bonds – power seemed still to radiate from the Earl of Warwick. The source had been extinguished, but the halo of light remained.

Jack had entered first and turned to close the door, but Clifford was blocking the entrance, as if undecided. Jack glanced around the silent room. "Leave us if you will, gentlemen," he murmured, to those of Warwick's entourage who hovered about the table with an air of fierce absorption.

There was a reluctant mustering and the attendants filed off through the far door. And still neither man had moved. Then, in the same instant that Warwick scraped his chair and stood, Clifford strode forward. They met halfway. Warwick bowed, and, as befitted his lesser rank, Clifford bowed lower. And then, as though it were always intended, as though they had long been practising, they moved together and grasped each other's arms. Not a full-blown embrace; a clasp above the elbow.

"Cousin," said Warwick.

Clifford nodded. "Cousin," said he.

Jack clapped both men on the shoulder.

"Will you sit with me, Cousin?" Warwick' voice was rusty as a hermit's. He shuffled his papers, a reflex, and tipped his head left and then right. The ensuing crack was audible; comically loud.

Clifford examined the old enemy. "Here we are. After all these years." He knew what he wanted, but not how to begin.

Now was the moment for Jack to assist, and he did so, sounding tense and unnatural. "It is good to come together after all these years, to put aside our differences for the sake of King Henry and the realm, working together for the common good."

Clifford leaned back, grinning openly. He didn't doubt they'd all be turning on each other the moment Edward of York was defeated. Never mind – he could be sentential, too. "Indeed, it is well said. Let us put the past behind us. As King Henry exonerates the Earl of Warwick for his endless treasons, so I forgive him for the killing of my kin, and promise to love him as a cousin."

Warwick's face was a mask. "Likewise, I forgive Robert Clifford for the killing of my father and my brother Thomas, my uncle and my young cousin, Edmund of Rutland."

Edmund of Rutland. That grisly spectre was bound to make an appearance at some point. Clifford shook his head. "Ah, you have the wrong man, my lord. I'm not responsible for your father's death. Nor that of your uncle, nor your brother. I was on the field when they fell; that is all." Fleetingly, he thought to deny Rutland also, but he didn't think Warwick had a sense of humour.

Warwick had stopped bothering to open his mouth and was now speaking through a slit of gritted teeth. "You began the war when you attacked my brother Thomas at Heworth twenty-odd years ago."

Jack had raised his hands, pleading.

Clifford was looking mildly pained. "My father, perhaps? I was what – fourteen or fifteen years at the time?"

More like sixteen or seventeen when he'd tried – enthusiastically, if not with any great expertise – to kill Warwick's brother in that ambush at Heworth. Getting in everyone's way; he recalled his father's exasperation. In fact, he'd probably saved Thomas Neville's life. Accidentally. Only to slaughter him much later, at Wakefield, and that was the entire history of his relations with Warwick's younger brother. He grinned again. "If I'd tried to kill your brother, he'd be dead."

"He *is* dead. Oh, you Cliffords killed him, whichever of you wielded the weapon! He *is* dead, as are they all."

"As are they *all*."

"My lords! Please!" The meeting was spinning out of control; blades would be next. "Robert – my lord of Warwick has been in conference with the Queen, as you know, making plans for the invasion. To seal the alliance, they've agreed to marry their children. Our Prince is to wed the Earl's younger daughter, Anne."

Clifford displayed a polite interest. "And when does this marriage take place?"

Warwick had regained his composure. "As soon as the Papal dispensation is received. I would hope within the month – before I sail for England."

"And Queen Margaret has agreed to the marriage being perfected at once?" Clifford's face was mild, but his voice was alert.

Warwick hesitated. "The marriage will be consummated after I've vanquished Edward of York."

Never, then, thought Clifford. That marriage would never be consummated. The bride would be put aside as soon as Warwick had outlived his usefulness. The loyal lords would see to that, even if Queen Margaret meant to keep faith.

Now Jack had a misplaced note of triumph in his voice. "So the Earl of Warwick and Queen Margaret are in perfect amity. Say you're with us, Robert! Declare yourself: now is the chance, my friend."

"Wait on," said Clifford. "Does our Prince go with you to England?"

Warwick was back to his papers. "The Prince will remain in France with Queen Margaret and my wife and daughter until I've secured the kingdom."

So the Queen doesn't trust you either. The moment had come. 'My lands," said Clifford.

Jack leaned back. His smile blossomed and grew. "My lord of Warwick has agreed that the Clifford lands will be returned to you."

This must be Jack's doing, then. How hard must he have striven to wrest those estates from Warwick, so notoriously greedy? And giving up the Clifford lands would set a dangerous precedent. All the dispossessed would be yammering.

"There are conditions, naturally." Warwick eyed him coldly. "You must travel to England with me. You must raise the North for King Henry and bring Harry Percy, Earl of Northumberland, over to me. You must acknowledge my lead, and fight at my side, under my command. You must deliver the support of your friend, the Earl of Devon."

"The support of *all* the exiled lords; the Dukes of Somerset and Exeter also," put in Jack, swiftly, as though it were a rider he were used to adding.

Clifford leaned back and contemplated his hands. His left hand, naked and unadorned; he frowned at it. "I cannot travel with you to England: I must return to Flanders to conclude my affairs there, but I could be after you, quick enough. You know very well I cannot promise you the Earl of Northumberland. Dearly did I love Harry Percy's father and grandfather, but this little one is almost a stranger; I can but try. Devon is under my thumb and will do as I say. But Edmond of Somerset is a cautious man; I can do little with him. The Duke of Exeter will follow Edmond of Somerset; I have no influence there, though, again, I'll do what I can. But confirm me in my title and my lands, and I will follow you into the mouth of Hell."

Warwick was staring at him through his brows, very still. "There is a Clifford heir, is there not?" he said quietly. "Your elder brother's son, young Henry, I think. You intend that the boy be simply disregarded? Or, perhaps…he is no longer alive?"

"John fathered no heir. His wife whored herself with a man of the retinue, and a child was born. It matters not whether the little imposter is alive or dead." He made his practised parade of indifference. "I am John's heir."

Jack was nodding, impatient. "We'll consider each point, of course, but I'm sure we can reach agreement with you on this."

36

Warwick interjected. "And, since you raise it, nothing will be done for Edmond of Somerset until Edward of York is vanquished, and then I'll see how the dice land. Some will not survive the coming struggle, and some will not aid me. It would be rash to be too generous in the return of lands."

Jack was looking less happy at that, as well he might. Without those estates and the riches they brought, Somerset would be emasculated; a worthless brother-in-law.

"All true," Clifford agreed. "And England may prove too small to contain both you and the Duke of Somerset." Clifford clapped his hands on the arms of his chair, looking at both men expectantly, but they seemed to have finished. "You know my price," he said, and pushed himself up.

Warwick tidied his letters as they counted away Clifford's heavy tread.

Jack flashed his vain white smile. "That went well."

"God in Heaven, but I hate that family. I had forgot how much." Warwick's voice was dismally morose. "This is hard for me. You cannot know how hard. Strange: I thought it would be kneeling to Queen Margaret that would undo me, but after all these years, I've come to admire the woman."

"My friend," Jack's voice was both soothing and warning, "you knew when you came over to Lancaster that you would have to work with such men. Robert Clifford is a sharp fellow and a peerless soldier. He deserves your respect, if not your liking."

"Don't take that tone with me! I was making kings, Jack, when you were pissing the bed. And don't pretend you thirst for the return of the house of Lancaster; you're driven entirely by your hatred for Edward of York. You'll crown a donkey if that's what it takes to get revenge for your father and Aubrey." He reverted to Clifford. "The man's a veritable beast. When did he lose the eye? It hasn't improved him."

Jack twinkled at him. "You took the eye, my friend. Ten years ago."

"Is that so?" Warwick was staring out of the window, beyond Angers; much farther away.

"If he is hostile, he has some cause. In point of fact, your men killed his father also." Jack was laughing quietly. "He let you off lightly, I think."

"He's the butcher, not I. *Lord* Clifford" he continued, bitterly. "The man has some nerve, to call himself by his nephew's title."

Irrepressible, Jack had resumed the lofty tone. "Listen, you'll learn to rub along with him. It has cost the Queen some heart-wrenching to accept your...change in loyalties. She must have those she trusts around her, and she prizes the man highly."

"Prizes him for what? His charm? The lords of Lancaster are a spent force. Not a single man in England will welcome them back. Without those tattered shadows we're all better off, in more ways than one. There's not enough land to go around, and you know it. Getting rid of York is just a preliminary. The day we put King Henry back on the throne is the day the struggle begins in earnest."

* * *

Somehow Alice had moved through the week without encountering Lord Clifford. She had seen him, of course, and he had seen her, but neither was alone and he had kept his distance, staring at her hungrily and, she thought, menacingly. It was too much to hope that she would indefinitely avoid his reproaches.

And so it was. On the eve of Duke Edmond's arrival, she was entering the spiral stairway that led to her chamber when she chanced upon Lord Clifford, descending the steps. There was no call for him to be loitering in that quarter of the castle. Alice halted. It was too late to turn back.

"A good evening, my lord," she murmured as she passed.

He spun and gripped her elbow. "Why are you avoiding me? I can't touch you now."

"You are touching me. Please don't." Pity and disgust churned within, drowning out the familiar fear.

A cruel and humourless smile; he was dragging her towards him with spiteful fingers. By now it was hard to keep herself from crying out.

"I wish you joy of your marriage. Somerset is more to your taste, I've no doubt. He's a mild fellow. I doubt he'll know what to do with a woman."

At that, the pain was scorched away by a reckless flare of anger. Alice shook off his hand. "You make yourself ridiculous."

As the footsteps faded, he almost roared her name in a fury of despair, choking down the shameful impulse. Seeking her out was a sober enough intention: she had his ring, and he meant to take it from her. But at the sight of the girl, cogent thought had flown. Clifford leaned his hot face against the stone of the wall and listened to his own breathing. Was he to turn the other cheek while the Duke of Somerset purloined this gift from God? As he made his slow way to the guestchamber, he could not remember, ever, feeling so absolutely baffled.

Angers was overstuffed with visitors; there was barely standing room within. "Sir Reginald! I wish for speech with you alone."

It took an age for the chamber to empty. Loic was the last to gather himself, affording Monseigneur many a moment to motion him back, closing the door at last with a soft click, head high.

Clifford drew up a chair for his confessor and sank before him to his knees. It was hard to frame the words, but once he'd started, he couldn't stop. Not a confession, in truth, for he didn't want absolution; he wanted comfort.

Sir Reginald examined his master's fingers, clasped in his own. "Where is the Clifford ruby?"

The bewilderment burst out again. "She has it! Ah – she keeps my ring and weds another."

"Good. Jack de Vere directs her. Outwardly the girl obeys her brother; inwardly she cleaves only to you. Go to her, Lord Robert. Go alone. Allow God to guide your actions."

"What of Somerset?"

There were words to be found somewhere; words of consolation and truth. The priest withdrew his hands and pushed to his feet, casting around as if all the world's literature lay at their disposal. He knelt at a battered little chest. There, front and central, was an illuminated Life of St Cuthbert – uncompromising northern battleaxe. Beneath it lay a dog-eared St Dunstan, the hammer of the devil, defiantly unhelpful. No matter, for by now the verse he wanted had come to mind: a profane source, to be sure, but apt in the context. "Do you know this line? A dictum of the ancient master, Horace. I'll render it in English, as your Latin is creaky: *Rarely does Vengeance, though lame, fail to catch the guilty man, though far in front.*"

It wasn't a prophecy, still less the word of God, but, declaimed by Sir Reginald Grey, it carried much the same resonance.

"Vengeance is lame? Somerset may think himself safe, but for a season only?" On Clifford's face, the faintest trace of doubt, soon stifled, then a slow nodding.

Grey nodded in return. "Do not confide in others, Lord Robert. The household men love you well, but they're gifted with no very great wisdom. God guards your steps."

An hour later, Clifford had wandered to the chamber below his own, where his closest friend was lodged. Though Devon had dealt the cards, they lay untouched on the table. Clifford's mind was running, still, on Sir Reginald's words and he was in no mood for gaming. Moreover he must confess the morning's work to his friend, who was unlikely to take it well. Clifford swilled his wine. Behind him, a low and mellifluous murmuring: his own man, Jem Bodrugan, whispering in Cornish with Loic's servant, Benet – more boyish girl than girlish boy.

"Don't you wonder if they talk behind your back?" Devon jerked his head in the lads' direction.

"No."

"Christ – I would. My sodding household are such false and greedy layabouts. Always whining I don't pay them sufficient, nor liberal enough with the wine. It's my wine."

"You wage them better than I. Most of mine I don't pay at all." He tipped his chair, brooding on Warwick. "They follow for love alone."

Devon grunted. "It's because I wasn't brought up to it. They knew me all those years as a bare knight; a younger brother. The men still don't see me as their lord. Not really." He'd forgotten that Clifford was in the same position. And Jack de Vere. And Edmond of Somerset. The war had been most efficient at promoting younger sons.

There was nothing to be gained from putting it off. "I saw Warwick this morning."

"Eh?"

"I said, I had an audience with Warwick this morning. Warwick had an audience with me."

"You did what?" Devon slammed down his cup, spraying droplets of wine over Clifford's sleeve.

"And Jack de Vere. To discuss the enterprise to England."

Devon swept up the cards and threw them aside.

"The fewer who were present, the better."

"The better for whom?" Devon's voice was sharp.

Clifford held up a hand. "It wasn't the warmest reunion, as you can imagine. The killing of one's kin does tend to cast a pall. Ah – I thought of bringing you along, my friend. But you have this tendency to provoke others – you may have noticed."

Devon was sprawled back in his chair, eyeing Clifford, pink-cheeked. "You might have told me what you were purposing, even if you didn't want me there for some reason. I've a right to know what's being planned."

"Which is why I'm enlightening you now, if you'll allow me."

"You did tell them I must have my lands?" Devon was fully on his guard; his friend had a scant regard for the truth. He'd say whatever suited.

"I did. They know you'll not join otherwise. Warwick didn't commit, mind. He's trying to buy me as cheap as he can. And he doesn't want Somerset to join us, that much was clear today; he's not keen for a rival, or to return Edmond's estates. In fact I doubt Warwick even knows the Duke is on his way; Jack de Vere has played his cards close to his chest. Keeping a foot in both camps."

"That may be, but we need Edmond of Somerset, of course. The West Country gentry will follow him, for sure; they never took to me so well. Jealousy is at the root of it, I don't doubt. It always is."

"Is it?"

"Don't let your desire for the girl lead you astray, Robert, for we must keep Edmond sweet. I can't raise the West Country alone; I need him beside me. You do see that, don't you?" Devon was spraying him with spittle.

Clifford saw no such thing, but he didn't expect his friend to understand. Alas, poor Devon; he was handsome and irritating and couldn't hold his drink; the world wrote him off as a fool. He was not a fool, thought Clifford; when he was sober, he could be both tenacious and shrewd, though he hid it well. And he was right about Edmond of Somerset: no doubt it would be better to have him aboard. But the Duke didn't need to be married to Alice de Vere for that.

* * *

Later that night, as the chamberwoman undressed her mistress, the bruises came painfully to light.

"What's this, my lady?" demanded the old woman. The others craned in.

Alice opened her mouth and shut it again. "Lord Clifford seems to feel he's been slighted, Mitten."

Elyn was rapt. "It's like a song, Lady Alice! He's mad with love for you."

"Be quiet, you stupid girl," cried Constance. "You're well out of it, Lady Alice. Well out of it. The man is a beast."

"And what did you say, my lady?" asked Blanche.

"I told him he'd made himself ridiculous."

A circle of surprised faces; Alice exhaled and looked at the ceiling.

Blanche hesitated, loyalty tested for the very first time. While Loic was seeking her company she could ignore the warning in her heart; it was only a whisper, after all, and hard to hear above the drumbeat of passion. But now the Frenchman was revealed in all his calculating coldness, and now, in all likelihood, Sir Hugh would lapse back into complacency. She was wrung with a sudden and unforeseen rush of pity for Lord Clifford, who'd been snuffed out like a candle. "That was, perhaps, not very...wise," she ventured.

"Perhaps not, Blanche. I'm sorry now that I said it. But do not ask me to apologise." Alice made an abrupt cutting motion in the air. "Let us forget Lord Clifford. The Duke of Somerset arrives tomorrow."

* * *

42

Alice was not presented to Duke Edmond until some hours after his arrival in Angers. Jack was in one of his agitated moods, talking too fast, repeating himself. He'd ordered her to remain in her chamber, out of sight. Evidently he wished to unveil his sister with some fanfare; he had bidden her several times to wear her best gown and take especial care with her hair – as if such a reminder were necessary, even once.

Jack – the other version of Jack; the good-natured and unruffled Jack – was present to welcome Somerset with an embrace, with gifts and the warmest words. He carried the Duke off to his chamber and drank with him and bathed with him and urged the newcomer to share his bed and his quarters. Somerset was quite exhausted by the time he managed to shrug off the man so that he could go, alone, to the Queen. He devoutly hoped that Alice de Vere was not so charming as her brother. He didn't think he could bear it.

At last Edmond of Somerset came before Queen Margaret, petty disquiets forgotten. His heart leaped at the sight of her, unchanged in the five years he'd been in Bruges, with her beautiful, wan face and her majestic bearing. For her part, the Queen was warm in her affection, raising him at once from his knees and embracing him, calling down the blessing of Heaven upon him.

"Now that you're here, Edmond, my confidence is complete. The house of Lancaster and its loyal lords; all of us, reunited at last." As usual she'd overlooked her husband, the King, that poor prisoner in London. "And Alice de Vere? Your message was silent on that point."

"Madam," said he, humbly. "I've no doubt that de Vere's sister is entirely suitable and, if you still wish it, it would be an honour to please you in this way."

She smiled at that, and then suddenly laughed, and drew him down beside her to the window seat. "We should warn you to be gentle with our friend Robert Clifford on that score. He had hoped to wed the lady himself. You never saw such a long face!"

"There are many other noble ladies, Madam." *With respectable dowries,* he didn't say.

The Queen leaned in. "Hard to credit, but Lord Clifford fancies himself in love with the girl. Since we heard of your approach, he acts as though he's suffered a mortal blow."

She sat back to see how he would take it. It would do Edmond good to be the object of envy; he needed to be stirred, at such a time, and act the man, or Clifford would trample him, as usual.

But her words were distasteful and his reply was sharp. "I trust the lady has not compromised herself in a similar way?"

The Queen laughed again. "Hardly! The poor girl looked as though she were going to the gallows every time he spoke to her. Now she has a spring in her step and a smile on her face. Alice de Vere is a sweet little thing, and – in truth – we are glad for her, that she's not to be Lord Clifford's wife. None appreciate the man's courage and loyalty more than we, but who could wish such a fate on an innocent maiden?" Her mind was ten years back, mired in the sack of Stamford. No one who'd witnessed Robert Clifford at his work would easily forget it.

Edmond dismissed the matter. "I'm less sure, Madam, of this other marriage."

The Queen looked at her hands.

He continued, "You'll understand my misgivings over the Earl of Warwick's part in this alliance! Warwick was ever the vehement enemy of our King; he's done every one of your loyal lords the most grievous harm. Yet we have only Jack de Vere to vouch for him, Madam, and though I trust de Vere's intentions, he's been in Warwick's pocket for years, and is wed to the man's sister. And now," the quiet tones were ratcheting up, "I hear that Warwick's price is the marriage of his daughter to our Prince, as if it were his place to dictate terms to us!"

He was getting into his stride, she saw, wearily. Duke Charles of Burgundy would be next.

"The Prince should look much higher for a bride: the daughter of Charles of Burgundy is the obvious choice. I would be your ambassador, Madam; I know Duke Charles would look favourably on such a proposal. He is already sympathetic to us; he's been a generous patron and protector to your loyal lords through all our years in Flanders. If the Prince were his own son-in-law, he would supply us then with men and money as needed. And then you could turn your back on Warwick, Madam!"

"Charles of Burgundy? Charles of Burgundy chose to marry Edward of York's sister only a few years ago!" Now the Queen's voice was also rising. "We cannot trust the Duke of Burgundy after that. No, Edmond. We are grateful that Duke Charles has seen fit to support you – you and the other loyal lords. But we cleave to our cousin, the King of France, who has ever been our strong support. He favours the Earl of Warwick, and supports him strongly, and has urged this alliance and the marriage to seal it, and that goes far with us." King Louis had compelled her agreement, days since, and it was irksome to hear Edmond raise all the objections she'd made herself.

"Madam," said he, heavily. "I came to France at your bidding, to support you and the Prince, and counsel you, if you'll permit it. But I tell you now that I could never trust Warwick, and I will never work with him. I should be surprised if any of us would. Exeter, for sure, feels as I do. He's cursed Warwick without ceasing, all the way from Bruges." He looked into the Queen's face, desperately sad, wishing he could bring her joy instead of disappointment.

"The Prince is all that matters. Our son's birthright has led us to think the unthinkable, and embrace the Earl of Warwick. If we can do this, so can you. Think further on it, and speak with the Duke of Exeter, but do so away from our presence; his evil temper offends us. And Edmond – do not assume that all feel as you do. Lord Clifford will, I think, take ship with Warwick and Jack de Vere when they return to England. And as Clifford leads, Devon follows."

Edmond of Somerset came away from the presence chamber, intending to rest in de Vere's chamber while he could, knowing he would sleep little that night with a stranger beside him. But here was his host, lurking in wait. Here too was Jack's friend, William Beaumont – an easy, pleasant fellow, with his close-set eyes, loose limbs and drooping brows. The pair had been trying, evidently, to engage Edmond's young brother Jonkin in conversation, always an uphill struggle. Somerset paused in the doorway.

Jonkin turned to Edmond with relief. "Brother, it seems Alice de Vere is awaiting you. We're invited to meet her now, if you wish it?"

Inwardly, Edmond sighed. He'd been pushing away thoughts of the de Vere woman for weeks, and now he must encounter her before an interested crowd.

Jack lit Somerset with his winning smile and gestured all to rise and follow.

Impatient for a glimpse of the Duke, the ladies had already reached the great chamber and formed themselves into a stiff line. Alice's hands were trembling as her brother appeared in the doorway. Time had slowed, and so anxious was Alice that she forgot to smile. Jack was steering the newcomer in her direction. She had only begun to take him in when the huge figure of Lord Clifford unexpectedly intruded itself. As the men stood together, she could plainly read Jack's attempts to extricate the Duke, while Lord Clifford, hand gripping Somerset's sleeve, paid not the slightest heed. It was perfectly clear that he was impeding the man deliberately, with infantile ill-will, but he should gain no satisfaction from it, and so she turned her back on the room and spoke quietly to Blanche. She had no idea what she was saying and it did not matter, for Blanche was not listening, but staring into her eyes, communing without words. At last she heard her brother's merry voice at her shoulder and she turned, breathless, to behold her bridegroom.

She drank him in: the deep-set hazel eyes, the straight nose, the high cheekbones. Duke Edmond's hair was thick and sandy, and flicked back from his face in little wings. He was of a good height; the right height. Not particularly arresting, or especially notable, and at something of a disadvantage beside Jack, but to Alice, Edmond was handsome and manly and vastly welcome. On his face, a warm smile – a smile in which relief was the main ingredient, but such a sentiment is difficult to read in a stranger, and she did not read it. Alice felt then that every tribulation had resolved itself, and the trials through which she'd passed these last weeks were just that: trials; and she had triumphed.

The Duke kissed her courteously and made his appropriate speech of greeting, of which she remembered nothing, while she basked in gladness.

Alice was used to others remarking on her unusual hair, in its many shades from butter yellow to warm chestnut. But when the Duke did so, she was charmed, and blushed at his acute and flattering discernment. They talked pleasantly for a while, of Flanders and his journey, and his house in Bruges, and she hung upon his words and answered with shy eagerness.

After she had been taken to vespers on his arm, they dined beside the Queen, and he served her, and spoke to her quietly and easily. When the tables were moved back after the meal, he presented her with a gift: an emerald, not large, but exquisitely fashioned. He fastened it at her throat.

"An emerald, to match my eyes!"

The Duke peered into her eyes then, but she was inspecting the pendant and did not see. His choice of gemstone was no more than a happy accident, but Edmond was taking too little cheer in this stroke of luck. He knew what was required and what was fitting; that did not make the jewel any easier to relinquish. It had cost him a month's income, ill-spared. He'd been forced to borrow on his scanty credit.

Then the dancing commenced and Edmond performed with nimble proficiency, and Alice's cup of happiness overflowed.

Heaving a great sigh at these promising signs, Jack swept the room with his gaze and encountered the Earl of Warwick's eyes, not warming the couple, but drilling into him, uncomfortably penetrating, reading all his calculations, the subterfuge and stratagems.

Jack looked quickly away; straight at Clifford. Another mistake.

Later, when Jack bore Edmond of Somerset to his chamber, he learned to his great relief that the Duke was content with Alice, content with the marriage, and content to leave the arranging of it in her brother's hands, which was just as well, as Jack had already procured a licence for the pair to wed at once.

And away in his own chamber, Robert Clifford coiled upon the bed, inexpressibly wretched. Food had lost its savour and turned to ashes in his mouth, and colour had leached from the world, leaving only leaden grey, and cheer would never return. He had watched her through the evening: she had eyes for none but her bridegroom, whom she favoured with all the smiles she had never given him. Her joy was clear to see. And he could take no happiness in that joy – for all that he said he loved her – but was consumed by a sour and twisting rage, which flooded his belly in acid, and raked and rent his innards as if with talons, wickedly sharp.

* * *

On the following day, in the cathedral below the castle, Warwick arranged his own indemnity. Edward of Lancaster, Prince of Wales, only son of King Henry – an imprisoned king – and Queen Margaret – a queen in exile – was betrothed to Anne Neville, Warwick's younger daughter. The couple were distant cousins, within the prohibited degrees, but a papal dispensation for the marriage had been slow to appear, and the Earl was impatient to be off to England.

The company divided sharply between those, like Warwick and King Louis of France, who smiled and nodded and looked pleased, and those, like the Duke of Somerset, who looked as though they were attending a funeral.

Alice was so sincerely glad for Anne that it was awkward to follow the Duke's lead, and restrain the outward show of her feelings. But Edmond had barely glanced at her that morning, so it was easy enough to convey her true feelings to her friend.

After the feast, Lord Clifford deigned to honour his Queen, and King Louis, by playing and singing for the company, which he had not done all this time in France. Together with a number of his men, he played the quickest and merriest of dances, with such effortless grace that those who'd heard little of his gifts were astounded.

And with good reason. For when the music commenced, his butler, Walter Findern, in a moment of inattention, had begun at twice the speed they'd practised; easy enough for Findern on the drum, but producing eye-rolling dismay in Loic on the lute; worse yet for Clifford on the pipes, the elaborate trills virtually beyond him at such a pace. The players managed to stay together, but only just; the crowd held its breath, then released it in a burst of relieved laughter.

48

When the applause had died away, Clifford sang for the company with great poise and self-assurance. It was his masterpiece, *Farewell,* an exquisite, heart-rending song that told of long exile; the beauty of England; the yearning for his homeland.

The Earl of Warwick cast around at the faces of the ladies, many wet with tears, and was pierced by no more than a certain exasperated weariness. England was nothing like the Eden of this elegy; nothing at all. Black Clifford, it turned out, was no more than a maudlin and sentimental fool. Who would have thought it?

Alice had heard the song before, when they tarried in the woods, and yet she'd not given Lord Clifford's talent the attention it deserved. She wondered at herself, and tried – actively tried, for the first time – to recall that day, and study her reaction, but the memories slid sideways and evoked only a sharp sense of shame, that she should have promised herself openly to the man and then discarded him without a word, like a shabby gown when a better one is offered.

* * *

On the day following, there was to be hunting. In her hopefulness, Alice had imagined Duke Edmond leading her in the chase, just as she had been led before. It would be impossible to be ambushed a second time; she knew now what was expected. But when she descended the next morning, it was to learn that Edmond was already closeted with the Queen.

Coming upon his sister, Jack cheered her with the news that she was to be married in three days' time. With the quick spirits that characterised his feverish spells, he resolved at once to bear her to the hunt, where he was bound with William Beaumont.

And so she rode out with her familiars, and Lord Clifford was there, with his. By now his manner troubled her more than his presence. Shortly they would all be away to Flanders, and Duke Edmond must surely notice the man's brooding stares; it was urgently necessary that she and Lord Clifford should learn to discourse politely and indifferently together. Winding up her courage, she sought his gaze and smiled beseechingly.

Lord Clifford searched her face. "I hear you're to be married in a few days, my lady." He spoke low, so that Jack would not hear.

"So my brother has just told me, my lord."

She caught his scent as he leaned in. The man's boots were huge – dusty and scuffed; she couldn't stop looking at them, or rather, she couldn't look elsewhere.

"I am wounded and wretched. Remember me in your prayers, as I shall remember you." He stalked away, crushing the dry grass.

When the Duke joined her at dinner that evening, she asked respectfully of his discourse with the Queen, but he seemed dismayed at her interest. She turned instead to the tale of the hunt. This did not appear to interest him greatly, and though he made assenting noises, his mind was clearly elsewhere.

* * *

"What ails you, my lady?"

Blanche and Alice were alone in their guestchamber; Blanche busy at her spindle beneath the wide window, Alice sliding on her leather soles, breathing noisily. The gentlewoman had drawn her mistress away from the crowd. There was a dam inside Alice, and it was creaking.

Duty was clear, and the gentlewoman focused all her will on performing it, shutting her ears to the maddening whispers. That wretched Frenchman; wherever he was at this moment, he was not thinking of Blanche. "How do you like the Duke? A handsome man, is he not? And courteous, it seems."

There was only a guarded sound.

"Lady Alice?"

Now, a tiny fracture in the dam; words bursting forth in little spurts. "He is a handsome man, Blanche, very. Of course, he is busy and taken up with the Queen; I know that. He did not come to Angers to spend time with me; I know that. But he is not always occupied and yet he has not sought me out, or even looked for me; not once. I thought he would lead me in the hunt; I thought he would want…He has not so much as touched my hand."

This greed for attention: vulgar and unbefitting. Blanche paused, and

50

sighed. *Lord Clifford*, she thought. Alice was an untouched parchment; the finest vellum. That man had soiled her. She bore his grubby imprint.

"There are some men who are always around women. With their cunning, they flatter and snare the vain and heedless. Such men should be avoided. You are right that the Duke is not the sort of man to seek ladies' company, but you should rejoice in that, for it will make him a more honourable husband; one who'll not shame you. After the wedding, you'll be quite alone, and then you will commune fully, and you'll come to care for each other." Despite the brave speech, Loic had intruded himself; at the prospect of losing him forever, Blanche was hard pressed not to cover her face and groan aloud.

Alice listened with close attention. Blanche was ten years older and had once been married. When Alice considered further, she could recall no signs of heat between the Earl and Countess of Warwick, yet the Earl did not shame his wife; the marriage had made them both content. Indeed, as Alice grew to womanhood in their North Country household, that union had been the perfect pattern of mutual trust and confidence. The marriage of Blanche and her late husband may perhaps have been similar. Alice would seek a higher satisfaction in doing her duty than in desiring attention for herself.

* * *

At the dinner on the eve of her wedding, Alice began afresh. She wished to know Edmond – all of him. She sat at his side and begged that he tell her of his history. He began to speak, haltingly, but very soon grew weary and concluded that it was not a fitting topic. Alice ventured to hope that he might find the time to teach her once they were married, for she knew that she was ignorant, and feared she could be of little assistance without a better understanding of all that had passed in England, and why.

Somerset gave one of his rare laughs then. "I don't look to you for counsel in affairs of state, my lady. You'll help me best by learning to order my household, and doing as you're bid." He did not mean to hurt her and, seeing that he had, he added gently, "You are only twenty years of age, and have no experience of life; start slowly and all will be well."

"I have only reached my seventeenth birthday, my lord."

He frowned at her. "Your brother told me you were older."

The Duke was simply mistaken, and it was absurd to blame Jack for it. Alice poked at her food in silence, stifling the stirrings of resentment. Looking away along the table, she beheld Lord Clifford watching her, chin in hand. She could tell at a glance that he'd been looking a long while; his gaze had sunk into a groove. And various others had noticed, too, it seemed, for she was encountering curious or amused looks all along the board. Blushing, she wondered how much time would have to pass before she would cease to blush, and relations between them would steady.

She looked back at her lap. In some way she was mishandling the Duke, and the harder she tried, the less happy he seemed. He'd not been pleased since that first evening. Alice unstifled the stirrings of resentment and was startled by their strength.

Murmuring an excuse, she stood and slipped from the chamber. Blanche stood also, but Elizabeth Ullerton had seen Lord Clifford rise from the bench, and she hurried to follow, motioning Blanche to seat herself. Keeping her distance, Lady Ullerton trailed Alice up a flight of stairs towards the privy. Lord Clifford seemed to have disappeared out of another door, but when she reached the top of the stairs, there he was, a massive figure lounging in the half-dark. Passing him, she secreted herself in an alcove. As soon as she had done so, she wished she had not. It was right and proper for her to accompany Alice; she should have been attending the girl, instead of quailing at his presence and leaving him in possession of the field.

After a moment Alice emerged, shaking out her skirts, and wandered slowly back. From the shadows came a heavy hand upon her shoulder, and she started violently. Lord Clifford's teeth were glinting. "Why am I here?"

There was a long pause. He seemed to be awaiting an answer to the ominous question. She shook her head.

"You have the Clifford ruby."

She groaned, picturing the ring locked away in her chamber. "There was no opportunity to return it, my lord. I'm so very sorry."

"One of your gentlewomen should have brought it, as you were too ashamed to speak to me."

"Of course," she whispered. "I didn't think."

"You didn't think? You'll fetch it now. I'll not have you keep my ring as you break your vow and wed another."

Of course she must return it at once. She hastened to her room, her mind fidgeting on the subject of the Duke. Ignoring a request to remain where he was, Lord Clifford had followed a step behind, keeping pace with long strides, watching her hair flying. When they reached the chamber, she turned and motioned him to wait outside. She was relocking the door from within when he thrust it open, jarring her fingers, and stalked into the room, looking about, arms folded, head back. Alice made a little sound of shock and protest.

"So you'd add to my humiliation? Tether me outside, like a kicked cur, where all can see?"

There was no time to argue, nor could she push him bodily from the room and she'd allowed herself to be pierced by the words. Closing the door, Alice knelt to unlock the chest. Behind her, the man threw himself down on her bed; there could be no other cause than to make her anxious. With shaking hands she fumbled and dropped the key. It spun under the table.

From the bed, his sardonic tones: "Take your time."

The shutters were bolted against the summer evening and though there was daylight still outside, it was as dark as midnight in the room, her candle casting a poor and unsteady light. She felt for the key, and when at last the ring lay in her palm, she stood to face him. Then came a silent tussle. Sprawled back, he was a monstrous shadow, a great pit of darkness in the pale linen. He extended a hand, but she would not approach the bed.

At last he pushed himself up, smirking, and crossed the room. Face averted, Alice dropped the ring into his hand and scuffled to the door. Her fingernail was tapping the latch. Lord Clifford examined the jewel, unwinding the leather thong and dropping it to the floor. Twisting the ring back on to his finger, he inspected it at arm's length.

By now, the Duke must surely have remarked her long absence and might have remarked his absence also. Finally she was pleading with him. "Please! Please go now, Lord Clifford, before we're both missed."

At last, he walked forward. She lifted the latch but the door had scarcely started to swing when Lord Clifford reached over her shoulder and closed it again. He raised her other hand in his own and blew out the flame. As she looked with dismay on the dwindling ember, he knocked the candle with the back of his hand. She heard it break on the floor. Alice had the strangest impression that he was assaying her, testing his way. Her eyes were lowered when his hands fell upon her shoulders; when he pressed her firmly against the door.

Leaning in, his lips were muffled against her hair. "You promised you'd be mine."

As yet, she was dimly mindful of the Duke, waiting below, and somewhere was the consciousness that protesting was a possibility, and resisting, even better; at the very least, averting herself. But she trembled, and did none of these things to hinder him. She must have raised her face, for his lips found hers and her eyes closed in the darkness. This was nothing like the last touch, in the woods, when the panic overwhelmed all else. By now the heady aroma of his skin lulled and enveloped. Her fingers were upon him; perhaps warding him off. All was quiet. His hands were gentle at her back, and they did not stray. The line of his form was thrust against her. The scent of him and the taste of his kiss had become one; and his cadence was smooth, unhurried; and she was inside his lips; and time spun out. Then, with an abruptness all the more startling after that slow assize, Robert stepped back, releasing her. She opened her eyes but it was barely less dark.

"Look outside the door," he said, as if nothing had happened; as if she had imagined it all.

She glanced about in the dim emptiness; a hubbub floating up, faint and distant. Without a word, without a backward glance, he was gone. Alice groped for the key and fled the room.

All the while, the unlucky Lady Ullerton was hovering nearby. She was within her rights to follow the pair, to barge the door as Lord Clifford had done, but she was afraid of the man. Once his heavy step departed, she hurried after Alice and asked, sharply, where she had been all this while, but there was only an incomprehensible mutter.

Complicity had seeded, taken root and borne fruit, all within a matter of moments. A confession was already beyond Alice. With hectic colour she retook her seat beside the Duke, her heart pulsing in jagged starts. It was a long while before she dared to raise her eyes, but Robert had not returned.

At last she was released to her chamber. She lay within his heavy imprint, the sheet dusted still with the perfume of his body, and opened her mind to let in the triumph. For Alice had conquered. With one kiss, she'd banished the mortifying encounter in the woods. And that rough, inarticulate man: he had his wordless farewell, and could depart in peace. The longer she dwelled on it, the less lustful it became, and the more poetic. In her dealings with Robert, she was a grown woman; a duchess; gracious; magnanimous. By the time she fell asleep her feelings had bent and twisted into some semblance of wholesomeness.

In a far corner of the castle Loic slumbered, replete with the secret. Beside him lay his master, wakeful, mind soaring. Clifford had detected something imperfect in Alice; some facet in her, twisting slowly from the light. God, in his mercy, was showing him the other path, dimming the lustre of her virtue so he could see the way.

* * *

Early on the morning of the wedding, when the light was limpid and the blanketing clouds had yet to blow up, the Countess of Warwick called Alice, alone, to her chamber. The summons was not unexpected, although there'd been no precedent. In all those years in the Warwick household at Middleham, Alice had committed no transgression; no indiscretion – and so had endured no interview; no reproach; only the lady's serene favour.

Alice looked on the Countess with a love grown through years of respect and gratitude. The lady had crested the hill of youth and was descending into the valley of her age, although her face was lovely to Alice's eyes, as her own mother's never was. The hidden hair must now be as grey as the soft whiskers that dotted her upper lip. Alice's gaze travelled over the lady's aquiline nose and small receding chin; her dimples; her somewhat crowded mouth.

Alice had been pondering the content of this little talk; of the instructions that were bound to follow. Would they be practical, or tending to the ideal? The latter, she supposed. Now the Countess opened those large, pale eyes very round, as was her wont. "My little Alice! Of all the maidens in my charge, you are the dearest. You are the one I'll miss. So many have caused me pain or anxiety, but not you, my sweet girl: always the pattern of quietness, propriety and grace."

On impulse, Alice leaned in to kiss the downy cheek and was gently put aside.

"Now Alice, listen carefully. As you go as wife to the Duke, never *ever* forget my husband's goodness to you and how great the debt you owe him. My lord of Warwick took you in and gave you a home when the de Veres were sunk to the depths. He treated you as a daughter. Now you must show him the devotion due to a father – even if your husband proves less compliant." The Countess paused, and swallowed, holding Alice's breathless gaze. "The followers of King Henry are not a harmonious band. I'm not speaking out of turn; everyone knows this. Once they've ousted Edward of York, the alliance may begin to…weaken. There is too much bad blood; too many feuds. You and my Anne have grown up in the quiet of the North Country; the Earl and I never felt the need to burden you with the high cares of the court. But, my dear," the voice had become much softer and yet more emphatic, "bear in mind that as the Duke's wife you will be in the thick of things and, as such, perfectly placed to follow a noblewoman's calling, which is to disregard your own desires and feelings in the pursuit of peace. Alice, if you remember nothing else, I hope that you'll remember this lesson."

A lengthy silence ensued as the good woman gazed, wordless, into the future, dreading what lay ahead. Alice waited, proud recipient of grave and adult guidance.

At last the lady turned her head and resumed the day's work. There followed some commonplace directives on the role of a wife; Alice could have spouted them herself, had roles been reversed. And now the Countess was working up to the wedding night. Eyes widening further, she said, with slow solemnity: "I will tell you just what I tell all my charges: provided you do as you're bid, readily and without demur, no more can be asked of you."

Is that all? thought Alice. It was a ludicrously insufficient, not to say belated, preparation for the demands of men.

* * *

The composure that had smoothed Robert Clifford's pillow was, predictably enough, ebbing away.

He eased himself through the ceremony, watching the bride abstractedly; it was the same grey dress she'd worn in the vision and when first he saw her in the flesh; her best gown. He was quite unable to focus on anything but the previous night's encounter, his mind roving over his surrender and hers; for they had, both of them, proved in that moment more generous than the other had any cause to expect. He paused at the point at which he'd yielded to pity and called a halt, and examined his instincts, and found them wanting.

Then his attention was recalled to the present: there was no lightning strike to the tower, nor did Somerset suffer a fatal stroke on the steps of the church; the pair were now husband and wife.

At the wedding feast he'd meant to play the man, to hold up his head, to please the company, and so he'd forewarned his fellow musicians among the household. He'd sing *Tamlin of Carterhaugh*, and watch her blush. But when the moment arrived, the self-disgust was in full flow; that he should have given way to mercy at such a moment, when he might have taken it all and prevented this perversion of God's purpose. Sullen and bitter, he could not rise to the music despite their questioning looks. And all day long Devon bothered him like a horsefly.

Clifford was not the only unhappy man in the room. Warwick's mask kept slipping; a thunderous expression trouncing him as his gaze wandered again and again to the irrepressible Jack de Vere, so carelessly triumphant in his ducal alliance, his future secure.

* * *

Away in the castle, by this time, the horseplay would be raucous; the couple frolicked and manhandled up to the chamber – to the bed – that was Clifford's own until that morning.

There was never any prospect that he would be present at the bedding; it was beyond anything he could bear. The black and brooding thoughts were marked on his face, now, as he stood in the chamber of their unfamiliar lodgings in the town below the castle. Loic brushed his hair while Jem brushed his boots.

"Shall I be accompanying you, Monseigneur?"

"Not tonight. For once Devon is putting his hand in his purse for my entertainment, and he won't welcome another thirsty man. Besides, this is an important occasion, and you'll be busy with your particular duties."

There was a nasty smile on his face. Loic, who was inspecting Jem's handiwork, looked up enquiringly.

"Once the carousers have gone, you'll spend the night with your ear to Somerset's door and report to me all that occurs within."

Loic dropped the brush and came slowly to his feet, a flush spreading up his neck and into his cheeks. "The devil I will."

"You will if I say it!" shouted Clifford, spoiling for the collision. "Or you'll leave my service tonight and beg your bread in the streets."

Fury flared into Loic's face and he fairly stamped his foot, slipping from English to torrential French. "We Monclers have held our lands since the days of Charlemagne! I will not stoop so low, and care too much for your honour, into the bargain. Do you think I cannot find a master who would pay me twice as well and not ask such services of me?"

"What say you, Jem?" Clifford had gripped the manservant's shoulder and was drawing him in to the quarrel. "So: you shall be my companion. You shall share my bed, my bath and my women, and yet cheek me as you will, as ever Master Moncler did, for am I not meek and mild with those who serve me?" The voice was growing ever louder and more harsh; roaring, now.

Every man of the household had abandoned his business, engrossed.

"While this fine nobleman shall go to the Duke of Exeter – who desires him so ardently – and wear purple velvet, and eat from a golden dish as

Charlemagne intended, and take it up the arse until he cannot walk straight. Mark his words: it was Moncler's choice, to leave me thus."

Clifford flung out of the room, forgetful of his hat, purse and knife, which Loic rapidly secreted under the bed. Then he lay down, hands clasped beneath his head.

"There now, Jem." Loic patted the bed next to him. "None of us shall eavesdrop at Somerset's door. Monseigneur should not have asked it, and he'll see that, when he's not so angry. Away he goes to pick a fight, but without his knife, so it will come to nothing. Devon will carry him off to a tavern, and he'll not return till dawn, and then he'll have a woman with him, and he'll be very drunk. By noon tomorrow, he will humbly beg my pardon, as quiet as a lamb."

"So you'll not go to serve the Duke of Exeter?" breathed Jem.

"And take it up the arse until I cannot walk straight? I thank you, no! I shall go on just as before, paid half as much as Exeter offers, well supplied with girls and wine, and kept awake, as ever, by Monseigneur's nightmares and his snoring. This life is just to my taste, and he knows it. I will never leave him."

* * *

At long last, the revellers left them. Alice was greatly touched that Robert had the delicacy to absent himself.

For an eternity of moments, husband and wife lay like effigies in the stifling blackness. Then Edmond rose and tugged back the bed's curtains. Alice watched him cross the room. Swinging the shutters to let in the still air, he leaned on the sill, gazing out over the silver roofs of Angers. Her husband's form was beautiful to her eyes; neither huge nor fearsome, but shapely, compact; the muscles not obscene, but tight and appropriate. Covering his chest and forearms was a fair, curling down that faintly blurred his outline.

He returned to the bed, and knelt over her, drawing the sheet from her body so that it fell about her feet in soft, heavy folds. Her courage would fail her if he didn't speak; she had imagined him kind and reassuring. Perhaps it showed in her face, for he murmured, "Don't be afraid. I won't hurt you."

Lying close beside her, he kissed her cheek, one arm draped to her far shoulder. She turned her face. For the first time, he pressed his mouth to hers: once, and then again. It was not the kiss she was anticipating. His scent was tart and light and left no impression. Nudging her knees apart, he guided himself down upon her. Contrary to his promise, it did hurt, and the absence of pleasure was complete and unforeseen. While he was moving, Alice lay rigid, unsure what to do. It was quickly over, and then he laid himself down, uncovered, unspeaking, facing away. After she'd waited a little to be sure there was no more, she tucked the linen about her. Now she recalled the Countess's little speech of that morning. As ever, the lady was right: that was, indeed, all. She felt relieved and despondent. And then, not long afterwards, undisturbed by any significant emotion, she slipped into sleep.

Still awake some hours later, Edmond rose to relieve himself. The moon was brightening the chamber and, looking on himself, he noticed a dark crust, as of dried blood. He peered over to Alice's side of the bed. The girl had rolled in her sleep and the cover was trailing to the floor. There was a small dark smear on the undersheet. He recalled his assurance, no sooner given than forgotten. She hadn't made a sound. He would ask forgiveness when she woke. Washing himself clean with water from the basin, he lay down.

* * *

Alice appeared the next morning arrayed in a headdress, her locks for the first time pinned away out of sight. She had chosen it with care, this rigid cap in shades of dark green, adorned with gauzy wings that fluttered from delicate wires. She turned her head about, and walked up and down, catching the trembling chiffon with the corner of her eye.

As the Queen's council was assembling in the great chamber, the Earl of Devon watched Alice strolling beneath the window. He looked at her attendants, and followed their admiring gaze back to her headwear. Of course: the girl was now a wife, and dressing as one.

"Edmond!" Devon's tone was loud and bantering. He grinned as Somerset winced at the casual, public treatment of his name. "You've deprived us of the sight of your wife's beautiful hair! She's parading like a peacock in her new headdress," he tapped the window with his nail, "when we know what's hidden beneath is much lovelier."

"I apologise for my selfishness, my lords," Somerset responded, trying for the same tone. "From now on, that lovely hair is reserved for my eyes only."

In the act of settling himself at the table, Clifford kicked his chair with an indiscreet and angry jerk.

Somerset's young brother Jonkin entered the room and took his bearings, plucking at his sleeves. The Prince of Wales was seated in the place of honour, the Queen to his right, Edmond before the door to his left. There were several earls present, but as brother to a duke of the royal house, Jonkin's place must be to the right of Queen Margaret. He walked round the table. As he grasped his chair, Jasper Tudor, Earl of Pembroke, small, prickly and self-assured, placed both hands on his shoulders and unceremoniously moved him aside, taking the place. Jonkin gave way, abashed, muttering apologies. Half-brother to King Henry, Tudor must be right in assuming precedence. In that case, Jonkin should be seated to the left of his brother. He walked back around the table to the empty chair. Edmond's hand hovered over the seat, preventing him from sitting.

"*Exeter*," he murmured.

Colour flooded Jonkin's cheeks. Of course, this place was reserved for the Duke of Exeter. In that case, he should have stayed on the other side of the table, beside Jasper Tudor. Yet there sat Warwick, perusing his letters, ignoring proceedings. As Jonkin was shuffling uncertainly to the left of the absent Exeter, Jack de Vere threw himself casually into the vacant chair, and Jonkin was shunted still further down, almost to the foot of the table. He was gratefully pulling out the free chair between Jack and Clifford, desperate to sink from view, when, in a carrying voice from the window embrasure, Devon hailed him.

"Don't mind me, Jonkin: that place is yours, if you will it."

This could not be right. He knew for certain that he outranked Devon, just as he outranked Warwick, and de Vere, and he frowned at his grinning oppressor, hot and perplexed. Edmond motioned him down. Trying for nonchalance, Jonkin eased himself in, next to a scowling Lord Clifford. He was at once assailed by a gust of stale perfume.

Meanwhile, the bridegroom endured a barrage of backslapping and joshing on his weary looks. Somerset was, indeed, tired – a poor sleeper these days, and unhappy to be sharing his bed with a woman. But there was an undertone. Under the guise of camaraderie, Devon was needling him. And Robert Clifford, more grim than usual, radiating hostility. Somerset watched Clifford as the meeting commenced, his mind wandering away. For the first time he recalled the Queen's account of Robert's abortive courtship. The scales fell from his eyes and he wished they hadn't.

Warwick opened the meeting, doing much of the talking, Somerset interjecting at times, wrong-footed by his rival's easy assumption of leadership. Warwick passed to the conquest of England. All his plans seemed to hinge on his brother, John Neville, another man who'd spent the last twenty years trying to kill them all.

It'll be a wonder if York is stupid enough to fall for this, thought Somerset. He turned to remark as much to his neighbour, but when Jack de Vere smirked at him, he held his peace.

"It's a clever strategy, but can you be sure of your brother's part in this?" said Prince Edward. "From the very first, John Neville has been an ardent supporter of the pretender, Edward of York."

"As has my Lord of Warwick," observed Somerset, his voice icy. "You'll not have forgotten, my lord Prince, that this man overthrew your father and killed many of our dearest friends. Yet we're expected to take this miraculous conversion on trust!"

The Queen smacked the flat of her hand on the table, in warning.

"I have letters here from my brother," Warwick's voice was calm, "assenting to all I've described. He waits only for my signal to raise his men in the cause of Lancaster. Moreover," he glanced at the Queen, seeking her attention, before staring pointedly at Somerset, "I suggest we all put the past behind us and, in particular, avoid ascribing deaths on the field to any particular hand. It is always unhelpful, and usually inaccurate."

Though some were red-handed. Some were positively drenched with blood. Clifford smirked, tipping his chair, hands behind his head, and cast around the table, as if challenging any man to meet his gaze. No one seemed interested.

"Edward of York gave your brother my lands in the West Country," said Devon, with an irksome smile. "Does he plan to surrender them to me as I wade ashore?"

Warwick frowned across. "My brother has no particular attachment to your lands. They are a poor prize, buried in some backwater."

Jack de Vere intervened cheerfully. "When we've destroyed Edward of York, there'll be confiscated lands aplenty, more than enough to go around."

"There is not enough to go around, and you know it!" bellowed Exeter, who'd slipped in beside him, late and glowering. The man was always angry about something; this was a better cause than most.

"And what of Harry Percy?" said the Queen, ignoring the Duke of Exeter, as was her way. "The Percys of Northumberland were ever our loyal supporters."

"Harry Percy?" Clifford spoke for the first time. "If Harry Percy is forced to take sides, he may be driven towards Edward of York. He's only just been restored to the earldom of Northumberland. He won't risk losing it again to the Nevilles."

"Harry Percy would like to torture every Neville to death." Devon grinned. "Slowly. I should imagine. Just a guess."

"Harry Percy will lose more than his lands if he doesn't come out for us," said de Vere.

"Harry Percy will keep his earldom and his lands if he returns to Lancaster," said Warwick quietly, watching Clifford from under his brows. "Lord Clifford will tell him so. But if Percy cleaves to York, it will be the last thing he does."

"So: Harry Percy's to keep his lands, and I'm to have mine. Since there's no land left over for your poor brother, my lord, perhaps John Neville will be content with a hermitage? We have a picturesque one down in Tiverton…sea air…"

Devon couldn't help himself. Now he was sketching a tiny square in the air for Warwick's benefit. Clifford caught his eye with a warning shake of the head. Warwick was looking from one to the other, lips pinched. The Queen had closed her eyes.

The meeting maundered on. To make amends, Clifford repressed Devon where he could, and assayed a few comments in support of Warwick, drawing puzzled looks from Somerset. The Prince, who'd begun the meeting with such pugnacious attention, was now scratching horses on the table with the tip of his knife. At one point, attempting to interrupt a long digression, the Queen asked Jonkin for his opinion. The timing was unfortunate; the boy had been following the debate until someone began expounding a theory of kingship. All the room was looking at him.

"I agree with my brother Edmond's position, Madam," he muttered.

But Somerset had not expressed an opinion, not for half an hour past, and Jonkin's words were greeted with silence, broken by a snort of laughter from Devon. Somerset rubbed his temples.

When the meeting broke up, Jonkin was quick to exit, evading for a time the reproof that was bound to follow. But Somerset was otherwise engaged. As the men filed out, talking amongst themselves, he hung back, gazing out of the window at the town beyond. Clifford was still lounging in his chair, brow resting in his hand, conversing in a low voice with his friend, who was perched on the table before him, swinging his leg, flipping his knife in the air and reaching for it, over and over.

"Serves you right." Devon's voice was smug and self-righteous. "I spent a particularly dreary evening."

Clifford wiped his brow and murmured again, voice lost in his handkerchief.

Devon chuckled. "Don't be so ungrateful. As I promised: the day has come and gone, and you have lived to tell the tale."

Somerset had approached on the blind side, and laid his hand on Clifford's arm. The man jumped as if scalded.

Devon swivelled to the newcomer. "What do you want, Edmond, eh?'

Somerset's eyes were still on Clifford. "This is a mockery, is it not?" He gestured to the empty room. "You know that neither of us will see our lands returned? You do know that?"

Devon flipped and grasped, and flipped and missed, and the knife clattered noisily across the floor. "Strange. I do believe I'm still drunk."

"I have no interest in this shameful and unworkable plan and I assume you feel the same, Robert. You should speak to the Queen; she thinks you mean to join Warwick's invasion of England."

Devon retrieved the knife and spun it again. Clifford couldn't bring himself to look at Somerset. "No, I'll be heading back to Flanders, as will Devon."

Devon interjected. "Not for long, though! We'll be off to England soon enough, Edmond, or we shall lose our chance. You too, if you know what's good for you." He fumbled the knife and caught it, twanging, by the tip of the blade. He flipped it again.

Somerset clicked his tongue in irritation, eyes still on Clifford, who reached out and plucked the knife from the air, placing it silently on the table. Clifford was examining his ring as he spoke.

"Warwick is our best hope. With his name, his wealth and his men at our disposal, we're better placed than we've been in years. And once York is vanquished, we deal with Warwick."

Somerset shook his head. "There is no honour in that, and I'll have no part in it: to smile in a man's face and sharpen your dagger behind his back. If our King is restored, I will return then to serve him. But fight alongside the one who started the war, who killed my father and drove me into exile – intending all the while to dispatch the man after? By God, no; it would shame me. My honour is worth more than this."

"And that strikes me as no less shameful: seeking to keep your own hands lily-white; to profit once others have done your dirty work," grunted Clifford, meeting Somerset's gaze at last, heaving himself to his feet. "Ah – why marry Alice de Vere, if you never intended to back the invasion? Why?" He retrieved Devon's knife and slipped it into the sheath at his friend's belt.

Somerset hesitated, taken aback at the intrusion. "The Queen wished it," he said, grudgingly.

Clifford sneered and turned to Devon. "Let's go and bathe. I'm dripping with sweat and I stink of cheap quim."

Devon laughed. "Who could refuse such an invitation? You coming, Edmond? No?"

* * *

Jonkin made his way to Alice's chamber and, from there, he was directed on to the gardens. He found his new sister-in-law sitting with Anne Neville amidst their gentlewoman. As he couldn't drink the milk of her sympathy before that array of bright eyes, he settled himself at her feet, an audience for their singing. It was *Tamlin of Carterhaugh*, familiar to these North Country dwellers, but not to him. They delighted in teaching him the ballad, faintly racy in its theme, clapping their hands at his feigned disapproval.

Alice held a lute in her lap. Her voice was lovely, her fingers less adept. Wresting the instrument from her, Jonkin picked up the tune with natural ease. Alice was singing lustily when she observed Lords Clifford and Devon riding for the gatehouse with a small train of men. Clifford had caught the song and turned, hard, in the saddle with a speaking look. Devon reached across and seized his reins.

* * *

When Alice joined the Queen's ladies for the midday meal, she was hopeful of further polite admiration. Instead, from the start, she was the subject of distressing intrusion. Mitten had bundled the stained sheet from the chamber, but Alice might as well have been wearing it, for she was pulled about for the most intimate details of her husband's performance, and at length, mortified and unhappy, she declined to speak at all.

Blanche guessed the reticence was not due to modesty alone. "Did he hurt you, my lady?" she asked, when they were alone with Anne.

66

"He did, although he said he wouldn't."

"Trying to be gentle, I'm sure. He is a considerate man, I think."

If he were trying to be gentle, she'd seen no evidence of it. "It was not as I hoped," said Alice in a low voice. "I thought there would be kisses; caresses. I thought he would be more attentive."

Anne was staring, goggle-eyed, as her mind spun in wonder and apprehension. Blanche was silent also, reliving the frantic joy of her own wedding night. She was surprised to find Alice had formed any expectation at all, so little knowledge had she.

That night, resignation in place of anticipation. In spite of her resolve, Alice flinched beneath her husband's touch. Only then did Edmond recall the blood. He halted at once, abashed, and lay down at her side, stroking her hair. Grateful at his forbearance, she slipped under his arm and laid her head on his shoulder, arm across his chest. He was touched by the intimacy of the gesture and then dismayed when she fell asleep at once, pinning him on his back, hot and heavy.

* * *

Clifford's finger was upraised. "Attend carefully to this agent of King Louis. I'll say you're an Englishman and so, like most Englishmen, you know not a word of French. Take care lest he catch you out."

Loic nodded. "What does he want?"

"What does he want? He wants to buy me."

King Louis's agent was late and lukewarm and didn't look the part. A shrunken and twisted homunculus was Pierre du Chastel, when such men should only ever be fat, twinkling and expansive.

Eyed by their guest, Loic bustled about the sparsely furnished chambers with their view across the baking garrets of Angers. This man had but lately joined his service from England, Clifford explained; Monsieur du Chastel might speak freely before him. And so, straining to straighten in his chair beneath the fearsome visage of his host, du Chastel began.

There followed all the delicate preliminaries. So Gallic – and they went on so long – that Clifford's mind was soon elsewhere, composing a letter to his mistress, inviting Babette to celebrate the thumping bribe with the purchase of a new gown. And here was the woman herself before his mind's eye, parading in the proud dress, a good deal comelier than the figure opposite.

But du Chastel brushed aside the embellishment at last, and let Clifford see the scaffolding. "King Louis is all too aware of your inestimable worth to the house of Lancaster, Milor' de Clifford. He was astonished to discover that Duke Charles of Burgundy – who never did understand the duties of a patron – sets so little store by you that he pays a pension only half of what he pays the Dukes of Somerset and Exeter."

"I wonder how he knows that!"

"There is nothing King Louis does not know. Nothing. The affairs of Christendom lie open as the pages of a book, bared to his gaze. King Louis knows the other exiles are insignificant. He knows Duke Charles loves them only because they're in his pocket. And he knows that you have the wisdom and independence of mind to put old enmities aside and work with his great friend, the Earl of Warwick."

Clifford laughed. "Your king knows more of my intentions that I do myself. And what does King Louis mean to do with these naked insights?"

Du Chastel smiled. "Why are we here, Milor'? He means to overthrow Edward of York and restore his good cousin Henry to the throne of England." The eloquence was giving way to something altogether brisker. "The price for King Louis's support is, as you probably expected, the destruction of Charles of Burgundy. Milor' de Warwick has agreed that England will join France in an attack on Flanders as soon as Edward of York is defeated."

"Has he now? Ah – I've been wondering, Monsieur du Chastel, what the Earl of Warwick stands to gain from this. It cannot be influence with King Louis; already he has the good fortune to be your master's dear friend. It cannot be money; this is the richest noble in England, by a very wide margin. So I ask myself what he lacks. He lacks independence, and he lacks protection – from those of us who will now be around him; the loyal lords, with our long memories."

Du Chastel held his gaze. "You are as astute as men say, Milor' de Clifford. The marriage of Milor' de Warwick's daughter, the lady Anne, to Prince

Edward of Lancaster, will help to give him the protection he requires. Any attempt to put the bride aside – as we hear that some of your less astute friends have been threatening – would bring down the wrath of France upon the malefactors. But, more importantly," he lowered his voice, "King Louis has promised to bestow the lands of Holland and Zeeland on Milor' de Warwick once Flanders is in his hands."

"Ah - taking Warwick away from England and the fear of reprisal, and giving King Louis a devoted and grateful friend to hold those northern dominions for him! A shrewd plan."

"Indeed, Milor'. Indeed." Du Chastel winched his head a little higher, pained and blinking. "You've suffered much, with the deaths of your father and your brother, as have many of those who are now to be Milor' de Warwick's allies. It's difficult, perhaps, to conjure much love for the man you hold responsible for these losses. But King Louis feels certain you could work with Milor' de Warwick if you bear in mind that he will not be long among you in England."

"Ah – good news for Warwick and good news for me. The prospect of his departure might go some way to securing my involvement." Clifford rubbed his hands with an impatience he didn't trouble to conceal. "*Some* of the way." Indeed, he was troubling not to conceal it.

"Just so. Now then. Your host in Flanders is sure to stop your pension once you leave Bruges for England. Sooner, if Duke Charles perceives that you're a friend to France. King Louis is therefore desirous of smoothing your path. As he values you so highly, he would pay you a pension equal to that which Edmond of Somerset receives from Duke Charles."

Somewhat less than he hoped, when Clifford was picturing the King of France as some bottomless well of corruption. There was silence while the old man waited, glumly, for gratitude.

"And, of course, if Milor' de Warwick comes safe through these travails, King Louis will not be slow to reward the Earl's defenders."

Clifford licked his dry lips. "Ah. This is generous."

"In point of fact, I have the first instalment with me, if convenient?"

"Greatly convenient." He smirked.

"Naturally the King will require a receipt."

Clifford folded his arms. "That will not be possible."

The courtier twitched in pretended surprise. "But Milor' de Clifford! The King is a stickler in such matters."

"Then I must decline his generosity. A receipt would not aid him greatly, but it would make matters uncomfortably hot for me, if it got into the wrong hands. But then…I'll shortly take back my own lands in England. Perhaps King Louis' gift, although flattering, is not truly necessary."

"Come, my friend," sighed du Chastel. "It's little enough to ask. He'll never agree to make a payment without evidence that it's duly received."

"He must take your word for it, or we go our separate ways."

There was a small hesitation; not long enough for a man to change his mind.

"Very well," said du Chastel, equably. "I'll have the gold brought in."

He rose and hobbled off to oversee the transfer. Clifford evaded Loic's eyes. A small chest with a peaked lid was deposited in a corner. Then du Chastel bowed low to Clifford, and bowed also to Loic, pausing, before he reached the door. "It is a great honour to meet the renowned Milor' de Clifford, whose mind is as impressive as his physique. May I commend you particularly, Milor', on your exceptional command of the French tongue? It's unusual to meet any foreigner who speaks our language so well, and certainly rare in an Englishman. My compliments also to your chamberlain," he added, with a smile at Loic, "who has imparted not only fluency, but elegance of expression. As a Moncler, his own education was, doubtless, of the highest order."

And then he bowed again, and left them.

* * *

Alice knew Anne well enough to see that she was agitating with the need to ask. Under the pretext of examining their stitching, the two girls removed to the window seat.

"Was it terrible, Alice? It sounds as though it was."

70

"Not at all," said Alice stoutly. She yearned to speak; she was racked with it, but not about that, for that did not repay close interest. "Anne, if I tell you something secret, will you promise faithfully never to tell anyone? Lord Clifford…" But she found she couldn't, after all, tell it. Her throat had closed up.

Anne had covered her mouth with her hand, and then, when nothing was forthcoming, she removed it.

Now Alice had to offer up something. "I believe Lord Clifford is jealous of my husband. I fear Duke Edmond will notice."

Anne's eager hand returned to her mouth. "I have noticed it too," she whispered. "His eyes are on you constantly. It is not appropriate."

Surely not news to anyone. There was no call for Anne to look so furtive; she may as well proclaim it to the room in general.

Anne giggled. "Not *eyes*! I mean *eye*."

The dissident truth was skulking in the shadows. Alice longed to share the impossible burden. She was alone.

* * *

Clifford and Loic were occupied with a new song of the master's composing, a soaring and delicate hymn in honour of the Virgin. Clifford was sprawled upon the bed, the mattress slumping under his weight, its base a bare inch above the pointed lid of a small chest; the chest cramful of King Louis's gold. Practising on the pipes, he was doing something complicated with his tongue, shaping little runs and trills, over and over, at dizzying speed.

The chamberlain was below him on the floor, the lute in his lap, shoulders sagging. Loic had broken off to suck his stinging fingers, when his master put aside the music to interrogate him on the subject of Blanche Carbery.

"I must confess, I've not sought her out in a while, Monseigneur. Do you wish it?"

"Mm, before she thinks you've lost interest."

"She didn't think I was interested in the first place, Monseigneur."

"Then your aim must be off."

71

"And what am I to do with her?"

Clifford paused. "I want to know if Somerset is pleasing his wife. Does Alice have any complaints? Does she speak of me?"

Loic winced. There was not a hint of embarrassment in the request. He would humiliate himself, doubtless for nothing. "I suspect I'll get nowhere, Monseigneur."

"See what you can achieve. At least keep her warm. Take my purse; spend as you must."

"You wish me to go now?" asked Loic, between Scylla and Charybdis.

"No, no. You must perfect the piece today, now you've got so far. You'll see her tomorrow."

"You know, Monseigneur, I'm rather troubled in my mind, I must confess. The vision…by all of it. I don't doubt the vision!" he added, quickly. "God may have meant you to marry the Lady Alice. He did, of course. But now she's wed to another."

"Exactly so."

"But how can it be God's purpose for you to continue on? For that would mean the Lord was encouraging you both into adultery."

"That's just the sort of tedious comment I'd expect from Devon. I thought you had more sense."

Loic shrugged, sullen now.

"First, God's ways are mysterious, aren't they? Aren't they? That's an incontrovertible fact. Speak to Reginald Grey if the theology is beyond you. Second, Somerset is a wolf in sheep's clothing and I am an instrument of vengeance."

"Edmond of Somerset is your friend. He's been your friend, and your leader, for years now. He didn't even want to marry the woman; he hasn't done so to spite you."

"You think it possible a man could so contravene God's purpose without some inkling of his own wrongdoing? God will not have left him in ignorance. Do not fear, though. *Vengeance is lame, yet still she pursues the guilty man.* Or something like."

72

"Well. No one conveys an arresting image like Horace, Monseigneur, though your translation does him no favours. Yet I can't help wondering: who, here, is the guilty man?"

* * *

Blanche seemed pleased to see him, for her own sake and, Loic presumed, on account of poor Sir Hugh. But how to open, on such a delicate matter? The woman was so quick-witted. He began by complaining of his master, the perennial opening gambit of servants everywhere.

"I'm sorry to hear that, sir," said she, and he could hear the smile in her voice. "I know you two are generally in perfect harmony. And there – you have his purse about you, as usual. A mark of trust."

"Curse you! He is in an unjust temper, though, Mistress Carbery, and you know the reason."

They were lounging in the arbour where Clifford and Alice had sat together, Loic on the bench and Blanche reclining against him. Loic kissed her fingertips one by one, and she sighed against his chest.

"The last time I was alone with you, we were rudely interrupted," he whispered. "We should make plans to pick up where we left off."

She could listen to him forever. His English was near-perfect, fluent and idiomatic, but the accent was heavy, and charming to her ears. "What can I do for you, Master Moncler?"

"I told you." He was still whispering, and kissed her temple, the broad flaxen brow. "And you could also please me by accepting a keepsake, something I believe would look very handsome around your neck."

"I see. And to what do I owe this rush of generosity?"

"To the memory of a beautiful afternoon. But if you wanted to please me more, you could gratify my curiosity on a few points."

There it was. "Ask away," she said, rather grimly.

Loic sighed, and girded his loins to go on. "The Duke of Somerset: is he kind to his wife?"

"Very kind. Why should he not be?"

"And he has made her happy?"

"Very happy."

"Give me something, Blanche," he pleaded.

"Loïc!" She pushed herself upright. "Anything I tell you could have come from no one but me. It would be traced back at once. You're asking me to risk my position solely to gratify your master's sordid curiosity."

"Then I shall also entrust you with a secret that must go no further: the Lord God has indicated to Monseigneur in a vision that he will be her husband."

"Another vision? God is particularly obliging where that nobleman is concerned – presumably on account of his legendary virtue."

"Well, no – not another vision. There was just the one vision concerning the lady, as far as I know. But once such a promise is made, it is a given, even if God is moving in mysterious ways just at present. Anything that you can do to further this purpose will no doubt be richly rewarded, both in Heaven and here on earth, in the jeweller's workshop by the bridge."

She snorted. "You are absurd."

He pulled her in and kissed her lips. "What harm can it do? He has no one to talk to except me and he is very unhappy. Of your charity, see if you can find something to cheer him."

"He talks to the Earl of Devon."

"Not about this. Devon is always scolding him."

She was doomed from the start. "On the first night, the Duke hurt her and she complained that he was too hasty and it gave no pleasure. I admit I was surprised. For a girl who's never been kissed, she seemed to know what was missing."

"But no: she has kissed Monseigneur. He…"

"Nonsense! You saw the results of that attempt of his: it appalled her so much it made her sick. Lady Alice learned nothing from that disaster in the woods, believe me."

Loïc eyed her thoughtfully. "Please go on."

"So then she was too sore to let her husband near and, now she is better, he has not come to her again and she is fretting. I've told her to talk to him, but she won't."

"I see. Thank you. This will comfort my poor master; comfort him discreetly. One last thing…" He rolled his eyes behind her back, which made the question no less silly. "Does she ever speak of Monseigneur?"

"No, Loic. Why would she?"

"I thought as much." Loic wrapped his arms about her. "You have been very kind. I would like to show you this piece I told you of. Will you come with me into the town?"

* * *

The women were surprised when Blanche appeared among them wearing an unusual crucifix, skilfully worked with seed pearls and filigree of gold.

"Has Sir Hugh Dacre given you this present, Blanche?" asked Joanna.

Constance was dismissive. "Sir Hugh does not have the good taste to choose such a lovely thing."

Blanche lowered her eyes. "I had it from Loic Moncler."

There were murmurs.

"Is Master Moncler still courting you, Blanche?" asked Alice, curious.

"I trust he is courting her!" said Elizabeth Ullerton.

Alice turned to her. "I thought you disapproved of the gentleman, Lady Ullerton?"

"I do indeed. Well – in truth I know little enough of him. But like master, like man. He is hand-in-glove with Lord Clifford, and that is enough to damn him."

Most young men hovered near enough to damnation in those jaundiced eyes.

"But you said…"

"I may not commend the man, Elyn, but what matters is that he seeks Blanche only for the honest purpose intended by God." Lady Ullerton's voice was sharpening. For herself, she was profoundly weary in waiting for an honest

75

purpose to unfold. Here was she, born into the family of Loys, ancient and respectable, and (happy boast) related – rather distantly – to the Earl of Essex and the Archbishop of Canterbury, both. But what, in truth, had she? A brief marriage, twenty years back, to a bald knight three times her age with a mouth so rotten he spat green spittle; his discourse so dull, so repetitive, that her eyes would sometimes fill with mad tears. Yet here was Blanche: daughter of an esquire; widow of an esquire; enjoying the attentions of that pretty, wicked boy and courted by a knight who could call two barons and an earl *cousin*. Though one of those barons was Lord Clifford, who didn't really count. Her eye was twitching. "Given the company he keeps, I fear that Master Moncler is worming himself into her good graces with some heinous design."

It was clear enough what that design might be, but Alice's mind was troubled in another direction.

"Blanche, it's not necessary to voice this, I know, but as Master Moncler is so dear to his master, I have been fearing that matters we speak of could reach Lord Clifford's ears."

Like an autumn leaf that falls and lights at random, the words signified nothing, but Blanche felt as though her heart had stopped. Her cheeks flared with colour as she stammered out her disavowal and Alice, concerned that she had caused offence, compounded the distress by humbly begging her pardon.

* * *

From Loic's self-important bustling, Clifford could tell he had news aboard.

"Come, then: tell me what she says. That purse feels a good deal lighter. I trust I had value for money."

Loic relayed the news of drought in the marriage-bed.

"He's had her only once? They've been wed a week!" Clifford crowed with laughter.

"That's not the best of it, though, Monseigneur." Loic conveyed Alice's complaint. "The lady is not satisfied with her husband. And Mistress Carbery knows nothing of your kiss on the eve of the wedding. Lady Alice has kept it to herself."

Clifford sat and considered awhile, twisting his ring. It seemed she was comparing the two men; that the first experiences had spoiled the rest. Perhaps she was even recalling the raptures he'd promised in the wood. This was better than expected. Even the lack of honesty was promising; with care, it might be cultivated into a tendency to deceit. "Now: you shall not let your connection with Mistress Carbery drop off again; I do not wish us to warm a corpse every time we need a little information."

* * *

Lord Clifford was last of the noblemen to take his leave of the royal party; he had kept them waiting. Alice was bidding her farewells to Anne as he rode up. He turned, as if sensing her regard. Or perhaps not; he was always looking.

"He kissed me. That's what I meant to tell you." It came in a rush, as Anne clung to her beside the gate of Angers. "The night before the wedding. In my chamber. In the dark. Lord Clifford kissed me." Anne disentangled herself, abruptly, holding Alice with her fingertips at arm's length, as if she were contagious.

"Oh, how *horrible!*"

"Well, no. Not horrible, in truth. He was –" she strove to translate the touch, "reverent. It was his farewell. The perfect farewell, for he has let me go."

Perfect? Anne grimaced at her. But all the retinue was mounted by now, and Alice was bustled into the carriage. The cavalcade rumbled slowly into motion. Anne could see her friend waving, but her mind was elsewhere as she stood, gazing after the departing band, a long time, until Alice had become a little doll among the retreating forms, a tiny puppet with one moving part.

* * *

The journey from Angers to Bruges was a lengthy one, and wearisome, particularly for the riders. The women accommodated in a long, trundling carriage and soon settled themselves into accustomed places. Alice took the seat at the back where she would have the widest view, if she cared to look, and be near to Edmond, if he cared to escort her, though generally it was Jonkin, more comfortable in female company, who would ride behind the lumbering vehicle. Alice was glad of his company; the carriage was well to the rear and, placed as she was, she could not see what was occurring further up the column among its more interesting constituents.

The Dukes of Exeter and Somerset were riding towards the middle of the group, and latterly the Earl of Devon was tending to fix himself to Exeter's other side, no matter how smartly the Duke tried to shake him off. The purpose, as usual, was a childish and calculated insolence. For, now and again, when Exeter's glance would idle upon a man among their company – it was always a man, of course, for there were only men about them – Devon would follow the direction of his eyes, and look back and forth between the Duke and the object of the Duke's gaze, on his face a puzzled frown. For some long while now, Exeter had been ignoring it, unwilling to call attention to the humiliating persecution, but the rage was surging within him.

Finally, he could restrain himself no more, and when Edmond's attention was claimed, he turned and spat, "Why do you go on looking at me in that way? You insult me!"

Devon started, with an appearance of bewilderment. "Look at you, my friend? For sure, I did not intend to look at you." He even sounded apologetic, though naturally he wasn't. Then he glanced about him ostentatiously, garnering plenty of interest, and leaned in with a conspiratorial wink. "I was wondering only on young Loic Moncler there. It's said some depraved miscreant has offered the boy twice what Clifford pays, to entice him away, all for the love of those shapely buttocks. But Robert will not tell me who it is, and though I've racked my brain, I simply can't guess."

Exeter's skin churned a mottled purple with shame and fury. He showed his teeth, and reined in hard, falling back among his household, where the tormentor would not follow.

The devil was making work for Devon only because Clifford had drifted away to the back of the cavalcade, now intimidating Jonkin with his presence.

Against all expectation, relations between Alice and Lord Clifford were proving easier after the marriage than before it. As a discarded suitor, his manner had been sullen and brooding. Now he was as warm, as calmly possessive, as if it had been he and not Edmond who stood beside her, making their vows in Angers Cathedral. It was a simple matter to ignore the undertow, for it did not disrupt the serene course of their exchanges, ready and tranquil.

"My lord, may I ask you to share your knowledge and tell me something of the affairs of England?"

"Mm?"

"I know that I'm ignorant, my lord. I would know more of the war."

He looked at Alice and smiled. "Did you never think to ask the Earl of Warwick, my lady? You lived with him long enough. If anyone could give chapter and verse on this strife, it is he."

She laughed a little and dropped her eyes.

Robert stretched in the saddle, silent for some moments. Then he commenced, twenty years back, when the house of Lancaster had the throne, and their own King Henry wore the crown. He told her of those court peers staunch for Lancaster: the old Earl of Northumberland, the old Duke of Somerset, and Robert's own father, Lord Thomas. Then he moved on to those men – like the old Duke of York, and Richard Neville, Earl of Warwick – who were at odds with the house of Lancaster. There were many reasons for this enmity, he explained: vast debts unpaid by the crown, the control of offices and favours, local hostilities, murderous hatred and so forth. The rivalry had first transmuted into violence with the ambush at Heworth in '53. But she had never heard what happened, and so he told her now: a sparkle of private malice had inspired the Cliffords and Percys to assault the wedding procession of Thomas Neville, Warwick's youngest brother. The ambush turned into a sorry hash – he didn't feel the need to explain why – but after that, the feuding ratcheted up a notch and, a couple of years later, exploded into vast open warfare.

"You were present that day at Heworth, my lord?"

"Ah – I was."

"You would have been very young?"

"About your age."

"Did you strike a blow in the ambush? Did you take life?"

He was amused by the look on her face. *Bloodthirsty little thing.* The memories of Heworth, and the merciless banter that followed, had chafed for several years after. He'd killed many, many hundreds since then. The shame was ancient; the episode now faintly comic.

She waited for his answer. He was gazing away, and so she guessed: *probably not.* What would he have been at her age? She failed to conjure him, and hoped that he would speak of it. She could not grow tired of listening. His voice: so distinctive, and there was no harshness in it, but rumbling in its depth and accustomed to command. Surreptitiously she looked her fill, lost as he was in memories. Those looks were rough and brutal; nothing could pretty them up. But those looks, by now, were also intimately familiar, and intimacy had changed the landscape.

He was staring down at her. Unnoticed, Jonkin was gone, replaced by Edmond riding alongside.

"My wife seems to have an incurable thirst for knowledge," said the Duke, ducking his head to smile into the dimness.

Lord Clifford's voice was cold. "I see no harm in that."

Somerset shrugged. "You have more patience than I, my friend."

No one spoke for a time, then Edmond moved forward to join his brother, who was talking with Blanche at the front of the carriage.

Alice turned back to her escort, ready with another question.

"I'll not tire you further, my lady." Lord Clifford spurred forward to find Devon.

* * *

Over the next days, Alice learned how it played out, stitching together those parts she did not know with those she did: the deaths of the old lords of Lancaster, followed by the triumphant revenge of Robert and the other bereaved sons some five years later at the battle of Wakefield, with the killing of Warwick's father, and his brother, Thomas Neville; and the old Duke of York. And, of course, the old Duke's second son, Edmund of Rutland.

Time was slowing for Alice. Wakefield; Wakefield Bridge: she'd been anticipating it from the start, and now waited, breathless, for the man to exonerate himself of the sickening cruelty of Rutland's slaying. He slid straight over it, to her great puzzlement. Gone too was the brutal sack of Ludlow and those other Yorkist towns: the hideous deeds of which he and John Clifford were accused: all these vanished also from his history. She was in no degree valiant enough to broach those evils. He was smiling oddly, as if he could read her mind; as if his silence was neither innocence, nor regret, but an insolent challenge.

It seemed that was all she would hear, for his history was winding onwards, and now passed impassively to a veritable string of catastrophes: the death of his brother John; Warwick's elevation of a young cousin, the pretender Edward of York, to the throne. Next, the early years of exile, the wandering years in Scotland and the North when there was sometimes not enough to eat – a wretched time.

Where was Henry Clifford in all of this, Lord John's young heir? Robert Clifford was widely held to have murdered the boy, yet this too had slipped into the shadows and was gone.

Did your brother not have a son to inherit his title? These were the words she almost said, but lacked the courage. *When was the child last seen, and by whom?* Robert Clifford would have his own answer, for he called himself by the boy's title and so must believe him to be dead. Whatever it was, he chose not to share it with her.

As the tale unwound her face had grown ever more troubled. Now he leaned down, for her ears only: "Still curious?" He sat back, that strange little smile about his lips. "Curiosity is the scourge of contentment. Master it."

She scowled at him, angry and hurt. Still smiling, he rode off to join the others.

* * *

81

That night, Alice lay abed in the guesthouse of a monastery, brooding on a man's capacity for wickedness. "There are terrible things said of Lord Clifford, husband – like the sack of English cities. And yet he is your friend."

There was silence a moment, and then Edmond's unwilling answer. "You forget: I was not in England in those years. Warwick had me imprisoned in Calais. But the Queen herself was there, and yet she holds Robert in high regard for his bravery and his loyalty. For us, that is enough. Certainly you should not be thinking of such things."

But the point was too pressing for her to heed his warning. "When he was telling me the history of the war, he did not mention those episodes at all: not just the ruin of the towns, but the killing of Edmund of Rutland and the disappearance of his brother's heir. I cannot understand why he would not give his side of the story."

Edmond was roused from his usual composure. "By Jesu, Alice! I've been his companion these many years, and I have never insulted him by asking. You surely did not expect the man to sully your ears with such matters? Have you no sense of what is fitting? I'll prohibit you from speaking with him if you cannot control this unbecoming curiosity."

"Your pardon, husband," she said, sleepily. "I did not ask him, of course."

Wakeful, Edmond lay beside his wife, pondering her lack of judgment. She, who was always prattling about the Countess of Warwick had, apparently, picked up none of that lady's undoubted discretion and good sense.

That night, the Clifford brothers invaded her dreams. For the first time Alice encountered John Clifford, and knew then where to lay the blame.

* * *

For several days, Robert stayed clear of the carriage, but they both knew he had not finished the lesson, and at last he reined in beside Alice. Her fingers were running through a puff of white fur; what he'd thought a lapdog, was, in fact, a large and sour-faced cat, a fine chain fixed to its velvet collar.

"Well, my lady: shall I tell you of the last attempt to put our poor King back on his throne?"

82

She would like that very much. She was humbly grateful.

"So: Queen Margaret, who is the most enterprising being I ever met, had travelled with her son, the Prince, to the court of Duke Charles in Flanders, and thence to France, seeking aid to dislodge the usurper Edward of York. At last – it was some six or seven years ago now – her cousin, King Louis of France, supplied us with money and a small force of men, and we invaded the North Country and retook some of our fortresses."

"I remember this! This, I remember!"

"I was back in my castle of Skipton, and we were hopeful for a time."

"And I was only a few miles away, at Middleham! The place was in a tumult – some said we would be besieged by the rebels. Anne and I made plans to barricade our chamber."

"Truly? A child's fancy; Middleham is quite impregnable. So you know what happened next. We fought two battles and were defeated twice over by Warwick's brother, John Neville."

"John Neville is such a good man, kind and patient. He taught me to play chess."

"He killed many of my dear friends."

"Oh. But in war, no side has a dominion for good or ill. There are as many vantage points as there are men."

"Are there? Are there, now?"

She had his fierce attention, but couldn't capitalise on it. This was the Countess of Warwick's insight and not her own.

"Ah – so that was the end of that. King Henry was captured and has passed all these years in the Tower, as you know. I fled into exile again, with Somerset and Exeter and Devon. We went first to Koeur in France, where the Queen had limped off with her little court. For a time I was master-at-arms to the Prince."

"I'm sure he was glad to learn from a soldier of your renown, my lord."

"He was not. I'm a hard taskmaster and the Prince is wilful, and overrates his skills. He was unhappy under my tutelage, and all the loyal lords were restless and running low on funds. Eventually we left for Flanders, where Duke Charles became our patron. The Duke is a warmonger, and has always kept our weapons sharp." He lowered his voice and bent towards her. "By the time we reached Bruges, Exeter had got himself separated from us, and been robbed, even of his shoes. There he was, all in rags and barefoot, begging his bread door-to-door…I can never see Exeter now without thinking on it: *rat-a-tat-tat*."

They both laughed, sly and callous.

He sat up. "Duke Charles's natural sympathies lie with King Henry and our cause, but so great is his hatred for the King of France, he's always sure to do the opposite of whatever King Louis does. And as you know, Duke Charles lately married Edward of York's sister. That has made life awkward for we exiles, drawing him towards the house of York. And, of course, he hates Warwick like the very devil, and that, too, will prove awkward, now that Warwick has come over to us. Devon and I will leave Bruges for England as soon as we can, whether Edmond will join us or not." He paused, sucking his lip. "Your husband stands high in Duke Charles's favour; they're brothers under the skin: honest and without guile, rash warriors, both."

She was diverted by the unrecognisable description. Never had Alice pictured her husband as a warrior, still less a rash one, and now she conjured him into being, clad in full harness, sword aloft. Her imaginary Edmond looked the part, but he was asking his adversaries to excuse him as he threaded his dejected way across the battlefield. Not so much rash as lacklustre.

The nonsensical image was dismissed from her mind and, unthinking, she asked, "Can you work with the Earl of Warwick, my lord? It must be hard for you, and for the others, and for him, too, I think."

Then it occurred to her that this was dangerous ground; that her husband would be angry, and her brother Jack, too, in all likelihood, and she shut up her mouth tight, turning quickly towards Lady Ullerton. The woman was snoring. The others were clustered at the front of the carriage, teasing Jonkin.

"I can do so, easily enough, as, I hope, can Devon: that's the advantage of possessing subtle morals."

She raised a brow at that, lips firmly closed.

He continued, "Somerset and Exeter are stiff-necked fools who cannot think straight. If the rest of us manage to defeat York and put our King back on the throne, those two will make an attempt on Warwick within the year."

This time her mouth fell open. "But the marriage! Between the Prince and the Lady Anne Neville…"

"…will never be consummated. She'll be put aside." His face was grave. "Why was your brother in such a rush to marry you off to one of us? No, don't say it is to tie us all together; it is the opposite." He was staring at her, and she was staring back. "It is to bind the loyal lords to him when Warwick falls. Jack can see it coming."

Her mind was spinning then, in great relief that Jack was so wise as to forestall the threat to himself, and great unhappiness over the Earl of Warwick, whom she honoured as a second father.

Lord Clifford watched her. "Do not concern yourself overmuch with your friend Warwick. I have no particular interest in bringing him down, and his instincts are keen. He may prove more than a match for Somerset and Exeter. Never difficult, at the best of times."

What he said astonished her. These were invaluable insights, apparently hidden from her husband – who had begun to seem rather simple. She noted that Robert would take her into his confidence in such matters: not warning her to keep her mouth shut, nor imagining her incapable of distinguishing what was secret from what was not, as Jack and Edmond were wont to do. This man, at least, would treat her as a woman grown.

There was no one listening; there was no one counselling her to be careful what she wished for, as Alice sat proud and surveyed all their short history from her present vantage – which was anything but lofty. For the sake of her conscience she had atoned for the pain and shame she had caused him; for her peace of mind she had bidden him farewell and set him free. She had done her work, and there he was – just as she wanted him: ally, well-wisher, friend.

That evening, for the first time, Edmond addressed his wife on the subject of her conduct. "Sad to say, Englishwomen have a poor reputation in Flanders, as they do in France. So you must take care, Alice, lest by your behaviour or your speech you give rise to talk, or give our enemies a weapon to use against us." His tone was light and he was attempting a smile.

Alice stiffened. "I thank you for your thoughtfulness in warning me, Edmond. I trust that I shall never give you cause for reproach."

He was reluctant to speak, but she was so obtuse that there was no help for it. "And yet, my dear, you've spent much of this journey tête-à-tête with Robert Clifford, a man whose reputation with women is far from exemplary. I, myself, have seen you laughing with the man and speaking low, so that others cannot hear. This is not the right beginning, I'm afraid. I say this not because I doubt you, of course, but to warn you of what others will think and say once you're out among the world."

She bit her tongue, for she could not trust herself to speak. The best part of those efforts with Robert had been aimed at restraining and steadying the man; teaching him how to conduct himself, so as to protect Edmond's feelings, in which she had assuredly succeeded. Now her husband's unwitting ingratitude made her wish for a window on her heart, that she might prove how pure she was.

* * *

Bruges: a bustling and handsome metropolis; a trade entrepôt; wealthy, powerful and diverse. Within it was a citadel; a tiny English enclave; a circumscribed world. None of the exiled lords went much into society, being hindered by poor credit and a shortage of ready cash, their households small and mean, their recreations constrained and introspective. Somerset, alone, could boast a warm welcome at court – at least in the absence of Duke Charles's wife – the ever-hostile Margaret of York.

Laura, the wife of the Earl of Devon, was a welcome addition to Alice's circle. In round terms the lady was reticent and inclined to good sense, excepting her one quirk, the matter that absorbed all her interest. Alice soon heard, and then heard many times over, in relentless and limitless detail, the history of her disastrous marriage.

"Of course, I loved him the moment I set eyes on him; the handsomest man I ever saw. How I thanked God for my good fortune! And then, on our wedding night, I learned just how much I disgust him, when he screwed up his eyes and bade me keep silent, lest I spoil the pretence that I was his latest mistress."

Her voice would grow louder, as it always did when she entered on her favourite subject, trembling and careless in its vehemence.

"When my husband fled England into exile, I was carrying his child, otherwise he would have been glad to leave me behind. But the babe did not live, and since that time he has been growing ever crueller and colder, now coming to me only when he's so drunk he can barely recognise me."

Laura's tribulations startled Alice, who thanked God in her turn that Edmond did not consort with other women. And if her husband would not come to her as often as he should, at least he was never unkind or the worse for drink when he did his duty.

"He shuns my bed, but he's indiscriminate elsewhere; his regular mistress is a mercer's widow, a woman old enough to be his mother, almost, who fawns on him and decks him out in all the newest fashions."

Laura, too, was expensively dressed, thanks to the generosity of this infatuated woman, but the truth had been charged down by her sense of grievance, which trampled all before it. The particular object of Laura's animus was neither her deserving husband nor his long-standing and liberal-handed mistress, but a lady of the court of Flanders, Isabeau Woudhuysen.

"It's so unlucky that Lady Isabeau and her husband Philippe are among the few who offer us welcome and don't court hospitality in return." Laura's poison had begun its slow drip before Alice ever met its target. "Lord Philippe is a grave and gentle man – and blind. I don't mean blind to his wife's ways, but blind in truth, a happy accident for him."

As Laura had predicted, Lady Isabeau, with her glittering dark looks and tall, sinuous figure, soon made herself a regular in Alice's house. Isabeau's sardonic eyes were everywhere, observing everything; a sinister Argos, perceiving too much indeed, as though all her husband's missing sense had been gathered to her, augmenting her powers. Alice soon became an object of especial interest, and it was not long before Isabeau began to amuse herself at her new friend's expense.

* * *

The trouble commenced one evening shortly after their arrival in Bruges, the exiles being gathered at Lord Philippe's town house. After a quiet dinner, their host begged Lord Clifford to sing for the company. Alice clasped her hands in anticipation and moved aside to make room for Loic, who carried in the ubiquitous lute and a drum for Monseigneur.

In deference to her husband's wishes, Alice had spoken barely a word to Robert, evading his gaze all the evening, but at the early beats of the drum, resistance faltered. *Tamlin*, of course; he was not like to choose another song when he could draw her in so effortlessly. At once she slipped the alien city, its solid towers and crowding gables and jumbled roofscape, the wild sweeps of the North Country opening vast before her inner eye, in poignant yearning and delicious shudders of nostalgia.

Unbidden, unintended, her voice rose to his. While the music swelled on, Isabeau watched the pair with close attention, witnessing their smiles reach and meld, intriguingly intimate. As the song's two versions strayed apart, the couple were closeted alone in plain sight, now imperilling the melody with their ill-stifled mirth. Soon Isabeau, too, was laughing and, looking up, she enjoyed Devon's face also; he looked like he might spit. Somerset had stalked out.

"My compliments!" cried their hostess, when no more joy could be wrung from them. "I've rarely known a more perfectly matched couple; your voices married beautifully. I didn't understand a word, of course, but it was clearly indecent; Lady Alice was beside herself."

Watching the discomfiture quench the smile, Clifford reached to touch the girl's cheek with the tips of his fingers, desperately rash. "Just a love song, as all ballads are."

"I'm not familiar with that one," remarked Devon, his voice icy but very low. "From what I could understand above the sniggering, it seemed to tell rather of base seduction than love. While you're on the subject, Robert, why not sing *The Demon Lover*? You know the theme: a foolish wife tempted from her husband by the devil. Ends badly."

Devon's wife was breathing through her nose like a ox.

"And here is the Duke, returned to us!" announced Isabeau. "You've missed a rare treat, my lord. I wonder if Lord Clifford can tempt your wife again? Watching their pleasure is half the amusement. How I envy the insouciance of English ladies – so wonderfully free from restraint." Her hand was quick upon the arm of Devon's wife. "Not you, of course, Lady Laura!"

In her vexation Alice could have cried aloud. Her husband's louring displeasure rolled over her head, completing Isabeau's work, and Devon's, dousing her like a sopping cloud.

"You shall not sing again in company," said Edmond, his voice high in pitch, cold and controlled, when they were alone that night, "since this evening you have seen fit to draw attention to yourself in the most unbecoming manner."

"Of course not, my lord, if it displeases you." Her voice was small and hopeless.

* * *

They'd started early and still the tavern was theirs, several would-be drinkers having turned in and turned smartly out again. Clifford yawned, stretched and caught the eye of a second girl. A moment later she was sharing his lap. He leaned between his companions and smirked into Devon's petulant face. "What? Your pardon, my friend. The sermon has gone on *so long* I shall surely fall asleep if I don't keep myself amused."

"You're in the grip of madness, Robert. I've never known you like this. Were you watching Edmond last night? Of course not – you had eyes only for that little girl." His voice swooped from heated to wintry. "It's not as if she's anything to look at. Scrawny tits and a baby face. Not witty. Not lively."

Sometimes, of course, it's what the lover longs to hear, feeding the perverse pride in valuing what others cannot. Clifford was glad that Devon could not make her out. His friend had struck the wrong note.

But Devon ploughed on. "If you think her husband hasn't seen what's going on, you're way off. I warned you this would happen."

"I thank you for your concern. There's no call to distress yourself, or your bowels will start playing up. God has charge of the matter. Don't meddle."

"God?" exclaimed Devon. His voice was dripping with scorn. "You always think God is abetting you. God doesn't make plans to help man fornicate. It's lust that's directing your actions. It may be the devil has a hand in it, but not God. If he were minded to intervene, don't you think it more likely he'd assist an innocent husband than a lecher?"

One of the girls whispered in his ear, and Clifford was smirking again. "How can I foretell how His purpose will come about? Perhaps in due course I'll be the innocent husband."

"Your thoughts turn to murder now, is that it?"

Loic goggled at Devon, appalled. He was shaking his head so swiftly his whole frame quivered.

"When God intends to make me his instrument, he'll send me a sign. I suggest you speak to Reginald Grey. He'll explain it to you. In Latin verse, if you're lucky."

Devon too was shaking his head. "I do believe you're actually insane. Do you think you could tear yourself away long enough to recover your lands, or is that also something God will arrange in your absence?" He turned the scowl on Bellingham and Nield. "What are you two gawking at? Someone has to take him to task and I'm the only one with the wit to do so."

Clifford was now burrowing into both gowns at once. His voice was muffled. "You're boring me, my friend. I have my chamberlain for that."

* * *

When he arrived at the Woudhuysen townhouse, Clifford knew he was following Devon; it was easy to recognise his steeds in the yard. The man was always the target of shysters, being no judge of horseflesh, and he wouldn't listen to his marshal, who was. Clifford lifted his face to the sky, enjoying the sun. A beautiful day for hawking, cold and clear. Now came the moment: Edmond so often assented to such expeditions, only for his spirit to fail him at the last moment, and he would never permit his duchess to attend without him. Clifford had not seen Alice in days and he was all too conscious of time slipping away; indeed Devon and he were almost at the point of giving up on Edmond of Somerset. If the Duke would not come away to England, there was no excuse to linger in Bruges.

The house was familiar territory. Leaving his men with the horses, Clifford waved away Philippe Woudhuysen's page, and strode with Jem to the day room. Philippe was settling himself in a heavy chair before the fire, reaching for a cup of mulled wine. No candles lit the room; it was dim and thick with the steam of spices.

Clifford greeted Woudhuysen as he walked round to the fire, Philippe's sightless eyes following a little behind his steps. Glancing across to the chair opposite, he was arrested by the sight of his hostess, braced, silent and motionless behind it, her hands gripping the posts. He hailed Isabeau from something of a distance, diverted as he was by the spectacle beneath the chair legs: long, shapely calves and a pair of impractically pointed boots protruding from the full skirts of her gown, soles uppermost. Had the lady turned contortionist?

She spoke then. "Philippe, my dear – you've taken a wrong turn. The choir is already assembled, awaiting your presence. They've been practising new pieces for your enjoyment. I ride with Lord Robert today. We'll come to you and share the gossip on our return."

Philippe turned a little in his wife's direction. "Your pardon, Isabeau. I did not realise you were here. I had forgotten the music. Will you summon the page to me?"

Leering, Clifford came to her rescue. "No need to summon help, Philippe; young Jem here knows the way to the chapel, and he will lead you."

Clifford elbowed Jem in the ribs. The boy shook the astonished expression from his face and hurried to offer his arm. As Philippe stood, Clifford reached for his friend's shoulder.

"One of those pieces is my own composition, Philippe: *The Queen of Heaven*. I trust you'll enjoy it."

"I'm sure I shall, Robert. You're a fine musician; none better."

Clifford nodded – invisible to Philippe. He was exceedingly proud of this transcendent hymn in honour of the Virgin, to whom he had a particular devotion. Lately, though, he wondered if a more earthly woman had lurked in his mind as he composed the soaring counterpoint. For the music was rousing him, every time; a disconcertingly physical reaction.

The door closed behind Woudhuysen. Clifford and Isabeau regarded each other a moment longer.

"You can't ride in those ludicrous shoes," tossed Clifford over his shoulder, as he reached the door. "What were you thinking, man?" He found Somerset and Exeter with the ladies, milling in the yard.

"I should see Philippe before we set off," said Edmond.

"Philippe is with Devon in the chapel, listening to the choir. Lady Isabeau is making ready; she'll collect the Earl on her way." Clifford avoided the Countess of Devon's eyes.

They stood around in a desultory fashion with their cups of wine, Clifford unable to shake his gaze from Alice, who was scuffing the ground, digging a little hole. Some long moments later, Isabeau emerged with Devon.

"Forgive us, my lords and ladies!" she cried. "I found the Earl in my closet, perusing my romances. Such appreciation! I could not drag him away."

Laura Courtenay rolled her eyes openly, allowing herself to be raised behind her husband without a word.

Passing Devon's horse, Edmond looked askance at his footwear. "You cannot surely be meaning to ride in those shoes? Very fashionable, no doubt, but hardly practical. They need a chain to join the toe to your knee."

"He means you're walking like a duck." Clifford pushed the groom aside to lift Alice behind her husband. His hand trailed her thigh as he released her and she bit her lip behind Edmond's back. Clifford trotted out of the yard with Isabeau grasping his waist in her spidery fingers.

The heavy rain of the last few weeks had pent up the energies of the men, the hawks and the prey, and now the sport was good, every man wishing to spread his wings. Clifford rode beside Somerset, shadowing Alice, to Isabeau's disgust, for she was backwards to the company, with nothing to look upon but trees. As the hawks rested, the company rested too, for a time, standing around, for it was too sodden to sit. Still Clifford dogged Alice's steps, as she moved to the aid of Laura Courtenay, marooned between Devon and Isabeau, the sourest look upon her face. Devon glanced over his wife's shoulder, across the clearing, where Somerset shunned the party, conversing with the Duke of

Exeter. It was plain that the two were speaking of some private matter, Exeter throwing sidelong glances in their direction.

"Go over there and talk to Exeter, Robert," said Devon crossly.

"Not I. You go and talk to Exeter. He's looking ill-tempered, for a change."

"The devil I will!" expostulated Devon. "Someone has to stay here and stop you making a fool of yourself."

"Have you been eating something which disagrees with you, my friend? I know how weak is your stomach. Confine yourself to less exotic fare and your body will thank you for it."

Isabeau laughed.

Clifford turned to Alice and lowered his voice. "I've received a letter from your brother, my lady."

Alice had been trying to slink away. "Have you, my lord? What does he say? Please – tell me everything. I've not heard from Jack since we parted at Angers."

Taking her arm, he steered her a little way off, in plain sight, but out of earshot. "Only good news, much of which you will know: Jack and Warwick have entered London and freed King Henry. John Neville has come over to us, just as Warwick promised. The taking of the country proved easier than I would have believed possible."

Embarrassingly so, in fact. He wondered now why they'd hovered in exile all these years. Unless, perhaps, Warwick really was the key to the kingdom. "Edward of York has fled. He took ship from Norfolk; none knows where."

Actually, he was fairly sure he did know: here. It was a virtual certainty the usurper would pop up at the court of Flanders before too long, where his sister, Margaret of York, would reserve for him the warmest of welcomes. Let Somerset and Exeter struggle to keep Flanders loyal to Lancaster in the face of so hostile a challenge; Clifford had no great desire to encounter an alliance of Rutland's brother and sister. He'd be gone from Bruges by the time Edward of York made his entrance. But Alice was nodding, and he smiled into her eager face.

"Perhaps you'll be most glad to learn that your brother, on being appointed Constable of England, has already hounded down his predecessor in that office, the Earl of Worcester. Jack tells me the cur was caught hiding in a tree!" He grinned at her. As Constable, Worcester had been York's bloodthirsty dog, sniffing out Lancastrian sympathisers. An absurd and ignominious end to such a ruthless career. "Jack has pronounced the death sentence; you have justice at last for the execution of your brother Aubrey and your father."

Her lips parted and she sighed, seizing his hands in hers, raising them up, kissing them in her elation – a spontaneous gesture of joy and vengefulness. "Thank you, my lord! Thank you!"

He gave a low, delighted laugh.

"Lady Alice!" came Somerset's peremptory cry, like the stamp of a foot.

Clifford bristled, though Alice did not so much as turn her head. On the spur of the moment, he slid a hand into his undershirt and pulled from it Jack's letter, waving the folded missive between his fingers. She slipped the warm parchment into her sleeve.

On the return journey, Isabeau snaked her arms around Clifford's waist, the waywardness winding up within her. "I trust you'll be gentle with your English rose, my friend," she murmured. "The little Duchess is falling in love with you."

Clifford inclined his head to the side. "Lady Isabeau, you have more talent for mischief than any creature I ever met."

Devon had reined in, unnoticed, on Clifford's blind side. "Except you, Robert. You're displaying a talent even Isabeau couldn't match. But only the greatest fool would foul their own nest, so let's hope you put your evil genius to work elsewhere."

Clifford smiled at his friend. Isabeau laughed aloud. And behind Devon's back, Laura, who would still have suffered any trial for a shred of his notice, wept inwardly.

* * *

It was the first time that Edmond's wrath had flared forth in her face. Unheeded by each, their paths had diverged. Long since, he had judged and condemned, but with the handy advantage of that ever-present lethargy, he had restrained his temper – until now. When the storm broke, it was a culmination of weeks of frustration; for his wife, the lightning struck out of the blue.

The Duke was coldly furious, that she should have shamed him with these public demonstrations: taking the man's hands in hers, and kissing them, secreting a letter from him in her gown. With a shock, she saw her danger, and rowed back, hard. The blameless letter was produced with trembling hands. She tried to explain, inarticulate and appalled: she had not heard from her brother, and had been fearing and wondering – and Lord Clifford had news that was particularly pointed: the arrest of the vile Earl of Worcester, he who had condemned her father and brother Aubrey to death, and was now in his turn condemned by Jack, through the grace of God. She was overcome with emotion, then and now.

Edmond suffered a brief surge of sympathy, and sternly crushed it. He had, himself, received a letter from Jack two days earlier, and would have shared those parts that concerned her, had she only waited. But she had not curbed herself, and the disgusting, unfeminine display of triumph was played out for all to see. And naturally – naturally – Clifford had intended only to provoke. Jack was Edmond's brother–in–law; it wasn't clear to him why the man was writing to Clifford at all.

* * *

Somerset was standing at the shoulder of his patron, Duke Charles; standing before the new portrait of the Duchess Margaret, sister to Edward of York. To behold the lady becalmed in tints was perfectly tolerable; in the flesh he would not have ventured so near.

"Petrus Christus; I reckon him the finest painter in Flanders, Edmond – perhaps in Christendom. It's the very image of my wife, is it not?"

Somerset made vague murmurs of assent. He could not say whether the study was a good likeness; when he had the misfortune to encounter the sitter, he would raise his eyes an inch above her head and fix them there, no matter how lengthy the audience or how great the provocation.

"We shall find Master Christus new commissions, or he'll be off to Paris before we know it. That devil of France must always be poaching from the best of my court. De Gruuthuse said he would sit, but he has an abscess. Oh – your bride! He shall paint your bride! Of course."

Somerset trusted his tone was sufficiently eager, for his heart was sinking. This was precisely the sort of needless and wasteful expenditure he was desperate to avoid.

A week after the exasperating directive, Somerset was escorting his wife home for her second sitting. Slow and grave, Master Christus spent more time in studying the subject's face than in capturing it. After the first episode of solemn patience, Alice had crossed the distance between herself and the artist to peep at the sketch. Someone had once remarked her watchful expression and there it was: plain before her in the evolving image; undeniably a marvellous likeness, the subject less than carefree. The portrait was destined to be hung, prominent, in the house, where all could see and none, probably, would look.

As her eyes wandered from the artist to the window, Alice was jolted from her musings by the sight of Robert Clifford threading his great horse amongst the market stalls, attended by Loic Moncler and a few of his men. It would be hard to miss him, towering as he was. Robert's arm circled an attractive, black-haired boy, perhaps five years of age, who gestured imperiously at the array on a woodcarver's stall. Lord Clifford turned to his manservant, who stepped forward to purchase the desired object. The youth passed the gift to the child, who bounced the toy up Robert's arm. A wooden horse, she guessed. She was enchanted by the vignette, and wondered about the boy. A baseborn son, might it be? He had the dark looks.

Later in the day, as husband and wife warmed themselves at Devon's fireside, Alice was thinking still on the scene in the marketplace. She sidled to her host and remarked that she'd seen Lord Clifford riding with a pretty child. She thought herself discreet; Devon had been sharpening his tongue again, and Edmond was standing apart, soothing Laura.

"That'll be his son, Jean."

"His son?"

Devon said pointedly, trusting it would wound: "Robert Clifford? Of course! More bastards than any man I know. Surely you've heard enough of him that it would not surprise you?"

Predictably she coloured, and Devon, of a sudden exasperated almost beyond endurance, tilted his head aside and scanned the room. "May I offer some advice, my lady? Robert has been my friend these many years, and I love him well. But you should beware of him."

She gazed into his face with a troubled frown.

Devon leaned forward, frowning back, accusing her: "Why is he is challenging your husband so, when all our thoughts should be fixed on carrying Somerset to England? There's no reasoning with Robert. And his intentions are not honourable, no matter what he's told you." He leaned back with a sneer. "But I think – perhaps – you know that."

The blush deepened. She said stiffly, "You are ungallant, my lord. I have done nothing of which I should be ashamed. And Lord Clifford has always respected my person. Since I became a wife."

Devon lost patience entirely. "Who cares about you? It's your husband who matters. I don't know whether Robert is acting this way solely to anger Edmond, but it is deliberate provocation. *It must stop.* Soon we'll be away to England. Until that time, you should feign illness or make some excuse to avoid Robert. Much greater matters turn on this than the gratification of your vanity; if Edmond ceases to trust Robert, it imperils the whole enterprise. You are unwelcome; detrimental. Do you understand?"

Alice dropped her head and gave a tiny nod.

* * *

That night the Duke and Duchess lay immured in their own thoughts, the accustomed acres of cold linen between them. She was near sleep when Edmond spoke in what she now thought of as his *light* voice, higher in pitch than his normal speaking tones, and the voice she had begun to dread.

"What were you saying to Lord Devon this evening? He seemed agitated."

"Agitated, my lord? I don't know. I don't remember, I'm afraid."

"I heard Lord Clifford's name mentioned." *Again.*

"Oh – I think I was asking about a little boy I had seen ahorse with Lord Clifford. The Earl told me the child was a baseborn son."

"Not a fitting subject to discuss with the Earl of Devon, was it?" he rapped out.

"Your pardon, husband. I did not know it was Lord Clifford's child, when I asked."

"So: why did Devon become angry?"

There was no acceptable explanation. "I don't recall," she whispered.

"Your memory is poor of late, Alice. Are you quite well?"

There was unaccustomed sarcasm in his voice, but she took refuge in the question. "I am not well, husband, no. I think perhaps I am overtired. I shall keep to the house for some time now."

Overtired? Edmond knew how luxuriantly his wife slept; it was one of many minor irritations she had brought to the marriage. Along with the major one. But he paused at that, and his voice gentled a little. "Are you perhaps with child, do you think?"

A humiliating question. It was hardly likely, since he showed himself ever less inclined to get her so.

He sounded closer. "You are muttering. I cannot hear you. Do you think you could be with child?"

"I should imagine not, my lord. I believe more is required, for that to occur."

He clicked his tongue and turned away. His voice came to her distantly; by the sound, much further than the edge of the bed. "You are impertinent; if you have something to complain of, please speak in a straightforward manner."

There was a pause, during which he squared for a direct reproach, and she tried to recall the moment when he had become a tyrant.

When she remained still, he continued, "You should understand, Alice, that your manner does not incline me towards you. And I wish that you will not again discuss Robert Clifford with any of our acquaintance; do you hear me?"

She did not answer, and he did not pursue it, but lay there, silent in the dark, his eyes staring, brooding on his wrongs.

* * *

From an upper window, Gabriel Appledore saw Lady Ullerton enter the house, and ran down the stairs as quietly as he could. The Duke's steward had been seeking a moment alone with the senior gentlewoman, and she was hard to come by; if the household was modest in scale, the house was more modest still and moments of privacy were few and far between. There was a small parlour on the ground floor, and it was into this useful and industrious room that he drew her. Pressing the gentlewoman into one chair, he took the other, and thought to possess himself of her slim hand, but courage failed him.

"Lady Ullerton," he began, at something of a rush. "Forgive me for disturbing you at your duties. I've been meaning to speak to you on a matter of some delicacy."

"And what is that, Sir Gabriel?"

"As you know," he continued, self-conscious and trying not to pant, "I am an unmarried man. I wish it were not so, at my age, but there it is. Here in Flanders, we've had little chance to become acquainted with suitable English gentlewomen. But now, the marriage of the Duke provides an opportunity…" he gave a little, playful laugh, "most welcome."

She gazed at him, frowning. Where was he going with this? Joanna, Elyn or Constance: too young for him, surely, notwithstanding the common silliness of men on that score.

"Perhaps you have guessed, by now. The gentlewoman I have in mind has been married before, and may, I hope, provide me with steady and gracious companionship, to the advantage of both."

And then it struck her with tiresome inevitability: Blanche.

He smiled and fidgeted about. "While not perhaps in the giddy blush of youth, she is yet most attractive in her person."

99

Not in the giddy blush of youth? If that were his verdict, when Blanche was golden and dimpled and ten years her junior, what must he think of herself? Misery forced it grimly upon her: a skinny, dried-up stick, no doubt. Her resentful gaze roved the steward's pleasant looks; his earnest, creased eyes and coarse thatch.

The knight was regarding her anxiously. "If you can read my mind, Lady Ullerton, please tell me whether I have cause to hope. Do I have cause to hope, would you say? The thought of that pretty skin torments me all the day when I should be thinking of my duties!"

"Really, Sir Gabriel. I cannot say." Her voice was tart and his hands were squirming. "The gentlewoman of whom you speak has several admirers; that is, she is courted by a knight of the Earl of Warwick's retinue and pursued also by a foreign person, here in Bruges. I can only suggest you put your question plainly and see what answer you receive."

At that she rose, quit the room and stamped to the chamber to attend upon Alice.

* * *

"It would grieve me greatly, my lord, to leave Flanders without your blessing, and inconvenience me greatly to do so without your safe conduct. But if I must, so be it." He'd slip away with Devon, under his letters of safe conduct – no trouble there.

Duke Charles glared at Clifford. Somerset and others had been telling him for weeks that the man was behaving badly, and it certainly seemed so. Duke Charles's intemperance was legendary. Nevertheless he summoned his meagre patience, and tried to sound reasonable. "I do not think I ask for so very much, Lord Clifford, in return for all I have done, and continue to do for you. Where would you be, h'm, these last five years, without my protection and generosity?"

"In France, my lord. In France," said Clifford. "You have indeed been generous, my lord, and I trust you'll also acknowledge the value of my service over the years. But the time has come for me to take back my own and, while you'll always have a follower and champion in me, I cannot bind myself in writing in the way you request."

Charles loosed the reins on his temper. "I do more than request it, my man: I require it. You claim to wish the Earl of Warwick dead, and yet you will not commit to it."

"Not in writing, I won't. That would be imprudent, my lord, and play into the hands of my enemies."

"Yet the others are content to do so!"

He folded his arms and looked down on the Duke. "As I said, my lord: imprudent."

"Such a bond would lie in no hands but mine. Therefore, you are calling *me* your enemy." The temper had the upper hand now, hissing like a kettle, and would shortly cause merry hell if he didn't make a swift exit. "Very well, Lord Clifford, let me tell you what I do to my enemies: I cut them off at the knees. That pension which I've paid you so freely these past years stops this very day. I'll pay it instead to Edmond of Somerset, who means what he says when he speaks of loyalty! You live in such a way as to well exceed your income; this will ruin you. And don't think of slinking away without clearing your debts. I have a long arm."

The Duke's jaw thrust forward, pugnacious and challenging. Time to go, and the Englishman bowed and withdrew. It had been agreeable, drawing upon two pensions at once, but he always knew it couldn't last and he was sanguine. He went to find Devon, to be harangued for the second time that day.

* * *

Under present circumstances, extricating himself from his life in Flanders – most particularly the mustering creditors – was complicated and should have consumed his full attention, but after a fortnight from her presence, Clifford was distracted by his greed for Alice. He timed the charge well, lurking until Somerset was known to have gone to Duke Charles, and the senior gentlewoman, Elizabeth Ullerton, was entertaining a visitor – one Olivier Dumanois, a Flemish merchant of Somerset's orbit.

101

When Clifford appeared at the house, disingenuously enquiring after the absent Duke, Lady Ullerton was very much engaged elsewhere. Of late her expectations of Dumanois had been growing apace; she could not and would not abandon her guest at this interesting moment. Alice was in her chamber when Lord Clifford was announced. She was rent with indecision, and vacillated hopelessly. He knew she was within, she was certain of it, and he knew her husband was not. She paused long enough to have made herself discourteous and then decided she could not insult him.

At the bottom of the stairs stood Robert, his back toward her, in close examination of Master Christus' work. Fingers traced the very brushstrokes, his face two inches from the canvas as if breathing life into the image. He may probably have done the portrait some injury, but her husband would not notice. Robert turned at her step and shifted his study to the living woman. As usual, her eyes slid away.

"As it seems your husband is from home, may I beg some speech with you, my lady?" He had folded his arms, his manner more than usually insolent; he was going through the motions.

"Please, my lord – follow me within. My gentlewomen are entertaining a guest in the chamber upstairs."

She led him into the small parlour on the ground floor. Outwardly composed, she gestured him to one of the chairs before the fire and, closing the door, joined him in the other. At once Sir Gabriel knocked and offered refreshment. By the slow lifting of the lady's eyes she signalled the spy in their midst, but her tone was perfect. Lord Clifford lounged before the fire, ankles a yard apart, not venturing on any subject. Returning with a page in tow, Sir Gabriel loomed dourly while the wine was poured and, when he could no longer delay his departure, left the door open.

The visitor made his speech: the familiar theme of Somerset's inaction; his equivocation; the necessity for his presence in England. Clifford found that he was somewhat interested in her view, but she would do no more than listen.

Finally she answered him. "You are persuasive, my lord, but my husband must do as he thinks right and I have no influence. I shall tell him of your visit, of course."

Clifford rose then and turned his back to the fire, looking down on Alice, struck by the poignancy of what might be his very last chance. "You will not wish to be forsaken here, I think, when we're in England."

She glanced up, and back to the smouldering wood.

"All wives have influence, if they care to use it."

"Not in this case. Truly, the Duke will not consult me."

"I speak of the weapon every wife possesses – at least, every one beloved by her husband."

Alice stared up at him in surprise, and suddenly, she stood, in some agitation, and tears filled her eyes. "Forgive me, my lord."

There was a hanging pause. He glanced at the door. It was more than half-open, but standing as he was, he was concealed from passing view. Raising a hand, he stroked at the tears, skimming her cheek with his thumb. Her eyes closed. More tears seeped beneath the purple lids.

Alice covered her face, covering his hand, also, with hers. "Forgive me." She turned blindly to flee the room.

A few steps and he had quietly closed the door, committing himself. "What is it, Alice? Tell me. I am your friend."

Somewhere in her mind sparked the idea that he could advise her; show her where she went wrong, for was he not a man, like any other? It was the devil who urged it, but still she sobbed out, "I don't please him. He will not touch me. I don't know why."

The irony made Clifford groan, possibly aloud. Alice had turned from him, buffing a pink and shiny nose with the back of her hand. He was not aware of his breathing, though she was conscious of it: heavy and ragged; he was fixed on her averted eyes. Pushing back the folds of cloth from her neck, he leaned in and inhaled the subtle scent of her skin. Warm lips touched her throat. Her hand had risen to his face, fingers at his mouth in mute protest. Then the tips were between his lips. The heat warmed her, far too much, yet she shivered. This fire issued from the very gates of Hell and she knew it, but her eyes were already shut and, even as she let fall her hand, she wilted against him. Clifford took the hand and pressed it to his chest, hard and smooth against her palm.

Beneath the muscle, the heavy ribs and beneath the ribs, the great heart thudded. A mirror image, his other hand lay now upon her, unmoving; she could overlook it if she chose.

They drew in, an unmeasurable moment as the balance teetered. Then he was impelled to speak, and murmured, "You promised you'd be mine. I must have you before I leave for England."

Alice jerked backwards and knocked away his hand. There was shock also on his face: an abrupt severing of his hopes. He should have held his tongue. He saw it at once, silently cursing.

"Your promise means nothing, does it, Alice?" He was bitter – very – and he hoped it carried: the forbearance he'd shown, that night in Angers; recompense was wanting and the debt had fallen due. "I'm wounded and wretched. How will it be if I lose my life in England, when you have served me this way?" Even to his own ears, the tone signalled only petulance.

From the foot of the stairs, Lady Ullerton frowned towards the door, attention torn between the prospect offered by Olivier Dumanois and the peevish monologue emanating from the next room.

Clifford shook his head, as if in disbelief at her cruelty, and measured Alice, but there was no softening in those angry eyes. Cutting his losses, he strode from the chamber, tossing a hostile look in Elizabeth's direction and slamming the front door hard enough to dislodge the portrait.

Lady Ullerton peered through the open doorway. Tears streamed down the girl's face, darkening her gown in spreading patches of damp. Elizabeth bustled into the room. "Lady Alice! You must never be alone with that man. Have you really no sense?" She snorted at the tears. "What ails you? Has he insulted you?"

"Of course not! I am fearful for the Duke. I was telling Lord Clifford: I hope we can persuade my husband to stay here in safety for ever."

Certainly not the speech of which she'd had caught the tail end. Lady Ullerton no longer expected Alice to confide in her or tell the truth. She started mopping her mistress's messy face.

Gathering his small retinue, Clifford rode slowly back to his house, rolling with the tumultuous thoughts. The night he kissed her – the eve of the wedding – he'd expected nothing but a swift rejection; a horrified rebuff. It was surprise, no doubt, that had betrayed him into such a stupid act of clemency.

Today: a stumble in the opposite direction. Beneath his hands, Alice was inching to surrender when he'd blundered into frank vulgarity. Doubtless Somerset would turn up in England eventually, and doubtless the climb back to the place of his fall would be a slow and arduous one. Thank God she was so easy to manipulate – a hopeless puppet, tangled in strings of debt and promise.

* * *

Unusually, Loic had not accompanied his master. He was lying abed in Monseigneur's chamber, a cold to the throat turning him husky. Benet was attending by his pillow. They were unmoving – suspended – when Clifford entered, Loic gazing through the wide window into the wide window opposite, Benet's amber eyes fixed on Loic's face. The master wondered, briefly, idly, what they spoke of when he was absent. Nothing, probably; his own presence breathed life.

Reckless of the hot wine in his chamberlain's hands, Clifford threw himself down. Loic rocked, and swung his brimming cup with careful rhythm above the pitching bed. He eyed Monseigneur speculatively. Clifford heaved on to his side and the mattress tilted, dangerously, again.

"Ah – I fucked it up," he announced. "I got so far along, and then it went to hell."

He gave Loic a précis. Always, the desire for an equivocating reaction, at such a time. He didn't get it; Loic was aghast.

"It might have been worse! I might have entreated her for what I actually wanted," he said, diverting Loic and Benet momentarily with the crude particulars.

"That you curbed yourself from begging favours forbidden by the church, between husband and wife, even, is not greatly to your credit, Monseigneur."

Clifford waved a dismissive hand. "Ah – you sarcastic whoreson. What was I to do? Carry her upstairs, throw her on Somerset's bed? Hard to do so in silence."

"You should hang back until she is so willing, the arranging of it becomes her problem."

Easy to say if you were not in torment, and time was not of the essence. But he trusted in God; it was not the end.

"Well, Monseigneur, in due course, I shall speak with Mistress Blanche. If she has heard nothing of this, you may take it as a hopeful sign." Loic had laid himself open to being plagued incessantly, and Monseigneur opened his mouth at once. The chamberlain raised a warning finger, a gesture he'd learned somewhere. "We must wait to give Lady Alice the chance to speak to the gentlewoman, if she will; too hasty, and we can draw no conclusion. And I am not well," he added plaintively.

Some days later, when Loic dallied next with Blanche, he found that she had nothing of her mistress to share with him; she looked blankly into his questing face. Clifford took that for the hopeful sign it was.

* * *

Alice, meanwhile, who had no one to confide in and no one to set her right, was occupied with absolving the man. Had she not led him to this point, with her avowals and denials, her confidences and her frailty? With relief, she acknowledged the blame. The talismanic Countess of Warwick would have made short shrift of Robert Clifford. But that lady was far away, and Alice had guile enough to keep his actions from the full glare of the light.

Dreading lest Gabriel Appledore would attempt to waylay his returning master, for the next hour Alice fidgeted alone in the small chamber near to the street, pleading fatigue to cover her strange behaviour; not strange to Elizabeth Ullerton, who had already unravelled it for Sir Gabriel's benefit. Alice's patience was rewarded, for she contrived to snare Edmond as he entered the house, and towed him before the fire, where she made a full and frank confession of the first half of her encounter with Lord Clifford. It fell out well for Alice: her husband was in an unaccustomed good humour.

Edmond listened quietly to his wife's timid admissions: she had permitted Robert Clifford entry, and spoken with him alone. Somerset did not believe that Clifford intended to engage with his wife on any serious subject; the cur was simply trying his luck. What did strike him, though, was his wife's prompt disclosure. She was learning. It was the deceit, the furtive behaviour, that had riled him beyond measure; the fear of a plot behind his back. If she would continue candid, he would trust again. He would resume relations with her.

Edmond rewarded Alice by telling her of his audience with Duke Charles. It was clear that his value to his patron was rising in inverse proportion to his rival's. Duke Charles had given a full and imaginative account of the encounter with Clifford, and Edmond relayed the astonishing particulars to his wife. And so Alice heard that the man had conducted himself so outrageously that Duke Charles was eventually driven to declare, in spite of Clifford's grovelling pleas, that he would henceforth transfer Clifford's pension to Edmond; augmenting the latter's allowance by half, rewarding Edmond for his loyalty, binding him more closely. And when Clifford blustered and threatened, Duke Charles, exasperated beyond endurance, had no choice but to have the man thrown bodily from the audience chamber.

Somerset stared, pensive, into the fire, reliving Duke Charles's anger; Clifford had, finally, lost his way.

Alice sat very still, very straight, as her husband honoured her with his confidence. She triumphed in his pride. Much, much less happy was the consequence for Robert. Why the perplexing ingratitude to their patron? This was surely madness, when he had no other source of income. Would he dismiss his household? Live with Devon, perhaps? Serve him? And then she called to mind, with a shock like a slap, that she would see none of this. He was leaving the country.

In due course, Sir Gabriel regaled his master with the day's doings. He found that Lady Ullerton had the right of it, and when the Duke carelessly dismissed Appledore's account of the morning's shameful tête-à-tête, the man bled. Wordlessly, he drew Elizabeth again to that busy parlour, gesturing her into Alice's seat, while he took Lord Clifford's chair, and scraped it forward, until their heads almost touched.

"Lady Ullerton." Sir Gabriel's face was redolent of his misery. "Entrust me with what you know. If my master's honour is compromised, I beg you: unburden yourself to me.

Like Sir Gabriel, she scented the tang of impending scandal. And all the while, haunting her, that ill-starred incident: the eve of the wedding in Angers when she had failed in her duty and allowed the guilty pair to disappear and something – *something* – had eventuated in the closeting darkness, the thought of which was strumming at her nerves.

"Sir Gabriel, your concern for the Duke does you great credit. Let me think awhile on this matter; on whether I have anything to tell you."

* * *

Clifford wished Alice to be left clasping the memory of his martial skills, surpassing all others', and Devon too was not averse to showing his prowess before his numerous admirers. The city elders agreed to share with the two noblemen the cost of a valedictory tournament; the town to stage the joust; the fêted guests to put up the purse. There was some minor difficulty over raising the money, for the departing men's credit had shrunk to a nullity, and even when Clifford convinced his lenders that he could not fail to win back the gold, the circular transaction was, in the end, barely worth the bother.

Devon, tall, heroic and rather hungover, lingered with Isabeau in a corner of the viewing platform. He had so little time left. Suddenly, with a sharp, hissing breath: "Christ! Is she come just to spite us?"

Isabeau leaned on the rail, her back to Alice. "Why are you snarling at the poor little Duchess?"

"Don't waste your sympathy on that sly halfwit."

The lady's face was wreathed in smiles. "She's unlikely to be both; choose your insult and stick with it."

"Oh, you're wrong there," averred Devon. "She may look demure as the Queen of Heaven but she's sly enough to know exactly what she's doing to Robert. Which makes her a halfwit, for she will damage both of them no less than the rest of us. As I've tried to warn her."

Isabeau stroked his forearm, a tiny movement. "She's certainly irritating. But much as it pains me to criticise our beloved Robert, the blame lies with him. The Queen of Heaven hasn't set out to catch him. He's old enough and wicked enough to know exactly what he's doing." She gave a delicate yawn. "It's not your habit to act as another man's conscience. Your mischief is what so beguiles me; I don't warm to the saint you're becoming. Speak to Robert if you must tire him with these frets, but let us leave the subject." She stepped closer. "Who will divert me when you're gone? My God, but I shall miss you, my love. I'll be longing for the day when King Henry sends his loyal Earl on an embassy to Flanders. And there will be a child for you to greet."

He searched her glistening eyes. Often enough, Isabeau struggled with honesty, but here she was candid.

All that day, Alice did not approach Robert Clifford and Robert Clifford did not approach Alice. She watched him take the victory, but when he stepped forward to receive the winner's purse and searched the platform for a final glimpse, Somerset and his lady were gone.

The next day, Devon, Clifford and their retinues rode out through the gates of Bruges, heading for England.

Part II

The Tall Trees

In the great chamber of the Bishop of London's palace, Jack de Vere, Earl of Oxford, warmed himself before an impressive fire. Behind him at the table, Warwick was hunched, perusing the list that Jack had laid before him: the names of those men proposed for knighthood; a disparate set. Jack had been to and fro, canvassing, and his own contributions had been lengthy. Warwick had twitched the list from his secretary; it was his own quill that scuttled down the page, leaving little marks beside the names.

"There are plenty of your neighbours here, Jack. Your household men are knighted already, I suppose."

"Indeed. Those on my list are local men from Suffolk and Essex – all but Peredur."

"Where's Peredur?"

"Yvo Peredur; a cousin of mine. Bailiff of my Cornish estates."

"I forgot you'd estates down there. Your grandmother's, were they not? So: Fabyan; yes. Sheringham; yes. Yes, yes, yes. Piers Brixhemar: a mischievous fellow, but you have your reasons, no doubt. Aveline…what does that even say?"

De Vere crossed to his mentor's shoulder. "*Anthony*, eldest son of Alan Teague, of Foxwhelps."

"Dismiss your scribe; the handwriting is terrible."

111

"It's my writing – you know it."

"Just a moment. Nicholas Loys. Not a son of Simon Loys, is he?" Warwick's brows had twitched together.

"A younger half-brother. Another neighbour, at Danehill in Essex. A fine fellow. He will come out for me, if needed."

"Unlike Simon Loys, that sneering, self-interested whoreson. There's gratitude for you: I have done so much for that man through the years, and he abandons me at the very first hint of trouble." He continued scanning. "Devon: no one. What is this?"

Jack grinned, enjoying the tale again. "The Earl of Devon has fallen out with most of his household, and particularly requests that the King should honour none of them, which seems somewhat rash, but he must go his own way."

Warwick sighed. "Here we have Clifford. Another long list. Looks like he's put up much of his household. Indiscriminate." Warwick sighed again, and scanned the familiar, ominous names. "Walter Grey; Findern; Tailboys; Edward Bigod. Hugh Bigod's brother? I thought the Bigods were strong for us?"

Us! Instantly Warwick was struck by his blunder and passed a hand before his eyes, shaken that he could still be making such errors after months of practice. He began again. "I thought the Bigods were strong for *York?*"

Jack ignored both the slip and the correction. "I believe this is an uncle. At odds with the rest of the family and in exile the last ten years, like most of Clifford's men."

"I see. The other Findern; Whittingham; Gifford – why are they all called *Walter?* Does he rechristen them? So: Jansen. Bertrand Jansen. That huge drunken Dane! Wasn't he a mercenary? It is not sufficient for the man to be paid for his sword arm? Clifford cannot be serious. No, I don't accept that one. I shall strike it. Richard...*Earwig*, that reads." He tapped the page with his fingernail. "It says *Earwig*. It does. Dormer; Tunstall. God in Heaven; all the old names are here, aren't they? All of them."

In former days, when these were his sworn enemies, the thought of such men flooding back to England would have horrified him. It was horrifying him now. Recently, of a night, he'd awaken, disorientated, alone, running with sweat, convinced he was making – had already made – a catastrophic error; a fatal miscalculation.

He continued, in his calm, cold voice: "Lewis Jolly. Another divided family; brother will be fighting brother shortly. Who's Louis Moncler?"

"Not Louis: Luc. Loic? Little Frenchman; Robert's familiar. Shares his bed."

Warwick was counting the names. "You have confused Clifford with Exeter."

Jack laughed. "Moncler is his chamberlain."

"I don't sleep with my chamberlain."

Jack lowered his voice. "It's said Clifford is tormented by nightmares and dare not sleep alone."

"If any man in England deserves a turbulent conscience, it is Robert Clifford."

Jack yawned. "What news from Flanders?"

"Did you hear who welcomed Edward of York into Bruges? It was that arch-schemer, Louis de Gruuthuse. York's staying with him now."

"De Gruuthuse? He hosted me in Bruges earlier this year. He's a decent fellow."

"He is not. They say York's strutting about the town as if he owned the place, lifting skirts, knocking back the wine. I kick him out of his kingdom, and still he won't learn. Still putting pleasure before duty. I had high hopes for him, once."

"I can't think why. A lazy glutton and a thickhead to boot."

"York is, as you so aptly put it, a thickhead." Warwick sipped his wine. "For now, Duke Charles has turned a blind eye. He won't meet York – at least, not in public. The Duke fears handing King Louis an excuse for war."

Jack shook his head. "Events will overtake him. King Louis will declare war, come what may; he's itching to lay waste to Flanders."

"Good. This is good."

"Well – not if it drives Duke Charles to dispatch Edward of York back to England with a Flemish army at his back!"

Warwick placed his hands flat upon his papers and looked up at his brother-in-law. "If Flanders is menaced by the French, Duke Charles will hardly spare an army for a foreign war." Unlike Jack de Vere, that vain, dashing, hectic boy, he had riddled it every way round; there was little else on his mind. The Earl of Warwick could no more turn his back on Louis of France than he could fly to the moon. Provoking Duke Charles was an enormous risk, and could pay the greatest of dividends. He was utterly comfortable taking that risk.

* * *

A few days earlier, when Jack de Vere and William Beaumont had come calling for Clifford's list – the roll of those preferred for knighthood – they found the man distracted, impatient for the onward journey into the North.

"I'm surprised you're leaving so soon!" said Jack, and Beaumont added, "There's work to be done here, Robert: London is fretting at the French alliance.

"Warwick's problem. Ah – you two so lately left your lands; you cannot understand how I *need* to be home. Men say Skipton's a forbidding fortress; to me it's enchanted. I *ache* for the moors; the scent of heather; the sharp wind."

Beaumont rolled his eyes, embarrassed and a little queasy. "Sounds nippy."

"It's a wild beauty, and not for mocking!"

The man's voice was breaking, and Jack found himself first diverted and then beguiled. In those words of yearning he traced the source of *Farewell*, Robert's heart-strum of an elegy, a song that brought its listeners to tears; and Jack was, briefly, lured to the wellspring. "Go then, my friend. God speed you home."

And so Clifford was in the highest humour on the final approach into the North Country, the road to Skipton. For the last night of the traverse northward he steered hopefully, expectantly, toward the manor house at Begthorne, the residence of one Mistress Winter, a comfortable gentry heiress; twice widowed; newly remarried; yielding, even now, to the inclination to accommodate him. Her overborne bridegroom clutched dumbly at Clifford's Wyvern badge, and made way.

114

Before dinner, Clifford was taking his ease before the fire, knee-deep in a litter of little ones; the house was infested with nurslings. Among them strutted a bold fellow, just of an age with his youngest son, Jean. By the time the hostess joined them, the child was riding his knee and whipping about with a homemade crop.

Elizabeth Winter halted on the threshold. "What is this? Away with you, imps! Let his lordship be!" She knelt and raised Clifford's hand to her lips. "Your pardon, my lord. Now: here is someone you should meet."

The gentlewoman beckoned forth a lofty, slender youth with sleek locks and well-ordered features. Clifford raised her up and pushed to his feet. He looked on the boy and the boy looked on Clifford. "Well now! And who have we here?"

Then his fond arm was about her shoulder, fleetingly domestic, as the two old friends watched Will, their black-haired lad, jogging his mother's infants upon his back.

That night Clifford skimmed at the brink of sleep and rose before dawn, fervent for his homecoming, rousing the household with lusty singing. Master Winter was not sorry to discard the black sheep of his wife's engulfing brood and so, when Clifford rode north, he bore away young Will, his fine son.

* * *

All-unwilling, Sir Roger Clifford's mind wheeled backward over the years. Some thought Robert's bark was worse than his bite; some thought that grisly reputation unwarranted. Roger had no such illusions. His older brothers were, both of them, as vicious as they were dissolute and it pained him to recall himself as a youth, dazzled and distantly pursuing. Rutland's murder, John's death and a spell in the Tower had sobered Roger like a dunking in icy water. He remade himself as his brothers' antithesis: cautious, steady and respectable. Now he had a superstitious fear of Robert's company, of touching pitch and being defiled.

Then the message reached him, as he knew it would: Robert had come home.

115

The knight sprawled, brooding, before the fire in the dying hours of the day, as the rain slammed against the windows of his modest manor house. Drumming his fingers, awaiting the summons to the gatehouse. When at last it came, he lurched up, reaching for a torch. Lady Joan, her dear, pretty face tense with empathy, rose with her husband.

Robert's long hair was plastered down his neck. Like a hound he shook off the rain, stepping into the warm and flickering light. He was perhaps a trifle heavier, a little more grim. Essentially unchanged. By contrast, the younger man was creased and wholly grey, with the beginnings of bulk about the waist. Sir Roger startled himself by pulling Robert into a long, hard embrace. Unexpectedly affecting, seeing him thus in the flesh, and Roger exclaimed over his older brother, incoherent half-phrases of greeting and remembrance.

Robert flashed his sister-in-law a roguish smile, primly returned. Stooping in for a kiss, he slid his tongue absently between her lips. He wasn't even looking. She pushed him away with both hands. Clifford was staring over Joan's shoulder.

Five dark boys; his brood of sons. Twins on the crest of manhood; a couple of youngsters, and one in between. The little ones were breathless and quailing and Clifford gave them barely a glance; his attention was on the two eldest. With tousled black locks and eyes of palest blue, the twins were, at first sight, identical. And yet they were not identical: Guy, strikingly handsome and somewhat commonplace; Aymer, strikingly handsome – and somehow not: an arresting figure. They bristled with truculence and conceit, the tiresome posturing of youth. The middle boy, Robbie, was much younger, newly into his teens, but taller by some inches and disconcertingly plump; the lad, beneath his father's frowning appraisal, stared sadly at the floor.

After vespers, Robert joined Roger and his wife for dinner in their small panelled parlour. Lady Joan questioned her guest for tidings of her brother, the Earl of Devon, and Robert intrigued her with the tale of Devon's love affair with Isabeau Woudhuysen, the lady's blind husband soon to be gifted with a cuckoo. As rain cascaded down the shivering casements, they exchanged a flood of news and gossip: of neighbours, and of courts and kings.

But when Joan retired to bed, Roger squared for the fight. "You've been at it all evening, so we might as well clear the air."

"What?"

"'*When we face York.*' You've said it a dozen times. There is no '*we*', Robert. There's no way on God's earth I'm following you back to war. You're not to drag me under now. It doesn't matter what you say, so don't waste your breath."

"Mother of God. You cannot be serious." He was speaking very slowly, as if his brother's wits were askew. "This is for King Henry, Roger. What would our father say?"

"What *would* our father say, Robert? What would he make of Edmund of Rutland's disgusting fate, I wonder? My nephew's disappearance? Your alliance with Warwick? Spare me. I thank God Lord Thomas is not alive to see it."

"Lord Thomas would do just as I have done! Our father was no milksop. A Clifford who knew what he stood for. And who he stood for."

Roger threw up his hands, as incredulous as Robert – and bitter, with it. "How you pride yourself on your loyalty! Always boasting that you're ready to die for your king. The truth of it is you have no choice. There was no way back for you with York, not after what you and John did to Rutland. Life's a little less straightforward for those of us left behind. Look at me: son of one of the most powerful nobles in the country: six months in the Tower with death at my elbow, and here I live, in this mean little house, and marvel that my head is still on my shoulders. I don't trust my neighbours, and they don't trust me. These last years, while Warwick and Jack de Vere have been plotting and manoeuvring, I've been under close watch. You've no idea what it is to live like this. And you want to drag me deeper!"

Robert's head was titled aside, brow furrowed as if in compassion, but Roger was stung by the faint smile of mockery. "So you think me a coward? Maybe I am a coward. At least I'm no monster."

Robert clapped his hands to his knees. "Ah – enough, Brother. That's enough of a sermon for one night. If you're no coward, then I'm no monster –

let's agree to that. You've only a handful of layabouts anyway. I don't know why I bothered. Mother has more men, and they'll be coming with me."

One of Robert's younger sons approached to fill their cups. He caught the boy's wrist, drained the wine with one draught and gestured to the jug. After spilling a deal of it, the boy turned to go, but Robert was holding him still.

"Remind me of your name, lad. How old would you be?"

"My name's Peter, my lord. I'm nearly twelve years of age, my lord."

"And who's your mam?"

"Mary Maddox, my lord. Lady Joan's chamberwoman."

"Alas – how ill-mannered of me! My apologies, Roger, for this…accident in your house." He released the boy.

His brother closed his heavy lids, shutting out Robert's insufferable smirk, and stretched his legs towards the fire. "Which puts me in mind: I do have some men for you, as it happens. Guy and Aymer." Roger's contribution was to insist that Robert take the twins away with him. They were insubordinate and unruly youths, evoking difficult memories of another pair of brothers. "Aymer has some…" he shrugged, " some sort of *hold* over my layabouts, as you call them. And he frightens my wife. You'll need to watch him."

"What? Ah – for God's sake, Roger. Listen to yourself! This is embarrassing."

"Well – you'll see. And the middle boy, Robbie; he must go, too. He's biddable but he's lazy. He wants hardening, and you can do that better than I."

"It's fighting men I'm after, you mawk. Can these three hold their own in battle? I doubt it. Those twins are dwarves. Are you even sure they're mine? Their mam must be one of the little folk. And the younger boy's as fat as a hog. What have you been doing, Roger? But you never were one for training – always had to be dragged to the yard. I'm not bothering with shirkers. I've no time for this."

"You've no choice. They're your bloody sons, you ingrate. They've had a fair training, as it goes. You can't raise men of your own, so it's lucky you invested early; you've bred your own army. Go and see Mother. Go and see the Earl of Northumberland. There are bastard boys all over the place."

The next morning, Robert found the three elder sons packed and ready to move out. On Guy and Aymer's matched faces was a wary eagerness.

Roger accompanied him to the gate. "I take it you've not seen Triston?"

"Triston? What do you think? Of course not. Nor shall I."

"He would wish it, I'm sure."

"Naturally he'd wish it – now York is gone. Our little brother backed the wrong king."

Bidding a brusque farewell to Roger, he led his party back across the Westmorland moors towards Skipton.

It was a gloomy morning and Reginald Grey was resolved to make it gloomier. "Give some thought to these sons of yours. There must be rules, Lord Robert; strictures. Do not permit the country around to be estranged by their misconduct."

Patrick Nield wagged black brows at Walter Findern, who forced down the laughter with a hiccough. "*Misconduct*, Sir Reginald?"

An anonymous echo: "Clifford? *Misconduct*?" The laughter rippled out.

"God forbid," intoned Bellingham.

Grey had set them off. Now the men were competing to recall the ancient japes and misdemeanours. Arthur Castor, their baby-faced master-at-arms, turned about to observe Loic. These legends of antiquity – the well-loved tales and shared adventures – had kept the household warm through the long dark. To the Frenchman, though, they were nothing of the sort; an unwelcome reminder that Monseigneur had lived a whole history before their worlds collided.

"Enough!" cried Loic. "Bell shall see to the boys! Discipline is the marshal's prerogative."

Grey's voice was leaden. "Sir Cuthbert? *Discipline*? If those lads are aught like their father, they'll need a *strong* hand."

There was another swell of mirth, Bellingham's easy laugh joining with the others.

Clifford swivelled in the saddle. The twins had found a place beside young Will in the train of the senior men, while Robbie had slithered away to the rear of the column in a vain attempt to conceal himself behind the pages. They looked all-too-harmless.

Raising his voice, he hailed the twins. "I hear there are others of my sons in your grandmother's care. You know them well, I suppose?"

The pair spurred forward. "Indeed no, my lord." Guy sounded surprised. "Lady Clifford is quite infirm, so they say. We've not seen her in years. She'll not leave her estates, and Uncle Roger seldom strays from his. And when he does, my lord, he never takes your bastards with him."

Clifford grunted. "You may call me Father, for that is what I am." All night long he'd brooded on Roger and his shrinking timidity. He thought again of his own father: one son a traitor and another a coward. Thank God Lord Thomas was not alive to see this.

"And so we stay at home always, Father, and liven things up for Lady Joan," smirked Aymer. "She enjoys that."

"Guard your tongue, whelp! You'll not find me so shy with the belt as Roger."

Reginald Grey was shaking his darkling head.

It was soon clear that there was no alliance between Robbie and his elder half-brothers; quite the contrary, and he trailed his father, disconsolate, from the first. By dark, the twins had already assayed the castle and swaggered in to vespers late, dishevelled and boisterous, dragging Will in their train. They had settled to their role.

* * *

No more had been said by Gabriel Appledore on the subject of Blanche Carbery, and nothing at all had been said by Blanche on the subject of Sir Gabriel, which perplexed Lady Ullerton greatly. Perhaps Blanche had already dismissed one suitor in preference for another, or perhaps Sir Gabriel had thought better of his intention, disgusted at her antics with that pert little Frenchman. It was a mercy that Sir Hugh Dacre was not in Bruges to witness her flaunting; it would have broken his heart.

At length Lady Ullerton was curious enough to probe, and enquired, daintily, whether Blanche had given her promise to Lord Clifford's chamberlain before he left the city. "Master Moncler was so persistent in his attentions, Blanche, that I presume he means to make an honest woman of you."

When the moment had come for him to take his leave, Loic had done so with breezy cheer, pinching her bottom and leaving Blanche in no doubt that she'd be gone from his mind before he was upon the highroad. Lord Clifford would not have been pleased; he'd not invested so much coin in the woman only for his man to skip off like this, and Blanche suffered a brief, vengeful desire to run with tales to his master. She was, altogether, in a grievous temper, and not inclined to listen quietly to Lady Ullerton's insincere homilies.

"Well, my dear, if marriage was not his object – and I'm sincerely sorry for it – I trust for your sake that he was thwarted in his true intentions."

Blanche was not too steady to put out her tongue behind the lady's back.

* * *

Sir Roger was right. Within their mother's household there were indeed more Clifford boys to be found: Richie and the absurdly-named Bedivere; about the same age – seventeen or eighteen years – and Tom, who was two or three years younger.

Richie and Tom were heavy, broad-chested youths, swarthy and sable-maned. Bedivere was rather different. Slimmer and longer-limbed; hair darkish but not dark, ashy in hue but bleaching already at the temples, lending him interest; his eyes a greenish–grey, a calm winter sea. But a Clifford; certainly a Clifford. Tom's features were barely visible under a remarkable crop of pimples.

Clifford's trip to his mother's house was a little more fruitful than the visit to Roger. In addition to the three youths, he'd the promise of twenty or so men, when he chose to call on them. And it had done him good to see the lady. Fifteen years since Lord Thomas's death, and Lady Clifford was still in full mourning. She gave short shrift to Robert's reconciliation with his father's killer.

"Ah, there'll be no sweeter revenge. Warwick surrendered our lands without a peep and we have his name, his wealth and his men at our disposal. And when York is vanquished, Warwick will follow him to the grave, believe me." No need for that – not if King Louis made good on his promise to whisk Warwick away to those Flemish lordships – but he wished to make her happy. "Somerset can't stomach Warwick either, but now that Edward of York has popped up in Bruges, England must be calling to him."

As if reading his mind, she passed from Somerset to the question of Robert's marriage.

He repressed her. "Time enough for that when the kingdom is secure." Time enough for that when Somerset was lying dead on the field, leaving a young widow. He was increasingly convinced that it was God's plan, and the thought warmed him nicely.

She laid a hand on his arm. "Have you seen Triston, Robert?"

"No, nor will I."

"I lost your father and John, and it near killed me. Do not torment me in this way. Your brother would wish to be reconciled with you, I know."

Clifford took her hands. "I would do almost anything to make you happy, my lady, but do not speak to me of that little traitor, I beg you."

As they rode away from the house, Clifford examined young Richie, inspecting his profile, the dark shadows beneath his eyes bestowing a villainous air; the boy's nose too large and high amid the emergent planes and hollows of his face. Then on to Bedivere, a more pleasing prospect. "You, boy, must surely hail from my castle of Pendragon in Westmorland. I can't call your mam to mind, but the women about those parts are all for giving their children foolish names from the court of Camelot – Lancelot and the like."

Bedivere dipped his agreeable face. "My half-sister is named Guinevere, my lord."

Clifford regarded him with amusement, and cast round the faces of his senior household, at their grins. "There are some others of my sons awaiting you at Skipton who'll give you no peace, named as you are. As I'm too kind-hearted to expose you to Guy and Aymer's humour, henceforth we'll call you *Bede*."

Young Bede accepted his father's pronouncement with equanimity. Then he met Guy and Aymer, and he understood.

* * *

If Loic were fascinated by London, he was equally delighted with the North Country. So Clifford looked anew on his lands, strange after so many years and stranger still as seen through the Frenchman's eyes. Loic accompanied his lord and the core of the household as they journeyed out from Skipton to the Clifford strongholds of Pendragon, Brough, Appleby and Brougham. From Brougham the boys plundered the attractions of nearby Penrith, such as they were. A dirty little town; something about the wind. The wind blew from the wrong quarter. Pigshit, it brought. Sheepshit was the smell of home; pigshit was not so fine.

Clifford looked out from the heights of Brougham's haughty keep, over the gatehouse, over the valley, over the Eamont; the name causing Loic such trouble. From up here, the river looked placid enough, though it was always plotting to spill its banks. He raised his chin, the altitude unnerving him, as ever. There, scything through the rough pastureland, was the far-distant ribbon of Clifford boys, breaching the dawn; breaching the curfew of the day before. They were cantering towards the bridge, trailed by a clutch of servants – most of the grooms, who should have been toiling in his own stables. He couldn't make out the figure at the head of the column, but he knew who it was. *I shall name him as their master.* A natural-born leader; one who'd conquered his fellows with ease.

When Loic had smoothed every wrinkle from his master's hose he stood and took in the scene. "Late for chapel."

Clifford grinned. "Ah – leave them be. I was just as they are, once. Always on a loose rein, yet see how I turned out."

"Just so," came the priest's stony verdict, from the door. Loic held his peace.

Clifford's hands were at his chamberlain's shoulders, twisting him toward the stairs, shepherding him through the arch after Reginald Grey's departing steps. "Come, my good Sir Loic! Lead me slowly, and those poor lads may beat us to it."

Before him, Loic smiled. He wasn't thinking of the boys, he was burnishing his shiny knighthood. Clifford was thinking too, of that recent honour: a lucky stroke, anchoring and elevating his foreign favourite in the eyes of a distrustful and conservative gentry. Those turbulent old names of Bellingham, Findern, Tailboys and Grey still commanded respect, inspiring nostalgia for braver times. There was some good hunting and hawking to be had. If they'd not been forever seeking after the promise of troops, it would have been a diverting few weeks.

But pleasure was not the purpose, and Clifford pushed fiercely in his quest for men. As his objective became widely known, he had grown hardened to an embarrassed or downright frosty reception. Some would not give their reasons; some would not engage with him; some would meet him with gimlet eyes and grim mouths. In these houses, it was the fate of Lord John's heir that lay behind the stony silence; there may as well have been a banner hanging from the gates, proclaiming his murderous guilt. The cold disgust was ringing like a verdict.

In other houses, his offence was of a different character. Where the men in question had known him as a youth, it did not generally tend to his advantage. So many accused him of ruining their daughters and sisters in years gone by, that eventually, harassed and exasperated, Robert put family feeling aside and started blaming John as a matter of course. It had become a routine exchange to be endured before he could start importuning for his retinue. And soon he was forced to leave his sons behind, their family resemblance all too clear; their presence adding insult to injury.

On one such visit, he was gifted with another Clifford boy: John's son Oliver, a strapping lad whose uncle was a local esquire. This fellow was clearly sorry to part with the youth, but offered him up on the altar of war, an ostentatious sacrifice. His only sacrifice, no further promise forthcoming. Oliver was barely sixteen years of age, but so large and handy, so self-possessed, that Clifford welcomed him with open arms. He was now the proverbial beggar, taking whatever came his way.

Meanwhile, at another house, he learned the existence of a further bastard of his (or of John's, as he insisted); a lay brother at Fountains Abbey. The boy was apparently as huge as a bull and, if the resemblance were more than skin-deep, dramatically unsuited to the life of the cloister. Clifford didn't wish to make the journey to retrieve him, but the way the recruitment was going, he'd have no choice.

* * *

Just as Blanche's entanglement with Sir Gabriel had not resolved itself, so another putative betrothal was lying in abeyance, for still Lady Ullerton had not given her answer to Olivier Dumanois. Although the long-desired offer was come at last, she was wondering, dubious, at the vista before her.

If she resolved to accept her foreign admirer, she would be safe to confess to Sir Gabriel her failings in preventing the *something* that occurred in the bedchamber in Angers. Duchess Alice would be damned, no doubt – but that was no more than she deserved – and the uproar would barely touch the departing bride.

And yet Elizabeth was shrinking from the prospect. Dumanois was a wealthy man, but his money oozed from trade, and his teeth were ominous, and, besides, she could not – surely could not – consign herself forever to this strange city when the Duke of Somerset might at any point return to England, leaving her stranded among these Flemings.

In the event, there was only to be one further encounter with Dumanois. Elizabeth suffered the man to kiss her, and the teeth were all that were threatened. After that, there could be no more question of marriage, and she extricated herself, brusque and shuddering.

But once there was no prospect of escape, there was no prospect of confession. Tell Sir Gabriel of the *something* and she would be sucked down with her mistress. And worse – if the Duke were to banish his wife, there yawned before Elizabeth a truly dreadful prospect: an eternity of wearying, cloistered, feminine seclusion, buried in the West Country. An eternity endured in Flanders with the teeth of nightmares were better than that.

When Sir Gabriel broached again the conduct of Lady Alice, therefore, his friend repeated that his concern did him credit, and she promised to watch their mistress always with especial care, but beyond that, he had nothing but her vague sympathy.

* * *

In addition to his natural role in raising – or in this case failing to raise – the country round about, Clifford had been entrusted by Warwick with one task of major significance. He was to bring Harry Percy, Earl of Northumberland, back to the fold.

"Tell me if you will, Monseigneur, of this Percy whom you were meant to be seeing, but whom you've done nothing about."

They were back in Skipton by now, taking their ease. Clifford stretched his legs towards the fire and kicked a log that was threatening to fall. He was silent so long that Cuthbert Bellingham took up the tale. "Lord Robert and Lord John spent the last – what? – eight or so years of their boyhood as squires at Alnwick, serving the old Earl. Alnwick is the seat of the Earls of Northumberland. In the far, far north, away near the Scots border; the sun never rises and it never, ever stops snowing."

Loic smiled. "There are giants, too? Trolls?"

"Not so many as over the border! Harry Percy is the present Earl, and quite a young'un. How old would he be now, Lord Robert?"

"Mm? No idea."

"He's twenty-one," said Castor.

Nield picked up the tale. "When Warwick put Edward of York on the throne, they wouldn't have another Percy hold the most powerful place in the North. So our young Harry was sent in the Tower and he's been there ever since. York bestowed the earldom on John Neville, Warwick's brother. The Nevilles and the Percys were ever the bitterest rivals, you see. This was the Nevilles' reward."

"He has not been there since. Only a short while in the Tower – he was there with your brother Roger, actually, Lord Robert. Then under the care of

York's friend William Herbert, at Raglan. Along with Henry Tudor, Jasper's nephew. And of course he's been back home for last year." It was a widely acknowledged fact that Arthur Castor knew everything; he made sure the reputation was constantly refreshed.

"So when Edward of York began to mistrust Warwick, that's when he gave Harry Percy back his lands?" suggested Loic, joining up the story with what he'd heard of York's fall.

"Exactly." Nield gave his shout of laughter. "Which was particularly stupid of him, as John Neville had been loyal to York until then; after that, of course, Neville couldn't wait to throw York over and join his brother Warwick in rebellion."

"John Neville shall not have the earldom of Northumberland, though," said Clifford. "I'll not see a Neville again in Alnwick, and neither will the other loyal lords. The cur must look elsewhere for lands." He recalled the argument in the great chamber at Angers, Devon needling Warwick on the subject. He devoutly hoped John Neville would get himself killed some time soon.

Clifford stared into the fire as the men passed on to other topics. Now, as the storm clouds were gathering, Harry Percy stood aloof, mute and remote in his great northern fastness, giving no hint which way he would leap when York made the inevitable return. There was no question but that Clifford was the obvious choice for this mission; if anyone could sway Harry Percy, it was he.

Except that Clifford had no such confidence. All the way from London he'd been skirting the issue; it served only to dishearten him. The gist of Roger's tiresome and sanctimonious harangue had been repeated again and again as he made his weary way among the gentry of the North Country: they'd all lost so much in the war; very few were prepared to risk it all over again. Especially to put the Nevilles back in power. There was little to lose by doing nothing, and the whole of the North was sitting on its hands.

* * *

"Eleanor – forgive me for disturbing you. It's a matter of some moment." Harry Percy was very still, a diminutive figure at the vast table. His sister swept to the window.

"What is it, Harry? The Abbess is here; I had to leave her in mid-flow."

"Your marriage, my dear, again." He paused, but she did not join him. "I've not been able to do for you that which I should have done."

"Well – I know that, well enough. The Percys so long in the wilderness, and York's wife buying up every eligible noble for her never-ending sisters. We've spoken of it so many times. I'd rather leave the subject be."

"Now it's worse, of course. John Neville eyeing my lands again like some grotesque magpie, waiting the reward for treachery. It's no secret we're in some difficulty. I wish it were otherwise."

"And I grow no younger."

"I hope that will not prove an obstacle! At twenty-two years, you're hardly elderly. But – they scent our weakness." His gesture encompassed the wide world outside his windows. "It comes to something, does it not, when bare knights feel at liberty to pester the Earl of Northumberland for his sister's hand?" He waved a sheaf of letters.

A bitter gasp of laughter. "Who are these paragons, who deem themselves worthy?"

Percy blew out his cheeks. "This time? Sir Godfrey Cave; Sir James Thwaite; Sir Simon Loys."

Another gasp of laughter, scornful now. "Minikins! Creatures that slither under stones. And everyone knows Loys killed his first wife."

"We're of one mind, then." He'd not piss on any of them in a fire. He was furious. "As it happens, though, a highly eligible suitor has fallen into our lap, as it were." Percy clasped his hands and gazed earnestly at her back, a braid of thistly bone. Well-versed in court fashion, Eleanor preferred to display her slender form in close-fitting gowns of her own singular style. "A nobleman, and no friend to the Nevilles; a natural ally."

The lengthy preamble was at an end. She had turned at last and was eyeing him, beginning to guess, surely, and Percy twisted his courage to go through with it.

"Not, perhaps, an ideal husband, but a man suitable in so many respects, if one looks at the matter in the round; if one steps back." Frankly, the further one stepped back, the better. "Robert Clifford, Sister. Do you think you could bring yourself to it?" He would assert his authority if he must, but please God it would not come to that.

Eleanor was examining her hands, bare of adornment now, where she used, always, to wear their mother's ring, a plait of fine gold set with tiny sapphires. He wondered, fleetingly, what had become of it. Then she raised her head, and colour had flared in the pale cheeks. "Robert Clifford? I love him, Harry. With all my heart, I love him. I always have."

* * *

Weeks passed and still he made no move. So it was with surprise that Clifford received a messenger from Harry Percy asking him to Alnwick for the Christmas season. He wondered then if Percy had guessed his purpose and grown impatient at the delay. Surely a hopeful sign: Clifford wouldn't be summoned all the way to the Scots border only to be told Percy wouldn't join him.

As he prepared for the journey, he dithered over whether to take the boys. An unappealing choice: appear at Alnwick with an absurd escort of Clifford by-blows, or leave them to their own devices. Not masterless, to be sure, for Aymer had the rule of them – but his was no steady hand, and the senior men warned Clifford not to turn the boys loose in his absence. None of the lads had ventured beyond York and they clamoured to accompany him. And so, when the time came to leave, they all rode out together.

At Fountains Abbey, some thirty miles up the road, they rested the first night. In the morning Clifford surprised his boys by bidding them welcome another. He had to pay the Abbot handsomely to release young Edwin from service; more than he was worth. While the boy was impressive enough to look at, his sinews needed stiffening. Tearfully bewildered at the sudden and unforeseen reversal in his prospects, Edwin gazed around at his new companions. He shut them out, peeped and shut them out again, riding blind, yearning to find himself back in the shelter of the Abbey's kitchen garden.

His horse slithered in the mud and fouled Aymer's grey. "Watch yourself, boy."

Richie bayed in at treble the volume. "Yes, watch yourself, you crabby mawk! What d'you think you're playing at?"

Edwin flinched. "Your pardon. I'm not well-used to riding."

The other twin reached with idle fingers and flipped the boy's bonnet, bowling it off his head and into a puddle. As Edwin was mourning the drabble of his only headgear, his knife was slipped from its sheath. Then the point was at his throat.

"Not well-used to much, are you, bantam?" Guy twisted the blade.

Edwin clutched blindly, sheathing the steel in the palm of his sheepskin glove. Fortunately, it hadn't been sharpened in a while.

"Come aside, Cousin," Oliver muttered, from behind, "and keep from their path." He idled, Edwin's reins in his hand, until the tormentors had ambled out of earshot.

Four fresh faces encircled the newcomer. They looked kindly enough, though one was so swathed in pocks and pustules that he was indecipherable.

"I don't know who anyone is." Blood and tears were trickling, watery pink, into the coarse wool of Edwin's cloak. "I didn't catch a single name. Guy, is it?"

"Guy?" said Oliver. "It's not Guy you need to watch, it's Aymer. There is something wrong with Aymer."

"Will and Richie are good fellows, in truth."

"Richie is *not* a good fellow, Bede; he's so *not*. And yea far up Aymer's arse. A common bully, just like Guy."

Fervent nodding from a fat boy with an anxious face.

"Chin up, gentlemen," Oliver continued, "for change is in the air. Sir Cuthbert says there are other Cliffords up at Alnwick who'll put Aymer's nose out of joint. Ranking men of the Earl's household. Older than the twins, says Sir Cuthbert, and not like to bend the knee."

"Excellent hearing!" cried Bede. "I love them already."

* * *

It was a very cold winter in Bruges, colder than the North Country, even. But in the midst of the ice, relations with her husband had thawed. Somerset was less busy about the court now. He'd made his arguments, repeatedly, to Duke Charles: Burgundy's long ties with the house of Lancaster; Somerset's ready service to him; the need to prevent Lancaster from falling into the hands of Louis of France. But Duke Charles had heard it all, many a time, and would hear no more. He was inexorably, inevitably, tending towards his brother-in-law, Edward of York – a man who was now so horribly present and conspicuous about the city. So Edmond hovered close to home, spending much of his time with Jonkin, and the household men, and Exeter.

"I think it only a matter of time before we leave for England," remarked Jonkin suddenly, as if reading her thoughts, and Alice shifted uneasily in her seat. "My brother feels that Duke Charles is being driven into Edward of York's arms by Warwick and King Louis. If that is so, it does no good us staying here. Exeter thinks the same."

She nodded, sympathetically. *Thank God.*

* * *

After a four-day forge through wretched weather, the bedraggled group sighted Alnwick Castle. Clifford could not fault the welcome. The Earl himself was waiting at the barbican to embrace him and lead him to the day room. Ten years, it had been; they'd not seen each other since Percy was a boy. Clifford was alert for clues from the outset, but Harry Percy was a difficult man to read. In appearance he strongly resembled his father and grandfather, men with whom Clifford had been intimately familiar. The Percy look was small-boned and palely drab. While there was no hint even of a light down on Percy's cheeks, he'd already lost most of the hair on his crown, giving him the disconcerting look of an inverted egg. The Earl was so very young, and had lived nothing but luxurious confinement. For all the shared heritage of Lancaster and the North, they had little in common.

After an early flurry of talk, Clifford was standing with his back to the sumptuous fire, thawing himself with greedy gulps of warm spiced wine. He watched as Harry Percy rubbed his hands and craned round in his chair, beckoning a young page from the shadows.

"Who have we here? Little Kit Loys, is it?" Percy whispered in the child's ear, and dispatched him. "There are some men I'd like you to meet." He twinkled happily at Clifford.

"Let me guess," said Clifford drily.

This time, the two sons who appeared before him could not be described as boys. Henry and Waryn were grown men and rising in Percy's service. These two were polished and impressive, very tall and broad. Henry could almost have been Robert's own twin, so alike were they in looks. A third man, hovering to the side, was John Clifford's natural son, George: a little older than his cousins, a little shorter, more handsome, less imposing.

For some time the Cliffords talked, filling in the blanks while Percy listened. How disconcerting to learn that the three lads had served the old enemy, John Neville, when he took possession of Alnwick. But they found Neville a decent master, and they prospered. On young Percy's return to his own, they'd passed smoothly into his household. Feeling again like the outsider he'd become, Clifford remarked on the ease with which men were changing sides. Percy said nothing.

And all the while, as he smiled and talked, ancient and uncomfortable memories were creeping in; slight, queasy misgivings. Behind his sons there hovered a ghost, the shadow of a woman gone these many years: Mistress Janet Prynne. Henry and Waryn's mother; she'd been Robert's first, and no easy conquest for a clumsy twelve-year-old. But eventually, trembling with hope, a rash and heedless child, he had done the reckless deed; scorned the very last warning his father gave when settling his boys at Alnwick. Mastered by desire, Robert had uttered the magic words; the incantation that unlocked the door. He had married her.

They were all frowning at him, expectant, for he'd slipped away, twenty years into the past, and scrambled now to regain the present. Clifford shook himself, dispelling the unease. Janet was gone.

When the three Clifford sons were released to their duties, Percy sat back, grinning.

Did the man suppose him to be shocked? Clifford pretended a rueful look. "This brings the tally of my bastards to fifteen, so far. Thirteen sons." A rough estimate. Every time he counted, he got a different number.

Percy looked startled. "My God! I haven't any."

"That you know of," suggested Clifford.

"But you're unwed, as yet?"

"As yet." He wondered what Percy would say if he gave voice to his hopes on the matter, and lifted the cup to mask a smile.

Harry Percy leaned back and gazed at Clifford. "I have a sister, Eleanor. You may recall her, though she'd have been a little maiden when you left Alnwick for Skipton. I'm seeking a husband for her. Perhaps you'd consider it?" He sipped his wine.

The disappointment was a sword thrust to the chest. *There we have it,* thought Clifford. *He hasn't summoned me to plan our strategy against York. He's summoned me to dispose of his sister.* With enormous difficulty, he controlled his face. "It's an idea." It was an idea; a most unwelcome one. "I haven't given much thought to marriage, though."

"No, I understand," said Percy. "We'd need to wait…" He shifted in his chair. "You'll excuse my frankness, Robert, but if King Edward retakes the throne…a dead bridegroom wouldn't do me much good. We'd defer the marriage until…"

"Quite," said Clifford.

"She's here. You'll see her at dinner."

* * *

Away in the guestchamber, Jem hovered about, getting in Loic's way, passing articles he didn't want, at inconvenient moments – their master preferring, always, his chamberlain's deft touch. Clifford slumped in a chair while Loic shaved him for the second time that day, combed his hair and mused over a succession of shabby chains. Several pearls had strayed from one; on another, the enamel was scratched and pitted.

"This will not do. Time for a new wardrobe, Monseigneur. Slashed sleeves, needles for boots, doublets that do justice to those fine legs."

"Fine buttocks, you mean. Show off my fine buttocks, in the English style?" And then – "Ah – I cannot believe he won't come out for his king. Another coward. What has become of this land?"

Loic lowered himself to the bed. "So, Monseigneur – the Earl of Northumberland is sitting tight after all?"

"He hasn't plucked up the courage to confess it, but yes, it does look that way." His toes hammered the chair legs.

"My God, the boots!" shrieked Jem. "Please, no, Lord Robert, no!"

Loic sighed. "So instead you're to be paraded as a potential bridegroom?"

"I'll be a laughing stock at court."

"If you can't sway the man, Monseigneur, no one can. This Percy made up his mind long ago."

"That won't save me. If I could raise a decent force myself it would hurt less." And then, in a gloomy aside, he said, "There are three more of our bastard boys here, by the way." He scrubbed at his hair, disordering it again.

Drawn to the little window, Clifford pushed his manservant aside and leaned upon the sill. A hundred yards beyond the curtain wall stood the church of St Michael, its dumpy tower a charcoal blot in the drizzling winter dusk. Mute beneath the sodden ground was his appalling error of judgment. And there she must lie. Perhaps he would visit the grave: a plea for mercy; a plea for complicity – for, in life, Janet was a woman both merciful and complicit. And then he pictured the Wyverns trailing him down the lane, an interested audience. He turned away.

Loic bobbed on his toes to smooth the tousled locks and Clifford stalked down to dinner in a bleak mood.

* * *

The holly-decked chamber – large, commodious and very warm against the foul weather outside – was thronged with local gentry and clerics, none of whom looked keen to engage with Black Clifford.

Percy tripped across on his little feet, leading a young woman by the hand. Folding his arms, Clifford looked the lady over in lewd and open appraisal. A quick, imperious thing was Eleanor Percy, all ash, hazel and sand. Not tall for a woman, but tall for a Percy. The maiden surprised him with a playful smile, flashing her small and crooked teeth. As her brother slipped away, she leaned in as though they were old friends. Which in a way they were, though for his part Clifford could unearth no memories whatever. By contrast, the lady seemed to recall Robert and his history in astounding detail. If he'd expected an unattractive version of Alice, he was wrong-footed. Eleanor was quite different.

Seated beside him through the elaborate dinner, she chattered away, unexpectedly witty and well-informed, bestowing her full attention. He might have been flattered, had he not been fairly sure the admiration was feigned. She was into her twenties already, he guessed, and no great beauty; doubtless she'd been instructed to do all she could to attach him. Nevertheless, she was animated and intelligent and his ill-humour had lifted by the time the meal was done.

Robert, who prided himself on the ability to read others, was well off course. From her earliest years, Eleanor venerated the Clifford brothers; as she grew to womanhood they remained the very pattern of rampant masculinity. She was, in fact, reeling in her admiration at the massive shoulders, the great strong hands, that leather eyepatch, which had so disgusted Alice, doing nothing to diminish the man's dangerous allure.

After dinner, guests were invited to play for the company. Here Clifford came into his own: meticulously rehearsed, ever-prepared, a player whose talents put most minstrels to shame. Now he summoned Loic and two of the Walters to accompany him on lute, timbrel and drum as he took up the pipes and executed a dance so quick and intricate that his fingers became a blur. He cast around the crowd, these aloof borderers. The music was whirling, ever more complex and exciting. Many smiled their incredulous delight; everywhere, a nodding and a tapping of feet. When the Wyverns finished there was an uproar of approval. Clifford was urged on all sides to play again.

With Loic beside him on the lute, Clifford sang his own composition, *Farewell*, his wrenching study of exile. Exile, not from England, but from

Alice, all the song's passionate intensity converging on the absent girl. He accompanied himself on the drum, the song as lingering and heartfelt as the dance had been rapid and contagious. Again, there was a storm of applause and he was begged to continue. He declined, smugly, knowing when to halt. A sidelong glance at Eleanor: her lashes wet with tears. If she'd not been his before, she was by then. Clifford gave her an intimate smile. He did not expect the marriage ever to take place, but there was no harm in nudging matters a little further forward.

* * *

So here was a prize indeed: Robert, Lord Clifford, a great Northern baron – best not to enquire too closely into the circumstance of his inheritance – and great hater of all things Neville. And very welcome he was, too. But a hazardous ally, nonetheless; one who might imperil Percy's cautious path, if not handled with particular care.

Harry Percy was a watchful man and a wary one, but he was ready for Clifford. Directly after matins on the next morning he came to the guestchamber and delivered the expected blow: he would not oppose King Edward's landing when it came, nor permit his affinity to do so.

"I know this is not what you were seeking."

"Hardly!"

"You must try to understand my position, Robert. My family lost everything for a time. I will not repeat the damage by backing the wrong side now."

Clifford sneered. "The wrong side?"

"Either side, frankly. Unlike my father, I don't really care who rules in London. If I come out for King Henry, and King Edward triumphs, I'll lose my head. If I declare for King Edward, and King Henry wins out, John Neville will be Earl of Northumberland again within the month." He sat back and examined Clifford, trimming his thumbnail with little teeth. "I don't imagine you'd relish delivering that news at court, however."

"I'm not afraid of Warwick!"

136

"Of course not." There was another silence. "How do you like Eleanor?"

"Well enough. I like her well enough."

"Well then. Here's my proposal: I suggest you tell Warwick – and Queen Margaret and so forth – that it was you who persuaded me not to come out for King Edward; to keep my men at home. If King Henry prevails, I'll need you to ensure that Warwick and his brother leave me and my lands alone. But if you want to bring them down, and I'm guessing that you do, we'll join forces. And you marry Eleanor as soon as Edward of York is dead."

Clifford rose to it slowly, unsure he understood. "You're content for me to go about saying you'd intended to support York, and I persuaded you otherwise?"

There was a weary roll of the eyes. "Robert – you'll do that in any case. I'm just acknowledging the obvious. I don't know if you heard the news from France, but the Papal dispensation came through, at last: Warwick's little girl has wed Prince Edward. With the Nevilles in the ascendant again, I need allies."

Clifford thought for a moment. "And if York prevails?"

"King Edward is grateful I haven't brought the North out against him; Eleanor marries any noble that his ghastly Woodville in-laws haven't already snatched for one of their own…" Percy was ticking off the outcomes on his fingers. "…and you and the Nevilles are in your graves."

Clifford gave an unwilling laugh. "You leave me little choice, Harry, though I should destroy you for this."

"And how would you accomplish that, I wonder? My retinue is fifteen hundred strong. I hear you're struggling to muster a hundred. And most of those seem to be your progeny."

* * *

Margaret de Vere thought she might be with child. At that, Jack insisted his wife remain at Wivenhoe for the whole spell, for his pace would surely exhaust her.

Making his frenetic rounds in the Christmas season, Jack's smile had become frozen, the muscles in a permanent rictus; another and another mumming, marvellously similar, more disguisings, more tortured puns, more wobbly props, at least one of which would always fall over at an inconvenient moment; more bad acting, bad dancing, bad carolling, bad playing; every manor breaking out its proudest wine, which he dutifully sampled; everywhere enormous, wanton spreads; dutifully sampled. Examining his belly, it seemed also to be wantonly spreading, and that filled him with dismay.

Among those families of Essex where Jack de Vere's influence had procured a knighthood or favour, he was doubly welcome, if that were possible. After Christmas, he moved on to the house of Nicholas Loys, young, courteous and handsome, a great favourite with the Earl, and his pretty wife – not that she was to Jack's taste, being of the fair, blue-eyed, apple-cheeked variety. Their repartee was more diverting than any play-acting, all quick-witted spite, the lady having much the best of it.

And then on to the house of Nick Loys's brother-in-law, Adam Ewelme, a most good-natured man, and on to the house shared by Mark Rohips, a most cantankerous man, and his nephew, Piers Brixhemar, a most amusing fellow. Jack had meant to visit all his grateful nominees, but by then it was well past Twelfth Night and Margaret was growing raucous.

Jack had so many promises of men that it was almost embarrassing, as he told Warwick, self-deprecating, in one of his many missives. And then, because Warwick had so much to do with getting the French treaty past the Council and ready for Parliament, Jack was compelled to forgo the reunion with his wife and head straight back to London.

* * *

Percy and Clifford passed the rest of the festive season in dispassionate harmony. Clifford was succumbing to a wary respect for the Earl, so quick and level-headed, despite his youth and inexperience.

"Will you be purloining my fine Clifford lads, Robert? The three of them are sworn to me, but I guess that won't stop you; you're a veritable Pied Piper, emptying the hearths of the North. Losing them would cause me a pang, but to tell the truth, I feel sorry for you."

The offer sowed dissension. It was briskly dismissed by Robert's second son, who closely resembled Sir Roger in temperament. Waryn had no wish to give up his comfortable, profitable position with the Earl to throw in his lot with his notorious father.

For Robert's eldest the prospect was different. All his life had been tending towards this point. Though memories of Robert were hazy, he had reverenced the man from afar. The tantalising call, when it came, coincided with a dramatic acceleration in the young man's fortunes: already under-steward by the age of twenty and highly valued, he expected to soar in the Earl's service. And, by now, he was a father in his turn, with two young sons dwelling close by. But nothing would deter him.

Waryn worked strenuously upon his elder brother's feelings, contrasting the honour of their position with the trail of mayhem, sin and slaughter that was their father's legacy. "And don't say I've made it sound enticing, Brother! You owe the Earl more in gratitude and respect than that."

The only response: a grin. Lowering himself into a chair before his brother, Waryn clasped his hands, stately and reproachful. "So you'll leave Grandfather Prynne all alone, infirm as he is, and skip off, heedless?"

"Not alone, Waryn. The old man will want for nothing while you are here."

Waryn shook his head darkly. "And your sons – who is to care for them? And your sweetheart Dorcas also?"

"Be reasonable, Waryn. We can't expect Father to give me a position until I've proved myself, so it's likely I'll be short of money for a time. But meanwhile, you'll take my place as under-steward the moment I'm gone. I'd expect you to be a good fellow and see them right. You may do with Dorcas as you please."

"You've ruined the poor girl; don't try to palm her off on me. And stop smirking in that revolting fashion. You have decidedly too much of Father in you."

The elder brother gave his little family no further thought. Off he went to his father before the packing-up commenced, and asked leave to join the Wyverns. Clifford embraced the young man with strong emotion.

"I am most glad that you have come to me, Henry; you cannot know how contented this makes me! My firstborn; my eldest; my fine, fine son."

"It is an honour. Call me *Hal*, Father – none but my mam ever called me *Henry*."

Clifford startled at the mention of Janet and swiftly stilled himself. The woman – he never would think of her as a wife – had died so long ago; it was clear their son knew nothing, and would settle to his proper place, the place that Clifford assigned, at the head of the bastard boys. As her shadow waned, he gazed into the face of their son, exploring the astonishing, eerie resemblance, a mirror to himself. "I am twice blessed, for young George offered his service days ago, before the Earl raised the question, even. There's another fine, strapping fellow, though Percy doesn't seem unduly disappointed!"

Hal smiled back. "You know George is acting master-at-arms for the Earl? He's very handy and quick, Father, but he does have a talent for trouble. He likes to keep his weapon sharp."

"Ah well." Clifford was thinking on the turbulent band he'd assembled. "He's wasted here. You've met the twins?"

"Oh yes, Father. I have taken their measure." He couldn't take Aymer's measure; something was amiss there. "George and Guy have set to brawling."

Clifford clicked his tongue. "You shall lead them for me, Hal. You shall master them. As my eldest, it is your place to do so. And what of Waryn?"

Hal shook his head. "My brother would never have joined us. To tell the truth, Father, Waryn's a clever man, and dear to me, but you'd not find him convivial company. He suits the Earl, and the Earl suits him. He's better off here."

* * *

The sojourn in Alnwick had refreshed them all, and given Clifford a sense of perspective. He'd made an ally of sorts in young Harry Percy, who would no doubt prove useful if they won through. Eleanor's feelings had become clear. He felt himself grown fond of her, though he could well envisage how she'd mature as wife: possessive and overbearing.

140

Brough Castle, he thought, would be the perfect place to consign her. She would manage his Westmorland estates from that stronghold. Brough was an aerie, lofty and exposed, always blowing a gale. It was hard to hear oneself think, and perfect for drowning her out. He would visit Eleanor and breed from her, an heir to a high and noble bloodline, not some poor mongrel like Hal. He'd live sometimes at Skipton and sometimes at court, where he could see Alice and couldn't hear Eleanor.

"And if you wed the lady, Monseigneur, and Somerset dies thereafter, leaving a widow – what then?"

"Mm. Then I imagine Reginald Grey will push Eleanor down the stairs and rid me of the impediment."

"I'd say he's itching to do so already."

"You have the right of it there. Poor Eleanor." Clifford tipped his chair and contemplated his chamberlain. "For now, the lady has charms of her own – enthusiasm not least among them. But I'm a patient man. There's nothing to be gained from rolling this one under a hedge."

"That would shake Northumberland from his present detachment, Monseigneur, and no mistake! Imagine having to admit to Warwick that Harry Percy raised the North for Edward of York because you…"

"Stop fretting, mon petit. I tell you: I have myself well in hand."

Meanwhile – naturally – the contrasting prospect of Alice grew ever more alluring. After months from her presence, he was tormented with desire and longing.

On the last night of his visit, Eleanor had dressed with more care than ever. Her fine pale hair lay in spirals that owned nothing to nature and those sandy lashes were black with soot. Plaguing him in vain to dance with her, she performed before him with self-conscious steps.

"I never dance; it's not that I lack the talent, for I dance very well. I'm so great in size that I choose not to disport myself in that way. But if it pleases you, I will dance on our wedding day."

It did please her. "I have waited all these years to dance with you, my lord. It pains me still, that you've no recollection of me, when my own memories are so

141

fresh." She pouted playfully. "Come – even the winter of '59, when you and your brother returned to spend Christmas with us? I was twelve years old by then."

"You would not have been of much interest to me at that age."

"The snow was early that year; a bitter winter. Surely you recall hawking with your brother on Christmas Eve? As you rode to the barbican, I was waiting on the wall above, my snowballs at the ready – do you remember that? How Lord John cursed; he turned the air blue! You were laughing so hard, and you said – " she forced her voice as low as it would go, " *'You've soused my new bonnet, you little trull. Come down here and beg my forgiveness!'*"

Clifford laughed again, and turned to pinch her cheek. "Ah – at last, you have nudged me to a recollection. I don't suppose you were foolish enough to come down to me, and never had the spanking you deserve." They had been wandering together, and he paused in a dim and convenient alcove, a hand warming her hip.

The moment was come for his Twelfth Night gift: a crucifix purchased by Loic in Angers as a handy stand-by, a twin of the one gifted to Blanche. Clifford was grateful for his chamberlain's foresight. He hadn't been grateful at the time; it seemed an unnecessary extravagance. He stroked back Eleanor's soft, light hair, the spirals wilted now to faint ripples, and fixed the necklace at her throat. Radiant and trembling, she took his hands and he drew her in. His mind strayed away to that perfect kiss in the summer darkness. He tried to conjure Alice, but she tasted different. His body was slow to respond.

But Eleanor had waited so desperately long for this. She brimmed with a passion her body could not sustain; her head reeled; she was drowning. As his hands began their work it was too much, unbearable beneath his touch, and she twisted, wordless, from the caress, and fled. Clifford started after her, a few uncertain steps, and abandoned the attempt. The lady was, clearly, unready for him. He smirked to himself. More like Alice than he'd thought.

Eleanor flew to her chamber and flung herself on the bed like a little girl. Flushed and panting, she stretched and shivered in a perfect anguish of overwrought longing. Marjorie Verrier – her gentlewoman and bosom friend – was poised for her confidences.

When every aspect of the man's conduct had been explored in sufficient minuteness, Marjorie ventured upon a subject more to her taste. "Have you remarked Lord Clifford's twin sons? What do you make of them?"

Eleanor opened her eyes. "You forget: the boys shall be my sons also when I wed, residing in my household at Skipton. They are short fellows and do not share the Clifford look."

The Clifford look left Marjorie unruffled. "But Guy and Aymer are such handsome men, are they not? Their colouring…a certain air they have about them. Especially Master Aymer. It puts me strongly in mind of Sir Miles."

"Miles Randall?" The eyes had closed again. "I barely remember him, though of course you'd recall his looks better than I." Now Marjorie would start upon the subject of the Cliffords' lost chamberlain, gone these many years, and Eleanor would dismiss the voice, for she was raging with the fever that Robert had, this night, released within her.

The next day, Clifford took his leave. Eleanor was weeping and waving her handkerchief, on and on, until the cavalcade moved out of sight. It seemed an excess of emotion. Only George waved back.

* * *

The day was lodged, ever-after, in her memory, the happiest time Alice spent with Edmond.

The canals had frozen over, and he suggested they go skating together, which was so unexpected that she'd gaped at him. But go they did, and he had good balance and comfortable strength, which made it easy. Alice was looking sideways at the unaccustomed grin – wide and boyish and charming – the waves of hair flicking under his bonnet, disordered by the wind, and a flush of pink across those high cheekbones. Her gentlewomen were there, excepting Lady Ullerton, as were Jonkin and the household men she favoured, not the prying Sir Gabriel. And afterwards, when they were sweating and cold at the same time, they warmed their hands and bellies with hot cinnamon-scented wine.

That night the couple lay beneath a swathe of furs and as she drowsed,

Edmond pulled her close against him so that she woke again, smiling and welcoming. She could not do enough to please him.

* * *

The band that left Alnwick was a little larger and a deal merrier than the band that arrived three weeks before. Clifford cast around at his boys. All these sons – his and John's – the seeds sown once upon a time, and John so long gone, and he had walked away, neither nourishing nor tending the saplings but returning, years later, to the orchard, to walk among the tall trees. It moved him.

"They should be Cliffords, Loic, but they have no true name." Hal and Waryn had every right to the name, though he was fierce in his refusal to contemplate it.

"They are the Clifford boys, Monseigneur."

"And what shall they be called, when they're no longer boys? George is not a boy, try as he might. Hal is no boy. I shall give them their own name, as the Beauforts were given a name."

Loic started in surprise. "Edmond of Somerset is baseborn?"

"Of course not. His grandfather was baseborn. And the grandfather's father – John of Gaunt – named the brood after his lands in France."

"Really? Well, this I never knew, Monseigneur. Duke Edmond is not so fine, after all!"

"Well, perhaps not," smirked Clifford. "But attend: the *FitzCliffords*, we'll call them. I shall write a song about them, perhaps."

"Wait till the FitzCliffords have triumphed in feats of arms, Monseigneur. Or the song will be very short, and concerned mostly with the heroes pissing on each other and pestering girls."

Clifford threw back his head and laughed. "Very true. Ah – but I tell you who I'm missing, greatly, Loic, among all those hefty lads: my fine little soldier."

"You did not know these others as infants, I suppose." *You, who came early to fatherhood and late to love.* "Your Jean is a fine boy. We'll send for him in

144

due course; him and my little Charles both, so they may continue to keep each other company. How the thought warms me! Ah – have you written to Madame Babette, Monseigneur?"

"You know I haven't!"

"Now we're more comfortable, I'll send her a little gold, shall I, for the clothing and feeding of your children? Your Jean must have some schooling, or my Charles's wits will put him to shame. You'll write poor Madame Babette a letter – a very brief one will suffice to please her – and I'll enclose it with the money."

"Send the gold to Bruges. You write to her; I won't, for now. Babette understands how busy I am. Which reminds me…" As the castle disappeared behind them, Clifford announced his intention to make all haste for Newcastle; in his day there'd been an excellent whorehouse in the town. "Others may have been luckier, but I've been living like a monk these past few weeks. I intend to make up for it."

The household men made cheerful assent. The expressions of the older FitzCliffords ranged from jaded to jubilant. Oliver, Tom and Robbie were looking anxious, Edwin on the brink of tears again.

On reaching the tavern, the men scattered to their business. As so often, Aymer found himself unmoved. He dawdled in the shadows, watching Reginald Grey shepherd a lost sheep with zealous hands, ministering to the fallen. Turning, Aymer contemplated Castor: the man's unwilling countenance. Perhaps the two of them would sit it out; play some cards. He'd a strong sense Sir Arthur Castor would repay attention. But his twin's hand was insistent at Aymer's shoulder and the knight turned and trailed away.

Reserving his own choice, Clifford paid over the coin for the boys and instructed the novices. Once he'd dispatched them all, he was left with Loic, who asked, as so often at this point, more in habit than in hope, "Shall we take her together, Monseigneur?"

"No."

"All right." Loic was settling, equable, with his drink. "I'll have her straight after, when she's warm."

"Say it aloud, and it puts me off my stride."

Loic shrugged. "We share the same tastes, Monseigneur."

"That's not what you said when you saw the Lady Alice." Clifford stalked after the whore. He was particular, and this distraction was taking the edge off the experience – and hardly for the first time. He would stop bringing Loic along. Before the man had finished his drink, Clifford was back.

The chamberlain stood and stretched.

"Hurry up, then! Mother of God – what a waste of coin." Clifford drummed his fingers. "And she'll not feel you, after me." But the thought didn't dampen Loic's ardour; not at all.

* * *

Elizabeth Ullerton had pleaded her age to be excused from skating, the only time she owned to that particular infirmity. Gabriel Appledore had sprained his ankle in an earlier bout with his fellows and so, alone among the senior household, these two were abandoned. The house lying at their disposal, the pair chose the upstairs chamber, Sir Gabriel resting his foot on a cushion before the fire, Lady Ullerton to his side in the window seat, remarking on the passers-by for the steward's benefit. Her sharp commentary was amusing him, and they passed a merry hour before Sir Gabriel reverted to the subject that had already made her irritable.

"I wonder, Lady Ullerton," he struck up, his voice an octave higher than a moment before, "whether you've thought further on the matter we discussed some weeks ago?"

She believed he was pursuing her with his inquisitions into the *something*, and her shoulders sagged.

"I will, of course, desist if the subject pains you, but you bade me ask the lady directly, and so, with some trepidation, I do."

Frowning, she glanced across.

He hurried on, as if rushing her objections. "My dear lady, I beg you to give me your consideration. I know I'm not so wealthy as your Flemish admirer, but I am a true Englishman; I do not have your exalted connections, certainly, but my family is rising, and I believe my standing with Duke Edmond lends a certain distinction."

Still she stared at him, until he became flustered.

"Alas, I have offended you. I shall say no more."

* * *

Travelling on from Newcastle, the boys had become more, rather than less, boisterous, their energies not slaked as Clifford had hoped. He was thinking ruefully of the extra coin he'd had to lay out afterwards; when Guy persuaded Aymer to join him, things had got out of hand. Clifford would have sent the landlord away with a flea in his ear, but he was nostalgic about the house and would no doubt patronise it again. And then he couldn't be bothered to give the twins a proper dressing-down; he and John had caused mayhem on occasion, and probably in the same establishment. Though he didn't recall Father ever putting his hand in his purse to smooth it over.

Now the boys were urging each other to havoc on the road, racing and harassing other travellers, George, John's boy and the oldest of them all, wishing ever to be in the thick of it, while Hal chose to ride with his father, well away at the front of the cavalcade. So Clifford found himself flanked by Hal and Loic, who'd not yet found a way to coexist.

Somewhere to the rear was Aymer, watching Hal's huge figure from a brooding distance; his eyes spitting the broad shoulders like an awl; loathing this interloper with unbridled force, as he had never known loathing until now. Aymer's place was up there, at the head, beside his father. Dominion was all. He'd let slip his chance.

As they approached the friary at Yarm, their next halt, Clifford was ignoring a fresh outbreak of rowdy mirth. He pulled up sharp on hearing Eleanor Percy's name bandied behind him. "Find out what they're saying, Hal."

"I know what they're saying, Father." Hal smiled. "George is speaking of the Earl's sister. You could say she has a liking for tall, dark men, but in all honesty, she just has a liking for Cliffords. *Any* of the Cliffords; you know how we run to type. George has had her."

Loic looked across in alarm as Clifford turned on his eldest with a thunderous expression.

Hal stared in surprise "What is it, Father?"

"I cannot credit what I'm hearing."

"Yes," Hal agreed. "She's an unusual girl."

* * *

"Right," said Clifford when Loic undressed him that evening in the friary guesthouse. "That was an unsavoury surprise, and no mistake. How am I to put a stop to this?"

"To the marriage or to the talk, Monseigneur?"

"To the talk – the marriage can take care of itself."

"Better that Master George is warned to hold his tongue, and as soon as possible."

"Agreed. Call George in. And Hal."

George entered warily and shot Loic a narrow glance. Following him, his cousin Hal.

Clifford plunged in. "You'll not yet be aware, George, that I'm considering marriage with the Earl of Northumberland's sister." George froze. Hal pondered the floor. "Today I heard you speak of Eleanor Percy. What did you mean by it?"

They could almost see the useless thoughts dissolving as George cast about to extricate himself. "Well," he said at last, "I did flirt with her, a little, my lord. I did kiss her."

Even the way he phrased it suggested a bigger admission lurking. Everyone looked sceptical, not least the unhappy youth.

"And no more than that?"

George shook his head, a tiny motion.

"Understand this, George: all you boys will stick to that tale, if it ever comes to light. A kiss, and it meant nothing. But it's not to be discussed any further, by any of you, or I'll turn you out into the street to beg your bread. Do I make myself clear?" He waved George away and looked steadily at his eldest son. "Take charge. Your task is to protect her reputation."

"I will do all in my power, Father." Hal hesitated. "If you'd taken me into your confidence earlier, I could have prevented this."

* * *

In their chamber George hovered, agitated and indignant. "What the fuck did you have to tell him for?"

"How was I to know he was taking her in marriage? And you were hardly discreet yourself. You never are."

"Did he believe me?" asked George, needlessly.

"Of course not."

"God's bones!" the elder burst out. "He *can't* marry her – can you imagine it? She, married to him, living in our household? Sooner or later…there'll be a catastrophe."

"Like Potiphar's wife."

"What?" The biblical reference was wasted on George.

Hal was sanguine. "He only said he was considering it. He'll do nothing until we've defeated York. You've time enough to worry about this later."

"All very well for you to say! I'll be worrying about it all the time now. God's bones – I wish I hadn't gone near her. But she's so bloody persuasive."

"Not persuasive. Just persistent."

George nodded despondently.

* * *

Once Sir Gabriel and his love had unravelled the muddle, to much relieved hilarity, they could make their happy plans. The steward was proud to boast that Duke Edmond not only consented to the match, but had condescended to advise Sir Gabriel on the wooing, which inspired Lady Ullerton with no very great respect for either man's insight.

The others displayed an unflattering uniformity of astonishment. Alice and Blanche at least made the attempt to conceal their surprise, Alice reflecting glumly that her ill-wishers had joined forces. The younger ladies' reactions were natural and healthy. The pair were elderly and desiccated; their laboured compliments, their tittering and blushing: it was, all of it, entirely revolting.

* * *

On their arrival back in Skipton, the boys resumed their training in martial skills. Here, Hal and George were proving an asset. These two were well-drilled, and competitive, and blessed with the best of the Clifford physique. Hal was just of a height with his father, and overtopped Aymer and Guy by half a foot, though he was some way off Clifford's weight and the twins were stockier. The others fell somewhere between.

Clifford took a very personal interest in their progress. He was doomed to make a poor showing when the call came; but if his little force were few in number, they'd do a lot of damage. And he wanted them to survive the encounter. It was in these moments that he was calmest, down in the yard, morning after morning, shouting and demonstrating, untiring.

"You have the knack of it there, Aymer. Elegant. Whoever taught you, it surely wasn't your Uncle Roger. Take this lad and this one into the space yonder and show them how; Bede's clinging on for dear life and Robbie's grip is limp." He raised his voice. "Hear me! From now on, young Robbie is not to sit on his arse unless it's to arm-wrestle; best way to strengthen a man's wrist. When yanking hasn't done the trick."

Robbie and Bede straggled after their elder brother.

"Guy! Use the flail like a mace! Like a mace!" Clifford ducked instinctively, wincing as the spiked ball made a wild swerve, its blunted studs connecting heavily with Guy's shoulderblade. "Stop concentrating on the tail – use it like a mace and the tail will follow." The same thing happened again. "Don't ignore the tail; just don't be fascinated by it. It's slowing you down. Your man will be upon you by the time it changes direction. You see?" He waited until Guy swung the weapon back and punched him in the face.

"I hate this fucking thing." Guy was panting. "Why can't I just wield a mace then? It's much easier. My lord."

"Anyone can slam with a mace. A flail has a longer reach and is harder to counter. That gives you an advantage. This is a matter of life and death. You should *want* to master it." And then to Richie, "What are you muttering about?"

"Your pardon, Father, but why train with something so testing? You said the weapon should feel just like your hand, but I'd never choose a flail; I don't want to waste time on it."

Clifford shook his head. *So naive.* "You think a battle's like a joust? Arms laid out neatly for you? Listen, all of you. Even if you start the day with the weapon of your choice, it's common to lose it at some point, especially when you're raw. You need to be deadly with whatever comes to hand. In any case, I've spent the last five years fighting someone else's war, someone else's way, in someone else's army. I hadn't the luxury of picking and choosing. If this all goes to hell, we'll end up in Granada, fighting the Moors – so get your heads down and concentrate."

It was easy to lapse into making speeches, but they had to understand how it would be. Even George and Hal had no experience of the chaos of real warfare. Most of them were cursed, also, with stupidity.

He strode across to where Tom and Edwin were practising against two of the Walters. The boys managed to tangle the chains of their flails just as their father approached. "Use it like a mace!"

All that day the phrase was sniggered wherever they went: spearing meat at dinner – "Use it like a mace!" To a page clearing a chamberpot – "Use it like a mace!" It was funny the first few times, but they never knew when to stop, and each training session was producing a new tag to irritate the household. Ah well. At least the repetition dinned it into their heads. With any luck, if they found themselves wielding a flail for real, they'd use it like a mace.

* * *

After the mild commotion, life in Somerset's house reverted to its usual torpor.

Edmond was increasingly despondent in those days, conscious that he was losing his patron to Edward of York. At last, the inevitable, ghastly mishap occurred: Edmond found himself in the same room as this bitter enemy – encountering York as the man swept into the court, laughing, talking over his shoulder just as Somerset paused, frigid, on the threshold. Their eyes met – one shuddering moment – before Edmond averted his face and, shaking, stalked on. Somehow he gained the next corner, one foot and then another, before he could collapse against a wall and still his heart.

He looked at the sky, and he looked at his hands. King Henry was being led into war on France's side; Duke Charles was grave and stern with him now, where once they'd soldiered shoulder to shoulder, sharing a tent. Edmond should be in England.

And within the city of Bruges the hostility to the house of Lancaster was now palpable. Alice had no wish to encounter it; she might as well have been in a convent, for all that she went out among her equals. Isabeau had dropped all pretence of friendship, making merry amongst the lords of York now much about the court, delighting them with her talents. Before long, Alice's name was bandied freely among them, a cheap and easy target. It caused Edmond as much pain as the renunciation by his patron.

Their departure was, at last, imminent. Alice was surprised that Duke Charles was co-operating even so far as to assist them with provisions and safe conducts; what concessions had he exacted from her husband? She knew better than to ask.

* * *

His father's body lay in the Abbey of St Albans, two hundred miles south, where Robert had no hope of communing with him. He wondered now why he and John had forsaken Thomas Clifford all those years – the early years, when power and wealth were theirs, and they could have brought him home. They were young and heedless when he died. They were at war.

Having fallen in the North Country, Lord John lay close by, in Bolton Priory where their mother had interred him, half-mad with grief. At his homecoming, Robert had paid his respects, creeping on his knees to his brother's tomb; laying out a small fortune in masses for his soul. Masses too, for his father, and masses for the soul of another. When the coming clash was done, when he could draw breath, he meant to re-inter his father and brother's remains with resplendent ceremony, as Warwick had famously done for his own kin, those who'd fallen at Wakefield. Clifford wondered where York buried his dead; where Edmund of Rutland lay now. Not scattered over Wakefield Bridge where John and he had spilled the lad. *Squire for me.*

Now he would make another pilgrimage to his brother's side, taking only his intimates. He would bring Hal and George along, underscoring his wish that there should be distance between this pair – his eldest and John's eldest – and the other boys.

As the favoured ones clattered out through the castle's massive barbican, there were watchers at the windows. The hoofbeats of the horses faded away up the Knaresborough road.

"It's a wonder you should be left behind, Aymer! You were the beloved until that great knave muscled in. Father will grow tired of him, I don't doubt – Hal is that full of himself."

"For Christ's sake, Richie," muttered Guy, offended on several counts.

Rigid upon the bed in their shared chamber, Aymer closed his eyes, closing out the world. In his graceless way, Richie was meaning to help, no doubt, but there was no help for it. Talking would not right this wrong; something more emphatic was required.

That evening, a few miles distant, Clifford dined alone with Prior William Man, a gentle soul he'd known for many years; the man who'd been prior when the Lords of Skipton were great in the North. Clifford shared his vision for the magnificent translation of his father and brother's remains, and Prior William dreamed along with him, for there was honour and profit in it, and the priory was deep in debt.

He noticed, at length, that his guest had eaten very little; a dainty feeder for so great a body. Was the dinner not to Lord Robert's taste? The prior abased himself. It was, truly, not good eating; the house was poor and growing poorer; the sheep had died in numbers that past autumn, rotting in the heavy rains, and the River Wharfe had flooded widely, swamping fields and drowning several labourers. Clifford, who knew that his own estates were not yielding as they should, listened abstractedly. The prior mumbled on. While all the landowners had suffered, some had taken matters into their own hands to remedy their losses. Most particularly Gawain Threlkeld, who'd raided down into Wharfedale and seized a quarter of the priory flock, which they could ill-afford to lose. Worse, he'd hidden the sheep away when Prior William journeyed to his moorland house to remonstrate, accusing the prior of letting his flock wander and graze other men's land.

The priory was a foundation of the Lords of Skipton and under their protection, and Prior Man felt that if anyone would sympathise, it would be Robert Clifford. He had not expected quite such an enthusiastic champion, however, and trembled before the man's great thunderclap of rage.

"Threlkeld shall rue the day he was born! That family is hell-spawn. Let me tell you."

The prior looked like he was panicking, for the name of Threlkeld presaged the vilest of all Clifford chronicles; dredged up from the very depths.

"You and I have known Gawain Threlkeld for years, and what a shitty little varlet he is! But that's as nothing – *nothing* – compared to his brother. You remember? You will do. Sir fucking peacock: Lancelot Threlkeld? One of our retinue; he ravened after John's wife?" Even the thinking on it, so many years later, and his jaw was trembling.

The prior had set down his wine, eyeing his patron with alarm, but the man was well beyond reach.

"That wicked pair were cuckolding John, weren't they?

"They were, my lord? I really couldn't say."

"I say they were! Lancelot Threlkeld got Margaret with child, didn't he?" One avowal after another, all of them couched as questions. They were not questions. "The *pretty little Henry*. Those two foisted that bastard whelp on my brother; called him a Clifford, but he was no Clifford, and anyone could tell it at a glance. Puny, fair, blue-eyed. A bit of a give-away, no? I told my brother: look into that fucking face, I told him, and Miles Randall – you remember our chamberlain – Miles told him, too, but no, John was in thrall to that bitch of a wife. And lo and behold: my brother was cold a bare month when the whore took Lancelot Threlkeld as her husband and laughed in my very face. What surer proof could a man need?"

Again, the prior was not looking as he should: he seemed to be scuffling inwardly. The yarn had ended, prematurely, without a resolution. *When was the child last seen, and by whom?* William Man might have asked it, but – like Alice – he did not.

Assuring the prior that he would take the theft of the flock well in hand, on the next morning Clifford led his party the few miles back to Skipton, full of grim resolve.

* * *

It was the day before their departure from Bruges. While harrying the servants at the back door, Alice noticed a figure hovering close by: a young woman, soberly dressed, regarding her narrowly. The woman had been speaking with the under-steward, and now he turned uncertainly to his mistress and slipped away. If the onlooker seemed in some way familiar, it must have been because her looks were unnervingly similar to Alice's own, and compelled her presence. The woman was perhaps ten years her elder; pale and slender, with a pointed chin and slanted, wary eyes. Alice took a deep, steadying breath, unwilling to stay or to go.

The woman approached, eyes downcast, and spoke in halting English. "My lady, my name is Babette Delaurin. I supply the sea and river fish to your household and I am…I was a friend of Lord Robert Clifford, if it please you."

It did not please her, and Alice almost turned to go in that moment, there being no honour in this meeting.

"Please, my lady – might I know if it's true you leave for England in the next days?"

"This is no concern of yours. Go about your business, woman."

"Please, my lady – may I humbly beg you to bear a message to him – to Lord Robert? He promised he would write often, to let me know how he does, and where he is, but he's not done so – not once. I need him to hear of some…news."

155

Speculating, sourly, at the news, Alice drew herself up to her full, inconsiderable height, some inches shorter than the other. "How dare you approach me so impertinently? Lord Clifford is nothing to me…I'll not bear sordid messages. Be gone!"

Silent tears slid down Madame Delaurin's face and it was this that stayed Alice from closing the door.

"My lady." The woman placed her trembling palms together, as if praying. "Lord Robert's little daughter, Marguerite: she has died, and was buried this morning. He must hear it. Please help us, of your charity."

Alice pulled the door close behind her. "How old was your little maiden, Madame Delaurin? Of what has she perished?"

"She was just past her second birthday, my lady. We lost her to a fever. The other two have recovered their health, thank God."

"The other two?" An irrepressible, tell-tale curiosity.

"Young Jean, and little Marie. I have the letter here, my lady. Would you take pity on us, and give it to him? Lord Robert has spoken of you so often that I know you to be a tender and gracious lady."

Alice bit her lip at that, extending a trembling hand. "I cannot say whether or when I shall see Lord Clifford," said she, in a low voice, "but I will do what I can to pass the sad news to him. I grieve for your loss, Madame Delaurin."

* * *

Back in his own bed, Clifford lay unquiet. It should, by rights, have been a nightmare. It was proving anything but; a luscious recollection.

Janet's father was a trapper, in a small way. Fox and rabbit fur at various stages of treatment or decay swung and dangled all over the dark little house that crouched at the edge of Alnwick. The stench was remarkable, but never mind that.

There stood the oversized boy, twisting his bonnet in maladroit hands, gawking at Janet.

"Where is Master Prynne?"

"Father's away in the woods. Trapping. Gone all day."

He felt faint. She offered him ale, moving about the room, shaking out her dark locks, knowing his eyes were feasting on her. A grown woman of eighteen years – impossibly beyond a twelve-year-old Robert. He just wanted her to take her clothes off.

"Ah – may I take one look, Mistress Prynne? A look, not a touch, I promise. Then I'll be on my way. I cannot eat my dinner for thinking of you."

In his sleep, Clifford yelped with laughter, and Loic's eyes flew open.

"That's not good hearing, sir," she answered, gravely. "That's bad news for your health."

Naturally, the glimpse did not improve matters. He would touch her. His palms scuffed at the rough yarn of her bodice. Worse and worse. Nonsense was coming out of his mouth. Pure fuckwittery.

"Give me your purse." Brushing aside his posy of prickly jasmine, she shook the meagre innards upon the worktable: two farthings and little gleaming ring, long outgrown. "That's not much. Not a fair exchange, sir. All the risk on my side. If you want more, you must promise more."

Anything; he would promise anything. Way more than he could deliver. The perfumes of Araby. Precious gems. Silks. Velvets. Gold.

Now she placed her hands on his shoulders, craning up, and he took his first shivering, slavering kiss. As she dropped back, tendrils of drool stretched from lip to lip; clear, slender spans, bowing under their own weight. She mopped her mouth on the back of her sleeve. By now he was perfectly lost, the world around them growing dim; he was slipping and his heels would find no purchase.

Observing the descent, Clifford laughed once more, in horrified glee.

"Eh? Monseigneur! You're upon your back again. Hush."

Loic nudged him, and his master rolled, face to face with the chamberlain.

"Watch now," cried the dreamer. "Watch and take warning."

When the man's words were lucid, they would, as a rule, hail from Wakefield Bridge, heralding tears and groaning. But Monseigneur was somewhere else tonight. Loic took his hand.

Janet took his hand. She drew Robert around the corner, up a splintering ladder to her pallet on its platform beneath the eaves. There they sat, side by side. The boy swung his legs in the chilly, smoky air.

"You shall not dishonour me. Make me your wife. Speak the words, and you may disrobe me here and now, and I will lead you to heaven."

Something Lord Thomas had said was buzzing distantly, like a fly at the glass, but the blood was now roaring in Robert's ears, deafening, a thunderous torrent.

* * *

A day or two to make the necessary preparation and await propitious weather and then, with the clouds whipping clear and the ground like iron, they set off along the road north-east to Barden.

The way wound up and up, through bracken and cloudberry, harbingers of the moor. As the morning wore on, Hal had fallen back to ride with George, as sometimes he would when his father and Loic lapsed from English into rapid French. It was Loic who first switched tongues; it always was. And then Hal would ride in awkward silence for a while, feeling the lack of his brother Waryn, holding his face impassive and hoping they'd revert to English. And eventually they would, but sometimes he couldn't wait it out.

Today there was a wound-up energy about the boys, a fug of restless, virile expectancy hanging over the column and unsettling the dogs. Hal felt it himself: well-trained they might be, but not one among them had been tested as men.

The sun began to wane, but as luck would have it, they encountered a flock bearing the priory mark well before they reached the house. Threlkeld's shepherds showed no inclination to resist and assisted the Wyverns to herd the flock. Many of Threlkeld's own animals mingled among them, and that was all to the good.

It was quickly accomplished, but Clifford would not ride tamely away nor squander the chance to teach Gawain Threlkeld a sharp lesson. He instructed his shepherds to drive the herd down the moor to the priory, and then they continued on.

Before too long, the house came into view, long and low and old-fashioned, its fortifications decayed; imprudent, for the Scots had raided these lands in years past and would do again, no doubt. It was sited in a shallow depression – much smaller than a valley; more of a hollow – snugly protected from the winds but also from the warning of attack.

The gatehouse was manned by a few very surprised men and held them up for a matter of minutes. Soon they were within the walls and could do as they willed. Clifford learned then that Gawain Threlkeld and his wife and sons were from home, visiting Sir Lancelot himself, as irony would have it. They should be quick and efficient, he reminded them, and that meant leaving the women be, save for their jewels.

He was interrupted by the tremendous pealing of a bell behind the house, and dispatched Guy and Aymer to silence it. Then he divided the rest of the men and set about the ransacking.

The bell was tolling so vigorously that the twins imagined there to be several men about it, and stole around the corner, swords drawn. They were brought up short by the sight of a strapping girl hauling on the rope with all her sweaty might. When Aymer gestured her away with his blade, she dropped the rope, her back to the wall. Guy came up beside her and threw Aymer an apologetic look.

"Must you?" said Aymer in disgust. "Look at her."

"I must; but only because of George," pleaded Guy. "I have time, don't I?"

"You've plenty of time, if you're content for the others to divide the spoils without you."

"Father would take it from us anyway." Guy was looking around for a suitable place.

"I thought so!" George had appeared behind them. "I knew you'd be trying to get one over on me." He gave the girl a cheery smile and started prising himself from his plates.

"For God's sake," said Aymer, irritably. "If you're both going to have her, there's no point; you'll cancel each other out."

"That's true." George stopped mid-buckle.

Disregarded, the girl had sidled forward and repossessed herself of the rope. She managed a few hefty heaves, sending the bell pealing again, clanging and carrying through the still air, before Aymer stepped up and struck her across the mouth with the back of his gauntlet. She ceased abruptly, spitting blood and broken teeth and staring at her gown in horror.

"What did you do that for?" demanded Guy and George in unison.

"Go on then, if you're going to."

George glared at Aymer. "She's in such a state now, I can't bring myself to it." He struggled to do himself up. "Your pardon, hen," he mumbled, his attention on his straps.

Aymer turned to Guy, who shook his head and stalked off. The other two followed him around the house. Before the door they found Tailboys and Jolly, two of the household, guarding a small group of Threlkeld's men. The captives floundered on their faces, hands bound, while Leonard Tailboys circled, methodical, kicking each one in the groin. Lewis Jolly was relieving himself in a wide and equitable arc.

By now Clifford and his contingent were upstairs. Light peeped from under a door, fast-bolted. With dismay, he realised that they'd forgotten the axes; it was a long time since he'd gone house-wrecking. He tested the door with a thump and then rapped upon it.

"You in there!" he hailed them. "Open up for me, will you? I shall surely come in, one way or another."

"Of course not, you scoundrel." It was deep voice, but female.

He sent Jem Bodrugan for a pillow. Every piece of harness was specially made, and expensive, on account of his size; he'd no wish to dent it. Jem hovered by the hinge, face averted, holding the pillow at arm's length. At the second attempt, the lock burst asunder and the door swung open with a tremendous crash. Clifford tumbled down a couple of steps and landed with all his weight on his left knee, jarring it agonisingly. For a moment he beat the floor with his fist, forgetful of his audience both within and without.

As he pushed awkwardly to his feet the others crowded in behind. The room was large but sparsely furnished and very hot, flames roaring in the hearth. A pair of elderly biddies cowered together from the intruders. Propped against the pillows was a woman, comb, mirror and nightcap in her lap. She was in early middle age, with light brown hair abundant across her shoulders, a deep frown etched between her brows and a sulky mouth. The nightgown was undone more than was seemly and when she saw him looking, she threw him a disdainful glance. There was no surprise in her face.

"Robert Clifford. Of course it would be you."

He tilted his head and bit his lip, tantalised.

"Catherine Pawleyne," she spat. "My sister is wed to Gawain Threlkeld, in whose house you are trespassing."

Surely not. Certainly he remembered Catherine Pawleyne; so pretty and slight and artless, but it was hard to reconcile that image with the sullen, rather overripe woman before him.

Hal, who guessed what was coming, had begun to rifle the room at speed. Loic snatched up a jug of wine from the bedside and tossed it over the fire, giving them all some respite. Hal was attacking a large chest – the only enticement he could find – with his knife when Mistress Pawleyne clicked her tongue at him and shook a ring of keys. As he bent to retrieve it and she looked him full in the face – and from Hal to Robert – the surly look left her, and there was a sardonic smile.

"Tell me, Mistress Pawleyne," said Clifford, conspiratorially. "Do you have another such as he tucked away somewhere? I have collected quite a number already."

The smile faded. "It was John. I bore a child to your brother, when you had already ruined me, but it did not live."

He groaned. He wasn't sure how many more of these reproaches he could bear. None of these women took responsibility for her own actions.

"I was too young to know what you were about! You took advantage of my innocence."

"Possibly, the first time." He raised his brow. "After that, could you not keep the lesson in mind? And when John came to you: you had forgotten all over again?"

There was some muffled laughter. Mistress Pawleyne glared round at her rapt audience. "Get out! All of you!"

To Clifford's surprise, the men turned and filed obediently from the room. Hal dropped the chest on to the spindly shoulder of his manservant, and stalked off. Shooing the old women before him like geese, Loic pulled the door to, instructing Jem to wait; Monseigneur would shortly have need of a squire.

Clifford ducked and peered through the low windows, first one side of the room, and then the other. A crowd of tenants and neighbours had begun to assemble outside the gates, summoned by the urgency of the bell, though none looked likely to raise a hand, and he was not surprised: the Wyvern of Clifford was prominent on the chest of each of his men. But they should not be long about it. It was growing dark. He turned back to the woman in the bed.

"You knew we were here. Did you not think to get up and clothe yourself?" His arms were folded, but he was smiling.

"I am not well." She coughed belatedly. "In any case, you've always taken what you want – what difference would it make?"

There was an open invitation, if ever he heard one.

* * *

If it were hot in Mistress Pawleyne's chamber, it was soon to grow much hotter, as the flames were quick to reach her door, to catch and take hold. Clifford had cautioned the woman to dress warmly, for it was a clear night, bitterly cold already and chilling all the while as he'd propelled her out of the room and down to her attendants in the yard. There she'd gazed at him with narrowed eyes, and he wondered, in that moment, if she wished him to carry her away. He had a brief, droll vision of Eleanor, confined at Brough, attended by Mistress Pawleyne and a numberless host of other resentful females. But she had turned away, and so had he.

Clifford had not singled out this old friend for special favour: all of Threlkeld's household had fair warning before the Wyverns fired the house.

"Ah – Bell, I'm sure I used to burn them out." Clifford leaned on the marshal's shoulder. "I must be growing soft with age."

Cuthbert Bellingham nodded, smiling. "You did, Lord Robert. You are."

There they all stood, the marauders and victims and onlookers, waiting. A long pause, as salamandrine tongues teased at the stones, then the tinder box touched, and the house flared beautifully into the freezing night. A communal sigh among the bystanders as the ground floor ceiling crumpled with a roar and a great shower of sparks exploded upwards towards the cold stars.

"Come away!" cried Clifford. Swiftly, the Wyverns mounted and filed off through the gatehouse, bearing their torches and their plunder. He halted amid the throng before the walls. "Tell Threlkeld from me," Clifford bellowed above the blaze, "to cherish the priory henceforth. He got off easy this time."

As they rode up the side of the hollow, the upper floor of the house collapsed in on itself, like a dejected face, and there was another great and noisy billow of flame and red ember into the blackness beyond. Then they crested the hill and turned south, out of sight, following the beck on its path downwards to the River Wharfe, which led to the priory.

* * *

Time to face Warwick.

Making south for the capital, the cavalcade passed not so far from Wakefield – an interesting site – and not so far from Conisbrough – Lord Robert's birthplace – but there was no detour, and the group rode on to the monastery at Rufford. Clifford was holding them to a smart pace; it was said the Duchess of Somerset was nearing London.

"Right," growled Aymer, slinging his bag upon a pallet in their guestchamber that evening. "Why is Notch in here, when we are not?" He stalked on, the usual threatening grace. "Notch, what in God's name are you about?"

Richie's eyes had slid round in dismay, but Will, for once, was looking offended, and that emboldened the boy. "I supposed you wouldn't mind, this one time," muttered Richie, pulling on his shirt. "I'm sore in need of a rub down, my neck is that stiff; I've cricked it. And my man Pleydell has a queue waiting; all the others."

"No!" Aymer's voice was sharp. "Notch is ours alone. George and Hal are allowed a manservant apiece, while Guy and I have to share Notch. And *that* I permit only because twins are not two men, in truth, but one." He defied Will's mutinous face. "So St Gregory tells us, perhaps. Or St Thomas Aquinas. Two bodies; a single soul. So it's not unbecoming that twins should share."

Richie's shoulders sagged. The ground was collapsing beneath him, as so often when he felt his feet most firmly planted. So warming, of late: Aymer hearing him out, encompassing him, amused at his antics. And now: a moment's rash presumption and this slap. He longed, only in that instant, to laugh down the tyrant and turn his back upon the man's inexplicable allure, wickedly glittering. But the other boys; his good fellows: they were leaden fare. He couldn't let go.

"We'll let it pass, just this once. You may carry on, Notch," said Guy carelessly. "Don't summon him again, Richie, or the others will jibe, and say Notch is serving the four of us."

"No! *Not* this once. *Pleydell* is his man; *Pleydell* shall do for him." Unconsciously, Aymer had adopted Robert Clifford's thundering tones and, for good measure, his pettiness.

"You are the eldest of the youngsters, Richie," assented Guy, "and must have first demand upon your manservant. Assert yourself, or that great donkey Bede will have Pleydell running at his beck and call."

Richie turned with slow rancour to dismiss Notch, and found the manservant already kneeling at Aymer's side, attending to his nails with a careful blade as the youth lounged, ankles crossed upon the sill, the intimate service beneath his notice.

* * *

"There you begin again! You strike me, Master Hal, as an ever-curious fellow who wishes to know everything about everyone." Cuthbert Bellingham was wearing his affable smile. "Well, in my case, there are no dark secrets. I had the honour of serving under your father in the French wars, and…"

Hal interrupted. "Are you sure, Sir Cuthbert?"

Bellingham gave a sudden laugh. "Your *grandfather*! Oh your pardon, Master Hal – every time I look at you I see only Lord Robert!" He shook his head, grinning. "I served with your *grandfather*, Lord Thomas: a magnificent man, an able soldier and a dear friend."

"Tell them about Agincourt, Bell," interjected Arthur Castor, giving Hal and Bede a broad wink. Castor's snub nose was sprinkled with freckles; an incongruously youthful, naughty face.

"Isn't our Arthur a witty man? That was my father – Knight Banneret at Agincourt – but since it was before I was born, young masters, I can't speak from experience. To return to your question: I've known your father all his life, and as marshal to Lord Thomas it was, of course, my unpleasant duty to discipline Lord Robert and his brothers as boys."

"And, generally, too soft to make a proper go of it!" Nield's voice carried years of affection.

Cuthbert Bellingham smiled sheepishly at Bede and Hal. "I had found a way of making the staff swish so it sounded much worse than it was. But your grandfather was satisfied."

"...while his sons got away with murder. So it's Bell's fault that Lord Robert turned out as he did," finished Castor.

"Murder," breathed Bede.

"No doubt true, Arthur. I mourn it now!"

"No you don't, or you'd have mended your ways." Patrick Nield grinned. "Only last month – the boys' pissing contest that got out of hand and moistened Sir Reginald? You were supposed to give young Tom a good hiding; anyone would think you were tickling him. You and I should exchange roles, Bell: you to be steward and sneak more meat into the household and me to be marshal and dish out the thrashings that cause you such heartache!"

"Indeed, Patrick. Not the first time you've said it. So," continued Bellingham, addressing himself again to the two lads, "it is sixteen years since the battle at St Albans, but the loss of Lord Thomas is raw with me yet. After he was killed, I served your uncle, Lord John, as marshal, and when he fell, I passed into your father's service in the same position, and here I am still, after so many years. What more? I have one daughter, abiding in Sedbergh with her huntsman husband and a bevy of little ones, and three sons, that I know of: Maurice, who is subprior on Holy Island; Cuthbert the Younger, a sharp lawyer in London, with grown sons of his own, who does very well for himself and hankers not at all after my presence, and last but not least, Charles, my golden-haired infant, left behind in Bruges. You'll not credit it, young masters, but my Charles could speak English, French and Flemish like a native when he was but two years old!"

The lads looked duly impressed.

"I have never married, though Lord Robert swears he'll not rest till he finds an heiress half my age to care for me in my dotage. I grow no younger, and yet there is not one of them beseeching my hand, as you can see. But I envy no man. And that is all there is to tell."

"He should assign the quest to our Loic," remarked Castor. "There's a man who can conjure a girl out of thin air. Though this task may be beyond anyone."

Bellingham laughed good-naturedly, and they rode on in silence for a time.

"When I was growing up," Hal's voice was steady, "I was forever hearing tales of my father and Lord John; everyone knew of them. Are the reports true, gentlemen, would you say?"

Bellingham and Castor exchanged glances. "Some of them, no doubt," said Castor, rubbing a hand through his rebellious mop of brown hair.

"We cannot all be perfect knights when the blood is up or crying for vengeance," added Cuthbert Bellingham kindly. "Don't lose sleep."

Hal persisted. "Edmund, Earl of Rutland – gentlemen: were you present at Wakefield when he fell?"

Bede's eyes were perfectly round.

"Neither of us was on that bridge when it happened," said Castor, with a repressive frown. "But there was no dishonour in killing the man; he would have killed any of us, if he could."

No dishonour in the bare fact of his killing: old enough to fight, and old enough to die, and a sure rebel against King Henry. The manner of the lad's slaughter, though: there was no honour in that, and it was idle to suggest

166

otherwise. Just now, though, it was not Edmund of Rutland who fretted at Hal's mind, for the accounts were in agreement there. Young Henry Clifford, it was, who tantalised his imaginings.

Castor's droll humour seemed to have faded as he forestalled Hal. "And don't start on Lord John's so-called heir, if you please! You'll find none in the household willing to venture on it, and you'll enrage your father to no good purpose."

* * *

As the party entered London, it was amusing to watch the FitzCliffords' expressions. Most of the boys had visited York; they had taken Newcastle in their stride, but all the bravado evaporated as they rode through the gates and into the city proper. Clifford's glance flicked to Loic, all self-conscious insouciance, as though he had not been just as they, a few short months before. The boys' eyes could not swivel fast enough for the thronging crowds, the workshops, the churches, the taverns, the great houses. Clifford brought them home to his house in Farringdon.

"Southwark, south of the Bridge: the stews, dog-fighting, bear-baiting. Keep an eye on the youngsters, a hand on your purse and don't come crying to me if you're fleeced." And then he turned them loose, and gave them no further thought.

Warwick now. To bring Harry Percy back to Lancaster: the commission he'd taken in the great chamber of Angers; the undertaking he'd given in return for his lands. The mission had not been an unalloyed success, and he'd no idea how the outcome would be received; he didn't know Warwick well enough. Accompanied by his entourage, he rode for the Bishop of London's magnificent palace, where the Earl was lodging with King Henry.

Cautiously Clifford began his tale, testing Warwick's reaction. Harry Percy was strongly of the view that everything he had, he owed to Edward of York, Clifford explained. And so it was that Percy was utterly determined to come out for York, his family's old adherence to Lancaster forgotten. Clifford enjoyed the dawning despair, and eventually lifted a staying hand.

"Ah – I've worked hard upon him, my friend; believe me. I have worked with all my power. I cannot bring him out for King Henry – and if I cannot, no one could. But I did, at last, persuade him to keep his affinity at home. Percy has promised to sit tight, and disregard York's summons when it comes."

It was not what was needed or desired; it was not nearly sufficient, but the man rose at once and clapped Clifford's shoulder with evident pleasure and relief. At that, Clifford relaxed and expanded, parading his martyrdom.

"Percy drives a hard bargain: I find I must shackle myself to his sister, when I had no thought of marriage, and meant to stay true to the Duchess of Somerset. Now I think I shall break her heart."

Warwick eyed Clifford speculatively. He'd heard the rumours, of course. There was no less likely harlot than Alice de Vere, and her husband Somerset was a great fool. But if Clifford would make jokes like this, he wasn't helping himself. Or Alice.

"You've heard the absurd rumours, of course. Mother of God." Clifford gave a great gusting sigh. After a moment, he put Alice aside and, peering close, examined the Earl's face. Warwick looked utterly exhausted. There was a small muscle drumming insistently in his jaw, irritating enough to watch – it must be greatly irritating to endure. "What's the matter? Is King Louis harassing us for troops?"

Warwick's mouth was hanging as if he were struggling for breath. "A ten-year treaty to destroy Duke Charles of Burgundy; three thousand men-at-arms to attack Flanders – those to be dispatched within the fortnight – countless more footmen to follow under my command shortly thereafter, and ten thousand archers. How can I get this through? I can't. The Commons is in free revolt. It's a rabble in there."

"I see." Warwick's face was naturally rather grey, but now Clifford wondered that he had not registered the man's ghastly pallor. "We've been at war with France for a hundred years. What did you expect? Seriously, my friend, no man must leave England until we've seen off York. He is coming. You're right that the French have distracted Duke Charles, but York was never relying on a Flemish army; he'll land here, and raise an English army."

Warwick looked perilously close to tears.

Clifford continued gently, "Shall I tell you what I advise? Don't fear the French ambassadors; King Louis will take whatever he's given, in the end. Keep spinning him along. Be more flagrant with the promise of Flemish lands to buy up those we can't trust: Essex, Stanley, Shrewsbury. It worked with you – it will work with them."

Clifford made a soothing motion with both hands, for Warwick's eyes were skidding around like a startled animal's. "King Louis has promised you Holland and Zeeland. I've long known it. Du Chastel told me himself, actually, when we were in Angers. It's an excellent plan. Now: let's make better use of French bounty while the envoys are in a compliant mood. Meanwhile, clap the Dukes of Norfolk and Suffolk in the Tower – don't be shy. And the Archbishop of Canterbury, while you're about it."

Warwick was nodding mechanically. "Queen Margaret has lingered too long in France, Robert; we need her here. Somerset is on his way, God be praised. Exeter too."

"Somerset? Somerset loathes you. But I'll detach the Duke of Exeter from him if I can. We go back a long way. Mother of God – I'll offer him my unfortunate chamberlain, if I have to. I'll set to work the moment he arrives."

As though he were a third party, a detached onlooker, he observed the astounding spectacle of Richard Neville, Earl of Warwick – the author of every harm – clutching Robert Clifford like a drowning man. Men would always prate of the Wheel of Fortune when they meant only the natural ebb and flow of life. But here, truly, the Wheel was at work, wondrous and disquieting.

* * *

At long last Alice rode into London in the carriage, and looked about her hungrily. She had not been into the city since the Princess Elizabeth's christening, four years ago; her one and only visit to court. Not *Princess*, though: *Lady*. Lady Elizabeth; Edward of York's eldest. London was almost as unfamiliar as Bruges; unfamiliar, but not foreign. Huge and grand and welcoming.

169

When Alice pictured her return, she'd imagined the exiles reunited in London. She had not foreseen that her movements would be almost as curtailed as they were in Bruges. Her husband had drawn new life as they approached his homeland, sucking energy, and now, in London, he was wholly different from the modest and reticent man she had known. These days he was often – usually – from home, visiting old friends and acquaintances, seducing those supporters of York whom he felt would repay the attentions of duke of the royal house; for Edmond wore his rank heavily now, and its magnificence entered the room before he did.

When Alice ventured to ask when she might be presented to the King, Edmond clicked his tongue at her. "King Henry is indisposed. You know this. When the Queen and the Prince have joined us, then you'll go to court. Until that time, you'll abide here."

Even Jonkin was often absent, accompanying his brother hither and thither. Alice was more than glad to be reunited with Jack's wife, Margaret. The youngest of Warwick's sisters, Margaret was one of those who'd taken so kindly an interest in Alice as a child – a small stranger, uprooted from the lush beauty of Essex and deposited amid the barren uplands of Warwick's northern estates. Relations between the two women had advanced not at all in the intervening years: to Margaret, Alice was, and would ever be, the little lost lamb.

Jack visited Alice once or twice; of Lord Clifford, she had seen nothing, though he arrived in London as she did, and kept company with her brother and Warwick, dining often with each, to Edmond's chagrin.

It was a week before the Duke and Duchess of Somerset were asked to Jack's house. The quandary of Madame Delaurin's letter, which had so racked Alice since she left Bruges, presented itself with renewed urgency. If she cared less for the man, she would hand him the letter and scuttle off, as Blanche suggested, but that was the coward's way and she could not be so heartless.

As she entered the great chamber of her brother's house, Alice was at once conscious of Robert's presence, as he was of hers. Disregarding the dramatic conclusion to their last meeting, he moved to clasp her to him, but she was unyielding in his arms, awkward and stiff. Which was just as well, for Somerset was watching closely, and when he saw his wife's expression, lost interest.

All the while, Devon was dogging Clifford's steps with disruptive intent.

"I hear you passed Christmastide with the Earl of Northumberland, my lord. You spent your boyhood at Alnwick, did you not? I trust the return visit was a happy one."

He'd meant to tell her of Eleanor, of course; all the way south, Clifford's breast had flared with a small, mean surge of anticipation each time he thought on it. Not so easy now, with those lovely eyes upon him.

"Fruitful. I've persuaded Harry Percy to keep his affinity at home. Which was indeed a challenge, for he was dead set on calling out his men in support of York. But I always get what I want in the end. Your friend Warwick was most grateful."

She smiled. "All loyal men must be grateful, I should imagine, my lord! My husband among them, I'm sure."

"Mm…your husband. A difficult man to please, so I'm told." He smirked at her.

Devon laid a hand on Clifford's arm. Clifford shook him off. "Harry Percy has his price, of course." He hadn't meant to say that; he aimed to present the marriage as his idea. Now he was sounding reluctant to wed.

Alice tilted her face to his.

"I've consented to marry his sister, the Lady Eleanor."

He'd wrecked the delivery entirely, but when her face sank, briefly, he brightened. The unguarded expression was as forlorn as he could have wished. Perhaps she'd been envisaging her husband's death, and what might follow. As had he; unceasingly. Perhaps not.

Devon gaped. "You're to wed Northumberland's sister? You kept that quiet!" He turned to Alice, the satisfaction rolling off him in palpable waves, like heat. Spitefully, he pressed on. "So – tell us of the Lady Eleanor, Robert. Beautiful, no doubt?"

Clifford cleared his throat, caught out by Devon's unhealthy interest. "Eleanor Percy is a little older than Lady Alice here; a little taller." He was looking at Devon though his words were aimed elsewhere. "Eyes of blue-grey.

Slender, elegant, fair. She…" how could he put this? The truth was stranger than any story. "She is most eager for our marriage. The lady remembers me well from my years at Alnwick, and has, so she says, been aching for my return." He allowed himself a grubby smile.

Alice was paying particular attention. "But surely the lady was too young, all those years ago to…know you well, my lord? Unless she is now…rather old to be a bride?"

He grinned. "No, indeed. The Lady Eleanor is the right age for a bride. I'm rather memorable, is all."

Devon laughed, delighted, and then his attention was claimed by a passing acquaintance.

As Alice backed away, Lord Clifford caught her wrist, abruptly sombre. "Tell me," he murmured, searching her face, "are you still angry at what I wished from you? My words were not…delicate, but you know that I am always honest. Have pity, for I am wounded and wretched."

She lowered her eyes in warm confusion. As his fingers twined with her own, the Clifford ruby winked heavily. So! This time Robert had not pressed the ring upon his intended. Eleanor Percy might be his for the taking, but, clearly, he did not feel driven to insist upon her vow.

As he waited, breathless, for an answer, Clifford was soothed by the little smile.

Devon's attention had been claimed by another man, and the newcomer was studying Alice closely, his brows raised in frank interest; a pair of thick, dark crescents. She wished them away – this prying fellow and the Earl of Devon, both. But there was no help for it; the tragic letter was rustling in her sleeve. She stepped back to Robert, very close. "May I beg a moment with you before you depart, my lord? One moment, alone? Just before you depart…would be best."

He nodded, baffled, barely daring to hope, and she left him.

As it happened, Somerset was wishing to leave long before Clifford, who was well ensconced with Exeter when Sir Gabriel Appledore appeared before Alice, bidding her to make ready.

"Sir Hugh!" She turned, tremulous, to her old friend, who'd been renewing his acquaintance with Blanche. "Would you do something for me? I must speak with Lord Clifford. I have bad news for him, I'm afraid. I shall be waiting by the outer door. Please bring him to me quickly, if you would."

Hugh Dacre looked doubtful, questioning Blanche with his eyes. When she gave a peremptory nod, he hastened to obey. Across the room, Appledore bent and whispered in Edmond's ear. The Countess of Devon saw it, and reached for Alice, but too late. By then Clifford had appeared, trailed by Dacre. Blanche pulled the intrusive Sir Hugh aside, keeping Alice discreetly in view. Careless of onlookers, Clifford took her hands, drawing her close.

She pulled herself gently from his clasp. "I am charged to bring you sad tidings, my lord. It is your daughter, Marguerite; the Lord has taken her to himself."

"Marguerite?" The exultant manner fell from him at once. Slowly he eased himself against the wall, silent, absorbing the blow. "Such a merry little one," he murmured at last. "Her mother will have taken this hard. I should write to her." He scrubbed at his hair.

Dumbly, Alice drew Madame Delaurin's letter from her sleeve. He slipped it into his undershirt.

And then Somerset was between them. "May I take my wife away now, Clifford?" He spat the words. "That is, if you've finished with her for the night."

* * *

Nothing was said on the short ride home, Edmond's temper a matter of chilly indifference. The silence flowed on until they were lying beneath the sheets, the usual battleground.

Alice turned on him before he could commence with her. "Lord Clifford has lost a little daughter, my lord. Before we left Flanders I was charged by the mother to bring him the sad news."

"Charged by the mother? Babette Delaurin?"

He took the breath from her sails.

173

"You know the woman?"

"Of course. Madame Delaurin is a fishmonger's widow. She supplies the fish for my own household. She should have come to me in her trouble. Why would she seek you?"

Alice saw a way out there. "I think she wished to speak to you, my lord, but I was with the servants when she came, and she was in a wretched state, very tearful."

"Nevertheless, you should have told me of this, Alice; I've warned you already on this score." The pitch was rising. "That man is not suitable company for my wife. You spent much of the evening with him even before you chose to pass on that letter. *I will not have it.*"

"My lord." Her voice was withering in the darkness. "I've not seen Lord Clifford or the Earl of Devon for several months; it would be a strange thing to ignore them in my brother's house. Lord Clifford was telling us of his bride, for he's to marry Eleanor Percy, the Earl of Northumberland's sister."

Edmond lay silent with his thoughts, and Alice guessed he must now regret his cruel words to Robert.

"Well," he said at last. "The passing of one little maiden will barely bother the man. He has a great throng of his bastards about him now – grown men all; huge hulking brutes."

* * *

Robert Clifford had not been rash enough to torment Exeter – a pleasure Devon could never forego – but neither had he bothered to court the man, a surly and mistrustful fellow. Now he surely had his work cut out hauling Exeter aboard.

When he asked the Duke to his house, it was to offer him the prize of two Flemish counties as soon as Duke Charles had been destroyed. Not just any Flemish counties; he chose the lushest and the broadest. The names tripped readily to mind.

"Ah – my friend! Holland and Zeeland; envision the acres, dripping with fatness!" Warwick would have been most surprised. Perhaps he and Exeter

174

could toss a coin; share them, perhaps; or take it in turns. Clifford smothered a grin. "When King Louis has Flanders for his own, he'll prove a most indulgent seigneur. And don't concern yourself with that bond you were forced to sign against Warwick in Bruges." His hand was light upon Exeter's arm. "In exile, one does whatever one must to get by." *Rat-a-tat-tat.*

"You didn't," said Exeter coldly.

Clifford gave a rueful laugh. "Ah – I surely wished I had, though, when Duke Charles withdrew my pension. Something of a blunder on my part, alas. I was left with no income at all."

"Come, Robert, I know you too well for this. What is it they want from me in return for these lands of Flanders; so very generous?" Exeter eyed Clifford with open suspicion.

And so Clifford put his shoulder to the task, sprinkling a little of the truth to grease his way; flattering the man, but so very delicately; gracefully contrasting Exeter's experience and pragmatism with that of Somerset, whose sanity he gently queried. All the while, his chamberlain was making a quite unnecessary number of entrances, lashes demurely lowered. When Exeter followed with his eyes, Clifford changed tack. Of late, he remarked in a pensive tone, Loic Moncler seemed restless in his service. He watched the Duke's face.

Hours and hours had passed – the longest day of his life – by the time Exeter was captured and trussed for delivery to Warwick. Clifford rewarded himself and his complaisant man with the best of his wine, reclining together in a steaming bath as they toasted each other on a task well done.

* * *

On his way up to Clifford's day room, Jack de Vere's eyes swivelled left and right: every entrance was a warren of Clifford boys.

Stalking the Earl upwards through the gloom, Aymer missed the ankle outstretched in ambush and blundered, heavily, to his knees.

"*Careful*, little brother. You've crushed the toes of those pretty new boots."

Righting himself, Aymer mounted a step above Hal, their faces level, very close. "Out of my way, you *cock*. You *childish fucking cock*." The younger man was trembling, poisoned by the purest venom.

A shaft of sunlight caught Aymer's face, the lilting eyes and faultless features, but Hal had no scope for envy, snug in his own rough skin. Above them, the footsteps stilled. Hal pointed at the ceiling. "Ah – you've alerted the Earl. Run along now. I wish you better luck next time with the eavesdropping."

"How *dare* you? It's only a matter of time, Hal. I'm the better man; quicker, stronger, sharper. I *warn* you."

Hal grinned. "Father doesn't share that view. Bend your neck, little one, and the yoke will chafe you less."

Hal watched the unsteady hand drop to the knife, and strolled away.

Above them, the host embraced his guest. Jack helped himself to a chair before the fire and commenced at his usual rapid pace.

"My friend, we must talk plainly. These rumours…I should take up the cudgels on behalf of my sister, but I cannot understand the exact truth of this. What have you to say?

Clifford was looking down on the seated man, arms folded, but at that, he flung himself into a chair, his fingers gripping the arms. "This disgraceful slander! I heard it from Exeter; it beggars belief." His shoulders drooped; he fell still, opening his hands with simple sincerity: "Ah – Jack. I am innocent, I promise you that."

Jack nodded, more than half-convinced before the man had said a word. He was recalling his sister's face on learning that Somerset was approaching Angers: the look of wild, disbelieving hope that she might be freed from her terrifying suitor; he was recalling her hymns in praise of Duke Edmond's beauty and bearing. In point of fact – Jack ran a hand through his own locks, all flax and tawny - Somerset was not so fine. The man's colouring was undistinguished; he could be taller; his chin was weak. Jack stroked his own chin, its firm outline and manly cleft. But if Edmond were less than perfect, poor Robert was, frankly, hideous.

Jack looked as though he'd lost interest, but Clifford had much more to say. "I've long suspected that Somerset suffers a malady of the brain. These last years in Flanders, he lost his will and his drive, forever making promises and breaking them. You see how he has treated you: why would he marry your sister and then fail to support you and Warwick? And now the disease is taking its course, he's become deluded. Have you heard the evidence against me? To my knowledge, it is thus," His voice was softly derisive. "I have sung a ballad with your sister, in plain sight of her husband and a dozen others. When she was curious, I troubled myself to tell her all the history of this past conflict – again, in plain sight of her husband and two hundred men. Another time, I called upon the Duke and, finding him from home, spoke instead to the Lady Alice, begging her to intercede with him on your account; she said she would tell her husband, and straightly did so. Mother of God, I even left open the door through my short visit, purposely to spare her unease. What more? I passed over your letter to me. Ah – and she passed me a letter from a woman of my acquaintance, telling of the death of my daughter. I can produce it if you wish. Hardly enough to hang a man, is it?"

Clifford had comprehensively belittled the accusations, which dwindled away to nothing in Jack's eyes, and that was no wonder; the man had a long and illustrious career as a dissembler, mastering the art twenty years back.

Shortly afterwards, Jack de Vere left him and went to Warwick, scathing in his denunciations of Somerset.

* * *

The West Country was calling, and the Duke would shortly be away for home. A few days after the dinner at Jack's house, Alice spent the afternoon with Countess Laura, listening abstractedly to the lady's stale complaints. Edmond and Jonkin were closeted again with the Earl of Devon, planning their expedition and the raising of men.

Before vespers the ladies joined the menfolk in the great chamber for refreshment, and there – uninvited, unexpected and unwelcome – was Lord Clifford with a group of his men. He seemed to have put aside the grief for his little daughter, for the teeth were gleaming in his smile when he pulled Alice towards him. As he leaned in and she presented her cheek, he turned his face and their lips touched. It was neatly done, and looked like an accident, but he spoiled the effect by holding her in plain view and perceptibly too long. When she raised her eyes, Edmond and Robert were staring at each other, heads up, like dogs striving at the leash.

A page went among them, filling cups, disrupting the febrile air.

"You two look like you've been plotting. But where is Exeter, I wonder?" said Clifford loudly.

Devon bridled. "You know where Exeter is, Robert. You've been suborning him for the past week. He's with Warwick, no doubt, where you left him when you came here looking for trouble."

Clifford folded his arms, staring brazenly at Alice, who could do nothing but frown at the floor. Somerset turned his face to his wife, his eyes sliding sideways to the interloper.

"It turns out Exeter has better sense than you gave him credit for. You are such fools, both of you," Clifford pronounced, with Jonkin still beneath his notice. "How York must thank God for your idiocy."

It was Devon's house, but Somerset who spoke, grimly, raising a hand: "Ladies, leave us."

Laura made all haste to obey, gripping Alice's arm as if unsure of her compliance, tugging her up the stairs and into the bedchamber. Alice floated above the awful events playing out below. Of course men argued – she knew it, but not like this – threatening, bristling, ominous; her poor Jonkin, terror-stricken; Edmond was all he had. In the chamber above, Laura and Alice sat hand-in-hand, eyes lowered, their waiting women opposite, arrayed in silence.

Devon rubbed his eyes, knowing the moment had come at last. His guts were twisting sharply. He would be forced to leave them, for sure, and swayed from foot to foot, fending it off.

And now Edmond paced directly at his rival as if to stride through him, his hand on his knife. "Get out, Clifford. I have nothing to say to you."

It was Devon's house. His hand opened, reflexively, and closed again.

Clifford gave a small snort of derision, looking down on Somerset from his overbearing height.

The Duke was slowly shaking his head. "Run back to your master, Warwick, where you belong; guard him from us, while you can."

"From *us*." Clifford laughed aloud then. "Who is 'us'? Who stands beside you?" He turned and walked away, leaving open the door, an enticement, surely. So out stalked the Duke, out into the dark street, the cobbles glittering wetly, Devon trailing behind, hunched, dreading what would follow; inevitable now. Jonkin clutched at Devon's arm with fluttering hands. Clifford's men had spilled out behind him and scattered.

A few quick paces, flanked by his household men, and Somerset was within distance. "My God, how can you live with yourself? You, who took Duke Charles's gold all these years and fought at his side; now to join his enemies to bring him down, swallowing King Louis' bribes, shielding Warwick, the man who slew John and your father! What would your kin say to this?"

Clifford turned on his heel, reaching to push Somerset casually in the chest. Not too hard; the man rocked on his heels.

"Don't *dare* to speak their names! They would have done the same in my place. Warwick will not be long among us in England."

"You cur!" spat Somerset. "You have betrayed us all, and would now betray Warwick also? Truly, you have no shred of honour."

At last Clifford loosed his temper for real. "I'll kill any man who assails my honour! My life's work is to keep King Henry on his throne. Better for all if you followed my lead, or is your lust for the Queen so hot that you wish for dead man's shoes?"

Variety of expression had, apparently, failed Somerset and his face could manifest only fury. "How *dare* you speak so of the Queen? You condemn yourself out of your own mouth; you can't imagine serving a woman with reverence. You haven't stopped trying to seduce my wife since I wed her."

Jonkin and Devon looked at each other, queasy. Sweat pearled Devon's face, though the icy air was lapping his cheek.

"At least someone's seeing to your poor wife. But then again…she did promise herself to me – repeatedly – before ever she met you. I took it as it was meant; an invitation."

In the chamber above, Alice and Blanche exchanged looks, aghast. Blanche hurried to her side. Elizabeth Ullerton examined her nails.

Somerset was very close to Clifford now, and panting. "The Queen told me everything. My wife did only what was required of her. You have blackmailed her with her innocent words, you whoreson."

Cuthbert Bellingham was shouting for aid and a number of the Wyverns, who had vanished into the night, were returning at a run. Among Somerset's men, the rasp of blades; a dozen cold gleams.

"Convince yourself of that, if you can," Clifford jeered. "I could tell you how I have enjoyed her…but I'll restrain myself for the sake of the lady."

Devon gave a cry and limped forward. Too late. When Edmond drew his steel, it was fast: feinting left, striking right. But he was always too frenzied when the rage descended, and Clifford forestalled him. Ignoring the feint, he sidestepped the thrust, catching the man's wrist and twisting sharply. The knife spun into the gutter.

"What are you trying to do – bore me to death?"

Jonkin stamped on the knife, but Clifford had already turned, presenting his back, a huge and insolent target, offering himself up, strolling into the darkness without a glance. Devon lamented to himself through a clammy haze of hurt: *we have regained Edmond and lost Robert.*

Dragged inside by his spluttering brother, Somerset was terrible to behold. Deathly white, Alice was helped down to her husband by Lady Laura, who rose to the moment with quiet dignity, seeing them off into the night, for Devon had unaccountably disappeared.

Alone in their bedchamber, Alice laid a tremulous hand on Edmond's arm, greatly pitying him for what he had endured and greatly dreading lest she was encompassed in his wrath.

He pulled back sharply. "*Don't touch me.*"

Rigid and unspeaking, Alice lay down upon the bed. If she lived a hundred years, she would never speak to Lord Clifford again. For months now, in her vanity, she'd exalted in the taming of the beast. But it had not been so. She was baiting a bear, and it had turned on her.

PART III

THE RECKONING

Clifford awoke of a sudden the next morning, conscious that something was wrong. He lay back as images of the previous night reformed themselves. Long before dawn he was closeted with Reginald Grey, pouring his story into the priest's ears. Spare and bloodless, Grey leaned in his chair, hands behind his head, with no great appearance of interest, at length responding in the usual cold monotone.

"I told you that when God wishes you to be his instrument, he will send you a sign. He sent you the clearest of signs and you turned tail. You are recalcitrant." When Clifford didn't answer, his chaplain leaned forward, steepling his fingers. "That man has deflected God's purpose; so far steeped in wickedness as to attempt murder – the clearest indication of evil. Yet still you do nothing. An eye for an eye, Lord Robert, a tooth for a tooth. Now is the time."

Now is not the time. Of all the times...now isn't it. Somerset had urgent work to do in raising the West Country. As soon as he could extricate himself, Clifford made his excuses and left, shouting for Loic; he must get to the Earl of Warwick before the rumours had time to catch. The priest watched him go.

Down at the wharf, the chamberlain settled his master into a sturdy craft, well-wrapped in a new and splendid cloak. These pelts were plush and warm and didn't puff a cloud of moths at every movement; praise God for King Louis and the punctilious flow of French gold. Loic ruffled the fur about Clifford's throat.

"Stop fretting at me, boy!" It was always thus when he'd flouted Sir Reginald; always. On those rare occasions, Clifford felt as though he were defying his father.

"Your pardon, Monseigneur." Loic raised his voice. "Row on, you fellows! What do you dawdle for?" And then repeated himself when the watermen couldn't follow his accent. They followed well enough; all Frenchmen were unpalatable just at present.

Loic stretched his legs before him, an unconscious mirror to his master. He sneaked a sideways look. "Sir Reginald loves you well, Monseigneur. Sometimes, perhaps, his zeal leads him astray; it's hard not to confuse one's own will for the will of God when there is so much riding on it." Out of the corner of his eye he could see Castor studying him with close attention, but that was the man's custom.

The response was prompt, and should have been predictable. "Not your place to question Sir Reginald! A priest, and Christ's vicar on Earth. Go on along that road and you'll be deep in sacrilege before you know it, with the stake at your back and the flames at your feet. Take warning."

Up jumped Loic, and deposited himself on the bench opposite, beside Arthur Castor, who pressed the slender fingers, briefly, with his calloused palm.

"The heresies in this household don't originate with me!" A mutinous whisper, taken up by the wind and whipped into Clifford's ear.

But Loic had pricked his master into a reverse. "Walter!" roared Clifford above the heads of his men. All the Walters flinched, but it was Reginald Grey's lesser brother who was wanted. The almoner staggered over, slapped by the gusting sleet. "Make in my name a penitential gift: two great candles for the Church of the Holy Sepulchre. For I know now that I had closed my ears to the word of God; a very wretched sinner. Let every man among you examine his conscience in like manner."

He tugged the cloak over his mouth, brooding in malevolent silence until he was safe ashore. Then Clifford disturbed Warwick at his breakfast with a lurid tale of madness and murder.

"It seems that Edmond of Somerset has, finally, lost his mind," he concluded. "We cannot trust him now. Let us dissemble our doubts while he raises the West Country for King Henry, but when he shows signs of evil intent thereafter, we shall be ready."

Warwick sipped his ale. "I have to admit I'm baffled by Somerset. He's showing an utter disregard for the King's interests. Even now, he refuses to come to me. The man is a stiff-necked fool – but *evil intent?*"

"I wonder you haven't fathomed his purpose! There's no explanation save that he has hopes of the crown for himself. After the Prince, he is the King's most senior kinsman. If anything were to befall our Prince, he would be the heir of Lancaster. And he knows I can read his purpose. This is why he tries to discredit me with those ludicrous rumours concerning his poor wife. When that fails, he tries to slay me."

And if anything were to befall the Prince, then your daughter would never be queen. Clifford had dropped the stone, and watched the ripples. There were more stones where that came from, and he would pitch a greater one into the waters. He bit his lip with a troubled expression, and lowered himself down beside the Earl.

"My friend," he said, heavily, "perhaps I should have levelled with you from the first. I had no wish to alarm you by speaking of this, but now I think I must. You should know that Duke Charles of Burgundy threatened to stop our pensions if we exiles would not sign a secret accord to destroy you once you had secured the crown for King Henry."

Warwick set down his cup and gazed at Clifford.

"Somerset put his name to the bond; Duke Charles waved the man's seal in my face. Devon, too, though only because he was trying to persuade Somerset to keep faith with us and come away to England. Exeter may or may not have done so; I believe not." Exeter had put his name to the promise; eagerly. But having laboured to deliver up the man to Warwick, Clifford wished for Exeter's value to be preserved. "Naturally, I refused to countenance any such undertaking, for I had already pledged myself to work with you. In his fury, Duke Charles stripped me of my annuity that very day and paid it over to Somerset himself – as you've probably heard, for Duke Charles's fury was common knowledge; I had to creep away from Flanders under Devon's safe conduct."

"God in Heaven," said Warwick quietly. "So Somerset puts his own interests above the interests of Flanders, and the interests of Flanders above the interests of England. I'll speak with Jack de Vere directly."

Clifford was nodding until that last, when the nodding faltered. "Well…" he hesitated, thinking quickly. His story was ludicrous. Edmond was incapable of aiming at the throne; his loyalty to his King and the Prince was absolute; one didn't need to know him well to know that. "Somerset is wed to Jack's sister, of course. Be cautious…de Vere is no doubt an excellent fellow, but few men would not have their head turned by the idea of a sister becoming Queen of England."

The Earl was now looking thoroughly queasy, plucking papers at random from a sheaf before him, shuffling them, first one way and then the other. "I don't believe Jack is capable of striking of my interests in such a way; I have been as a father to him."

"Doubtless you're right." Clifford didn't want this to run away from him. "I merely wished to put you on your guard, in these dangerous times. Thank God I've managed to detach the Duke of Exeter from Somerset. You must capitalise on my work; keep Exeter close."

"Robert, you speak as if you will not be here: 'I should do this', and 'I should do that'…"

"Ah – but I shan't be here. I'm going north directly. Consider, Cousin: we're speaking of the most powerful noble in the kingdom." It was a low blow, and Warwick twitched. "Last night that man tried to kill me. While I remain within reach, my life is in danger."

Warwick had pushed himself to his feet. "Robert! You could see off Somerset blindfold with your hands bound."

Clifford folded his arms. "So next time he'll not strike so openly: a dagger in the crowd; an arrow in the back. But don't doubt me, my friend – I shall be ready when the call comes. When you face York, it will be with me at your side. I have given my word."

Warwick lowered himself back into the ornate chair, shaking his head. "And I was going to offer you a seat on the Council."

* * *

By the morning, Sir Gabriel's horror had abated not one whit. Lord Clifford's ominous taunts hung in his memory, ushering in all the earlier doubts. The steward could not settle to his duties. "Lady Ullerton, you heard what the brute said of the Duchess. What do you think he meant by it?"

"It is obvious what he meant by it, sir. Before the Duke arrived, she had given Lord Clifford her promise and he had, one must assume, tried to pre-empt the ceremony."

Sir Gabriel's eyes had opened very wide. So wide his eyeballs seemed at risk. "Do you think…?

She clicked her tongue. "Come, we're speaking of Black Clifford, a man steeped in iniquity; it's entirely possible. Certainly there was an ill-advised hunting excursion – sanctioned by her brother, I might add; an utterly careless man. In the depth of the woods, I gather, Blanche Carbery and that shameless Frenchman took themselves off, leaving my lady alone with the fiend. She was in a highly agitated state on her return." She might as well tell it all. "And, Sir Gabriel, there is worse: on the night before her wedding to Duke Edmond, my lady slipped out of the Queen's presence in company with Lord Clifford. They secreted themselves in her bedchamber for some while, together upon the bed…"

"How do you know this?" he broke in, sharply.

"I caught her as she left her room, and she lied to me. The bed was in disorder." She folded her hands demurely.

He had walked away and stood at the window for far too long. "You should have mentioned this before, surely, Lady Ullerton? It was on this very matter that I questioned you."

"I have my loyalties too, Sir Gabriel," said the gentlewoman with prim composure. "You'll understand that I wish to defend my mistress's honour, as you would wish to defend your master. I'm sure she is the victim here. She is very young, and that man is drenched in wickedness."

"And yet you choose to disclose this now." His voice was strangled.

"Now – as we're to be married, Sir Gabriel – I have other loyalties to consider. This matter, which I kept to myself by reason on my devotion to the Duchess, it's now right for me to share with you. You must do as you see fit; I trust your judgment implicitly."

Sir Gabriel stared at his intended. Elizabeth was a very slim woman, with clear, flushed skin – comely, but comelier had she been plumper; the lines were spreading like webs. Dominating her face, a pair of huge brown eyes. She had a predilection for jewels – poor ones, for no one had given her better – and opulent colours, and her movements were somewhat febrile. The effect, as he examined her with a critical eye, was of a damselfly, gaudy and hovering. He wondered if she were vulgar, or deficient in some way. But Lady Ullerton's cousin was the Archbishop of Canterbury and Sir Gabriel was the grandson of a yeoman farmer. There was but one course open to him. He would lay it all before the Duke: the epitome of honour and wisdom.

* * *

By mid-afternoon it was growing dark already in the bedchamber. *This is what comes of dwelling so far north*, thought Loic. And Skipton was darker even, and colder. The anchor to his life was always a person and not a place. Nonetheless, *Farewell* – Monseigneur's hymn to the North Country – had prepared him to love the moors and he found, already, that he did. Behind him the light warmed slowly as the page moved about, setting candles.

"Make ready; we leave for Skipton at first light."

Loic turned, quizzical. "I'll instruct Patrick and Bell directly, Monseigneur, but may I know the reason for this sudden resolve?"

"Somerset tries to murder me, and you ask that?"

Loic ushered Jem and the little page from the chamber, took up the manservant's brush and attended to the grooming of the new cloak. "Have you not always said the Duke has an ungovernable temper when roused? What did you call it: the *red mist*? It seems to me that by now he must regret his actions. And you were never at any risk, Monseigneur."

186

"Certainly he'll regret his actions, when he learns the result." Exultant, Clifford shared the morning's work with Loic. To his chagrin, there was no indulgence on his chamberlain's face; no admiring smile.

"Monseigneur…" Loic paused, his mouth twisting. "You've overreached yourself this time, I think. The Earl of Warwick has become very tense of late, has he not? This could end in the Duke of Somerset's death."

"You sound as though you would regret that! Believe me – I will never stop until I bring him down. That man tried to kill me. His incompetence in the attempt doesn't absolve him of the crime. But never fear: *Vengeance is lame,* and so forth."

"Oh yes. The slow limp of the cripple. And will the guilty man know the tap of the crutch when he hears it close behind?"

"I do hope so! I do hope he recognises Vengeance when she comes for him. In any case," Clifford smiled now, pride peeping out again, so that Loic's sour look returned. "Warwick is most sincerely grateful for my warning. Watch me rise as the Duke falls; I expect an earldom before long. Earl of Cumberland – why not?"

* * *

The women were particularly gentle with the Duchess in the days following, as if she were a fractured vessel.

Naturally, Alice was anxious to put distance between herself and London, and Lord Clifford and his pernicious dealings. But the day before their start for the West Country, Lady Laura brought the unexpected tidings that the man had pre-empted their departure; he had already left London. Perhaps Lord Clifford had resolved to give no further support to the loyal lords, going north to wed Eleanor Percy and sit tight with the Earl of Northumberland. *Such treachery.* She wished Jack would come to her.

"At last you've witnessed the man's malice openly at work. Lord Edmond is such a good and honourable man. We must hope that, in time, he will come to for…forget what has passed."

Alice could all but hear Devon's sanctimonious tones; husband and wife had found a rare harmony. Roused at once, she responded in just the way

Devon would have deplored: "And yet, Lady Laura, Jonkin told me that Edmond tried to stab Lord Clifford – who merely disarmed him, and did not raise a hand to retaliate."

"Oh, Lord Clifford did retaliate!" Laura contradicted her at once. "Indeed he did. The man wounded the Duke more deeply with his words than he could with any dagger."

"The man said very little, in point of fact," snapped Alice. "Lord Clifford's words were vague and meaningless, intended only to rile and irritate. Do not pay him the compliment of heeding him! I understood him to suggest that my husband desires the Queen, yet you do not see me consumed with jealousy."

Laura shook her head. "Lady Alice, have a care, for you are on a cliff-edge. Do not seek to absolve that scoundrel, even in the seclusion of your own mind."

The blood rose and foamed within her like an onrushing tide. "*Absolve him?* Robert Clifford is a vicious man; false and vindictive. *I* am his victim."

* * *

"Father," ventured Hal, after a day's ride of interminable dullness. "You've much on your mind. I can offer no counsel, of course, but if you chose to share your burdens with me, I'm sure I'd profit from any lesson you care to impart."

Clifford was testing his swollen knee, and would have limped off into the hostelry, but the words sparked a broad smile, and he turned back, clapping his eldest on the shoulder. "Delicately done, my son. But that curiosity is notorious enough to give you away. You're itching, are you not?"

Hal started to protest.

"Come – you know what is on my mind. You know that Edmond of Somerset set upon me in the street. You know how he tries to discredit me. You know that he'll not use the sense God gave him and work with Warwick. You know that Devon has abandoned us. You know that we have done a grand job upon Exeter." He swapped grins with Loic. "You know that, even now, York is preparing to sail for England; that a great clash is coming; that we must prepare ourselves for the final reckoning. All these things you already know. There is no more."

There is always the 'why', thought Hal. The Duchess of Somerset must be a rare creature, to have endangered a kingdom. He would very much like to have met her.

"And as to the *why*," continued his father, "of that you're not entirely in ignorance either, I suspect."

Hal glanced beyond his father. There was the chamberlain, framed in the doorway, head back, arms folded, presenting a miniature, quaint and presumably inadvertent parody of his master. Loic was the gatekeeper; Hal cast around thoughtfully for the key.

* * *

The day after the arrival in Skipton, Clifford made his way to his brother's house.

Swift as he'd travelled, the rumours were ahead of him. Roger regaled him with reports of a great rift and a clash.

"They say weapons were drawn and you stood between Warwick and Somerset in the street, shielding Warwick from the Duke's assault. Mystifying."

Clifford groaned. "Ah – Warwick wasn't there. Somerset picked the fight; he came at me with a knife. I didn't retaliate, obviously, or he'd be dead." The frustration exploded again. "Only an utter fool would behave like this. If the Queen can work with Warwick, so can we all, for now."

Sir Roger leaned back and crossed his ankles. "I see. The end justifies the means. So, Somerset attacked you unprovoked, did he? They also say you're tupping his wife, which I did think implausible, even for you, but when did that ever stand in the way of a good story?"

Arms folded, Robert stared away for a moment. Then, with a slight smile, he leaned forward and murmured in his brother's ear. Roger twitched. Conscious of others within earshot, he confined himself to an affronted shake of the head.

Robert laughed. "You judge so harshly! Yet not so long ago…"

Lady Joan swept in, encompassing them both in a serene smile. She offered to Robert the hind of a cheek – her neck, almost – a hand braced against his upper arm, fending him off. His pestering had long since lapsed to a mischievous habit, but the lady was blessed with a tranquil life; Robert was always more than she could comfortably handle. He was gazing at her, perceiving her plainly for the first time in years. Her likeness to her brother Devon was wringing his heart.

Her mind, too, was running on the Earl of Devon. At once she quizzed Robert on the rumours, seeking reassurance that her brother had taken no hurt from him, in what seemed, in retrospect, to have morphed into a vast public brawl. Joan, too, had heard whispers of the Duchess. She laughed at the unlikely tale, gently teasing her brother-in-law.

"Oh, don't start him on that!" exclaimed Roger. "I can't bear to hear him say it again."

Joan's eyes sank. Robert smirked from Roger to his wife. Poor Joan. How had his brother become such a prude? He'd been rather more entertaining in the old days.

"Ask me later," he mouthed at her. They both ignored him.

* * *

Nothing had been said by Edmond concerning that terrible night's work. He continued in distant courtesy. He continued to share his wife's bed. They left London and travelled, in proud state, towards the West Country. A south wind blew, and spring was catching everywhere, but there were no light spirits at the head of the cavalcade and it was worse among the women in the carriages.

Several days in, and they were passing the night in a religious house. As Edmond pinched the candle and the room faded away, Alice lay with her back to her husband, slipping swiftly towards sleep. He terrified her with his words.

"Has he touched you?" That ghastly tone, quiet and falsely light.

"What? My lord?" She may as well have signed the confession; her perfidious voice had betrayed her, sharp and breathless.

"Has Lord Clifford laid a hand on you, Alice? From what the man said, it seems so."

"Of course not, Husband. Why would you ask such a thing?"

"So, to be clear: never – not before I arrived in Angers even – has he touched you with any lustful intent? He has not kissed you; not once? Despite your brother's plan that you two should wed – the plan that you unaccountably failed to mention to me."

The silent struggle lasted no more than a moment, but the pause was more than sufficient to alert him.

She cleared her throat. "There was a kiss, my lord – before you arrived in Angers. It was in the gardens, on the first day, when he gave me his ring and asked if I would be his wife. Jack and my gentlewomen were present, of course." She had mastered her voice now, and with a supreme effort, by stilling her mind, Alice forced it to encompass a corrupted memory.

"I see." Somerset's tones were grave and sad. "I need hardly say that you should have made a clean breast of this to me at the outset. Do you not agree?"

He was making himself ridiculous, this grown man, but she braced her mind to remain within the chosen confines. "Jack directed me to speak to no one of his plans, my lord, yet I wish I had, for though the touch was so brief and unwelcome, it has driven a wedge between us."

"Which is as he would wish it. God has joined you and me in wedlock; Clifford has no right to put us asunder. And though that man is the very devil incarnate, I cannot hold you blameless. I trust you've prayed long and hard to be cleansed of your sin."

Alice closed her eyes so that she would not have to look at him. After a few moments he reached, and gently tugged her arm. She lay rigid. He tugged again, still gentle, and still she lay rigid.

"Alice! I do not require enthusiasm, but I do demand obedience."

She stared at the wall, grey in the gloom.

"Very well." His voice was icy. "It seems that even your duty is beyond you. I have no use for a disobedient wife."

She turned her head at last. "Edmond – please. I've no wish to disobey you. But you are hurting me so dreadfully with these suspicions. I am wounded and wretched."

191

The words had presented themselves, ready and apt. But when she recalled the speaker of those words, and the reason for his speech, she rolled on to her face in the darkness. Edmond removed his hand.

* * *

In so short a space, Clifford had exchanged his closest companions for Exeter and Warwick, a strange turn of events. Now he must make sure of another new ally.

They were only just settled in Skipton, when the message travelled swiftly among the men, filtering downwards: they were off to Alnwick again. But George's antics, and Hal's innocent warning, had given Clifford pause, and he felt he must leave the FitzCliffords behind, with Loic, perhaps; in his care. He was among a few of his sons when he mused on it.

"That gutless sodomite? I'll take no orders from him." Aymer's voice was the quietest among them and the comment was for Will's ears only. But there it hung, audible, in a moment of unlucky silence.

Clifford spun and grasped his son by the throat. "*Sir* Loic, as you shall call him, has fought many times alongside me, in the thick of battle, and acquitted himself ably." Loic was a liability on the field; Clifford had to nurse-maid him, which was a distraction, and hazardous. "A faithful knight and a dear friend. No sodomite, he; how dare you say it? Sir Loic has had more women than you could dream of. Treat him with respect." He flung his son from his hand.

Hal's face was wreathed in delight. Aymer glanced at his brother and a tremor ran through him, violent enough to be seen across the hall. Though his bow was scrappy, the youth managed an even stride through the door and across the clanging kitchen until he had gained a quiet stairwell and could sink to the cold stone. Inquisitive hounds nosed about, and a puppy curled itself in his lap.

By the time Aymer watched Arthur Castor emerging through the shadows, a wretched defiance had mastered him. Sir Arthur offered an obliging hand. Scooping the sleepy dog aside, Aymer heaved himself up and dusted the back of his hose.

"Your father will have forgotten by dinnertime."

"Whether he has or he hasn't, I'll take no orders from that mincing Frenchman." In the musty chill, Aymer's breath was spuming, hot and briny. "Of course Moncler's had more women. What a stupid jibe! He's years older and he's a randy little fucker."

"This, from the boy who needs tally sticks to keep count!"

"Tally sticks? No, that's Guy. I'm known for turning girls away. I've little interest in the flesh."

Castor's lip twitched. "Indeed?" The knight had an inch or so advantage over the other; now close enough that it seemed more.

A clangour of long, swinging strides signalled the approach of Reginald Grey. The priest pressed into the crowded nook, his bony face at Sir Arthur's ear. "Tell this puerile half-wit to grovel before Lord Robert and our chamberlain, or *I* shall take a hand in the matter." He probed Aymer with his skewering stare – tiny points of light in the murk – then passed on.

"Come, now. I can hear Master Hal holding forth in the hall. Your brother has sufficient grief in store for you; don't make enemies elsewhere."

"Fuck Hal. Either he goes, or I do." Aymer raised his voice, for it was possible Grey was still within earshot. "As for Moncler, I won't tolerate the way he looks at my father. Filthy little outlander. Who knows where his fingers stray in the darkness?"

"What a lively imagination! If those fingers stray, it's into his ears – to muffle your father's wails and shouting; the noisiest sleeper on God's earth." Castor shook his head. "Loic would lay down his life for Lord Robert. It is love, pure and tender."

"Hardly pure."

Castor felt a twinge of irritation. If any man had reconnoitred Loic's inner desires, it was he. But when their eyes met, he saw that Aymer hadn't simply blundered in; he *knew*. They studied each other in silence.

Then Sir Arthur leaned forward until the younger man was an inch from his throat, inhaling the comfortable smell of horseflesh and hay. One fingertip was deep in the meat of Aymer's shoulder. *"Don't judge me. Don't judge what you don't understand.* Sir Loic deserves your respect and probably – given your father's frequent cruelties – your pity." He stepped back. "But come: some sword-play in the yard will steady you. I want to see how you perform without Guy at your side."

* * *

The problem of who to take and who to leave continued to irritate Clifford for some long while. He was reminded of a puzzle he'd once heard concerning a fox, a hen and a bushel of wheat.

Clearly, George must stay at Skipton. And Hal, who'd been at Alnwick when George bedded Eleanor; Hal knew, and Eleanor probably knew that Hal knew; Hal must stay also. Hal and Aymer were locked in a private struggle for mastery; leave Aymer in Hal's charge and there'd be murder by nightfall. After what had just passed, he couldn't leave Loic in command; the man was instinctively high-handed and Aymer would be itching to teach him a lesson. And after what he'd learned of Eleanor's inclinations, it would surely be rash to take Aymer and Guy, the most handsome, most unbridled of the boys...and so it went on. Eventually, after his headache had driven him to consult the senior men, he abandoned the fox and the wheat: Guy, George, Hal and Richie remained at Skipton with Cuthbert Bellingham, while Clifford led Aymer and the rest northwards once more.

* * *

Alice believed she was to accompany her husband on his recruiting rounds; believed it until the moment she found herself abruptly discarded. The party spent a night at Cerne Abbey as they moved through the West Country, and when Edmond made ready to leave the next morning, he informed his wife that her presence was not required; that he would retrieve her when the Queen joined them.

Alice did not wish for Laura Courtenay's company after what had passed, but there was a malicious satisfaction in observing her fall, for the lady's sterling work on behalf of her husband had brought her no reward, and she too had been shrugged off at the first opportunity. And then the Countess was again loud in her denunciations of her treacherous husband, and amity was restored.

There followed some weary weeks with little news. The Duke did not write to Alice, and the Earl of Devon did not write to Laura. There is nothing to tell of that time, for nothing happened – nothing at all – and every day was identical, at once dreary and filled with dread. Each of their waiting women came to some sense of what the future might hold, with the two lords and their ladies estranged, and all the suffering – or the outward manifestation of it – on the ladies' side. Elizabeth Ullerton exulted. Her marriage would follow directly on the defeat of York, and then she would reside wherever the Duke chose to reside: at court, most likely, with her husband as steward to the foremost nobleman in England, and a fair train of servants to wait upon her.

* * *

Clifford arrived in Alnwick with a smaller escort than last time, though bolstered with several of his mother's men – she'd been fussing. The south wind that was thawing Wessex had petered out at the Pennines. They had left Skipton frosty and clear; Alnwick was icy and pizzling.

As before, the Earl of Northumberland did Clifford the honour of meeting him at the gatehouse, embracing him warmly as a brother; as the brother he was soon to be. And there, in the background, his sturdy son Waryn, earnest pleasure in his greeting. Just as Clifford looked in vain for Eleanor, Waryn looked in vain for George and Hal. The Earl led his guest to the great chamber and waited on him in person while he was warmed and refreshed. Behind the bland courtesies, Harry Percy couldn't conceal his eagerness over the quarrel with Somerset. The subject was unwelcome and Clifford's answers, unhelpful.

Percy kept pressing – only, he said, so as to establish the facts. "Warwick and Somerset are daggers-drawn by the Charing Cross; you throw yourself between them; Somerset tries to stab Warwick; you're injured under Warwick's arm – where are you injured? I can't see it…" And so it went on.

Clifford folded his arms. "The whole story is invented. It's a fabrication from start to finish. Edmond and I had a good laugh over this. Apologies, my friend; that's all there is."

Percy blinked his disappointment. For all his sober baby face, he was a mischief-maker like the rest. "Oh well. I devoutly trust you aren't in Warwick's pocket, Robert. They say you are."

"Ah – Harry. No one knows better than you what that man has cost us."

"And this rumour of Somerset's wife?"

Clifford shrugged. "Come now. Does it sound likely? A most virtuous woman. I wager if I laid a finger on her, she'd throw up." He'd amused himself with that one; not bad for the spur of the moment. He leaned back and looked down on Percy. "Seduce my best friend's wife? What sort of man do you think I am?"

Harry Percy would very much like to be in possession of the truth. He sat for a time after Clifford had left him, staring into the fire, and then dispatched little Kit Loys to summon his under-steward, Robert's second son, Waryn.

It was soon clear that Clifford had neglected to close down the conduits within his circle, for within the past week, Waryn had received a letter from his brother Hal. The under-steward surrendered the missive to his master. Much of it was puerile stuff: the disports of London; new harness and apparel; the minutiae of Hal's conquests, pivoting – entirely without irony – into a sermon on the rearing of some infants he'd abandoned in Alnwick.

Scanning the letter, Percy found the interesting passage. While Hal had not been present at the fight, he was in attendance when Clifford flung in, red with rage, and had the details from witnesses. Percy read slower. There had been a violent and noisy row; Clifford was accused of betraying his erstwhile patron Duke Charles; taking bribes from Louis of France and trying to seduce the Duchess. In reply, Clifford taunted Somerset on the subject of his wife. He'd hinted that Warwick would not outlive the year. Somerset had then tried to stab Clifford, who'd disarmed him and walked away unscathed.

Percy sat back, well satisfied. With delicacy, he made certain of Waryn's silence, and sought his permission to retain the letter for an hour. When the under-steward left him, Percy sent Kit to fetch a scribe and had the letter copied; all of it, not sparing Hal's explicit insights on life in that degenerate household. He dictated a covering note and instructed the page to dispatch the package by immediate courier to Louis de Gruuthuse, Edward of York's host in Bruges. He trusted King Edward would be suitably appreciative.

* * *

Edward of York was more appreciative than Harry Percy could have guessed. Not for the news only – adroitly gathered and greatly welcome – but for the reassurance to be inferred from Percy's prompt action: lately, the whole world seemed to have turned Lancastrian; signals of loyalty in this powerful and enigmatic lord were God-sent indeed.

For some days, the contents of the missive were teased apart by York's small retinue; in every breast a grim satisfaction that the diehard lords of Lancaster could not work in amity; that power had corrupted; that Warwick was showing himself as divisive within the Lancastrian camp as he'd proved amongst themselves. And of all the adherents of Lancaster, none was more reviled than Robert Clifford, the contemptible slayer of King Edward's favourite brother; despoiler of York's towns: Stamford, Ludlow and those other places so viciously ravaged by his forces at the height of the last conflict. The news that Clifford was in the King of France's pocket; that he'd brawled with his old companions; that he'd aligned himself with Warwick – it was, all of it, fascinating and unexpected.

Before York had wrung all he could from the letter, Louis de Gruuthuse had a further copy taken and passed it to his master, Duke Charles of Burgundy.

And so it was that Hal FitzClifford's trifling note, scrawled in careless haste when the lad was late for dinner, was to prove a mortal blow to the time-honoured bonds of northern Christendom. By the next morning, Duke Charles had abandoned King Henry and the House of Lancaster; he had thrown the might of Burgundy and Flanders behind Edward of York and his invasion of England.

* * *

The dinner that evening at Alnwick was an intimate affair compared with the sumptuous feasting of the previous visit. As before, Eleanor was seated beside Lord Clifford, but there was a constraint in her manner, and he could guess the reason. Percy confirmed it in a quiet word as they parted for the night.

"I believe Eleanor is distressed by the rumours out of London. Perhaps you may care to speak to her? If you wish for privacy, the small chamber will be free after matins. And Robert, I should caution you to be gentle. My sister takes your words very much to heart."

The next morning, after he'd endured, with bad grace, her incessant fidgeting in chapel, Clifford asked the lady to step aside.

As soon as he'd closed the door, Eleanor made her displeasure known. "Everyone is talking of this affair of the Duchess of Somerset! They say you hope for dead man's shoes. I'm waiting for your denial!"

How absurd she was to focus on that one detail, ignoring the attempt on his life! He would expect any wife of his to give more thought to his safety than his virtue. He raised his brow. "Edmond of Somerset is no older than I. Such patience is beyond me."

"Don't be flippant with me, my lord! Is there truth in what men say? It's disgusting to hear your name linked with another in this sordid way."

Clifford's smile frightened her and she took a step back.

"We are not lovers, the lady and I. If you want me to avow this, I will swear it on the Scriptures. Would that you could give me similar assurance!"

She halted, and by then her colour was draining. "What are you saying?"

The smile was truly nasty. "We both know what you've done, and with whom, Lady Eleanor. And yet you dare to question my conduct, like a shrew. This is not the way to endear yourself to a man."

She gasped, and groped for the table edge, her defiance collapsing. He had walked away and now turned back, the familiar, challenging pose. Eleanor was red and mottled and watery, twisting her sinuous fingers, but he sensed that beneath the show of contrition, her quick mind was at work; questing to see how far the rot had gone, and what he would do with the knowledge.

"You little whore! How could you degrade yourself in that way?" If George were more intelligent or independent of mind, Clifford could not have borne it. But the boy was no rival; the incident need be raised only once, and never raised again; he would terrify her, and it would be enough.

"How can I make you understand?" She was wailing now, but quietly. "It's terrible to speak of this to you, of all men. How am I to make you understand? My life's story is nothing without you in it. When I was born, you were already living among us. As I grew, I saw you every day. To my eyes, you were all that a man should be, and I watched you, Robert, and I loved you. Since I was a little maiden, I loved you. And then you left us, and went back to your father, and I felt my heart would break. When I learned that you had gone into exile, I believed I would never see you again. Then my brother took back his own and – with his household – your boys...the Clifford look. I was helpless. I know how this must sound – but at the time it seemed as though God had planned it."

"God?" exclaimed Clifford, his voice dripping with scorn. "God doesn't make plans to help man fornicate. It's lust that's directing your actions, my lady. It may be the devil has a hand in it, but not God."

Her head drooped and tears fell directly to the floor.

"All of it, Eleanor! You shall admit it all. Don't think of lying to me or it will go worse with you. Were there other men?"

"Oh no!" she exclaimed. "How – how could there be? Only those you know of."

"Only *those* I know of?" He repeated it slowly.

And that was just..." she tailed off, and tried again. "I would never think of other men in that way. It's just...and when my brother asked if I could bring myself to marry you, I so, *so* wished I'd saved myself for you!"

That wail was loud and heartfelt. She covered her face with her hands.

"Look at me! You shall acknowledge your shame by naming these men."

Now confusion was added to the dread. "As you know, my lord, it was George and Hal, the Clifford boys."

The breath left him. Clifford stared away, above her head, out of the window. He could not marry her. Not now. *Hal.* There was a sudden, absurd desire to laugh. *Hal? Hal, too?* He was all at sea.

"But you must understand…" While her gaze was grovelling, the resentment had reared up, to claw its way past the shame. "Hal's behaviour was as horrifying to me as it is to you! I had no wish to pleasure him in that most scandalous of ways, but once he learned…about George, he blackmailed me, forcing me to satisfy him, again and again in that way, until you came to us at Christmastide." She was creeping to him, and sank humbly to her knees, fumbling to clasp his hands.

Cold and pitiless, Clifford peeled her tentacle fingers from his wrists and twisted from her. His heavy tread alerted the listener beyond the door, allowing the man ample time to fade away before Clifford reached the threshold.

* * *

"*Hal?*" Loic's incredulity precisely matched his own.

They frowned into each other's faces, recalling all that had been said between them on the matter; and said by George; and by Hal himself – and then Loic began to laugh and laugh, in scandalised mirth.

"Monseigneur, God has smoothed your path. This is a blessing. How else could you keep the Earl as an ally, yet gain the freedom to wed another? The Earl of Northumberland will be grovelling; he cannot blame you for rejecting the lady now – you hold all the cards. But *Hal!* I thought Hal a decent man; rather a dry fellow. I wronged him!

"I, also."

"He is your son, in truth!"

"I'm overcome with pride," said Clifford heavily. "Never speak of this again."

* * *

Warwick had only to look into Jack de Vere's handsome, eager face for Clifford's warning to slip.

"What?" exclaimed Jack. "*What?* Edmond of Somerset? Do you know so little of the man that you could believe this of him? Somerset has shown himself a dolt, not a traitor. My God – you're spying conspiracies everywhere!"

"If I know little of him, whose fault is it? He will not come to me, will not work with me. That man is up to no good. Jack…" he pushed his papers aside and leaned, folding his arms, his chin tilted. "Tell me something. Why did you not consult me when you arranged Alice's marriage?"

The question had been so long in coming that Jack had forgotten his answer, honed as it once had been. He shrugged. "Why did you not consult me when you arranged your daughter's marriage to the Prince? Because we had the same purpose, of course: to strengthen our alliance with the stalwarts of Lancaster. For Christ's sake – get a grip on yourself! I'm not plotting against you! In point of fact, it is *I* who has been cold-shouldered. I've neither the time nor inclination to join the Council but I'm forever asked why I'm not a member. I can give no answer; I have been excluded – for no good reason that I can see. Meanwhile, you hang on every word that falls from Robert Clifford's lips. There's even a rumour you offered *him* a seat! I tell you what, my lord: if I believed something so preposterous, I'd leave London for good, and damn your troubles with the treaty."

Warwick threw up his hands. "A perfect illustration! This is the reason I give you no authority. You are infantile and overexcited. I *do* need Clifford on the Council."

The younger man's lip was quivering; his nostrils flared – the very picture of an overexcited infant. "I see! And when Clifford stirred you up over Somerset, did he think to mention the threat he made concerning you? Eh? I've heard from several men who were present that night, and all agree." A dramatic and irksome pause. "Clifford said: *'Warwick will not be long among us in England'*."

Warwick closed his eyes. Robert and his dreadful, irrepressible, disastrous sense of humour; he could all but hear the man's voice. He wasn't about to enlighten Jack as to the meaning behind those words, and smartly turned the subject.

"We'll not quarrel amongst ourselves – we've more than enough to deal with. You realise there's no chance of getting this through Parliament in the form King Louis expects? The ambassadors are pushing for a ten-year treaty of open warfare against Duke Charles. We'll be lucky to get a vague promise to be enemies of each other's enemies."

Jack was still looking confused. "You've had coins struck bearing the insignia of France, for God's sake. Louis has already lost patience at your tortuous speed and invaded Flanders. How can such a feeble offer satisfy him?" Jack's gaze wandered anxiously over the dry lines at his friend's eyes and lips.

"What are the ambassadors for, if not to apprise him of the difficulties? The French know I'll have a reckoning with Edward of York before I can make good on my personal vows. Clifford has explained it to them."

Indeed, as a token of his good faith, the Calais garrison – small but pugnacious – was already making merry hell in Duke Charles's western dominions. The leading of a great English army into Flanders: it would happen; certainly it would happen, as soon as he was rid of Edward of York – his cousin, his protégé, his one-time pupil. And when Jack beheld his friend Warwick invested as Count of Holland and Zeeland and no longer among them in England, the significance of Robert Clifford's enigmatic remark would, at last, unravel itself.

* * *

It was late afternoon, and Harry Percy had not seen his sister since matins. He ushered away her women. She went on with her stitching.

"Eleanor!" His voice was peremptory – he wanted to observe her eyes. "Did Lord Clifford speak to you?"

Reluctantly she raised her face. Not a pretty sight, alas.

She said, "Why? Did he speak to you?"

"We've been together much of the afternoon, as it happens, playing at chess." He patted his swollen purse; it chinked fatly. "The fellow's no strategist – all headlong frontal assault. But I trust he put your mind at rest?"

"I did think he was displeased with me, but perhaps…"

"I warned you to be careful, Eleanor. Where Clifford is concerned, you seem to have abandoned all good sense. This is not a man you can browbeat.

Remember, my dear," he added, more gently, "that one should not attach too much weight to fidelity. It's perfectly possible for marriage to bring contentment where one party has not been chaste beforehand, or, indeed, constant afterwards."

Wise words, surely, but she did not seem to be attending. "Oh Harry, I love Robert to distraction, and well he knows it."

Harry Percy lowered himself into the window seat, stripping his nails. *Incredible.* That man was *Long Lankin* made flesh; the butcher from a ballad that had horrified him as a child. Were Percy a maiden, Robert Clifford – hideous, depraved and brutal as he was – would be the last man on earth he would desire as a husband. The veil, and possibly the grave, would tempt him more.

"I am glad, for he is a worthy man. But do not be betrayed by your feelings. Remember that if King Edward triumphs, as I expect he will, you'll never see Lord Clifford again."

* * *

And so this visit turned out very differently from the last, Eleanor avoiding her beloved as though he had the pox. Yet when they were forced together, Clifford was scrupulously polite.

She could see that between Robert and her brother, the remainder of the sojourn passed easily enough; the usual muted amity. It was clear that Lord Clifford had not shared his discovery with Harry. Hope blossomed afresh and slowly her eyes returned to linger on him, over his form. He took it all in, and was disgusted anew.

All the while, Eleanor was thanking God for her presence of mind in exposing Hal's covert intimidation. The consequences of his son's indefensible betrayal, on which the father was darkly brooding, were of no concern to her. Had she seen the damage, she would have been the better pleased.

Clifford had not any idea how this little tragedy had come to pass, and might have had more sympathy with Eleanor if he knew the whole of it; or perhaps not. Perhaps he would have drawn grim amusement from Hal's part in the tale or perhaps felt some pity for George, who had been so comprehensively outclassed.

After a few weary days of enforced civility, Clifford rode away from Alnwick, his boyhood home over many happy years, hoping never to set foot in the place again. George had been granted a lucky escape. Hal had not.

* * *

In these last weeks, Somerset had excelled in the raising of men, filling his listeners with a nostalgic and quite inaccurate fervour for the good old days of King Henry; the talismanic Beaufort name playing well in the West Country heartlands. Yet still there was no sign of their Queen or their Prince, pinned in Normandy by the adverse winds. When he heard that Warwick had left London on his recruiting drive, he began to think of returning to the capital himself. Warwick gone, he was drawn to possess the person of his cousin, the hapless King.

He summoned the Earl of Devon to accompany him to London. Devon was well content to quit his ancestral estates, for he discovered he'd not Somerset's gift for inspiring respect. His was a contentious family, long inclined to feuding and violence, and as Devon traversed his county, old enmities made their presence felt, hemming him on every side.

The two men travelled eastwards via Cerne, where both their wives were still immured.

"I'll bring Laura back to London with me. My wife's presence may be of value; it'll remind her father Essex to keep faith once York invades." Moreover, Devon was not adverse to a little breathless reverence at this juncture; balm to his irritated spirits.

Somerset shook his head dismissively. "The Earl of Essex will rush to York's side at the drop of a hat; he'll not regard his daughter's feelings. To think Warwick believed he had bought the fellow! What a fool. But do as you think best."

Neither lord had bothered to alert the ladies of their approach, and thus Alice had no time to compose her feelings or refresh her story. The reunion

204

was stilted; he was abstracted and she was watchful, and very little passed between them, until the next morning, when Edmond informed Alice that he planned to forsake her in the West Country, now – and from now on.

"You wish we had never wed; that much is clear to me!" The last dregs of feeling made her strain for a contradiction; there was none forthcoming. "But you cannot annul our marriage, my lord, and you know it. We were both of an age; there was no coercion; the marriage was properly dispensed and conducted." Her heart drummed in her throat.

"You seem to have given the matter plenty of thought."

"I've been shut in this house for weeks with nothing to do but to brood on your injustice to me. May I ask, my lord, whether you have spoken to my brother? Jack will not sit idly by while his sister is humiliated in this way."

He turned directly to face her. "Oh, your brother is well aware. He has discussed your conduct with the Earl of Devon, yet still Jack has not dared to come to me in person."

"With the Earl of Devon? That troublemaker. I can imagine what fables he has told of me."

"I've known Devon all my life; a man who shared my exile these ten years, a most true and loyal lord, while so many of those who now court King Henry were disporting themselves as followers and favourites of Edward of York. I'll not hear his name abused in your mouth."

The noblemen rode on to London alone.

"I tell you what, Edmond: I couldn't endure to look on my wife a moment longer. Christ, but she disgusts me. I've never known a woman so sweaty. And her legs –all thick and veined."

Somerset turned away, queasy, but Devon trundled on regardless.

"Christ. Lift her gown and you'd think there was some ancient, shrivelled crone squatting under there, what with the sour stench, and her…"

At last he noticed Somerset's rising panic and swerved from the mishap just in time.

"…*presence* being of no value to us; Essex will rush to York's side at the drop of a hat; he'll not regard his daughter's feelings. Do you know, I believe the man actually dislikes me, for all that I'm his son-in-law. I tell you what, Edmond: when all this is over, and the court is restored, I'll feather myself a tidy nest in Westminster, and Laura will live in the West Country, minding my estates. Wives are ever more trouble than they're worth. Especially when they can't manage to produce an heir" – he'd forgot his audience, again – "no matter how many weary times you empty yourself into them. Slack and wrinkled…"

"Enough!" Somerset cried. "This is intolerable. You *must* stop."

"You're right – quite right. I should have stopped long ago, in point of fact, but the woman desires me and I've always been too soft-hearted for my own good. Not that I can get the marriage annulled, of course, but that doesn't mean I have to lie with my wife. It doesn't mean I have to live with her. You must follow my lead, else Lady Alice will be forever running those sly eyes of hers over Robert Clifford and you'll have no peace."

Somerset grunted, nauseous. He'd long since determined to do just this – divide himself from his wife. He hated to have it gnawed over by the Earl of Devon.

* * *

The story was commonplace enough: a variation on a theme playing out day-by-day in houses great and small across the country. The more Eleanor thought on it, the less she held herself to blame. For she had passed much of her girlhood in obscure penury while the Nevilles lorded it over the North; once her brother was restored to the pinnacle, and potency had come again to the Percys, she was greedy for life. When she'd returned to take her place at Alnwick, she'd been jolted by the presence of Clifford boys so close at hand. She had told Robert the truth.

Of course, she'd soon noticed that George was looking at her, and the more he looked at her, the more she looked at him; or perhaps it was the other way round. Eventually, inevitably, the looking was not sufficient. George's failings were of a mundane nature, and his response was predictable. Just as he was dreading the consequences, his head was turned in equal measure by the imagining of an encounter, and the desire to boast of it afterwards.

The lad was hanging back, uncertain, from the fatal step when Eleanor took up the reins. A number of times she contrived to press past him or brush his hand. Encouraged by his yearning looks, she advanced at length to the heady step of summoning him by way of a scribbled note. George – to whom the written word was a mystery – turned to Hal in his trouble, entreating his cousin to decipher the marks. Hal read aloud to George the note Eleanor might have written but hadn't, inventively praising his cousin's manly demeanour and handsome looks, but omitting the crucial details of time and place. And so Eleanor waited in vain, with dawning dismay, at the appointed tryst, and the budding romance was confounded for a time.

One December evening – it was the year before Lord Clifford's Christmas visit – George had dawdled alone to the lower door to call in the hounds. Outside, the first snow of winter cast its lonely drifting spell into the darkness. His reverie was interrupted by an abrupt, wordless tug to the hand. Turning with a frown, he beheld the Lady Eleanor before him in the quiet shadows and, surrendering at once to the commands of Fate, he pulled her in and kissed her with clumsy greed. Of course, she gasped and sighed, and her hands were in his hair, and that was enough for the foolish lad, for all sense had flown. He lifted her gown, tore the cloth beneath her skirts, freed himself and hoisted her against him. It was so shocking and perfect that she clung to him and cried out and did not guess that the stupid, stupid boy had lost control, not withdrawing at the last, but completing what he'd started, at great peril to them both.

Hal marvelled that God had given George not so much sense as a sheep, that he should have risked this, when all his future depended on the Earl her brother, and the Earl's good opinion. Too many household men had been regaled with the braggart tale before Hal could prevail upon his cousin to shut his mouth. In truth, George had not seen fit to finish the story, omitting to mention the stinging slap to the face he'd received directly after, when Eleanor understood the harm he had done her and, furious, swept away with what little dignity she could muster.

In the weeks that followed, the lady continued fretful and angry and would not look at George, even when it became clear that the worst had not happened, and she would not have to go to her brother and break the shameful news. And because George was so foolish, his ardour grew in direct proportion to her disdain; he had begun all this by thinking little enough of her, but by now he was frantic even for a smile. And so Eleanor discovered, by accident, the joys of persecution, and when she deigned to notice him, it was to allow him less than he wanted and keep him dangling after her.

And meanwhile, Hal, whose guile far exceeded that of his hapless cousin, saw a way to profit from his predecessor's fall and commenced with Eleanor himself, too shrewd to commit any of George's errors. He would stare at her on occasion, smouldering and brazen, and ignore her at all other times, agitating her with his attention and his inattention until the unlucky George was forgotten entirely and she thought of no one and nothing but Hal; Robert Clifford incarnate.

Hal did not approach her for a long, lingering time. One summer evening, half a year before his father returned to fetch him away – when Hal had been tormenting Eleanor for months – he sauntered into her bedchamber, released his cod-piece with a flourish and stared down on the lady, chin raised and arms folded.

Had he not conquered her so well, she would have laughed, so ludicrous was his appearance – and he knew it, and cursed that he could not make his entrance over again. But by now, for her, there was no amusement to be found anywhere.

"Come, girl; kneel before me and take me in your mouth," he ordered, in his deep and commanding voice. "Or I shall go straight to the Earl your brother and tell him what evil you have done with my cousin."

They each considered, for a brief moment, whether he would, if necessary, follow through with his threat and each suspected that he would not, but the menace was sufficient excuse and she obeyed him then and on many occasions thereafter. Soon he ceased to bother looking at her at all, or pretending to blackmail her and, needless to say, told no one of his sport. If Eleanor wished for more from him, she dared not say, for she was entirely awe-struck, and feared and adored him with all her heart. And so it continued until late that year, when Robert Clifford himself returned to Alnwick after ten years' absence and wiped Hal utterly from her mind.

But Robert Clifford knew none of this and, while the revulsion was fresh with him, he cared not how it had come about or at whose door the fault lay. Eleanor had lost her way, and lost her chance entirely. Brough Castle would not be far enough to banish her; she was no fit wife for him.

* * *

Sir Gabriel Appledore knew with certainty that he must unburden himself of the terrible disclosures Lady Ullerton had seen fit to make, passing them on to his innocent master like some revolting disease. Here in London he would prime the Duke, but when they returned to Cerne, Elizabeth herself must confess the ugly particulars and meet the Duke's questions. Awkward questions, no doubt, which would try her nerve. *Good.*

When he finished his faltering preliminaries, it was not going well for him.

Somerset, seated at the table, glared at his steward. "Is it not sufficient, Appledore, that we two consider this painful matter, man-to-man, without dragging Lady Ullerton into it?"

Sir Gabriel at once scrutinised himself. If the master were angry, he must have gone awry. But how could the Duke fathom this matter without the gentlewoman's help? It was, frankly, appalling that a man of such noble dignity should be forced to endure so vulgar a…

"Well, Appledore? You may tell me what she says, I think, without the gentlewoman herself being present. I'm surprised at you for suggesting so vulgar a thing."

Sir Gabriel's mind was emptying. The details began to elude him, and he stammered as he tried. "Lady Ullerton told me that the Duchess has possibly not behaved herself as you might probably have wished, my lord." This was terrible; it was beyond him. The Duke's fingers had steepled.

"By which I mean – or she means – Lady Ullerton, I mean – that my lady – that is, Lady Alice, was closeted alone with Lord Clifford in the lower chamber in your house in Bruges."

"I know this," interrupted Somerset ominously. "You have told me already. As, indeed, has my wife."

"But she was crying, Lord Edmond!"

Somerset's mouth twisted. "Crying? Perhaps she had a headache. I think I recall that she did. Why bring it to my attention now, when I'm entirely occupied with affairs of state?"

"Might I sit, my lord?" begged the drooping man.

"I think you had better not, Appledore. This will be more effectively done if you stay silent long enough to consider what you have to say, and then say it, swiftly and simply."

Sir Gabriel nodded, and looked around the magnificent panelled apartment, so marvellously different from the rooms of that mean and cramped house in which the Duchess had disported herself so shamelessly. In due course, the steward raised his head and began again. "On the night before your wedding, my lord, Lady Ullerton says that Lady Alice went from the great chamber where she was dining with you, and at her signal, Lord Clifford followed, and together they slipped to her bedchamber and were secluded within for a time, all alone. When Lady Alice emerged, her candle was broken and cold upon the floor. Lady Ullerton witnessed a great indent and a rumple upon the bed, though the chamberwoman had laid the sheets freshly that morning."

For a long while Somerset sat motionless, eyes wandering vacantly among the motes of dust on the tabletop.

Appledore watched his master's handsome face, drawn in a faint frown of inward contemplation. At last he was satisfied.

* * *

The other boys were doing rather better now; much faster, more skilled, more versatile, the imminence of the challenge concentrating every mind. They had improved markedly in his absence; George's influence, perhaps. Clifford watched them, arms folded, a detailed appraisal. "You've done well. Now see if you can take Robbie in hand." Clifford was leaning on George's shoulder. "If he's separated from us, he won't manage. Toughen him up, and close the kitchen to him. He's…" he gesticulated toward his own taut stomach, "…doughy."

"He's not *trying*." George's voice was quivering with disapproval; outrage, even. Unexpected, from one who would never be serious, and Clifford smiled with warm affection until he saw an identical smile on Hal's face, and scowled.

At that, Aymer chanced his arm. "On this occasion, George has the right of it. Since our return, I've spent a good part of every morning with Robbie. Your pardon, Father, but one who cannot fight is worse than useless: a danger to those around him. Perhaps you'd consider leaving the lad behind when we are summoned?"

The tone was respectful, but Clifford's scowl spread.

Castor laid a mild hand on Aymer's arm. "We leave no man behind. It's not our way."

"God shall be the judge." Another gnomic utterance from Reginald Grey.

Aymer promptly abandoned Robbie. Hal and George took up the unfortunate boy and succeeded in frightening him half to death, confusing him with a relentless barrage of correction and advice, being more expert in the performance than the instruction. The additional exertion made Robbie hungrier and more loath than ever. He spent so much time lurking about the kitchen that even the lowliest scullion lost patience and turned informer.

Were it not for Richie and Guy, he would have suffered agonies. But his brothers had come, unexpectedly, to his aid and rescued him with a ready supply of piecrust and soothing guidance, none of which bolstered his lessons – quite the contrary – but which proved, mercifully, a good deal easier to swallow.

* * *

After Robert's devastating discoveries, Eleanor understood all too well the only course open to her: to hold her peace and allow the revelations to fade gently from the forefront of his mind. Knowing it was one thing, but her engulfing feelings were causing her anguish. For some days she drifted about Alnwick, spectral, racked by the fear that he had withdrawn himself from her; dreading the prospect of a vast, empty stretch of years cast from his presence.

As ever, Eleanor shared her inmost thoughts with her attendant and dearest friend, Marjorie Verrier, a woman cut from a similar cloth: the pattern alike, the quality not so fine.

"I asked him to write to me, Marjorie. As he left, I begged him to do so."

Marjorie nodded, encouraging. So coarse and weighty hung her hair that no mere move of the head could stir its tacky jumble.

"I should not have done that. I resolved not to do that. Now, when he writes, he will think of me, and when he thinks of me, he will remember."

"It is jealousy, Lady Eleanor. Pure and simple."

"Jealousy? No, I'm beyond that! Let Lord Clifford pursue every married woman in England! What does it matter, so long as he takes me for his wife?" Her suspicions, which had caused such agonies when the rumours first reached her, had been trampled by her fear and were nowhere, and she was, for the present, utterly unconcerned at his infidelities. It would not last, of course; jealousy was a dormant seed, poised to spring up and seek its place in the sun.

"His jealousy, not yours. The boys are younger than he; more appealing – and he fears them. He wants you all to himself. You could not have done better had you planned this outcome from the first."

Eleanor wished so very much to believe it, but the truth would persist in breaking in. "You did not see his face, Marjorie. You did not hear his voice. He was so filled with disappointment, so filled with contempt. I have disgusted him."

She crossed the floor, and stood motionless, her cheek on the other's shoulder, breathing the heavy scent, drawing comfort from the assurance of her friend: this gentlewoman, no older than her mistress, but ever ahead of her, an incitement to weakness and waywardness, falling, a headlong victim, for Miles Randall's sordid charms on the same day – so long ago – that little Eleanor was casting her innocent snowballs, thrilled by Robert's laughing reprimand.

* * *

Very quietly, Hal slipped open the door to the twins' chamber. As the designated master of the FitzCliffords, it behoved him to know the employments and endeavours of his underlings, Aymer most particularly.

Will was stretched on his low pallet, peacefully sleeping. Tucked beneath his arm, with her hair fanned across his chest, lay a pale, golden-headed girl. They made a sweet picture. Alongside, on a second pallet, lay Richie. As Hal watched from the threshold, there was a movement beneath the sheet and the older youth's great sallow paw emerged, his heavy fingers fondling the smooth white skin, clutching and groping. Hal was struck with an uncomfortable doubt: was this how he would appear to an observer – huge and ugly and bestial? Probably not; Richie's advances always seemed to be unwelcome.

Slowly, inevitably, the lad eased himself closer until he was hard behind the girl, beginning, furtively, to handle himself. Still Will and his girl slumbered on, she making small, untroubled snores against his chest. Hal leaned against the doorpost and reckoned the rhythm, watching until his brother reached the very cusp of abandonment. Then –

"Richie!" he shouted.

The youth slumped forward with a horrified groan. Opening a surprised eye, Will shrugged Richie away. The girl had turned in bewilderment, tugging the sheet to her neck.

"A good morning to all," continued Hal, placidly. "Listen, Richie – I'm sent with a message. Father is most heartily sick of you and the twins plaguing Bede with foolish donkey noises, and commands you to stop." It was doubtful Lord Clifford had noticed. "Father also says…" he cast about for another annoyance, "you're not giving Sir Cuthbert the respect he deserves. He will beat you for it, next time. That's all: you may carry on meddling with that poor lass now." He ducked back under the lintel and vanished.

Will raised a quizzical brow at Richie, who barked in reply. "He has made it all up, just to barge in and throw his weight around. My God, but I *hate* Hal! It was a dark day for us when Father fetched him from Alnwick. Why can you never summon the guts to take him on? Always leaving it to the rest of us. Hal should beware, for Aymer and I are fast losing patience. We shall give him a good drubbing if he goes on like this."

Richie pushed himself up, twitching the sheet from the pair. Crossing to the door, he bawled for the wretched Pleydell, who never would answer his summons. In a high temper he flung back, clothing himself with slipshod haste while the girl burrowed shyly against her lover and Will watched him with mild interest, stroking absently. With no word more Richie exited, banging the door, and went in search of Aymer. He was not halfway across the yard when he was accosted by Loic and Nield and chastised most angrily for daring to approach his father unwashed, unshaven and half-undone.

* * *

As Clifford's mother no longer desired to make the journey of some miles to Skipton, he travelled east to spend the day with her. The affray outside Devon's house was quickly raised and briskly dismissed as a drinking bout that had lurched out of control. She pursed her lips.

It would have been a tranquil visit, were Lady Clifford not so insistent in exploring his forthcoming marriage. There was no marriage forthcoming, but revealing that would lead to an inquisition. George's part in all this was bad enough; Hal's was beyond forgiveness. Not the act itself, or acts – many of them, apparently – nor the blackmail – grist to Clifford's mill – but the deceit; the furtive behaviour that riled him beyond measure; the inkling of a plot behind his back. There could be only one explanation, of course: Hal had intended his pleasures to continue after his father's marriage, as before it.

When her son's mood darkened Lady Clifford reluctantly abandoned Eleanor Percy, who seemed to have distressed him in some way. The pair had been playing chess, the lady's mind not on the game any more than her son's, though she was winning easily enough. He had forsaken the board and was standing with his back to his mother, staring from the window.

"My son – there are other tales about. Tell me, are you in love with the Duke of Somerset's wife?"

He turned and regarded her blankly for a moment, the lie composing itself, and then he turned back to the view. The loftiness of the moors held a different sort of beauty, more stirring, but his mother's house was set in a small lush valley, a fold in the land. A beck rushed by, deep and clear. It couldn't be seen from the house, but its music could be heard, and he listened.

"I am, for God Himself showed the girl to me in a vision. We were to marry. Then Somerset appeared in Angers, and I was cast aside."

"Oh, my poor son! And now you're jealous of Somerset. This led you to provoke him, I suppose."

"Yes and no. Like you, my lady, the Duke does not approve of my alliance with Warwick."

He broke off at the interruption of a messenger. While Robert leaned on the sill, Lady Clifford broke the seal and scanned the missive. He turned sharply at her scudding intake of breath.

She had risen and crossed quickly to him. "Edward of York has landed at Ravenspur with a small force. Kingston upon Hull denied him entry, but the city of York has admitted him."

Robert nodded, unruffled. "We'll await Warwick's command. Warn your men." He held out his hand. "The letter, if you please."

She snatched it behind her back. "This is a private matter."

When he stood impassive, her hand returned slowly to her side. Robert twitched the letter from her grasp and held it above his face where she had no hope of reaching it.

"Ah – it is from Triston, of course." His voice was savage as he read on. "So well informed, because, naturally, it is he, himself, who opened the gates of the city. And now, at long last, the little traitor has his knighthood: for admitting John's killer through the very gate on which John's killer impaled John's head."

"Oh no, my son! Edward of York did not kill John. Warwick killed your brother, just as Warwick killed your father, and it is you – *you* – who have betrayed all we hold dear to do the killer's bidding!"

"I work with the man in the cause of our King!" He was shouting at her, and she was trembling, though not from fear. "In the cause of our *King*! I, who

215

have lost so much; I am as far from a traitor as it is possible to be: one of the few loyal lords left in this benighted country."

"How dare you speak to me like that? I would not *spit* on Warwick – I, who lost so much more than you! My husband, my eldest son, his heir…"

That startled him. Never had she raised the subject of John's heir; there was a tacit agreement not to speak of young Henry. He believed she had closed her mind to the subject and, certainly, he would not refer to it. Not now. Not with an uncertain grip on his temper. He flung out of the chamber without taking leave.

Halfway to Skipton, he was already regretting the quarrel. Loic must write to the lady without delay, and excuse his master's wretched temper. Clifford sketched for his intimates a brief outline and waited for them to soothe him.

"Passing strange – until this year, I never even heard that you had a second brother, Monseigneur."

"A third brother, Loic. Triston is my *third* brother."

Loic closed his eyes. "Ah – of course, Monseigneur: a third brother. My apologies; to you, and to the lost Lord John. How I wish I had known him."

"Don't delude yourself," said Clifford, momentarily diverted. "He would have loathed you."

Cuthbert Bellingham and Patrick Nield exchanged glances of poignant memory before the chamberlain's affronted face. Nield reached to pat his shoulder. "You see, Loic, Lord John was a superb man, in his way, but not mild, not tolerant, as is our Lord Robert. Eh, Bell?"

"No, indeed, Loic," Sir Cuthbert concurred, abstracted, brooding on their master long dead. "Certainly he had no sympathy with men of your…" his voice faltered away.

"Country?" supplied Nield.

"Country," agreed Clifford, with a gurgle of laughter.

Nield leant close. "Imagine Aymer…but born to vast power."

* * *

Somerset had wronged his steward; he knew it now. It was quite proper for Sir Gabriel to come to him, to persist when his master closed his ears. Appledore's

216

revelation was terrifying in its implications. What evil had that girl attempted – from the outset – for all her gentle grace?

There was no prospect of an annulment; Alice had the right of it there. But it was not too late to evade a worse outcome, and he was determined on a permanent separation. While she lived – and she would probably outlive him – he could not take another wife. But he would, at least, prevent a bastard child being foisted upon him as his own. Edmond spoke with his brother, the only man to whom he would expose this raw and weeping sore.

"Oh, Edmond. I suffer for you in your pain, believe me, but you judge too hastily; I know it. The lady you describe is not the Alice I know. She is full of sweetness and charity and everything that's proper and gracious in a woman. Her manner is never light or forward, but everything one would wish in a Christian wife: courteous, cheerful and virtuous."

"But this is how she has deluded us, Jonkin; with just such a manner. There can be no innocent explanation for her behaviour." He held up a hand to silence the other. "I hope I'm a good Christian, too, Brother. I would hardly condemn her unheard. When we return to the West Country, we'll travel via Cerne, and I will speak first to Lady Ullerton, and then to Alice herself. I will put to her what I've learned, and hear out her excuses."

Jonkin slipped his bonds. "It seems to me that already you have condemned her unheard! At the least, let me be present, Edmond. If Alice sees some friendly face, she'll take heart and know that not everyone has abandoned her."

So very unlikely that Edmond, of all men, would agree to such a suggestion, both improper and disloyal as it was, and, with stern and affronted words, he chased his brother away. Jonkin knew nothing of the world.

* * *

Hal was riding now beside George, for it was clear he had offended his father in some way. Better to hold himself aloof until the fault was forgotten, whatever it may be. York was heading south; discussion turned to the coming battle, and indeed other matters were rarely mentioned now. Hal had noted that the sight of the Wyvern on their breasts had a tendency to provoke fear before they'd even resorted to weapons. George agreed wholeheartedly; he saw it, too, and with war, finally, in imminent prospect, it was a gratifying advantage to be riding into the storm beside Robert Clifford. The two cousins were congratulating themselves on their good fortune and their proud, if defective, ancestry, when the other boys, less eager for battle, perhaps – or less self-assured – felt duty-bound to bring them back to earth.

Robert Clifford might be a famous warrior – was the general view – but living with him was not unalloyed joy; his extreme piety was irksome, and they pulled that about for a while, and not for the first time; the way it permeated their mode of life, imposing hours of prayer and attendance at divine office, and severely curtailing the consumption of meat in the household. And if they were somewhat used to it by now, and found ways to supplement their diet, still it were better if he would be less rigid in his observance. Someone ventured to hope that Reginald Grey, their terrifying chaplain, might suffer a fatal clump to the head in the coming engagement, and someone else volunteered to help matters discreetly along.

And then: Robert Clifford's addiction to music was also an irritant, they agreed. Sometimes he'd play dances so contagious it was impossible to control one's feet and they'd dance even if they didn't want to, even with each other, hand-in-hand, which left them sheepish once the notes had died away. Just as often, he'd expect them to attend to singing that was tiresomely dreary or extravagantly mournful. And, worst of all: the pretty anthems in honour of the Virgin.

After hearing out their complaints for a time, Richie leaned slyly to the others to confide that he'd found a way to hear out the music with equanimity, even enjoyment. The key to it, he explained, was to imagine that the subject of every song, regardless of its title and avowed subject matter, was the Duchess of Somerset.

"So: *The Queen of Heaven*, his latest dirge. Not his reverence for the Blessed Virgin; his desire for the Duchess Alice. Listen to the words with that in mind, and you'll enjoy it too."

There was silence as every mind ran over the pious verses, which now took on an obscene tinge, and then came the crows of laughter and the delighted clapping.

Even George, who plagued Richie where he could, was grinning. "*Farewell*," he agreed. "Not exile from England, but exile from his mistress, who is wed to another." More hilarity.

Placed halfway, as it were, between his father and the FitzCliffords, it ill-became Hal to take amusement in their puerile impudence; Lord Clifford was deadly serious on the subject of his music. Hal sighed and peeled off towards the front of the group.

A short while later, Clifford turned sharply aside, raising a forefinger to silence the men. *The Queen of Heaven* was being inharmoniously shouted behind them. Loic exchanged glances with Hal and both turned to grimace at the household. It was surely impossible that anyone, however self-regarding, could delude themselves that such sudden enthusiasm for the hymn was complimentary, or intended as such; the boys were simply too overexcited to keep quiet. But, incredibly, Clifford was looking gratified, and when they stopped for the night and sat out before the tents, he stretched his long legs comfortably towards the fire, settling the lute in his lap and, closing his good eye, sang lustily to please them. The household men shuffled about; in wordless agreement moving forward to hide the worst of it. For it was plain to them, if not to their master, that most of his boys were beside themselves with suppressed laughter; the less controlled among them were actually crying.

Hal stood aloof, watching the FitzCliffords from a cold distance. He wondered at his father: the man's humour so quick and lively when it came to the follies of others, so inexplicably blind to his own absurdities.

* * *

Harry Percy kept his word to Robert Clifford. He kept to the letter of their agreement. Not one amongst his affinity rose in support of either king, just as he'd promised, and when Clifford boasted to Warwick that he alone had kept Harry Percy from joining York, no word came south to contradict him.

219

The spirit of the agreement, though, was long since in tatters. The missive with which Percy had intrigued Louis de Gruuthuse and his guests was a tempting morsel, a signal of intent. When Triston Clifford threw open the gates of York, King Edward was carrying – parading – a file of letters from his loyal Earl of Northumberland; letters which addressed him reverently as king, proffering news and intelligence which should have been of the utmost value.

Harry Percy loved no creature in this world, and cared for barely any one. Yet Eleanor and he were a close pair, sharing swift wits, a flexible code and roughshod ambition. It was his habit to inform his sister of his plans and stratagems. She was ever interested, and generally full of advice, all of which he heard, and some of which he followed.

In this matter, though, the Earl and his sister were not to see eye to eye. Percy had tried from the first to keep Eleanor in ignorance of his machinations, guessing at her wholesale and inconvenient conversion to the house of Lancaster. He made an inexpert job of it; his silence was too sudden and his activities, too furtive.

"There is a great bustle of messengers these days, Harry. I wonder what you're so busy with."

"Forgive me, Sister." He rose above the mocking note. "I meant to tell you at once. It's just as we predicted; exactly as we predicted." He lowered himself into the chair before her, hands quiet in his lap. "Edward of York has detached his brother George from Warwick and persuaded him to rejoin the fold. What a great Judas George of Clarence has turned out to be! I wouldn't trust that renegade in a dark alley. He'd knife a man for the price of a drink."

"But where is Robert Clifford, in all this? I've had no letter, though he promised to write."

"And while Warwick and Somerset were rambling about the country making speeches, the fools have let Edward of York enter London, and take custody of Henry of Lancaster. There'll be carnage soon enough"

Eleanor's hand slid along the table edge. All her future swayed in the balance. "Where is Robert? It's twenty-four days since he left us."

Percy shrugged. "Doing whatever Warwick bids him, as ever. Oh – and remember Robert's little brother Triston? This will amuse you: it is Triston himself who opened the gates of York to King Edward. What a family! They're all as bad as each other. They're all the same."

Eleanor had turned away. "We've precious little to brag of ourselves, Harry, on that score."

But her own loyalty lay on the far side of dubious. By now, all her energies were focused on wresting control of the nexus between the castle and the world. And so a small enterprise cranked into life: couriers were relieved of their cargo, letters teased apart and transformed, and the lady made free with her brother's seal. Eleanor was a daring and intelligent woman and a quick learner, but when she rewrote the dispatches Percy had prepared for Edward of York, she did not grasp the importance of credibility; she did not anticipate how closely the information would be inspected.

York had other sources against which to check her fabrications, of course. Perhaps it was clumsy of her not to warn him of certain obvious dangers, and she erred in focusing, in perplexing detail, on the daring and imaginary exploits of Robert Clifford, with whom, alas, York was not unduly concerned. But when Robert's brother Triston was invited to review the sheaf of letters, and dismissed much of its baffling contents, York's confidence in Percy's judgment was severely dented, and Eleanor had muddled through to an imperfect success.

* * *

Clifford was brooding not only on the estrangement from his eldest, but on the loss of Eleanor also; a loss which had been forced upon him, quite against his will. The three of them: they could not live together and, wounded though he was, he would not turn his son away. He pictured the woman, too often: the blue-grey eyes and beautiful hands, the particular way she walked; that assured and elegant sweep of her gown.

"I should have had her," he announced, as Loic trooped doggedly towards sleep. They were approaching London; they were approaching Edward of York: rest was crucial.

"Who, Monseigneur?"

"Eleanor Percy, of course."

Loic lurched on to his back. "You said there was nothing to be gained from rolling the lady under a hedge. I distinctly remember it."

"With my luck, that was all I was ever likely to get. You should have known that, you mawk. You should have pointed it out. She was so hot for me, and now I've nothing."

"I thought it was the Lady Alice on whom all your desires were fixed?" muttered the chamberlain.

"I haven't had her either."

Loic clicked his tongue audibly.

"How old is Exeter's daughter?" An abrupt change of tone. "Ah – you wouldn't know, of course. The Duke has a daughter, raised in England: his only child; his heiress. I wonder if he has a husband in mind for her. Fetch Castor."

Poor Arthur stalked in some moments later, eyes crumpled against the light. Clifford waved him on to the bed.

"How old is Exeter's daughter?"

"What? The Duke of Exeter's daughter? Er – let me see. Somewhere between fifteen and twenty years, Lord Robert. May I ask why? I understood…"

"I'm thirty-four years old, with no heir. I must wed, of course. Of all the noblemen in England, I'm the most worthy. Wouldn't you agree, Arthur?"

"Oh no, Lord Robert. I wouldn't say that. Certainly not. The Earl of Northumberland: he's unmarried, is he not? The Earl of Lincoln – the Duke of Suffolk's heir – I don't believe he's married. The Duke of Somerset's brother: he's unmarried. Thomas, Earl of Arundel: he's a widower. Jasper Tudor, Earl of Pembroke; he's King Henry's half-brother and he's not married either. That's five earls I've counted, without even putting my mind to it."

Clifford grunted. "All right. If I were Exeter, though, I'd prefer to marry the girl to me; I stand well with Warwick. I'm the finest soldier in the land. Exeter and I go back a long way. I expect he will, if I ask him. You may go now, Arthur."

"And you're the biggest. And you've the best singing voice, Lord Robert," murmured Castor, bowing. "Also a help, no doubt."

Loic laughed quietly.

"I heard that, Arthur. *Arthur*!" Castor turned in the doorway. " I've decided not to wed Lady Eleanor. Ah – we had a disagreement of sorts. I don't want her name mentioned again among the household."

Castor raised his brows, tilting his enquiry towards Loic.

"I may well marry the Duke of Exeter's daughter. I shall sound him out. What's her name?"

Castor was still digesting the interesting morsel; their news came so rarely from the horse's mouth. "Er – it's irrelevant, Lord Robert. The girl's married already. To Edward of York's stepson."

* * *

Devon rode straight from London towards his manor of Tiverton in the West Country; Somerset made sure of that. The man had been pestering Edmond to accompany him into his lands, trusting that the Beaufort name would work some spell upon the recalcitrant gentry. Edmond made only vague assenting noises, which Devon heard as promises. So the Earl was taken aback when his leader made a break for freedom as they moved west, pleading – an absurd excuse – Sir Gabriel Appledore's desperation to see his betrothed. Devon rode on, disappointed and cross.

Again, there was no forewarning when the large and resplendent party shattered the Abbey's serenity. If Edmond's manner was chilly as he left for London, it was frigid now. When Alice and her gentlewomen were ordered to retire at once to their quarters, the Duchess was struck with a sense of foreboding, anticipating news of another clash between Edmond and Lord Clifford, whose whereabouts were a mystery to her. Her fear grew towards dread when Lady Ullerton was summoned, alone, to the Duke. Silent and composed, the gentlewoman swept from the chamber.

Before the door fell to, Alice glimpsed her brother-in-law, a slim silhouette against the outer arch, staring at the pale sky, hands clasped, fingertips pressed to his lips. She lifted the catch, but the under-chamberlain had positioned himself on the threshold, courteous and abashed, ushering her gently backwards.

223

"Please, my lady – if you would? The Duke has asked that you remain within until he summons you."

Desperate, she discarded her dignity and called quietly for Jonkin, but when he did not appear, she turned away and the door closed.

Sir Gabriel led Lady Ullerton – in silence, and not by the hand – to a large, light-filled chamber on the upper floor where the Duke was waiting, seated and still. Bowing, Appledore backed out of the room before her eyes could entreat him to stay.

"Please be seated, Lady Ullerton. You know on which subject I wish to question you. I need hardly say that I request – require – both scrupulous honesty and utmost discretion. It is the Duchess whose conduct is at issue."

She bowed her head and folded her hands.

"Tell me, please, of the incident on the evening before my wedding."

She told him, just as she had told Sir Gabriel.

"You should have spoken out before, Lady Ullerton. That much is obvious. Why disclose this now?"

"My lord – I could never conceive that the Duchess was caught up in any wrongdoing. I was incapable of imagining it." Her tone was too prim; she had misjudged him. "It was not until we ladies overheard the quarrel in the street, those terrible, base taunts of Lord Clifford, that my eyes were opened. Then I recalled the strange events of that evening last year in Angers, and it began to seem that there was no other interpretation to put upon them."

There was a lip-licking eagerness about the woman that sparked an immediate revolt. "That is as may be. My wife is young and naive. She was pure in body when she came to me. I am sure of it. Once I've defeated Edward of York and we can look to the future, I shall protect her by allowing her to retire to the West Country while I reside at court."

Elizabeth's ace lay tranquil in her sleeve. She slid it into the light. "My lord, this matter is not so simple as you suppose. Lady Alice is already with child."

* * *

It was early in the morning, and the Wyverns were some few miles south-east of St Albans on the London road.

There was a lacklustre air amongst the men. Many of them – the senior household and the FitzCliffords – had spent the best part of the preceding night on their knees in St Albans Abbey, whether they wished it or no, praying at the cobwebbed tomb of Lord Thomas Clifford. The vigil was a trial. They'd commenced in a tidy-enough pattern, Hal beside his father, resolved to hold himself rigid – as became his position – while his mind wandered at will. The household was arrayed behind, Nield heading the men at Clifford's back, with Cuthbert Bellingham to one side, reaching to tap Hal's shoulder when he began to slump. Loic and Castor were beyond.

To the left of Hal were George and Guy, pursuing their campaign of spats and skirmishes, trying now, softly, unobtrusively, to break each other's fingers. Some while later, like puppies, the pair abruptly slept, propped precariously and shallow in their breathing. Availing himself of Castor's discreet and indulgent hands, Aymer whiled away the time in gently arranging their pliant bodies: braced together, throats and shoulders interlocking, a dovetail joint in the flesh.

Further along, Richie flinched from Bede's insistent murmuring. His twitching grew, quite apparent to those around, until they could plainly hear the exasperated whisper: "Why must you be such a donkey, Bede? I know what I'm about. He's amusing. I *want* to spend all my time with him."

Aymer's dark face pivoted slowly. In the half-light, his expression was unreadable.

Craning round the conjoined figures at his side, Hal glared down Richie – the great fool – parading his shameful enslavement. And Bede, too: neither the time nor the place for such an inquisition. Next along: Will – observant, as ever; Edwin – all exemplary concentration; Oliver and Tom, also silent, bent double, shielding their playing cards from intrusive view. Hal glanced to his right. Beside him, Robert Clifford prayed, still tranquil, still deep in remembrances of his father, despite the noise from the far end of the row: Robbie, an oversized piglet, snoring softly, unregarded.

And now, in the morning light, with some of the more seasoned men napping in the saddle, those who hadn't learned the trick were turning fractious or aggrieved. Hal slowed until he divided Castor from Nield. "I've no experience of soldiery, gentlemen, but I thought we'd aim to be well-rested. It seems rash to be heading into combat so weary as we now are."

Castor gave an involuntary yawn. "We'll see no fighting today. And if we all join your grandfather in the grave tomorrow, you may sleep as long as you will."

"Cheerful thought," commented Nield, briefly opening an eye. "You'll slumber soundly tonight, Master Hal, and that's what matters."

Hal glanced at his father, jesting with Bertrand Jansen. The man was in a lively humour, last night's antics going unremarked.

"Yes, he's in fine fettle," whispered Castor. "For when he believes he's kneeling at prayer, he's usually wedged upright, dozing. It's Sir Cuthbert's job to rescue everyone else, lamenting the strain on his ancient bones."

"Master Hal, do you know what caused the breach between Lord Robert and Lady Eleanor?" Patrick Nield had opened both eyes. "Arthur here hadn't the guts to ask him."

Castor clicked his tongue. "We were speaking of something else – it wasn't convenient. Besides, I assumed Loic would prove as leaky as ever – but not this time."

Hal felt as though he'd run, full-tilt, into a wall. A horrifying possibility opened before him: could Eleanor have told Robert Clifford of the lewd demands his son had made upon her? Surely not. No confession was less likely. Which didn't explain why his father was sending him such black looks. Hal rode on, frowning his disquiet. If only Loic had warmed to him – if he had discovered the key to the fellow – he might have learned the truth.

"Well, Master Hal?"

"Sorry, Sir Patrick. I've no idea."

"Not so quick to share your own thoughts as you are to delve into others', eh?" Castor's tone was grating, and silence fell.

York's force was massing in London. Such was the news coming north – but not massing with any great urgency and not expected to set out in the next hours. They might possibly see no fighting tomorrow either, or the next day, perhaps, if the enemy dawdled on at this rate.

Eventually the cavalcade reached a fork, the right-hand road bearing south to the village of Barnet, the left, to a swathe of open land. They halted at the junction.

"Left, then, my lord" said their gruff local guide. "Left here to Gladmore Heath. That's where you'll find the noblemen for Lancaster drawn up already with a vast crowd of their men. I'll part with you here, by your leave."

"How far is Barnet?" asked Clifford, motioning Walter Grey to open his purse.

"Down that lane, my lord; a few minutes' ride."

"Excellent," said Clifford, and they all turned right.

"Large, is it? This village?" Loic wondered as they approached.

"Not large, I'd say. But large enough for you, my friends." Bellingham had comfortable faith in the foraging skills of Nield and Moncler.

They ambled along. Woodsmoke wafted idly above Barnet village, but beneath the smoke, a tell-tale smudge of dark dust. With one accord, the men at the head of the column slackened their pace. By now, there was heard some distant shouting.

"York?" cried Clifford, hand aloft. "York!"

They'd already wheeled about, uncertain, when a thunder of hooves produced a heart-stopping moment. The band of riders surging from the village were flaunting the Ragged Staff of Warwick, but a brief distance to the rear of Warwick's men came another force, streaming out of the hamlet, pursuing.

Catching sight of the Wyvern standard, Warwick's party swept them up in their flight for the Earl's camp. York's own harbingers were now very close behind, and with the worst possible timing, Robbie's horse stumbled in a rut, and the boy lost his uncertain seat. By a measure of dumb luck, he had Richie close on one side and Bede to the other, each of whom shot out an instinctive arm to steady him, sharing a brief, shaky laugh as the pursuers began to falter and fall away. And then Richie dropped his gaze, evading Bede's eyes.

The Wyverns straggled on to the swarming heath, thwarted, dishevelled and panting, fronted by a sweating Lord Clifford, staring straight ahead between his horse's ears. In his mind's eye, he'd swaggered into camp – late and conspicuous, as was his custom – laden with his necessaries, drawing looks and whispers: admiration, apprehension or envy. But not like this. Now his men hastened past a forest of pennons bearing the Star of Oxford, seeking Exeter's retinue, and pitched camp with tetchy efficiency.

Clifford, at least, had a warm reception, borne away to Warwick's vast and magnificent pavilion, all crimson and gold, to find Exeter, Beaumont and Jack de Vere already at hand. And John Neville, also, awaiting his presence. Between Clifford and Warwick's brother there roiled a vast ocean of blood. He'd a very wary welcome, returned with matching enthusiasm. Then the two men traded no further words, though Neville's gaze was tethered to Clifford's face.

The nobles were lounging at the campaign table or craning sideways at a plan pinned beneath Warwick's elbow. Now the company was complete, conversation turned to the dispositions in the coming encounter.

John Neville took the centre division. Steely and reserved, battled-hardened, Neville's record on the field easily outmatched that of any man present. He lounged back with a slight smirk, as if waiting for Clifford to object. He didn't object. When Warwick asked Clifford and Exeter to share the left wing, Jack drummed his testy hands on the table, awaiting another outburst that didn't come. Clifford had promised to fight under Warwick's command; he would keep that promise.

Completing the divisions: William Beaumont and Jack de Vere on the right wing. Warwick would take the rearguard; the better, thought Clifford, to flee the field if necessary. The man was an audacious statesman; rather a jumpy soldier. "My friend, you must join the rest of us, attacking on foot this time. Not your usual practice, but if you won't fight among them, the men lose heart."

John Neville couldn't resist a curt nod at that, and Beaumont smiled into his sleeve.

In mild tones Warwick responded. "My thoughts exactly, Robert. I'll be in close attendance, ready to come forward wherever needed."

Clifford looked round at the others. Jack had waged no more than the odd skirmish, as far as he knew. Untried...but tall, charismatic; imposing in the training yard at Angers; he'd probably do well, if he could only calm himself a little. Beaumont, of gentle, slightly hapless appearance, was a dogged soldier, holding his own beside Clifford at Towton, and probably elsewhere, though by now all Clifford's defeats were starting to merge into each other. Exeter, he'd soldiered with many a time; gangling and awkward to watch, but a sounder leader than one might have expected. John Neville was formidable; only a fool would deny it. They would do well tomorrow, he thought. They should do well.

Exeter pushed back from the table; it was time to pray. The others rose also. Clifford wondered if it were worth sounding the Duke on the subject of his daughter – he still didn't know her name – just so the man would know he was in the market. If her husband fell in action tomorrow, there could be a sudden charge for the woman.

While he paused, Warwick spoke in his ear. "A word, Robert, before you go."

John Neville hesitated, and Warwick pinched his brother's sleeve, keeping him back. Clifford sat down and Warwick at once slumped over on one elbow, as though standing had pained him. His face was sunken. The man had been masking some private grief.

"Something unendurable has happened."

Clifford's mind raced.

"King Louis has signed a truce with Duke Charles of Burgundy."

His first response was a rather inappropriate relief; that it wasn't something worse, something truly unendurable. "Ah – a great pity, my friend, but not, in fact, so very unexpected." But then the significance started to seep in. His estates: mismanaged for a decade, now inadequate to support him; he badly needed that French pension. Recent extravagances pressed upon him: a fashionable wardrobe furnished on King Louis' credit: ornate chains; silk hose; velvet doublets, scandalously brief. Likewise for his boys; ah – his poor, provincial hobbledehoys: all round-toed boots and shapeless, dun-coloured gowns. And not just their new garb; kitting them out with decent armour and weaponry had cost an arm and a leg. He'd even started paying his men. The creditors would jostle in, now. A rich wife was suddenly an urgent necessity. He closed his good eye. And then the consequences flowed on: those lands of Flanders which should have freed him from his new companions: gone. He was stuck with the Earl of Warwick.

He tapped his teeth and turned, as Warwick pushed himself up, breathing like one wounded. Clifford grasped the man's wrist – and did all he could do. "For now, you'll content yourself as the most powerful man in England, Cousin – and in due course, father-in-law to the King. Don't brood on this; don't respond to the King of France until we've beaten that whoreson of York; King Louis will fall out with Duke Charles soon enough, and everything will right itself."

He squeezed Warwick's shoulder, bowed punctiliously to John Neville and left them, before the bitter disappointment could betray him.

Warwick's brother watched him go. "You may be seduced, but that man's an arrant troublemaker, short-sighted, stupid, and a poor leader of men." Neville had raised a staying hand. "I know! You say he's steadied. The North's not ringing with ugly rumours like the old days, but I will never trust him. And, perhaps, you don't either, or you'd have confessed that you've already dispatched that recklessly offensive letter to Louis of France, and burned all our bridges."

* * *

Early in the confrontation, the lady's natural humility had flown. Alice interrupted her husband with angry contempt. "I did not *conceal* this child from you, my lord! What an absurd idea! I wonder who can have put it into your head." She paused and tried to thaw the ice in her voice. "I hope and trust that I am with child. But it is early days – some few months before I might feel it quicken – and I did not want to raise false hopes. It was wholly wrong of Lady Ullerton to take it upon herself to tell you. I'm minded to dismiss her. She is becoming pernicious."

"No. It is Mistress Carbery who will be dismissed. I've learned that the gentlewoman is more concerned with gratifying her own desires than guarding your virtue. She has misbehaved herself with Lord Clifford's chamberlain, that lewd and tricksy Frenchman. We have very probably harboured a spy in our midst."

The back of her hand was over her lips. Not her beloved Blanche; she could not survive without Blanche.

"Lady Ullerton will keep close attendance until the babe comes. Once this child is born – believe me – I will know its father at a glance."

She was crying freely. "Edmond! These words belong in a fable, not real life. Your wits are fevered! You are the father, of course – I have never betrayed you."

There was no hint, now, of the *light* voice; his tones were rough with rage, the words splintering through his teeth, and he'd seized her by the arms. She sensed that he was but a moment from shaking her.

"Woman, I know where you were on the night before our wedding, and with whom; in the dark; upon the bed."

"Upon the bed?" She shook her head, the scene all too clear: Lord Clifford lounging in the shadows, taunting her with his presence. She breathed and held her husband's eyes. "Edmond – that night, he had surprised me when I was answering the call of nature. Lord Clifford jeered at me, for I had not returned his ring. I went to fetch it, and gave it to him; that is all. How could you believe there was more? Was I not a maiden when I came to you? You know it."

It was not clear that he was listening or hearing. He pushed her towards the door, not roughly now, but resolutely.

As she stumbled blindly across the threshold, Jonkin was there to enfold her in his arms. When he had tried his helpless sympathy on her, his futile pledges, he led her back to the women's chamber where another dramatic scene was, apparently, in the act of closing. As they entered, Elizabeth Ullerton was standing opposite the door, presenting her rigid back to the room, while Blanche hovered close beside the Countess of Devon, sorting coloured flax for the lady with fierce absorption.

231

"Lady Alice!" Laura hailed her, loud and self-conscious. "I regret to inform you that Lady Ullerton has not been displaying the good sense or proper deference one might expect in the presence of her betters. I shall be forced to bring her lapse to the Duke's attention, and that of his steward. Meanwhile, we hear that Mistress Carbery has been unfortunate enough to lose her place in your household. But I, at least, value her judgment and humility, and I've offered her a place in my own. As long as you and I keep each other company, she'll comfort and serve you as ever she did."

And then the tears coursed forth, and Laura and her dear ones came to her.

* * *

Weighted by the mustering woes, Clifford found he couldn't face Exeter at that moment and trudged on to his tent in the gathering gloom, lowering himself wearily to the pallet, napping with an arm thrown over his face as the men bustled around him. He was wakened by a commotion: York's army was, at last, approaching through Barnet village. By now it was near full dark and a fine drizzle dampened the air and the spirits. The flames of the campfires cowered. Soon they could hear the distant trudge of York's army – though the enemy was all but tiptoeing – and when the foe pitched camp it was in whispering darkness.

Beneath stuttering torches, escorted by a number of his gentlemen, Clifford strode back to Warwick's pavilion, where he found the master-gunners taking orders. John Neville lounged, sipping wine, his ankles crossed, considering Clifford once more.

"We're about to open fire, Robert," said Warwick. "We'll unsettle them from the start. Tell your men to gird themselves ready for the return."

"Very well," grunted Clifford. He distrusted guns; as had his brother; as had their father – they'd never have gunners in their own force. Not that arrows had been his friend. He beckoned to Jem, who passed his open-faced sallet. Tugging on the cloth skull cap, he tipped the helmet on to his head.

"Not quite yet," said John Neville, with a dry smile. "Half an hour, perhaps, for the men to prepare. Then I'll give the signal."

Crossly, Clifford shrugged the helmet off again.

Warwick was frowning. "Is that the best you have? Here: take any one of my spares; you must wear a visor, my friend."

"Visor down, he'd be virtually blind," remarked John Neville.

"As your brother so delicately puts it," snarled Clifford to Warwick. He wanted sleep. No chance of that now; they'd spend the night in full harness.

* * *

A few hours later, and he was back.

"My teeth are aching. Why no return of fire? I'll tell you why – you're aiming at the wrong place."

"So I believe," said John Neville. "We've sent out scouts."

"And?"

"They haven't returned."

"Send more."

"They haven't returned either."

Clifford was shaking his head. "Then stop firing. Mother of God. What time are we up, again?"

"At four, Robert," said Warwick. "I want to be at it by dawn."

Clifford was growling now. "Ah – cease firing. You'll run through our shot and leave us weak."

Warwick gave him a weary smile. "We're virtually drained already."

"Then at least we might get some sleep. Mother of God."

* * *

The archers' speed was shocking. There it was, just as he'd been taught; the lengthy exchange of fire between the opposing sides, holding firm and waiting it out. But Hal had not even begun to imagine how it would feel. The tension was almost unendurable, and couldn't be shared. The armoured men were visor-down, immured within their discrete worlds, dark, muted metal, noisy breathing, slits of light, hunched against the storm. Then an arrow struck his

233

shoulder, alarming him, throwing him off balance. It skittered off his harness, followed by several more. To the side, cowering, a group of grooms, in their open helms and padded jacks, vulnerable, and they knew it, twitching. Pacing among them, Robert Clifford, who chose, always, the open-faced helmet with its Wyvern finial, shouting into faces, clapping backs, bolstering his febrile men with that massive figure and that vaunting assurance.

Then, out of the mist, the gunfire. Even Clifford jumped. The noise of the barrage astounded and shattered. And it was all on the wrong side; Warwick had exhausted their shot with his vain volleys through the night. Everywhere, men cringed, and morale shuddered. Hal was braced between Tom and Edwin, teeth clenched, a hand steady on the shoulder of each boy. And then the inevitable explosion of gore and one of the grooms toppled in a loose swoop, head gone, legs writhing, blood bucking everywhere. The two youngsters, in perfect rhythm, staggered and went to their knees. With Bede's help, Hal hauled them up and shouted, like his father, into their faces, but they couldn't hear his voice and he couldn't hear his voice.

And then, before he'd registered it, the signal was somewhere given, and his father made a great gathering motion with both arms, and they began to run.

"Desormais! Desormais!" Hal found himself crying, which was fitting, but his helmet filled with hot breath and no one heeded him, so the shouting lapsed and he allowed himself to grunt at will.

Quickly into his stride, it was just – *just* – as he'd prayed: stirring, yet calmly unthinking; his mace connecting with such satisfying power, equally happy in either hand. He was a leviathan; never had he felt such potency. Nothing else came close. After a joyful while, he settled to the rapture, and began to notice more. The youngsters were making a fine showing, that relentless drilling wholly vindicated. Oliver in particular in need of no help; the composed and affable boy was brutal and spattered at their side. With George at one end and Hal at the other, the line was strung like a fishing net, snagging bodies in the mesh and dispatching them.

Behind them, the twins. Guy and Aymer would be shielding younger boys between them, as he and George were doing. But no: glancing over his shoulder, Hal saw Will and Richie abandoned to their own devices while the twins were virtually entwined, vicious and swift; moving strangely. He stared at them for a heartbeat, then dismissed them from his mind, pressing on. The household men spread out behind them, a reversal of the usual order, and further back, the levies and his father's undersized affinity, dawdling somewhat.

Lord Clifford was pushing forward, carving his path, already well ahead of the standard, disappearing and re-appearing through the mist. By now, he'd the curious combination of sword in the left hand and a splintered poleaxe in the right; flanked – martyred – by Loic and Robbie. Loic was leaping ahead, flitting heedlessly between the combatants, prancing like a goat, skittish. And Robbie, so much slower; he was slipping behind; impelled again and again by the flat of a blade on his rump – whoever was nearest.

Clifford kept shouting at Exeter's standard-bearer to spread his men left; the Wyverns were crowded at the flank, and, naturally, it was the other force who must give ground. The wretched man wouldn't look over, and Clifford tossed away the poleaxe to cup hand to mouth as he roared. Eventually, the message got through, and they had the space then to wheel some degrees over, to charge the surging oncomers – Richard of Gloucester's men.

Still Hal and George came on, panting, shepherding the others. The foe much heavier here, crossing at an oblique angle, rupturing their tight formation.

Exeter himself was now within sight, trying to sweep his men out of Clifford's way, spidery limbs flailing. Fleetingly distracted, his feet were hewn from under him, and in one horrifying instant he was gone, trampled under foot. His followers stuttered to a halt and the men at their back rushed into them, tumbling a few to the ground. George and Hal faltered together. Another outburst of commotion, and Hal spun as Exeter's dazed standard-bearer was dragged bodily by Arthur Castor and the twins into the Wyverns' knot of men, and then Exeter's force steadied and rallied and they all went forward again, much slower.

Clifford ran on, leading no one, knocking men down, unchecked, losing his fellows, summoned by the heart-stopping sight of his chamberlain cut off and slashing wildly amidst a press of Gloucester's men. The cousins ploughed forward bearing Robbie, the other youngsters falling behind with the twins. Clifford had smashed his way into the mob before their approach, all his impulse bent on Loic, one protective arm thrown out, the other carelessly hammering and hacking; Robbie, in a rare moment of agility, skipping just as the heedless sword swung low: it would have taken him off at the knees. Clifford seized his man from the reach of the assailants and dragged him close. With slow wonder, Loic raised his visor, gazing into the face of his champion: Patroclus to Robert's Achilles. Robert slammed it shut.

Spent, they had fallen back awhile – panting, some doubled over, some vomiting, some shouting, deafened, heads close – as fresher men took up the assault, contenting themselves with sporadic swipes at foemen streaming through the foremost ranks. Light was broken now, the mist hindering vision. The ground was a treacherous mess. Then they began again; rested again; began again.

Hal had no idea how long they'd been at it. It was broad day, and he was desperately thirsty, the elation fading. The fog was heavy still, and drifting, concealing much of the field, carrying puffs of ferocious stench. It barely occurred to wonder who was winning. But either their line had twisted by a quarter turn, or Gloucester's had wheeled again, for the enemy was now coming fully side-on and they began to be swept up in the press. Exeter's standard had finally fallen. Still the Wyverns struggled on.

And then, just as Hal was trembling with exhaustion in every limb, of a sudden Robert Clifford wheeled before them, face to livid face, sending them backwards with both palms, bellowing to turn about and make for the horses. Bewildered, the boys obeyed unquestioningly, though the reverse was frighteningly abrupt. But Clifford's instincts were much the keener, for his men had only just cleared their wing when it broke completely, and the carnage began in earnest.

* * *

Through a blend of expedient illness and pragmatic shifts of allegiance, Hugh Dacre had contrived to avoid every one of the great battles that had rent the country since his youth. His luck had run out. Here he was at Barnet, hemmed in the rearguard, the safest place to be, keeping a keen distance from that conspicuous target, the Earl of Warwick.

To Dacre's inexpert eyes, the battle looked like it was going well for them until it stopped going well and started going very badly indeed. Something truly bizarre was happening out on the right wing. Though the field was partly obscured by the drifting mist, it looked like Jack de Vere's men had driven through the enemy's vanguard and circled back to attack their own allies in John Neville's division. About him on all sides was the Star badge of de Vere, just where it shouldn't be. Warwick's rearguard charged forward and collided with the ebbing centre. Dacre watched, open-mouthed, as Warwick's brother was cut down just fifty feet off, and the line immediately started to break up. He'd known John Neville all his life. Stunned and queasy, Dacre was wrenched from his stupor by the sight of York's men flooding towards him in number, hacking at Neville's fleeing force. With his few attendants, he clanked around and made a break to retrieve the horses. They reached the baggage park only just ahead of York's men.

It was better once Dacre was mounted, well above the heads of the rabble. A footsoldier came in to slash his thigh. He kicked the man in the mouth and watched him reel away. He kicked another in the back of the head and trampled him as he fell; one of their own, in fact, but no one saw. Everywhere there were parts of men, and men missing parts, and the all-pervading stench of shit. It was all more horrific and confused than he could possibly have dreamed. Then a knot of York's men closed in on him. Dacre swung his poleaxe, more in warning than with any considered intent, and sliced off the ear of his own horse, dragging out a clump of its scalp. Blood sprayed across his helmet and now some of it was inside his visor, rust-scented and dripping. Gorge rising, he shook his head violently, moaning as the horse's knees buckled and he started to tumble headlong down its neck. The light was snuffed out.

A short time later, he came to and stumbled upright. The assailants were gone, but so too were his horse, helmet, axe and companions. He started to run awkwardly among the rest of John Neville's men, most of whom were less encumbered with armour and easily outpacing him. A little later the cry went up that Warwick had fled; now some were shouting that he'd fallen. His leader. His lord. This was beyond belief. Winded now, Dacre was running slower and slower, his dagger bouncing in his hand, but he was somewhat sheltered by trees and the thinning mist, and the pursuers seemed to be heading at a tangent.

Sir Hugh tried to think and run and keep a sharp look out, all at once – taxing, when his head throbbed so much. At all costs he must accomplish his surrender before flight into exile became the only option. He had no money, no lord and no belly to continue down the appalling path of treason. Somehow he must throw himself on the mercy of King Edward before he was picked off by one of the marauding men-at-arms. He jogged on wearily towards, he hoped, York's camp, a stitch in his side, lamenting to himself as he went.

"Where do you think you're going, Dacre?"

The voice behind was distantly familiar: arrogant and very deep. With a sinking heart he turned. There, towering above him like a fiend, was Robert Clifford and, off to the side, that little shit, Loic Moncler.

Just when he thought it couldn't go any worse. "Oh Jesu, *Jesu...*" was coming out of his mouth.

"Let's find Sir Hugh a horse, Rawn. Quick, now."

Clifford stared down on Dacre from his gigantic mount. The little groom soon returned with a horse that was somewhat the worse for wear, blood congealed in a long streak below a missing ear. Sir Hugh looked away. The horse caught his scent, snorted and shied, but eventually two grooms held it still and trembling long enough for Dacre to clamber up. One of the men passed him an archer's helmet and an elderly sword.

When he raised his head to survey the unwelcome rescue party, Sir Hugh realised he was still concussed. Now there appeared before him a dozen of Clifford, a ghastly hallucination. He swayed his head back and forth, tentatively and then more vehemently. They were still there. But on closer inspection, the replicas were younger, and fully-sighted. Moncler was watching him, a malicious gleam in his eye. *Jesu, they must all be Clifford's spawn. Jesu. How frightful.*

* * *

With one accord, the company wheeled and rode on, mired in their own thoughts, until they'd put some miles of safety between themselves and the field of carnage.

As they steadied, a querulous Nield was interrogating Lord Robert, as was his habit; as though each engagement they suffered through were entertainment for his diversion, and he expected his money back.

"I can't be sure, Patrick. I can't be sure what went wrong *this time.*" Clifford had no very great urge to defend himself. He was used to leading his men to defeat; it felt normal. "Who was commanding York's vanguard? That soak Hastings? Whoever it was, Jack's men broke through their line early on, probably beyond the field for a while. The divisions weren't even aligned to begin with; I couldn't straighten our wing to face Richard of Gloucester head on, and by then, the whole field had spun." He motioned in a circle. "If Jack de Vere brought his men back in at that point, through the mist, he would have hit John Neville in our centre, thinking he was attacking York. That's quite enough to cause a rout."

"There was plenty of shouting about treason," suggested Findern.

"When is there ever not? Men always suspect treason where there is only incompetence. You know that, Walter. Jack de Vere honoured Warwick as a father. I'm certain he never intended…"

Nield was examining his gauntlets.

"You're thinking that God does not look favourably on our cause, Patrick? Or on me, perhaps?" he added heavily.

"Hard to say, Lord Robert. His ways are mysterious. Who knows what the future may hold? Sir Reginald will unravel it for us."

So the voluble Nield would not share his thoughts. That was ominous. At least Jack de Vere was alive, Clifford was sure of it. With William Beaumont, he'd been sighted by many folk fleeing northeast, heading into East Anglia

239

with a small retinue. But wrathful and thwarted as Clifford was, it made no sense to pursue de Vere blindly about the country in the hope of catching up with him. Jack would lie low, no doubt, and await the Queen.

His thoughts turned to Exeter. The Duke had been loping nearby on long, raw-boned legs, swinging at the foe in that awkward, erratic way of his. One moment, there he was; the next, he was gone: fallen, dispatched with daggers. There was a numb feeling of surprise; he'd known Exeter all his life, for all that the man was hard to love.

John Neville, though, he'd never tried to love. He'd borne arms against that lord many a time. Pecking at other men's lands like a magpie. No loss there.

And Warwick…Clifford rode on with his thoughts.

* * *

The cavalcade was at sixes and sevens; George leading, with Hal close beside, wordless for now. They could not part, not yet, nor return to accustomed roles, the ordeal dragging on their minds like a sea anchor, heavy and silent. Later, the inquisition would begin, and then it would be hard to draw breath.

Lord Clifford was behind with Cuthbert Bellingham and the household. The men were unusually gentle with their fellows just now; grave and peaceable.

Further down the column, though, irreverent talk struck up, untimely and jarring. The fresh horrors of the field had slid off the pitiless carapace and Aymer's vindictive tones, soft as they were, carried to the rider at his back.

"Brothers – we have witnessed the perfect rescue. Like something from the tales of King Arthur, let's say: the Shouty Knight and his delicate maiden. I was moved."

"It was, truly, an inspiring sight, and beautiful to witness." Guy's voice, always husky, and now the note was exaggerated, in a mockery of passion.

"Beautiful indeed. I was blinded by tears," agreed Richie. "Dangerous for me, but not near so dangerous as stranding oneself in the midst of all those men, if you've no fucking clue which end of a sword is which."

240

"Oh, the maiden had a tight enough grip on her little sword, I reckon, with all those men pressing in on her body. She didn't know who to have first." Guy gave a light, dirty laugh.

Aymer glanced behind him: they had the quarry's full, quivering attention, while the hunter's pulse was cool. "And yet…I did expect our strident hero to be rewarded on risking his life to save the beloved. A kiss would have been fitting. And I thought a kiss was offered, but the Shouty Knight was too tense, perhaps. Jealous, perhaps."

Two of the Walters interrupted, oblivious, with a noisy, intensifying debate on the relative merits of crossbows and artillery.

* * *

For the second time, Clifford's son Waryn rose to assist Dorcas, Hal's forsaken drab; on this occasion, in pouring the ale.

"You're too kind, sir. So, as I say, Stepfather was well enough yesterday. In his accustomed temper, and boxed my ears just as usual. But last night – of a sudden gone from us, with an apoplexy. It was very frightening, sir. He was all I had left, sir. Now I don't know how I'll manage. There is small prospect of a husband."

Her eyes were salmon-pink. Her linen could be cleaner. The children could be much cleaner. Of a husband, there was no prospect.

"You have this little place, though." A swift look around. The cottage – it was a hovel, really – had once been well kept, when Dorcas was a sweet little thing, neatly turned-out and much too eager to please. "Your stepfather had no kin of his own, I think?"

"How will we live?" She was whispering.

Waryn rubbed his mouth, profoundly angry; not, in the main, with her.

But she added, "Worse, sir: I'm with child again."

"*Really?*" He couldn't keep the disgust from his voice, though her shrivelled eyes were brimming over. "Hal's, is it?"

"*Of course* Master Hal is the father. Why would you ask me that?" Her voice was sharp, as if succumbing in that loathsome way dignified her, and he'd failed to notice. "Oh, sir – forgive me for speaking in that tone! Please forgive me. I'm at my wits' end."

"Hush, I've already disregarded it. Now then, Dorcas. I have an idea for the better governance of your household and provision for all these infants."

She knelt at his chair, a humble, exhausted child.

* * *

"Lord Robert, we must make all haste to the West Country to await the Queen and the Prince. We'll lose the men we have raised; we cannot delay."

They had pulled up to rest awhile and refresh themselves under cover of a copse around a stream.

"No, Bell – I'll not wander blindly around the West Country until we're captured. We make towards home, pending news. Curse Somerset for his idiocy; if he had joined us, we would have destroyed York together, but, ah no, he must go his own way, and this is the result." And worse yet: his dread lest the news of Warwick's death reach the Queen before she stepped on to the ship. She might never place her foot aboard. But Clifford kept that fear to himself.

"You saw we weren't the only Wyverns on the field today?" prompted Bellingham.

Clifford gazed at him, and realisation dawned. "Mother of God – *Triston* was there? I did not see. And a good thing, too, or my mam would have suffered another loss. Which division?"

"The centre – York's own."

"Makes sense," sneered Clifford. "Aiming high, is Triston Clifford." He shook his head, and then dismissed the turncoat from his mind. "Warwick, Bell: we shall never see his like again."

"My father used to say that of King Henry the Fifth, Lord Robert. I always resolved that I would never declare it of any man – it's what the old say, when they have done with the world."

"Nevertheless, sometimes, it's the truth. This was a rare man. I'm sorely grieved at his loss. Don't let the others jeer at him."

Clifford walked away among the men, searching for his elusive chamberlain.

"Ah – Loic," he began, face severe, voice low. The man crumpled. "You're stronger than you look, and quick on your feet. Too quick. Too far ahead, this time. Too rash." He looked on, unspeaking, and after a moment, Loic raised his stinging eyes, and tried, unobtrusively, to slip from his master's fingers.

"Your pardon, Monseigneur, please" – barely above a whisper. "I am shamed."

Clifford released him, unsmiling. "Very well. We'll say no more."

Some way behind, Sir Hugh Dacre sat dumbly astride his sorry horse, neck drooping. There were too many about him to slip off unnoticed. With a sigh, he dismounted and steeled himself to face down the devil.

"My Lord Clifford." He cleared his throat, twice, for he had no one's notice. "My Lord Clifford? I am, of course, deeply indebted to you for furnishing me with a mount after my unfortunate experience. This will be of great value in assisting me to continue my travels, but my intention was always to return to London, so if you'll excuse me, I'll be on my way."

Clifford was in a sombre mood, but Sir Hugh lightened it. "I couldn't think of parting with you, Cousin Dacre." He clapped the man on the back, causing his knees to buckle. "We shall not abandon you, nor has the chance of glory escaped: shortly you'll restore your honour fighting for your Prince – never fear."

He did fear, greatly, seeing his slim chance of redemption disappearing south. Lord Clifford was licking his lips at him like a wolf, and with an effort, Sir Hugh quelled the weary tears that threatened to unman him. "Oh – indeed. I thank you, my lord. This was all I was seeking: your reassurance that I might serve you."

Clifford smiled, which was worse than the licking, and turned away. "Findern there will give you my badge."

"Your pardon, my lord – which is Findern?" His voice was wobbling unmanageably.

The huge man paused. "Walter! A Wyvern badge for our friend here."

Walter Findern shook a small sack bulging with metalwork. "How many may I press on you, Sir Hugh? I've plenty, as you see; sparkly-new; never been worn, alas."

"Five-score should do it, Walter." Clifford smirked. "Festoon him with Wyverns."

Sir Hugh accepted a badge from the grinning Findern, and fiddled with the clasp for a moment. The emblem was cheaply made. The pin twisted and snapped in his hand. It dropped through his fingers and he trod on it, for good measure, grinding it into the dirt.

As Dacre began to edge towards the cover of the trees, Clifford seized his arm and tugged him about among the senior household. Bellingham, rangy, tanned, old, clapped him on the back in welcome, making him stagger, again; from then on, Sir Hugh kept his wary distance. The master-at-arms – a merry, overgrown child; some giant, blond Viking; a cold-eyed priest; a lot of men called Walter. Next, Patrick Nield, stocky, short – a Scot, for God's sake – but as dark as a Moor, gleaming with springy vigour, and last, the hateful Moncler, jabbering his foreign nonsense while Sir Hugh mutinied in his mind.

Finally Dacre neared the horrid throng of offspring. Clifford started to present them, but losing concentration halfway through, he named some twice and some not at all; carelessly crediting John Clifford with the majority – more than his fair share. To Dacre's surprise, the two eldest were known to him from their days in John Neville's household. That calmed him a little, and when they started off again, he was riding between the pair.

The defeat had passed George by. He prattled away. His uncle was an exceptional fellow, he assured the captive audience. If Sir Hugh had the good fortune to follow Lord Clifford into battle, the knight's respect would, like his own, deepen to ardent admiration. To pass the time, George chose to regale Sir Hugh with a full history: all the petty dullness of his life in Alnwick, but, in deference to his uncle's orders, omitting the only episode that would have interested his listener. Hal had the grace to look uncomfortable, and removed himself at that point to join his father, leaving Sir Hugh stranded with George.

Dacre was doubtless intrigued to hear that Skipton was a vast improvement on Alnwick. He learned that the boys were kept on a very free rein, George describing, in exquisite detail, their every prank and amusement. Now Dacre could hear Lord Clifford making his way through the company, scattering praise where it was due, and encouragement where it wasn't. When the nobleman reined in beside George, he was unsparing in his acclaim, ruffling the lad's hair, hailing his prize soldier; the youth soon spilling with gratified and noisy emotion. By now utterly desperate, Sir Hugh contrived to wriggle his way rearwards through the cavalcade. For a short while, he cleaved to a kindred spirit in Sir Lewis Jolly, another very glum knight, but after an hour in the man's company he was tantalised by the prospect of cutting his own throat.

At long last, Bellingham and Nield took pity and sought out Sir Hugh, soothing him with their cheerful banter; promising ample wine and a good dinner, until his eyes lost their wild look.

* * *

Clifford continued his way along the column. Confidence was essential to prowess, and as he neared Robbie, he had manacled his tongue. "You're improving in some measure, my lad." He wasn't. He seemed to have gone backward since George took him in hand. "But you cannot rely on me to protect you, and you cannot rely on weight alone against a well-trained opponent."

Robbie was nodding emphatically, his empty eyes wandering away.

Clenching the hand that itched to drive home the message, Clifford proffered the advice that aimed to save his life: "Aspire to speed, if skill is beyond you." He wheeled about and stood off, pensive. The boy was beyond help; it would be a miracle if he survived another bout.

Then he scanned the column for the twins. These two had been the veritable revelation. Somewhat flippant in the training yard, they'd excelled in the slaughter. In the past he had pitied shorter men, but in the snatches he'd seen, the twins seemed almost to hug the ground; mighty, savage, impossible to bring down.

Clifford reined in beside Will and Richie: bold boys, garnering praise and a few pointers. Turning with enthusiasm to their companions: "My fearsome, *fearsome* sons! How greatly you've impressed me! What you lack in height is more than balanced by strength and skill." His hand was upon Guy's shoulder, and the youth flushed, wine-dark. "Yet still you're fighting as one man. How will it go for the other, if one of you should fall?"

"No chance of that, Father," said Aymer airily. "Guy and I: in truth, we are the same man; two bodies, sharing one soul..."

The rebuke was on Clifford's lips when Guy interrupted: "If one body falls..."

"...the other falls with it. So St Augustine tells us, or St Paul, perhaps." And then, with a cruel smirk, Aymer added, "It must have been taxing to rescue our reckless little Sir Loic, Father, with that slack-bellied oaf dangling from your elbow. Fattie is the runt of the litter. Someone should put him out of his misery."

Clifford said nothing, askance at Aymer's heretical nonsense.

The twins exchanged glances. "Can he truly be yours, Father?" prodded Guy. "Even Edwin can fight, when he must."

"Robbie? Of course. The Clifford look never lies." Clifford made as if to turn aside.

"The Lady Joan had ever a dislike to Fattie," said the sly-grinning Aymer. "We think he is the bastard of our Uncle Roger – who's no great soldier himself."

Clifford tilted his head, amused. "The Lady Joan has a dislike to you also, child. It does not make you Roger's son."

"Only because I would not lie with her," pronounced Aymer in his quiet drawl.

"Mother of God, Aymer!" Clifford shook his head, offended all over again, and cantered away.

"He's a jealous one."

* * *

The bleak silence of Cerne Abbey was shattered, at last, by the arrival of the Queen herself. And beside the Queen: the Prince and his wife, Alice's beloved Anne. It was Queen Margaret who brought the shocking news; disastrous news: the deaths of the Earl of Warwick and John Neville and the Duke of Exeter upon the field.

The Earl of Warwick; the great, constant, North Star of her life. The shock was too great to absorb, and while Alice heaved tearless cries, she reached for his daughter. She was repelled.

For Anne was now different indeed from the eager, candid, tactless girl Alice had left in Angers. Her sanity seemed almost at issue; she was filled with animosity for everyone and everything she contemplated: the Queen and the Prince; her own mother, the Countess, who'd slipped into sanctuary on hearing the dreadful news. When Alice tried to protest, appalled, Jack de Vere was excoriated also, and Anne passed swiftly on to the Duchess Alice herself.

"Beware the Queen's wrath, Lady Alice! All the French court has been picking over your adultery with Lord Clifford, and the Queen says she'll not have you about her."

"Anne – what do you mean? What can you mean? *You* surely do not believe this of me, you who have known me so long, and loved me so well?"

It was an open target, and Anne took aim. "*Lady* Anne, if you please. Should I not believe it when you, yourself, boasted of that base, carnal embrace on the night before your wedding? I trust you've confessed all to your husband, begging his forgiveness? I see from your face that you have not."

Alice's horrified stammering had become quite incoherent. She fled to her chamber, retreating from the hate-filled voice, and when Edmond returned to the Abbey that evening to greet his Queen, he found his wife still hiding.

Queen Margaret dragged in her wake a somewhat unwilling recruit: Lord Wenlock, long-time adherent of the Earl of Warwick and friend to Sir Hugh Dacre. Wenlock, too, had learned of the Earl's death only that morning. He was still groggy.

Somerset and Devon gave this old turncoat a most chilly welcome.

"Madam," began Devon, once he and the Duke were closeted with the Queen. "Let us kick Wenlock from our force. With Warwick dead we needn't keep up the pretence."

Sighing, the Queen turned to Edmond, trusting that his sense, at least, had not deserted him.

"Your Grace, we should certainly keep Lord Wenlock beside us. He's a well-worn soldier. Without him, there is none of sufficient stature to lead the third division. Your pardon, my lord." He bowed to the Queen's son, whose arms were folded. "Untried as you are, you must, I feel, have support."

The Queen nodded. "You have done well, my lords, in the raising of men, but where are the nobles who should have joined us? We shall summon Lord Clifford – who must, by now, have returned to Skipton – though we cannot be sure he'll reach us in time..." Jonkin looked up sharply, but the Queen passed on. "And where is Jack de Vere? Where is Lord Beaumont? It's said they've not been seen since the engagement at Barnet. Where is the Earl of Shrewsbury? Unreliable as ever. At least Lord Wenlock cannot defect."

Devon laughed. "Clifford cannot defect either, Madam. Oh, York would be delighted to see him, no doubt; he'd not long survive that welcoming embrace. I'll write to him myself; I know he'll join us before long."

* * *

Eleanor Percy heard out the tidings of battle, hand hard against her ribs. Her colour drained and her lungs rebelled against the rush of air as her brother helped her to a chair before the window.

"An indecisive outcome; long may it continue! The Neville brothers slain: the best news I had in years; and their lap-dogs – de Vere, Beaumont, Clifford – in free flight. Queen Margaret joining Edmond of Somerset in the West Country – well received, so I hear. We're nicely placed, sister. The true danger is passed. Whichever side gains the final victory, at last, thank God, the Percys are secure."

Robert! She yearned for him with all her will; bent all her mind to reach him – wherever he may be. He *must* sense it. If he would only come for her. If only. She would follow him to the last; to the utmost bounds of the darksome earth: penniless, adrift and barefoot.

* * *

Over the next days, Hugh Dacre adjusted to his predicament – half retainer, half hostage. This company of men, though few in number, was not so very different from Warwick's household; he could live among them, now that he had sorted the wheat from the chaff. Bellingham and Patrick Nield were good fellows, and some of the others – Castor, Findern and one of the other Walters – were agreeable company. Lord Clifford, though, he could not stomach; the man had a strong whiff of sulphur about him, as though he'd sold his soul.

Riding with Sir Cuthbert Bellingham, Dacre riddled the man, hoping to winkle out a fellow-sufferer. He was doomed to disappointment.

"You don't want to believe all you hear, Sir Hugh; Lord Robert savours that wicked reputation, you see, otherwise he'd set the story straight. There were others about him, in the old days, whose sins he has shouldered."

Robert Clifford, Christ-like: an image preposterously implausible. Dacre frowned away, across the easy-sloping hills coming on to full green. Bellingham was either disingenuous, or desperately naive.

Sir Cuthbert ambled on. "A man most easy to love. Open-handed. Open-hearted." He waved an expansive hand. "And, of course, a matchless soldier." Then Dacre endured another paean on Robert Clifford's skill at slaying people.

"But that appalling clan of his? he assayed, hopefully. "With the ridiculous name: those Dumbfoundlings?"

Bellingham had caught his breath, and startled Dacre with a bellow of laughter. "Oh, Sir Hugh! *Dumbfoundlings*? The *FitzCliffords*, Lord Robert named them. *Dumbfoundlings*! Wonderful!"

"It wasn't I who coined the tag! Your chaplain…Sir Reginald, is it? He doesn't seem to like them either."

Bellingham was wiping his eyes.

Sir Hugh came at last to the wellspring of animus. "But, sir, it cannot please you to dwell alongside a pert little French fellow who gives himself such intolerable airs?"

"Sir Loic?" Bellingham beamed. "Not hard to fathom what you have against him, Sir Hugh! He's been meddling with Blanche Carbery and you hoped to meddle there yourself, did you not? She's had her head turned by our pretty boy!"

"Not at all," said Sir Hugh crossly. "There is an understanding between us. Promises…"

"Not on her side, apparently! Loic made free use of the gentlewoman in Bruges, my friend. You've lost your down-payment there!"

Dacre was muttering furiously to himself, of which only snatches were audible: "…filthy little arsehole…dirty foreign paws on her…"

"Calm yourself, Sir Hugh," exclaimed Bellingham, a little contrite. "I don't believe my friend planned to displace you permanently. Loic Moncler worships only one creature in this world, and it is not Mistress Carbery. Do not think so hardly of him. Sir Loic is one of the cleverest men I know and more noble-born than Lord Robert himself, as well as being rather a charming little foreign arsehole."

"I suppose he's a famous warrior, also?" sneered Dacre.

"Not a bit of it. Entirely hopeless." Sir Cuthbert was smiling broadly. "We all keep an eye on the fellow. A danger to himself and all around him."

They seemed intent on owning him, these men: with every badge he mislaid, a new wyvern found its way about his person. And there was more chaff than wheat: Lord Clifford, and his man Moncler; the alarming chaplain; Leonard Tailboys, whom rumour credited with the most repulsive of practices, and, of course, all of the Dumbfoundlings, excepting only Hal, perhaps – a decent-enough fellow despite his chilling appearance, and oddly unappreciated by his father.

But then Dacre could make neither head nor tail of it: that a man who murdered his brother's heir should treat his other nephews – those he hadn't killed – exactly as he treated his sons; quite indistinguishable, and often muddled. Not that he acted the father in any case; chastising only when irritated beyond indolence, and so, of course, they ran amok; a large portion of the party resembling nothing so much as a mobile, aggressive orphanage.

* * *

With the Queen's arrival, Alice was, at least, at last, released from captivity. Belying Anne's threat, Queen Margaret would not countenance the Duchess of Somerset or the Countess of Devon remaining at the Abbey. Shortly the entire party moved out, recruiting as they went. Laura was made most welcome among the Queen's small retinue, Devon's evident aversion only working in the lady's favour. On the subject of Alice, Edmond had just begun his wretched tale, when Queen Margaret cut him short.

"We have heard it all at King Louis's court. Does it not occur to you, my dear Edmond, that this, and worse, was whispered of your Queen in times past? Your own father it was, in point of fact, to whom the world ascribed the siring of Prince Edward."

Edmond flushed hotly, but she was not inclined to softness, and continued, with what was almost a sneer. "Do *you* believe the Prince to be your brother, my lord? No? No? Then no more would we believe that the Duchess's child was fathered by Robert Clifford. Open your eyes."

"Madam," said he, stiffly. "Your pardon, but it is not the same. No sane man would believe such evil of you. In my wife's case, though, I have heard and seen the way he sings to her, looks at her, pursues her. Now I learn that he followed her within the bedchamber the night before I married her…"

"Listen to yourself, my lord! Your complaints should be against him, not your poor little wife. Robert Clifford is a great and loyal warrior in our cause – that much should, in fairness, be said of him – but he is also a thoroughly wicked man, with morals to make Satan blush. Fortunate for you – captive at Calais when he was wreaking his worst on those wretched towns; you were spared the dilemma we faced in witnessing it. Believe us: your wife would never permit such a man to approach her."

Edmond had forgotten Jonkin's presence and, turning, he was disconcerted by his brother's steady gaze.

* * *

Percy was playing the long game; his favoured game. He'd while away entire days at chess, if he could. His sister was not the preferred partner; always Eleanor would begin with a beady enthusiasm, turn reckless and end with martyrdom. Their play had taken just such a downward course when the page entered.

"Sir Simon Loys sends word that he's an hour from Alnwick, my lord. He begs an audience, if you have the leisure."

"Up. Up, Kit. Hop off, then. Await your father at the gate, and tell him to come to me when he's rested. Let Master Waryn prepare a guestchamber."

Eleanor paused as the little feet pattered away. The boy's father had materialised in her mind, briefly ousting its customary occupant. "He cannot take no for an answer, that one. I'd rather wed any of the others. Any one of them! Not that I would, of course. Wed any of them."

"Of course not! But marriage will be the last thing on Simon Loys's mind just at present. He's come to discover my plans. If he'd join my affinity, I'd offer him a place on my council. Yes, Eleanor – I should welcome him. As a councillor, mind, not as a brother-in-law. Clever as a rat."

"A man who murdered his first wife?"

"Not so, Eleanor. Loys was studying overseas when his first wife died. He was telling me of his travels the last time I saw him."

"Second wife, then. Poison. And they say he practises sorcery."

Percy shrugged. "Then he should probably practise harder."

"If Loys stays, I dine in my chamber. I'm in no mood for his insolence."

"Again – you are not his object."

By evening, the low rays of sun picked out the two men alone in Percy's day room, examining a sword fresh out of Milan, a commission of the Earl's design – pristine and beautiful and destined to remain so.

"You've come to ask my advice, Simon?" It was Percy's little joke; Loys was the elder by a decade, a man who'd never doubted his own mind.

"I've come to discover your plans, my lord, if you'll share them." Loys raised the sword on his upstretched palm, weighing it. "You held back your affinity from Barnet; I can't fault your prudence there. But everything changed when Warwick fell. The cause of Lancaster is doomed." Loys's back was squarely to the Earl – that want of deference so vexing to Eleanor. He pivoted, wheeling the blade, enjoying its perfect balance, but by then Percy was settled at the table, and the point gusted the hairs at his throat. Both men caught their breath. "Your pardon! Christ."

"Or perhaps the cause of Lancaster is stronger without Warwick. It turns out they were all squabbling like cats in a sack. Take a look at this." Percy retrieved a strongbox and rifled for a copy of Hal's letter, the scrap that had wrought such inadvertent mayhem.

Skimming at first, Loys slowed over the confrontation at Charing Cross. "Who is this imbecile?" He inspected the extravagant signature. "One of Clifford's whelps? Christ." He returned the parchment. "None of the lords of Lancaster is fit for high office – not that they'll get a chance to prove it. We may know Edward of York for an idle gallivant, but he plays the king and assuredly fights like one. York never lost a battle; he won't start now."

Loys strolled to the window, lounging at his ease against the sill while Percy examined his profile, fingertips slipping to his teeth, as usual; little snippings.

Why would a man wear his hair so short? The Earl was somewhat preoccupied with hair, having so little of his own. Sir Simon's locks were a rich chestnut; neither greying nor thinned, but that close-cropped style did nothing to flatter a long nose and sneering lips. A face well-known at Alnwick, though not well-loved. Here was a man in a tight corner, thought Percy, happily; wealth sufficient for his needs but not for his wants, for while his needs were modest, his wants were prodigious – a man of untrammelled ambition. And lordless, too, since Warwick came adrift of his moorings and ran aground. This last twelvemonth was as squally and rudderless for Sir Simon as for the rest of his class. Worse, probably. And now Loys was rolling the dice again: double or quits, which was not how Percy played the game. The Earl cleared his throat. "Nevertheless, my retinue will sit tight. If you march south to join York, Simon, you'll not be wearing my badge."

"Just as you say, my lord: I shall join York, and I shan't be wearing your badge."

"Go your own way, then; prey for the poachers. We of the North should stick together. Your father knew that – a Percy man to the last. And his father before him. But you've no family feeling."

"Rather too much of it, perhaps. A month ago my brother Nick was fighting under Jack de Vere at Barnet – did you not hear? Now it falls to me to undo the damage."

* * *

The loyal army continued its trundle north to the Severn crossing to join King Henry's half-brother, Jasper Tudor, recruiting across the river in Monmouthshire. The ladies paid little heed to their direction, glad to be out in the world once more.

Edmond was bewildering: at times, acting with gentle consideration; at others, eyeing Alice with chilly suspicion. Jonkin did his best to remedy the deficit, riding beside her carriage, cleaving to her with a public show of faith. Lady Ullerton had positioned herself at the front, well away from her mistress, and as Anne was sharing the other carriage with the Queen, Alice and her brother-in-law were left to converse in peace.

"It is the babe that's so unsettled him," murmured Jonkin.

"He acts as though this child were proof of something terrible. It's proof only that I've done my duty!"

"Hush! When he sees the little imp, he'll know it as his own, never fear."

"All newborns are dark, no? He will accuse me…" Her voice soared, a tiny shriek.

"Hush! Am I not dark myself – his own blood, as I am? Our mother was dark. If he has forgot, I will call it to his mind."

Her voice was a whimper. "Oh, Jonkin. What would I do without your kindness?"

The other carriage had slowed before them and drew close to broach a mud-filled, deep-sucking ford. Alice could see Anne, seated at the rear and watching her with close attention. Losing its wheelhold, the first wagon slithered to within a few feet. Jonkin's horse reared and skittered, and he struggled briefly at the reins of the frightened animal. Leaning from the window, Anne mouthed, barely audible, but clear to see: "When shall you confess it?"

One hand was thrown forward, blindly warding off the words and then the Duchess, who had not eaten well in weeks, alarmed her brother-in-law by sinking slowly to her knees and collapsing on to the cushioned bench.

* * *

Days ago now, and three hundred miles distant, the Queen had come ashore; the Prince had gathered many to his banner, a swelling band.

As they clattered in though the great gatehouse of Skipton, the Wyverns knew nothing of this. Clifford was poised to collapse into the undemanding ease of home. Awaiting him was a summons from the Queen, peremptory and stiff in tone.

The senior men were confounded when he crumpled it, half-read, and tossed it aside.

"I'll go south alone, if I must! Jesu! No man shall assail Patrick Nield's honour."

"You'll not be alone, Patrick. You'll not be alone."

Reginald Grey rounded on them, ready with the supercilious defence. "Edmond of Somerset is a greater enemy to God than Edward of York, if you but knew it; this household should confine itself to its duties and leave the thinking to those of us gifted with greater insight." His reasoning was as inscrutable as ever and, for once, it cut no ice.

"Oh, give over, Grey!"

"We shouldn't have unsaddled the horses."

Loic took Cuthbert Bellingham aside. "I cannot lead Monseigneur, Bell. On matters of war, your guidance is preferred." Which was Loic's way of admitting that he knew his limitations. Bellingham savoured the moment, and then went to his master, asking leave to give his counsel, and Clifford was growling even before he commenced.

"How little you value my skin! The man tries to murder me and you would offer me up so he can finish the job."

"Not so, Lord Robert. I merely suggest you make all speed to the Queen's side, to the Prince, where you belong. Not one of us believes the Duke of Somerset has any hope of killing you, but you would not want men to say that you fear him. And meanwhile, he is no doubt filling the Queen's ears with *lies*."

Bellingham's mouth was set straight – absolutely straight – though Clifford knew him well enough to find the mirth buried in his gaze. "And there are others about the Queen whom you must, by now, be hungry to see."

Clifford's lip quirked up at that, and then Bellingham added, soberly, "By which I mean the Earl of Devon, of course." And they both laughed.

And that very afternoon, a letter found its way from Devon himself. The rambling missive, a muddle-headed blend of sermon, plea and falsehood, touched Clifford sincerely, containing as it did the very essence of his friend:

"I cannot pretend Somerset is sorry for his actions of that night, and I cannot pretend that I blame him, though he is tiresome to live with and tedious. You have brought this on yourself, Robert. I warned you enough times. But your place is here, with us, and if you will just be prudent, I know the Duke will forgive you, for I have encouraged him to put all the blame on his Duchess, and he fairly hates the woman now. The Queen seems very cross, and very distressed too about Warwick, though the news has cheered the rest of us nicely, and surely no one could regret the loss of Exeter!"

Clifford winced.

"I wish you will hurry south, for I have no one sensible to talk to. I had to dismiss several of my senior men for disloyalty, by which I mean they were bitching behind my back..." And so on and so on, apparently tending nowhere, but the real import was relegated to the last lines: Edward of York had moved out from London, mustering his levies, readying to strike west; to strike with force; to intercept the loyal army as it advanced towards the Severn seeking Jasper Tudor's host. Devon ended in something like a howl: "In the name of God, Robert, do not fail us in this, our final trial."

They had failed him at Barnet, with disastrous results. But Clifford had no intention of returning the favour, despite the household's flutterings. The trick of it was to time their arrival so as to emerge upon the field of battle itself. That way, he marched nowhere in Somerset's shadow and that way, he could charge in wherever he chose – the hero of the hour.

This time Clifford had no commission to array troops, and his retinue was harder to rouse even than before; a myriad specious reasons for absence. As more apologies trickled in, the boys entertained themselves in predicting the excuses, each suggestion more absurd than the last. By the time Richie was speculating on a drunken visit from the Four Horsemen of the Apocalypse,

Clifford had ordered all letters to be opened in private. The game went on, but at least he was spared the hearing of it.

When, finally, he issued his summons, a few local knights straggled in; his mother dispatched her recalcitrant men and the poor tenants had no choice. Shortly the pitiful force moved south once more.

* * *

Like many without imagination, Clifford's son Waryn enjoyed profound confidence in his own powers. He had formulated a plan to solve several problems at a stroke; it did not occur to him that others would not fall in happily.

His grandfather, Master Prynne, was not truly a difficult man – loving and indulgent, as far as his small means and lack of patience would permit. But Waryn had not ventured the idea gracefully. His grandfather rebelled at once: Hal's woman Dorcas was a trull; a little whore, and he would not have her in his house.

"She should not have done as she has, certainly, Grandfather, though she's not the first young girl to fall in this way! But Hal is older, and it's he who ruined and abandoned her. You know her to be a mild and sweet-tempered woman, and the little ones are merry boys. Having them about will keep you young – that's what everyone says, isn't it?"

"Hal is a wicked, wicked boy – I never said he wasn't. But what will folks think if a fallen girl comes here to live? They'll jeer at me, and bring up your mam Janet again."

"No more than they have jeered at me, for helping Dorcas. It is a Christian duty. We'll put her stepfather's cottage out to rent and you shall take the money to feed the little ones while she keeps house for you. It's a good arrangement."

The muttering went on for some time. Waryn omitted to mention that there was another little one on the way.

"I'll test it and see. I'll turn her out if she's light or disagreeable. Only don't you try the same trick. If you must have female company, make sure you marry, as Christian folk should."

"I shall, Grandfather, I shall. In fact I'm to be married very shortly, you'll be glad to hear. The Earl has given his blessing and the banns will be called directly."

"Eh, Waryn? What's all this? You're a sly one! Who's the girl who caught your eye?"

"She's no girl. You may know of her: Anna, the widow of Master Murrow. Anna Thwaite, she was born; sister to Sir James Thwaite of Belforth. I'm honoured she's accepted me, a gentlewoman as she is. Mistress Murrow has lately suffered a blow: she's lost her jointure through a lawsuit with Murrow's family, which, to speak plainly, is to my advantage, or she would be too far above me."

Master Prynne was standing straighter, his chest straining to fill his shapeless shirt.

"Well, now! And her brother a landed knight! This is a fine thing indeed, Waryn. How does our good Sir James welcome the news?"

"Very ill. He says he'll not speak to his sister again and he's named his eldest bastard son as heir to Belforth."

"But he was always a spite-filled, bitter fellow, even as a youngster dwelling up at the castle. Ingrate! It's a prouder marriage for the gentlewoman than for you, if James Thwaite but knew it. Your bloodline is noble and pure enough for any lady in the kingdom."

"What? An eccentric judgment, Grandfather! I'll fetch Dorcas and the boys now, shall I?"

"One day Hal should be lord of Skipton – not that he deserves it – and you should be Sir Waryn Clifford of somewhere fine, if all had their rights. I'll not hold my peace. Why should I? What did Robert Clifford ever do for me or my poor Janet that I should keep such wickedness a secret? I'm an old man; I'll speak as I choose."

Waryn gazed at Master Prynne, uncertain how to meet such peculiar assertions. "If you've riddled some confidence out of my father, I can only suggest you keep it to yourself, Grandfather. Lord Clifford would make a dangerous enemy. Let us all abide in peace."

Master Prynne had turned away and reverted to the muttering.

* * *

The loyal army paused some days in the city of Exeter, as supporters flooded in. Alice and her husband were residing with Jonkin in one of its finest houses, proudly relinquished by its owner for their use.

Now she was conscious of Anne's eyes always upon her, threatening her with that terrible, fateful confidence so impulsively shared – so recklessly blurted out – at the departure of the cavalcade to Flanders, nine long months before. Alice fluttered in her mind, around and over the secret, until her wits were tattered, until she came to wish the kiss ungiven, untaken. As she had kept the secret even from Blanche, why could she not have kept it also from Anne, who had so much less understanding? Nothing now could prevent the eventual unmasking. Alice evaded Anne where she could, but she could not, generally, evade her, and any speech between the Princess and Lady Ullerton left her faint.

At last the burden became too much for her shattered nerves. Alice sought out Jonkin and, trembling, took him into her confidence: stammering out the bare fact of the kiss on the eve of the wedding, giving him the impression of a most startling and terrifying intrusion.

If the truth had in any sense resembled the fiction, Edmond would have nothing to fear from Robert Clifford. It did not, of course, though Jonkin, unlearned in the ways of the world, did not see it. Nevertheless, the disappointment in his eyes gave her almost bodily pain.

"Oh *Alice!*" cried her brother-in-law. "All this time I have defended you, and now I learn that *I* am the dupe. Is this the sum of it, at last, or are there revelations yet to come?"

Every fibre strained to deny the truth, but even now, before Jonkin's very eyes, she was tugged away to another insistent scene: the well-worn, familiar episode in the small chamber of the house in Bruges: the overmastering scent of him; the brush of Robert's long hair against her cheek as he licked the tears from her throat; her touch at his lips, within his lips; his tongue upon her fingertips; her hand upon his breast, as his hand was upon hers. And the words of urgent desire that spilled from him, breaking the languorous spell. The words that had, in truth, saved her.

"No. Truly, Jonkin, there is nothing more. Lord Clifford has respected my person since I became a wife."

He sat then, rubbing his face with his hands. "Who shall tell my brother? Who shall bear this task? Once more, you have made a denial, only for worse to emerge. Which person shared the secret of that shameful kiss, whom you so feared that you must pre-empt the talebearer?" He answered himself, when she did not. "It is the Lady Anne, I suppose." When her desperate looks concurred, Jonkin pressed the heels of his hands to his eyes. The words were wrenched out of him: "I shall tell him."

* * *

"This is a joke. I've spent so much time ahorse this last month that I'm walking bandy-legged."

"It'll all be worth it when we get there, Aymer. We'll fight under the Prince's banner; we'll win renown; we'll have another good scrap." Even a knighthood…It was not impossible, but Richie wouldn't risk thinking it aloud.

Aymer threw him a pitying glance. "You're enjoying this, aren't you?"

Before Richie could disclaim any particular enjoyment, Guy cut in, tones dark with significance. "Oh, we've made worse journeys, you and I."

At once Richie was assailed with the habitual, querulous resentment. *Why must they talk in riddles?*

Guy had not taken his eyes from his twin. "Well-fed, well-dressed, well-mounted. Aymer…you have forgotten where we came from."

Where had they come from? They'd come from Sir Roger's snug manor, surely. Richie craned round at Will, saw a similar confusion, and was somewhat mollified.

But the portentous utterances had no effect. "I already know I'm better than any man here with a weapon in my hand. I don't need to keep proving it."

A small, mutinous noise from Guy.

"What I really wish for?" Aymer continued, "I'd like to sack a city. There seemed to be rather a lot of sacking last time round. Father did much of it, so we hear: Ludlow…Stamford…*I'd* like to slaughter children; rape nuns;

260

desecrate a church or two; I'd torture fat merchants – rob their treasure, let's say. So: riding round and round the country, very quickly? No, it doesn't excite me."

"You should go and fight the Moors, Aymer," Richie suggested. "You could do anything you fancy in Granada."

Aymer stretched his back and rolled his neck. "And the next city, I'd bugger merchants with my sword, perhaps. Rob churches; desecrate children; torture nuns. There's this device I've heard of…" he dropped his reins, the better to demonstrate "…I'll have one made."

Poor Sir Hugh, riding before them, attending with half an ear to one of Castor's yarns, revolted by all he overheard. That ghastly Aymer. Easy enough to tell the twins apart: in manner; speech and measure of evil. They were said to be identical. They weren't.

"Granada, Aymer; you could do a lot of nasty things in Granada," repeated Richie. "We all could."

Aymer sighed, restless, by now, and disenchanted. There'd been so much promise in his father. Black Clifford. The dismemberment of Rutland was the very template of egregious wickedness. "Father has gone soft. It'll be worse if we win. If we win, he'll get fat and idle, wed that Percy whore, breed hundreds of trueborn sons and we won't see a penny. Bellingham will die and Hal will be marshal. We can't have him in charge of discipline; just imagine it; imagine Hal with the marshal's staff in his sweaty grip. I'll never have lands of my own in England. If we win, I'll go to Granada, perhaps. Do a lot of nasty things, and get absolved of my sins."

"If you get absolved of your sins for killing Moors, and then you commit more sins, do you go on getting absolved for ever?" wondered Richie.

Will was shaking his head.

"Yes," said Aymer. "You do."

* * *

If Alice supposed the roof would tumble in while she waited, hunched, against the collapse, she waited in vain. Long since, her ladies had ceased to probe the awful subject, and those who loved her spoke of anything but the state of her marriage. Edmond avoided her person, as he now shunned her bed. When she saw him, he was flanked always by the loyal cohort: Humphrey Audley, little James Delves, Appledore, Chowne and the rest. Where he slept, she did not know, for they spoke as little as they could. Jonkin spent no less time with the ladies than before, though when he spoke, he now addressed himself to all of them at once, rather than Alice foremost.

"Tell me, my lord," commenced Anne on one such occasion, as they shared a hurried meal. "Has the Queen any news yet of Lord Clifford? She wrote many days ago. Is it Edward of York that he fears the more – or your brother, do you think?"

Alice was reminded forcefully of Isabeau Woudhuysen. Jonkin blushed and mumbled.

"No news, you say? How shameful. I hear Lord Clifford is to wed the Earl of Northumberland's sister. No doubt he's keeping the lady company, away in the North, far from danger; he and that other coward, Harry Percy. And what of the valiant Jack de Vere? Another truant. The Prince is not well served. He should have their heads for this."

For Jonkin, who strove always to be just, it was hard to remain silent. Alice did not attempt it.

"Lord Clifford and my brother have in the last weeks risked their lives beside your father, Madam, fighting for King Henry. Our Prince and the Queen shall reckon their service more justly than you do."

"Aha! *There* speaks the guilty voice. You're hardly an impartial observer, Lady Alice. It would be prudent to hold your tongue, no?"

Blanche and the Countess of Devon were, each of them, sending Alice furious signals. Lady Ullerton nodded sagely.

* * *

The Wyverns were not halfway to the West Country when they came upon the rumour that Edward of York had indeed struck west from Windsor and was bearing down at speed upon the loyal army. Lord Robert had badly mistimed his intervention – dragging his feet – was the general muttering, and by now even Bellingham was scathing.

"As I told him, his absence has let the Duke whisper at will in the Queen's ear, and God alone knows what she makes of their fight by now; you heard the tone of her letter."

"Worse than that, Cuthbert," said Nield. "The Queen will never forgive him if he puts the life of the Prince in danger. He can forget that dreamed-of earldom. We'll be packed off home with our tails between our legs."

Castor pouted like a giant baby. "Pride is at the root of it. He cannot abide to follow Somerset, who is, after all, only a duke of the royal house, as well as our acknowledged leader for all these last years. If we miss the combat, we'll be a laughing stock. Remember the ribbing when Norfolk arrived a day late for the battle of St Albans? Life will not be worth living."

"Gentlemen, we cannot allow ourselves to be shamed like this." Nield's voice was soft. "The Wyverns had always the greatest name for courage and daring. He must mend his ways."

* * *

The loyal army had marched out from the city of Exeter and was moving again, towards Bristol now, at gruelling speed, seeking Jasper Tudor's forces before York's army could overtake them.

All the while the army swelled. Not every man was stirred by the same ideals: when they reached the walls of Wells, the ladies were hastened away to safety at the first signs of what was to become a minor riot, the advance guard doing what levies are wont to do: misbehaving themselves freely. Alice learned that her husband had, fleetingly, lost all control of his force, then resorted to hanging to restore order. The Queen kept her composure – she'd witnessed far worse. Alice thought, again, of the sack of York's towns. Had Robert Clifford shrugged and joined in? Or did he lead the soldiery into barbarism? The man was no docile follower.

Briefly they rested, revictualled and reinforced, at Bristol, but greater troubles now pressed upon the loyal army. York's forces were advanced too close, and while Queen Margaret sent out scout after scout, still Jasper Tudor had not mustered his Welshmen sufficient to strike out from Chepstow and

263

cross the Severn. The army had now begun a headlong rush northwards to the river, for if Tudor could not come to them, they must get to him.

How terrible for the men, knowing they must fight but unable to choose the where or the when. York was close behind them now. By this time, the cavalcade was making pell-mell for Gloucester, the first crossing point into Wales, stretching the exhausted foot-soldiers, York's force gaining all the while. Now the Queen had left the women and was riding astride her own horse, leading the column beside the Prince and their lords.

* * *

Heading towards the loyal army, and many miles distant, Clifford was riding behind the head of the column. To his right was his butler, the button-eyed Findern, crackly ginger hair whipping about his scowl. To his left, his marshal, also more sombre than usual. Hal was some way further back, but tall enough to watch his father over the heads of the household. His eyes wandered over the back of Cuthbert Bellingham's head. On the far side of fifty, with an unfashionable close-cropped beard and hair of silver, the man wore his years lightly; strapping and vigorous, with regular, suntanned features. Clifford's dearest intimate amongst his household, excepting, of course, Moncler. Hal cast around the men. How fortunate, his father, to have attracted and retained such a group. Naturally, there were a few Hal didn't care for: Reginald Grey, of course; Leonard Tailboys, with his distasteful interests, and Lewis Jolly, preposterously misnamed: at best sour, and usually an unmitigated pain in the arse, his moaning so habitual it was never heeded.

And then there was Loic. Hal's eyes slid aside, watching the young man discreetly. This cocky Frenchman was different, to be sure, from Robert Clifford's other followers. His sway over his rowdy master – indeed, over all the household: it was unfathomable.

"What's on your mind, Master Hal?" said Loic, after an awkward moment.

"I was thinking, Sir Loic, on my father's household. The loyalty; the constancy. Unquestioning fidelity. He's truly blessed."

Hal was surprised by Moncler's air of baffled incredulity – vexation, even – when he'd disparaged neither his father nor the men. Perhaps the chamberlain had mistook his meaning.

"And of all the Wyverns, you are the most devoted." The look didn't abate. He conjectured, again, on the mystery of Loic. Somewhere, he felt, there was a key; the gate must swing easily before him, if he could but find it. Hal tried again. "Ah – and I was wondering how you came to him, Sir Loic. I never heard."

At least Loic had stopped eyeing him as if he were simple, and now there was a faraway look.

"The Monclers are an ancient family – so much older than your English nobility – hailing from Bar." He turned. "That's in eastern France, near Burgundy. Some years before I was born, there was a quarrel between my grandfather and his older brother, back and forth. My grandfather seized lands and a castle. After those two brothers died, my father and his cousin Raoul continued the quarrel. It went to court, and Raoul won the case, but my father still would not give up the estate. Then my father died suddenly when I was just a boy, and my sister Claude a little older; sixteen years or so. We were helpless when Raoul and his men arrived take possession. He beat me half to death, and left his men to finish me. I was praying for a miracle, for that was all that would save us. Just at that moment, a huge champion rode in on a white horse. Monseigneur, with his household men, though I'd no idea they were English. I thought they'd been sent by God."

"Eh? How so?" Hal considered his father's wandering exile, the details of which were rather hazy. "What was he doing there?"

"At that time – this was years back, when York had lately usurped the throne and before the loyal lords drifted off to Flanders – Monseigneur was living at the Queen's little court at Koeur, tutor-at-arms to the Prince. Monseigneur had heard of the raid on my home, and came by looking for trouble. He likes to interfere, of course, and they were all out for some fun. So, he and his men saw off my cousin's retinue, wounded Raoul and rescued Claude and me. My cousin took back the lands, of course – that was a lost cause. But we were alive and safe."

"And your sister?" Hal raised a heavy brow.

"No, no." The chamberlain bristled. "Of course not! So we had nothing beyond what Monseigneur's men managed to gather: a little money, plate, a few horses, but there wasn't much, and nowhere to go, so Monseigneur took my sister to a convent, and there she is still, I should think. I joined his household. Not as chamberlain though, not then, for Monseigneur had an acting chamberlain, at that time. Osbert Dormer, it was."

Up went both brows. "*Acting* chamberlain, Sir Loic?"

"Ah – his true chamberlain, *Randall*," Loic practically spat the name, " the previous man...he was gone." He hesitated, and continued. "So, a little later when Osbert fell, at Montlhéry, in '65, I had his place. And I've been caring for Monseigneur ever since, as if I were his wife, and he, my husband."

Hal turned on him, distracted; disconcerted. "Your English has let you down, my friend."

"I think not."

* * *

Abandoned, for the most part, and speculating hopelessly, the ladies were perplexed to witness from their place at the rear a great rushing of soldiers to and fro. Then a sizable group broke from the main party, galloping eastwards towards – presumably – York's force.

Jonkin dropped back to speak with the Countess of Devon, and soon a rumour rustled through the women: Edmond had dispatched a decoy host to draw away the enemy, while the main body continued its sprint north for the city of Gloucester. Alice listened with surprise. She'd not credited her husband with the capacity for such a spirited deception. Perhaps she'd made a hundred such mistakes, but it was too late to learn him now. And her grasp of the world beyond the numbing confines of the carriage was ebbing away, for at the worst possible moment the child was making its presence felt, impelling Alice to bring up any morsel she swallowed; reducing her to gasping, shivering misery. At least, for the women, there was the chance to rest in the carriages; the men – the nobles, even – were ragged.

266

For a time it seemed as though Edmond's bold ploy had sprung them from the snare. Edward of York was, indeed, beguiled by the false harbingers to some place out east, expecting to give battle, well removed from their fleeing column. But as the enemy had been wrongfooted, so, shortly, he took his revenge.

After a dreadful forced march, pounding on through the night, barely halting even in the darkest hours, they sighted Gloucester at last. And there, with horror, they found the gates barred against them. Exhausted and hounded as they were, it was a most bitter blow.

Nor was that all, for as the Queen flung her desperate host northwards towards the next crossing point, a marauding band erupted from the hostile city at their back and assailed the rear of the column. There was a brief but terrifying commotion as the carriages were encircled by defenders and marshalled swiftly forward. Though the women were unharmed, much of the baggage and most of the artillery train, which could not be hastened, was lost to them: looted, picked off and dispatched, with brutal irony, to join the pursuing army.

It was Jonkin, escorting the carriages on one of his periodic visits to the back of the cavalcade, who had led the brave defence of the rearguard; Edmond and Devon dashing on with their knights, forcing the army forward, flanking their Queen and their Prince.

"Now I see that he has, at last, utterly forsaken his wife and his poor child!" These were the words she wished to cry to her brother-in-law, but Jonkin was attending at the other carriage and would not approach. This was how matters stood, then, when she looked the truth in its face.

In that moment, had the arch-fiend himself charged in – huge and dark and probably perfidious – Alice might well have flung herself into those familiar arms.

* * *

There was no prospect of parading such defiance. Clifford was adrift. He'd no idea whether the Queen's army had joined Jasper's force somewhere into

Wales or was still en route, this side of the Severn. And his retinue was too small to risk dispatching scouts every which way, the ground they'd have to cover being a great deal too vast.

The senior men were watching him; watching him grow irascible, isolated as he was. Soon the childish and arrogant misjudgement loomed so large that he was picturing his shame in tangible form: a vast black pennon fluttering over the cavalcade, proclaiming itself to all within the widest radius, visible to the Queen's elusive army, visible even to Edward of York, wherever he may be.

To follow the Severn south was his shred of a plan, searching after news at the crossing points as he came. When night fell, Clifford fought the impulse to press on; to rise before dawn, instead, forcing himself and his men to a more leisurely pace, lest the household note the sudden speed and read it as panic. Rising up behind him, a murmuring that could be sensed like a tremor even when it could not be heard. Resisting the appeal of his open-hearted boys, he passed among the household. The laughter was flown and the singing was silenced. The impassive looks on those well-loved faces – their conscious restraint – pricked him to a treacherous urge: the unburdening of himself, the exposure of his mortal frailty, a plea for understanding.

"Ah, Monseigneur, you are their lord, not their fellow. This is the hour in which you must not falter. Never admit the fault; lead them; stand strong."

The chamberlain, with the steadfast help of Reginald Grey, doing all he could among his companions, behind the master's back: pleading, soothing, heartening. It seemed to Loic then that the fragile sorcery that animated these tattered shadows must surely vanish, like morning mist, at a peep of sunlight, a puff of breeze.

In the darkness Monseigneur would toss and turn and pin Loic too close for comfort, and then the master would sleep, and his dreams would wake the other men.

* * *

When at last the loyal army gained the river crossing at Tewkesbury, it was already too late. York, taking the high ridge over the hills, was fast closing;

parched and weary as his soldiers were, they had thrust on the more swiftly. The deep route – the hedged and rutted lanes through which Queen Margaret led her men – had condemned them. By late afternoon, after twenty-five miles of another dogged march, they were spent.

Between Edmond and Lord Wenlock there sparked a brief and ugly spat. Wenlock demanded that they make the ferry crossing towards Wales, even now, protracted as it may be; exhausted as they were. They must join Tudor at all costs.

The Queen raised a hand to shield her eyes from the low, sweltering sun. Edmond was right; Tudor was lost to them, and they would end it here, one way or the other. She opened her mouth.

"By God, no!" Somerset exclaimed, losing the shreds of his composure. "I'll not be caught and drowned by York." His quiet voice was grown thunderous. "We stand and fight at dawn, and Tudor, still abed in Monmouthshire, shall curse he were not here to claim the victory, and hold his manhood cheap. By tomorrow noon, Edward of York shall lie, slain, before me – my foot upon his neck."

Roused, the Prince bared his teeth and shook his fist before him, while Devon pounded Edmond on the back. "This is the spirit that shall gain us England!" he shouted in Wenlock's face.

As the man twisted aside, the Queen caught Wenlock's look of thwarted fury.

"My lord," she said, with quiet gravity. "Will you lead the mainward? Will you defend the life of the King's only son, in this, his first engagement? You have more experience than any man here; we know we can entrust this immeasurable task to you."

The old man stood a little straighter. "Madam, it would be an honour to die in this cause. My only care is to preserve the royal house."

The Queen lit Somerset's eyes with a tiny, reproving smile. He searched her face for a moment, as if to commit it to memory. He bowed.

An hour later and a few miles distant, Edward of York pitched camp. There would be battle at dawn.

Turning their backs on the beautiful evening, the ladies settled themselves into a gloomy and low-windowed house behind the men's lines. Edmond was somewhere at hand, talking with the Queen – Alice heard the muted tones, on and on, an hour or more – but he did not come to her. She took herself to bed. As Blanche stroked her hair, Alice slipped to a shallow sleep. She found herself once more in the North Country of her girlhood. Middleham: the castle under siege by a rebel army in countless number, its vast walls proving all-too-pregnable; crumbling before the onslaught. She was not there to witness its fall: closeted inside her chamber, the bed barricading the door. And all the while, the tumult swelled until a heavy footfall shook the floor, the bolt banged in the lock and the hinges shuddered. Crouched in the shadows, Alice cradled her knees in her arms and sobbed for the Earl of Warwick.

Well before dawn, Blanche shook her awake. The army was on its feet, arming, praying, making ready. The baggage – what was left of it – was stowed once more in the carriages, for the women would await the outcome in a place of surer safety. One last time the commanders came to them, with their farewells. Alice watched with surprise as the Prince gathered the Lady Anne for a lingering kiss, embracing her as if they were sweethearts; the Earl of Devon followed suit with his wife. Laura stood, after, hands clutched at her breast, her eyes raised to the low and grubby ceiling; whether she was beseeching God or stemming the tears, Alice could not tell.

Jonkin, who'd not addressed her in a week or more, now approached, resting his forehead against hers, a kiss to each cheek, holding her against him. When the boy could find no words, they clasped each other in silence.

At last Edmond entered: knelt, silent, before the Queen, holding her palms against his face, pressing kisses to her skin. Then came a moment when Alice believed her husband would pass direct from the Queen to the door. But no: he paused before her, also unspeaking. A kiss of distant solemnity, a hand light upon her neck. And then he was gone.

Sir John Fortescue, the Queen's chamberlain, old and lame, led the escort party northwards, and Sir Andrew Chowne, the Duke's chamberlain, not so old but also lame, rode beside the carriage as they travelled to the place of lingering: the Priory at Little Malvern, high above the next river crossing at Upton.

Brittle with nerves, Andrew Chowne chattered incessantly. Before many miles he was grating unbearably. Within the carriage the Queen prayed, the tears streaming freely upon her cheeks. Her confessor intoned above her, shouting down Sir Andrew. Under cover of the din, Elyn turned to her half-sister, struck by a sudden alarm.

"Lady Alice – what happens if York wins?"

A strangled squeal of outrage from Constance. "Oh, you stupid, stupid..."

"Yes – do hold your tongue, Elyn. This is beyond anything." Blanche wiped her forehead with a handkerchief, tugging the linen coif over the greasy yellow hairline.

Alice stroked her belly with protective hands. There was no belly to be seen – she was as flat as a board.

When the party reached the small religious house that was to be their shelter, the prior conveyed the Queen, almost unrecognisable, her face blotched and swollen, to his own chamber, where she fell upon her knees with her confessor and resumed her fervent entreaties. Lady Ullerton followed the Queen's example. A dreadful, listless waiting commenced.

* * *

Hard on the heels of the departing Queen, at the break of day Edward of York led his army the few remaining miles to Tewkesbury, up a gentle incline until at last he beheld the enemy arrayed before him.

There was the Beaufort standard, as expected; the vanguard, positioned to the right. York could not recall facing Edmond Beaufort in battle; if the man had been present at past encounters it was only as a cadet, buried somewhere in another lord's division. Since then, though, exile had burnished the fellow until he'd acquired something of a reputation. And York was smarting, still smarting, at that enterprising decoy which had lured him from Lancaster's main force, leaving him to kick his heels for hours, awaiting an army that never came; losing him precious time; making him an open dupe.

271

York's eyes wandered west, to a low wooded hillock near the Severn. Hunkered beneath the fresh foliage, a band of two hundred horse, a free and mobile detachment, ready with their own little surprise in case Edmond Beaufort tried any more tricks.

His gaze tracked back. Over on the left wing: Courtenay, a man who called himself Earl of Devon: a jouster; a nothing. And somewhere beneath that rippling standard, leading the centre – leading the army – the very young Edward of Lancaster, utterly untried. The boy he must and would dispatch, to end it here. York sighed and scanned the standards again with impatient eyes. One foe was missing, one who'd eluded him too long. Where was Robert Clifford? His sword hand twitched.

From the opposite ridge, Edmond of Somerset watched in his turn. There was Richard of Gloucester, York's brother, heading the vanguard. Clearly York was short of commanders, for the lad must be no older than Jonkin. And they said Gloucester was a cripple. But then, they said a lot of things – few of them true.

Edmond was enjoying the muddle over the enemy's dispositions: their vanguard, over to the left, where the other wing ought to have been. A topsy-turvy arrangement, for York's faith in Lord Hastings had faltered after the latter's dismal showing at Barnet, when he allowed Jack de Vere's division to punch straight through his line. The débâcle might have proved conclusive…had not Clifford's ineptitude spun a sure victory for Lancaster into a rout. Robert Clifford, for all his personal prowess, proving himself, yet again, a sorry commander: rash, unimaginative, over-reliant on brute force. How Somerset had savoured the news, when tidings reached him in the West Country! Warwick slain, Clifford shamed.

And yet, in spite of his resolve, in spite of all he'd suffered, Edmond found himself craning northwards, scouring the country behind, as though no worthless woman had ever come between them; as though, even at this moment, Robert Clifford would be charging towards them, racing to support his brothers-in-arms. Devon had assured him that Clifford would appear that day upon the field – but Devon was a fool.

* * *

"My God! Simon! Where did you spring from?"

Spring? Even the thought was exhausting – hot, stiff and disgruntled as he was. Simon Loys had, in fact, been wilting there a considerable while, joggled by a shifting melee of Gloucester's men, examining the pocket of dust nestled in every hinge of his gauntlets. Eventually he removed the gloves to find his hands stinking and slippery. Others were watching by now; an array of measuring eyes. Without doubt the King's brother knew he was waiting. Eventually Duke Richard broke off the debate with his captains, sauntering up. He clapped Loys on the shoulder, and the spectators busied themselves.

"My lord." Sir Simon's bow was as deep as deference demanded, though he had to thrust against his knees to regain the vertical. Sweat trickled, front and back, into his pungent crotch. "I thank God I reached you in time."

"Just in time. Emerging on the very field of battle itself, eh? The hero of the hour! We were disappointed not to see you at Barnet, Simon. But better your absence than bearing arms for Lancaster."

"I trust King Edward will find it in his heart to forgive my brother for that folly. Nick is young, and moved by a misplaced devotion to Jack de Vere."

At last Gloucester dropped the mocking tone. "The King has somewhat greater matters at hand. Your presence here will do much to assist Nicholas – and much to assist you also, no doubt. Your fortunes are on the rise. Now then. Where do you place yourself, lordless as you are? Follow me today, and we'll see how we agree." The confidential and charming smile, catching him out, as it always did. "Don't let poor Hastings pick you up, or it may be the last thing you do. De Vere ran rings around him at Barnet. Drunk, as usual."

* * *

It was barely an hour after the Queen's party crossed the Severn at Upton that a party of horsemen in full array entered the same village, heading south. The group halted on the baked earth by the bridge, and looked about them.

Reginald Grey and Loic Moncler swung down and headed off in search of news. At last there was news to be had, a small group of eager villagers encircling them, sniffing out a reward. The tidings could not be fresher:

Queen Margaret had just passed through with the Prince's wife and a small escort, heading for the priory upon the hill, there to await the outcome.

"The *outcome*?" faltered Loic. Ice crystals furled in his lungs, constricting his breathing.

A young man obliged. "The two forces, engaged at Tewkesbury, sir, below the town. They'll have set to, this last hour or more."

"Last hour?" scoffed another. "They've been hard at it since dawn. We'll hear the ending soon enough."

"What of Jasper Tudor?" barked Grey. "The Earl of Pembroke: has he crossed the river to join the Queen's force?"

Slow shrugs greeted his words. There was no force for Lancaster but the Queen's army, lately come up from Bristol. There was a small force holding Chepstow, folk said, but the Welshmen had ventured no nearer. Grey was still a moment, drumming his forehead with slender fingers. He dropped a few mean coins into the jostling hands – fewer than expected and there were muted curses as he spun, stalking back towards his lord. Loic scampered beside the priest's swinging stride, their faces setting the scene before they reached the motionless men.

Clifford sprang from his horse as if his armour were thistledown. Grasping Grey's arms, bearing him backwards a few long steps out of range, he inclined his ear for the worst. When it came, he was hard-pressed not to groan aloud. Nodding to his chamberlain and his priest, Clifford forced a bold smile and turned about, squinting into the sun.

"A couple more miles, my men, and we'll be upon them. Ah – it seems our friend Somerset has started without us, but we'll excuse his wretched manners if he has spared us bodies for the slaughter. Come!"

His gaze was angled only on his boys, whose keen faces filled him with a doleful warmth. The three men remounted, wheeled about and led off the cold-eyed household, abandoning the languid pretence, speeding as fast as they could go.

* * *

There it was, just as he'd been taught; the lengthy exchange of fire between the opposing sides, holding firm and waiting it out. Learning it was one thing; nothing could prepare a man for this. Jonkin had imagined moving freely beside his brother, step to his step, but instead he was immured within the dark, sonorous world of his helm, hunched before the storm. Every time he lifted his flinching face and peered through the slit of light, Edmond had moved again: now here, now there – shouting into faces, pointing, gesturing – now vanished. Jonkin couldn't trot at his heels like a puppy, so he stayed. Then a hand clapped heavy on his shoulder, alarming him, throwing him off balance. He spun, with a nervy oath. It was only James Delves, his friend recklessly tilting the visor to give an exaggerated wink.

"Drop it! *Drop it!*" Jonkin motioned, frantically. To the side, a groom toppled like a felled tree, two arrows splitting his mouth.

When Jonkin pictured the scene, he now realised, he'd not thought to add sound to the images. The barrage of incoming fire was stunningly loud. And some of the artillery was theirs, no doubt: the pieces captured outside Gloucester. Alas, he'd done his best, defended that which he could, but the ladies were so much more important than the guns. So he'd thought. Now he wasn't sure.

There was Edmond again, feet stilled but arms aloft, drawing men's eyes. Above him, the standard unfurled in the breeze: the arms of England, proclaiming the royal blood – the border denoting the Beauforts' bastard descent. Jonkin was gazing upward, watching the fabric flutter, enjoying as always the symbol of his family's proud name, when Delves careered into him, hands drumming madly, and he saw with dismay that he'd missed the signal – the trumpets drowned by the roar of the guns – and leapt at once to a loping run.

Drawing his sword as he went, he waved it wonderingly, but the weapon seemed woefully slight and he slid it back in its sheath, passing the heavy mace from left to right, and that felt better.

Gloucester's men must have been further off than they looked, for Somerset's vanguard was jogging for some while before it encountered any foe.

Downhill they went, beneath the trees, along hedges and ditches, speeding up, eventually and rather suddenly breaking upon the enemy. They had been tending eastwards, it was now clear, for as they emerged from cover they split the enemy's left wing from its centre, crashing into Edward of York's own division. An unorthodox manoeuvre. Was it deliberate? Edmond had not shared his plans.

Their sudden appearance was causing consternation, so they all set to the slaughter with a right good will. Unexpectedly easy to kill a man, as it turned out, and Jonkin struck about him, again and again, with increasing zest.

The vanguard's advance must have taken the rest of the loyal army by surprise also, for the other divisions were, as yet, loitering upon the hill. When Edmond paused to draw breath, Jonkin followed his gaze behind, where Devon's distant figure had broken into an answering run and then vanished as his wing hurtled towards Lord Hastings.

Ominous to behold: the knot of men in the centre division, the men beneath the royal standard of Lancaster, had moved not an inch.

By now York's right wing was distracted, Lord Hastings fully engaged in holding off Devon's frontal assault. Somerset was fighting like a man demented, his poleaxe whirling; so much more savage than Jonkin's imaginings. Their brave knights, Audley, Appledore and the rest, each giving of their best. For a brief instant, or an hour or more – he could not know – there was a sort of ecstasy in the slaughter. But with the loyal army's mainward still immobile upon the slope, York had regrouped, turning his force inward upon their numbers, skewering them against his brother Gloucester's vanguard.

As they faltered, panting, weapons weighing their hands, without warning a great force of mounted men slammed into the flank, springing from God knows where, and that was the immediate end of their assault. The division hunched together. Jonkin saw his brother dragged away by his knights – not the snaking way they'd come, but in open flight, straight towards the royal standard fluttering above the Prince. The Duke was roaring, not resisting them now, but racing uphill with a renewed belt of strength. Jonkin struggled to keep Edmond in sight, stumbling after him, exhausted, legs quaking upon each dogged step. James Delves took his hand and heaved.

But of a sudden, from somewhere unseen, he was struck with a tremendous blow; something monstrous splicing him. He'd no idea what it was or where it was when he was launched forward through the air, pitched on his face in the churned filth. After a stunned moment, with the greatest of effort, Jonkin raised his head, but he could see nothing at all, not in any direction, all light extinguished within the helm. Time slid on, and with it a certain warm and jaded languor. There was no profit in holding his head at this defiant angle. It would be easier to rest, and so, after a while, he did.

Sobbing, choking, vomit sopping his chinstrap, James Delves pushed himself, trembling, to his feet and stumbled on after his leader, in the direction his leader had gone. By the time he caught his fellows, matters were worse. The knot of them was huddled over another fallen figure, visors up, careless of the risk.

A shriek was rising; it was rising from Delves's own throat. The Duke raised a desolate face and Delves saw that it was not Somerset who'd gone down, but their Prince; their bright hope. Somerset shook the limp form once, then with increasing force, pounding the Prince's mangled breastplate. There were cries of protest. The Duke was heaved to his feet, dark blood besliming his gauntlets, and he slumped against Gabriel Appledore's shoulder, casting about him. Catching sight of Delves, Edmond passed on, searching for Jonkin. After a circuit, his wild eyes returned to Delves, the Duke's face an open question. Delves shook his head, and his mouth crumpled, and mercifully this was all that was required. He did not pronounce the dreadful words.

The danger was fully upon them. Devon's line must surely have broken, for there were foes of all colours bearing down. The men collected themselves and ran again, spent, Somerset rifling the corpses with exhausted eyes as he went, searching for one man among the dead. He was driven on by his veterans, shunning the many streams and ditches clotted with gore where the slaughter was deepest. Then the heavy tower of the Abbey presented itself to their view like a beacon, and they steered by that.

James Delves was dropping further and further behind. At last his leader was lost to him. At the far reaches of exhaustion he clodded to a halt, juddered a moment and fell to the ground. He could not even await his fate; he'd the not the spirit for it. He merely endured until his fate found him.

As the Duke's men overtook a small band of fugitives, Humphrey Audley's hand thudded upon Lord Wenlock's shoulder, the old man panting and blowing as though his heart would burst. Audley made to gather Wenlock among them, but Wenlock had spun upon the Duke with a stare of such thunderous fury that Audley faltered a step. At last Somerset found his target, slamming into Wenlock, knocking him down, their incoherent bellowing joined in a violent uproar of rage. Wenlock was no less maddened than his assailant, spitting curses, screaming. Before anyone could guess what would follow, Edmond hefted his poleaxe and swung the weapon in a heavy arc. With one shattering blow he split the man's head, raising a vast spume of blood, raining matter in all directions.

* * *

It was into the confused and macabre postscript that Clifford and his Wyverns galloped, timing their arrival so as to emerge upon the field of battle itself – just as Clifford had promised himself, days ago. And so he achieved his aim, marching nowhere in Somerset's shadow, charging in where he chose. But hardly – hardly now – the hero of the hour.

The field of battle opened before them. The boys looked about in disappointment. The faces of the household were eloquent, rather, of savage despair, the significance breaking upon them with desperate force.

They'd circled a large thicket to come upon the northern outskirts of the field, somewhat concealed from view. Even for those of the enemy who would spy them out, this fresh, mounted and well-armed band offered no inducement, and the foemen skirted them widely; there was easier prey aplenty.

Aymer dismounted, unbidden, at his father's back. Sword drawn, he stalked a few steps behind them. Richie watched, intrigued as ever: the man's senses were so very keen, verging on the uncanny. Sure enough, as if to order, a few of York's men came jogging around the trees, stumbling quite by accident upon the rear of the group. Aymer welcomed them, venting his frustration in the most fitting way he knew. Clifford turned and eyed the tangled bodies, his mind elsewhere.

Then there was a ripple within the copse itself. Fugitives could be glimpsed concealing themselves amid the undergrowth, a refuge only for the most desperate. A commanding voice hailed the buried men, triggering panic, drawing them out in hasty fright to stifle the ringing tones.

Careless of their predicament, Clifford bade the furtive men deliver their news. The fate of the Prince was his first imperative. Dead; he was certainly dead. One of the fugitives raged at Somerset's impulsive, inexplicable attempt to crush York and Gloucester together. Not so, was the others' view: the blame lying squarely with Wenlock, who'd failed to support the charge despite a plain view of combat, despite the clear peril to the vanguard.

"The Earl of Devon?"

Devon had fought strongly, valiantly; fleeing at the last for his horse. After that, nothing was known. Clifford nodded. Perhaps the most he could hope for. He'd a strong suspicion his friend was alive.

"What of Lord Wenlock?" quavered Sir Hugh, repeatedly, until he was heard.

A gentleman in Somerset's livery turned on him, delivering the verdict in a voice of cold satisfaction: "The Duke slew him for his treachery."

The sweating soldiers crept closer to the shelter of the coppice.

Into the pregnant silence Loic pitched himself. "Ah – Edmond Beaufort: what of him?" But he'd pronounced the name in the French manner, and met only puzzlement. "*Beaufort*? What of *Beaufort*?" he repeated.

"For Christ's sake!" barked Grey. "Somerset: dead or alive?"

The Duke's man looked pained. "My lord is alive and unharmed, within the sanctuary of the Abbey – may God defend him always."

There was a general sober nodding among the household; assenting murmurs, intended only to irk him, Clifford assumed. The trees had closed once more upon the runaways. Lifting his eyes to scan the land, he hesitated, transfixed with doubt. If he rode on now, he'd no certainty his men would follow.

Mother of God, he felt like crying. *It's not like you have a choice. It's all over. Follow me back into exile, or throw yourselves on York's mercy.* It was exile or death.

After an agonising moment Clifford folded his arms and addressed his household.

"So it seems the day is already done. Ah – fight enough battles, and this is bound to happen eventually. But meanwhile, Jasper Tudor, our friend and ally, is near at hand. York will turn on him now. Tudor stands in dire need of our aid, and it shall not be said that we Wyverns deserted him. Nor shall we desert our defenceless Queen. Malvern Priory lies on the road into Wales, with many a young lady yearning to be rescued. Come!" He led off at a steady pace.

With alacrity, the FitzCliffords wheeled their mounts. Moncler and Reginald Grey came on with a parade of readiness, pursued by Hugh Dacre, for reasons of his own. Clifford twisted in the pretence of consulting them. The others had not moved. A lifetime's unbearable pause; the tang of blood upon his lip.

Hal had halted again and eyed his friends, misliking what he saw. He turned towards his father – now staring fixedly at the Abbey tower. Then Walter Grey trotted up, cowed by his brother's ferocious scowl. In grim resignation, Bellingham kicked on his horse. At last, led by Castor and Nield, their faces stern, the household followed. Loic glanced across with a tiny pensive sigh. Clifford breathed and spurred forward.

PART IV
INTO THE WOODS

The ladies tarried in strained and listless silence. Now and then a shrill cry would tear the stillness, as if at the first advent of dire tidings, as if, each time, the grim news were freshly broken.

An hour or more, now, since the messenger vaulted from the foaming, wild-eyed horse and pelted up the stairs to the Queen; rushing to pierce a mother's heart with tidings as sharp as any dagger: the death of her only son. An hour or more, since the house was rent with the first shrieks of her agony – terrible to hear; unbearable to witness.

Someone would come, a man of significance; perhaps, even now, crossing the Severn, seeking after the quarry. Each of the women endured her private turmoil of hopes and dreads.

And then he came: the dreary hush was smashed by a sudden clatter of many hooves.

Joanna had been loitering at the window, and now exclaimed, "Good God – it is Lord Clifford!"

Alice started violently and pressed her trembling hands together, the stitching tumbled in her lap. She looked across at Anne, lately a princess, new-widowed: a nobody, now. The girl's eyes were narrowed.

"He," said Anne contemptuously. "Whatever can he want?"

Alice darted to the window. Robert Clifford had removed his helmet and was casting about him while his men assembled in the courtyard.

"He has his force beside him!" The triumph was strong in her voice. "Such lies were told, yet he *has* taken the field, fresh from one engagement to the other! He is come to deliver us!"

"Deliver us from what?" Anne was sharp. "I'm going nowhere."

Clifford had turned to scan the guesthouse, but the glass was mirrors of gold in the sun. She watched him dismount and walk among the men, clapping backs and thighs, a few words here and there; leave-taking. All the ladies but Anne and Laura were now crowded into the window embrasure. Anne continued at her stitching, the needle rending the linen in sloppy twitches. Laura stared vacantly at the wall. A number of the soldiers, mounted on an odd assortment of steeds, began to file away through the gate, leaving a group of horsemen. Most of these, Alice knew as Robert's household. Those she didn't know were variations on a familiar theme: the Clifford boys. She gazed on their fresh faces.

"They're leaving," said Constance.

"Only his retinue. Why so few? They'll have a long journey back," remarked Blanche. "See all those new men? My God – we don't have to wonder who they are, do we? And look! What is our Sir Hugh doing among them, I wonder? He doesn't look very happy."

The household and the boys loitered in the courtyard below, stretching, drinking and talking amongst themselves as Clifford disappeared beneath the window. The deep thrum of his voice could be heard in conversation with the prior and Alice's chamberlain, Andrew Chowne; after a few moments, his heavy step upon the stair. Alice walked forward, chin up, hands pressed together. Robert Clifford clanked in. He'd never stood before her in full harness; he dwarfed the room.

"Alice," he said quietly, improperly, and pulled her in. She proffered a cheek, but he grasped her, hard and still, pinioned against his sharp edges.

When she spoke his Christian name for the first time, with a tremulous smile, there was no answering smile; he looked haggard.

Clifford scanned the chamber. "Where is the Queen?"

Blanche answered him. "She's in the prior's chamber with Sir John Fortescue. Prostrate with grief, poor lady."

He nodded. "I will go to her, and you must all make ready to leave upon the instant."

He swept past Alice and knelt before Anne, taking her reluctant hand. "My lady, your forgiveness for the question, but may I know if you carry our Prince's heir?"

Anne stood abruptly, shaking him off with a motion of disgust.

"You are impertinent!" The voice was unnaturally high. "I cannot be with child. Leave me be. I remain here to await my victorious cousin, King Edward."

A shocked exclamation broke from Alice's lips. Clifford heaved himself up. "So that's how it stands?" he sneered. "Then stay here, and welcome."

Turning about him, Clifford caught Laura's eye. She gave him a clouded smile. "I think you'll find the Queen will not depart with you either, my lord. I will remain here to attend her."

"Devon's fate is unknown, my lady. If he is alive, as I hope to find, better you're with me than in the hands of Edward of York."

"I do not believe the Earl lives," she said calmly. "I dreamed last night that my lord would fall. I'll abide here."

Shrugging, he turned from her. Devon would not miss his wife – that much was certain. "Lady Alice, come with me to the Queen. You others: I told you to look sharp about you. Make haste!"

Clifford took Alice by the elbow and drew her out, pulling the door behind him. Then his hands were upon her shoulders. Her eyes closed, then quickly opened again. He didn't seem to have noticed. "What now? You know they have Somerset trapped in the Abbey? I fear we'll never see him again."

She dropped her eyes. *You fear it? You were said to desire it, before.* "I am carrying his child, my lord. I will come away with you. Gladly."

He sucked a long breath and his hands dropped from her. "Take me to the Queen's chamber."

Queen Margaret was sprawled on the floor in a tumble of disorder, a dolorous lady kneeling at either side. She looked stupefied; stunned. Sir John was pacing the room, and came to meet Clifford as he entered. Clifford made his obeisance. It was not clear that she recognised him. He turned to the knight.

"Sir John, we must flee, and quickly, before York discovers the Queen."

The ponderous old man was shaking his head. "Alas, my good lord, God has abandoned our cause. Our Prince is lost. There is nothing left to fight for. We must abide here to await the coming of Edward of York. We must throw ourselves on his mercy."

"What's this?" shouted Clifford. "Do as you choose, you old dolt; the Queen comes with me! Humiliation and imprisonment – that's what awaits if she falls into those hands. We must join with Jasper Tudor and rally our cause." He knelt before her, urgent. "Madam, I humbly beg you to rouse yourself. All is not lost; this lady carries an heir for the house of Lancaster – Edmond of Somerset's child."

The Queen raised her terrible eyes to Alice; they were no more than bloody slits in the grey flesh. "My son!" she mewled. Her head dropped.

Clifford gazed at her. It would not do; she was gone from them. He raised her hands and kissed them with reverence. "I pray God you find the peace you deserve, Madam, after your heavy labours."

Standing to draw breath, he caught sight of Elizabeth Ullerton, red-eyed and motionless at the window.

"Lady Ullerton, your place is with the Duchess. Go back to her women and ensure all is ready. Discard what you can."

Elizabeth bolstered herself with a glance at Sir John's affronted face. "The Duchess will go nowhere with you! We do as Sir John bids, and await Edward of York's direction."

Clifford bared his teeth at her. "If you think so ill of me, my lady, then the Duchess has all the more need of a chaperone. Make haste."

Alice's face was even less welcoming.

"Lady Alice!" cried Elizabeth. "The Duke is alive and safe in sanctuary! I forbid you to leave with this evil man. He brings nothing but disgrace. Men say he is the father of your child, and your husband believes it likewise!"

"How dare you speak to me in this way?" Alice flared up. "Stay, then, and rot! I want nothing to do with you, you poisonous hag." Making an ungraceful homage to the insensate figure on the floor, Alice strode from the room. Bowing also, Clifford followed her. At the door he paused, gazing uncertainly at the broken doll of a queen. Alice was stalking towards the great chamber without a backward glance, and he turned and trailed after.

In the other chamber, all was in remarkably good order, the baggage pared down, neatly arrayed and travel-ready; it was clear the party had anticipated a hasty departure. Clifford leaned from the window, shouting instructions to Chowne, while the grooms and pages stowed belongings on the spare horses. When Lord Clifford stood ready to lead the ladies down, Alice paused awkwardly before Anne, who averted her face. She had a warmer leave-taking with Laura Courtenay. Then they passed out into the sunshine.

The boys were craning, open-mouthed, for the first glimpse of the Queen of Heaven; the woman who'd vanquished Lord Clifford and imperilled a kingdom; the woman endowed by each with the face and figure of their imaginings. This, at last, was she, her hand on his arm. *Surely not* was the silent but general verdict. This girl: so pale, so small and slight? One youth was lost from that moment, his heart a painful echo of Robert's own; others felt only a transitory disappointment.

Clifford turned to her, a hand possessive at her back. "Lady Alice – you know my household, and Sir Hugh Dacre, who's been good enough to join us."

Sir Hugh gave the ladies a tight smile.

"Wearing my badge today, Sir Hugh? I'm in luck. The others...no, don't dismount, we haven't time." Clifford frowned at the youths for a moment, defeated again by their number, "Are my boys or my brother John's." He rushed the task, confusing Guy and Aymer – the only man who did; relegating Richie from son to nephew; sliding over Bedivere's name so no one heard.

Still the FitzCliffords were staring at Alice. Then each lowered his head respectfully. All except Aymer; as Lord Clifford turned away, she was transfixed by the youth's insolent appraisal. His gaze slithered over her.

285

Clifford was encountering a dilemma. In the absence of any proper chaperone, the transport of this group of young women presented a delicate problem. He eyed the Queen's carriage. She was a spent force; it was likely they'd never meet again, but after a short internal struggle, he concluded that they'd be faster on horseback, and he stole not the carriage, but the pillion saddles.

Every female should be mounted behind an appropriate escort, but appropriate escorts were thin on the ground in this notorious company. Alice, the only one who truly mattered, was quickly disposed behind her own chamberlain, Andrew Chowne. Constance rode with Clifford's steward, Patrick Nield, her face rigid. He was, at least, an older man, and would follow orders. Joanna, he assigned to his marshal, Cuthbert Bellingham. Bellingham, too, had an eye for the ladies, although, from his imperturbable expression, not this lady. Mitten swamped Clifford's groom. Elyn, who looked as though she'd died and attained paradise, was difficult to place, but in the end Clifford threw her up behind Sir Leonard Tailboys. Wall-eyed and barrel-chested, a grubby fellow; chosen for his looks and not his morals; whoever carried Elyn was at risk from her, but this man was surely less at risk than others. Sir Hugh had, naturally enough, taken possession of Blanche.

As the horsemen clattered through the gate, Guy lost Aymer and discovered him at the front beside Loic.

"So you say he hasn't ridden her yet?" Now that Alice had become flesh, she had become interesting: a crucible of latent strife.

Uneasy, Guy scanned the men behind, but Lord Clifford was speaking with Bellingham some way back. His brother hadn't so much as turned his head.

Loic Moncler, fount of all knowledge, stared at Aymer with loathing. He'd said no such thing; not to this viper. A measure of his power derived from the flow of information, upward and downward, but mainly downward. He knew exactly what he'd said, to whom, and why.

Guy snatched up his brother's reins and dragged him back. "Don't even think of it! Our father would wallow in your guts."

Once they were set upon the road and skirting the high escarpment above the priory, the men were debating the route in earnest. By now there would be enemies scouring the country, competing to discover the Queen. A day or two's lead was the very most they could expect. Clifford had thought, by that night, to reach Goodrich Castle – seat of the shifty Earl of Shrewsbury; from there, they would head south to Chepstow to rendezvous with Jasper Tudor, and that would take another day; two at most. But it was now afternoon, the men were flagging and Alice, his precious burden, was looking wan. He fell in next to Andrew Chowne, who was chafing the hand of his mistress. In her lap lay the puff of white fur; her evil-looking cat. Clifford touched the girl's arm. Her eyes jerked open and she smiled weakly.

There was a pause, and Alice whispered, "Jonkin – my brother-in-law. We've had no news. I feel in my heart that he is lost."

Why the boy? That sweet, shy, dreamy youth. "He fell early."

Her lips were bloodless.

"It was very swift, so I hear; he did not suffer. And he never left his brother's side." He had no idea how it happened.

"Oh, my poor Jonkin!" The back of her hand was over her lips.

Sir Andrew craned around in the saddle. "Honourable, companionable and swift. My lady, no man could wish for a better end."

Clifford was frowning at Alice. In the hot sunlight she was insubstantial; a mere wisp. "You're unwell?" he said, brusquely.

"Lady Alice is suffering from sickness, my lord," said Chowne. "It comes and goes. Travel makes it worse, it seems."

Clifford had been right to abandon the idea of Goodrich and determined, instead, on Ledbury; on an old companion-in-arms who would, he hoped, offer a bed. Ledbury was an easy ride, much closer; they should reach Goodrich in good time tomorrow. Though whether its castellan would offer a welcome: that was less certain.

"My lord?" She interrupted the urgent inner debate. "The Countess of Warwick took refuge in Beaulieu Abbey when she heard of the Earl's death. What will become of her now?"

"What? I neither know nor care. Look to yourself. Look to your child."

Clifford passed through the column of horsemen. Dacre was behind him at the rear, shielding Blanche from Loic, who hadn't so much as glanced in her direction. Bede reined in beside Nield, drawing a chorus of donkey noises from the twins as he passed; their usual infantile malice. Bede was a nice-looking lad: large, soft eyes, long-lashed; perhaps he did look a touch like a donkey. And somewhat stupid. But so were they all, thought Clifford. A herd of great, stupid donkeys. The boy was gawking hopefully into the pallid, heart-shaped face of Alice's niece. Trapped sidewards on her pillion saddle, Constance was compelled to face him, but Bede's quest was more hopeless than he knew, and Clifford was content to let that one lie.

Meanwhile Leonard Tailboys had trotted forward to Aymer's side, forgetful of Clifford's instruction. The knight was tilting awkwardly in his saddle as Elyn craned around him, her bold, dark eyes sweeping the twins. Guy met her gaze and captured it, while Aymer yawned ostentatiously. Clifford could see her fate at a glance. Not on his watch: he ordered Tailboys to fall back with Dacre and Nield, and waved a warning finger in Guy's face.

"Monseigneur, how does it go with you? How does it go with you, now?" Clifford had made his way on to Loic and Hal at the head of the column.

"Better than when last you asked! I have the heir of Lancaster, don't I?"

Both of them turned to regard him, then Loic was repelling Hal across Clifford's chest.

"Ah – I have the heir of Lancaster, Loic. And she who carries the heir. Quite a fortune to salvage from the ruins of the day."

As so often, Loic's first impulse was to close out trespassers. He jerked his head towards the rear of the column. "I take it I'm released, then, Monseigneur?" Not content with the abrupt change in topic, he had changed languages also. Hal sighed and wheeled his horse about to partner Walter Findern.

Clifford grinned. "My good cousin Sir Hugh is making his intentions plain. I'm not sure even you could vanquish a proposal of marriage from so eligible a gentleman." He raised his brow at the chamberlain. "Unless you were to offer first?"

Hot words tripped over themselves before Clifford raised a hand. "I'm teasing you, mon petit!" He patted Loic's neck. "Mistress Blanche is not the one for you, I know it. Besides, how could I release you when I have no wife of my own?"

* * *

Ledbury was a comfortable if modest respite when they arrived several hours later through the warm dusk. The mistress of the house shepherded Alice and the ladies to their guestchamber.

It was unfortunate that the women were crowded together; Blanche had to speak and did not want an audience. She took a deep breath, and was at once interrupted.

"Jonkin is among the lost."

First the clamour of sorrow and then the swift reverse into solace: death was a kinder fate; Jonkin would not wish to live on without Duke Edmond. An unflattering verdict on Jonkin, in truth, who might, perhaps, have escaped his brother's shadow and grown to be a great man, but a spell had fallen, tempering the truth's sharp edges, enveloping the survivors in its merciful embrace.

"Duke Edmond is very much alive!" Blanche stared the catastrophe full in its face, determined to rouse the others.

Joanna blundered off. "Lady Alice, did you ask about the Countess of Warwick?" There was a circle of anxious faces.

Blanche turned on Joanna, but the others had gone blindly after.

"The Wyverns will ride to her rescue, of course. These are Arthurian knights, risen again."

"No, Elyn – I don't think so. Though I'm sure they'd wish to. In fact, Lord Clifford said he wished to, but she is far out west. It cannot be done, he said, alas."

"West, Lady Alice?" The quiet voice of Constance. "Beaulieu is south-east of us."

"Yes. That's what I meant. And that's what he said. The Countess is too far south-east of us, alas."

289

"Lady Alice." Blanche took her mistress's hands in her own. "Never mind the Countess of Warwick; there are great troubles closer at hand. It cannot be right, can it, to have abandoned your husband like this? Do you think it right, before God? We have made a grave mistake."

"My husband abandoned me, long since! He abandoned his child. Duke Edmond is a hollow man, wilful and unjust. He would have put me from him, soon enough; he said so. Annulled the marriage, if he could; shut me away, innocent as I am. God is punishing him."

It was a more brazen defence than Blanche expected. "Well! And where does this lead, in the end?"

"That is for Lord Clifford to say. Into Wales, I expect. It is strong for Lancaster. And thence to France?" She had not understood the question – possibly. "As long as we're safe, I care not."

"We were safe at Little Malvern."

"You may have been safe – my child was not!" The retort was sharp. "The babe would have been snatched from me to live out its days in the Tower, if nothing worse. King Henry's heir? Edward of York would never have lived easy with my child at large."

Blanche reached out and stroked her arm. "Yet many believe that the babe is Lord Clifford's get. No, don't be angry. I repeat only what men say. And can't you see how much worse it is now, when you've abandoned your husband and fled with this very man? The child will be smirched with these rumours, unable even to hold up its head, let alone restore the royal house."

"What can I do if I'm pursued by lies?" cried Alice. "Lord Clifford's first concern is for the house of Lancaster, always! He tried so hard to coax the Queen to flee the priory; you heard him ask if Anne carried the Prince's child. I was last in his thoughts. In fact," – here it hit her, with a chill, and her voice slowed – "he didn't even ask me; I told him. I told him I would gladly follow him."

"Well! You're always complaining that everyone treats you as child. Lord Clifford will not treat you as a child. You'll wish he had, before the end. You *are* a child, and because of it, you cannot see where this is headed." Alice was trembling by now, and Blanche found that she was trembling too. She drew a clear breath. "So here's what we shall do: we'll remain at Goodrich with the Countess of Shrewsbury. Lady Catherine's sister was wife to your brother Aubrey, was she not? Lady Catherine will stand for your good name. Sir Andrew and Sir Hugh will remain with us, I know. Sir Hugh's been saying from the first that we've got ourselves into the most terrible predicament."

Alice was deflating. "I'll speak with Lord Clifford. I do not think he'll permit it."

"Do not consult him! You owe him nothing. Say not a word until we reach Goodrich, then tell him you will go no further."

"Oh, I cannot do that," said Alice quickly.

Well then, thought Blanche, *you are in his thrall, and I can do no more, and I will leave you.*

* * *

Their host had not been present on the field that morning, though news was dribbling in from neighbours who knew more. The rumours on Devon's fate were, as yet, contradictory: some saying he'd been killed; others, that he'd fled the field and escaped west into Wales. Clifford was buoyed by that. In his experience, if a man were killed outright, the truth would soon spread. He pictured himself reaching Chepstow to find Devon awaiting him. It was more than possible. Jasper's presence would draw friends and enemies like a lure.

But the news on Somerset was as dire as he'd expected. York's men had already thrust their way in to Tewkesbury Abbey in the teeth of the Abbot's protests and dragged Somerset and his companions into custody. Tomorrow morning, they'd come before the new Constable of England: York's young brother, Richard of Gloucester.

It is the end. Clifford knew it. He'd not held out any real hope, yet the confirmation was the gravest blow. And clamouring at his mind was the fear of Edmond's dying curse; to the survivor, such words having an ominous power, arcane and dangerous.

The yawning men were ordered to early and crowded beds, but, drained as he was, sleep eluded him. Beside him, Loic breathed easily, while Clifford stared up into the darkness, slow waves of pity and self-pity washing over him. He ached, wept inside, for that good man, his friend through long adversity. And despite the last, desperate effort to conjure the savage resentment of this man – Alice's husband – on which he'd been gorging himself for months, he found it had deserted him.

Then his thoughts turned, inevitably, to his lands – his most beloved lands, further from his grasp than ever. Yet still he had Alice, who'd come to him willingly; perhaps a widow by morning. He had her child, the heir of Lancaster. His boys and his household had made it through unharmed. He had a hope of Devon to cling to. Eventually he slipped into a merciful sleep.

* * *

While Clifford suffered his torments, the focus of his agony was stretched upon the pallet in his stuffy cell, shifting his weight, regarding the low stone above his head. Edmond's frame ached from honest toil, his sword arm bruised and stiffening. Sleep would not come; not yet; perhaps not that night. But soon enough he would rest in peace eternal, and meanwhile his mind was filled with strange diversions, foremost of which was the evening's private visit from Richard of Gloucester.

When Duke Richard was announced, Somerset had pictured another Edward of York – loud, strapping and genial – so that his youngest brother was a downright shock: diminutive, slender and dark; humming with restless energy; a handsome, foxy face, his voice childish and reedy. An impressive entourage crowded him, shooed away at the door to loiter in the cool shadows while the two royal dukes took their leisure within. Gloucester acted the suppliant, exerting himself to charm; embracing Edmond as a cousin, hailing his spirited generalship; modest before the other's punctilious praise.

"I'll not speak of my own prowess, stripling as I am. But was it not a noble contest, Cousin? If Wenlock had played his part like a man, we'd all have been the better pleased. I hear you slew him with your own hand. The story spreads far and wide, and I acclaim you for it." Gloucester laughed confidingly. "And if your cause was riven with rifts, we've our own cross to bear in the shape of my

Janus-faced brother of Clarence. George has become so tricksy of late that he'll hop into bed with the strangest of fellows. He chose to fight with us this time, but it was a close-run thing. Did I say Janus? I meant Judas. I'm not convinced we'll hold George's interest long. But forgive me – it's not your challenge!"

The weathercock George of Clarence held no interest for Edmond. "Shall it be the Tower that is my journey's end, Cousin? So the world may take heed?"

"No, better not. We'll do it here. I'll try you tomorrow – as stern and cold as the King could wish…" The young man made an astonishing little play, parading back and forth with a haughty frown. "… and find you guilty of high treason, of course. You shall abandon all mortal care at the dawn following."

Somerset nodded.

"Truth be told," Duke Richard was confiding again, "there are too many of your friends about to risk carrying you back to London. The Kentish men have assaulted Southwark; the North is unsettled; Jack de Vere and William Beaumont at large; Jasper Tudor near at hand. And Robert Clifford still wandering about somewhere, begging directions. He seems to have got lost en route." He sniggered, as if to share the private joke.

Edmond looked away.

Speaking of which, thought Gloucester. "Where is your wife, by the by, Sir Edmond? And my cousin, Anne of Warwick? Where is Margaret, your would-be queen? If either of the younger ladies is with child, it would be a pity."

"Neither the Prince's wife nor my own carries a child. We spoke of it just as we parted. You may rest easy on that score, Cousin."

"Well: we shall see. For sure you wouldn't tell me, and I don't blame you for it."

* * *

The next morning, the travellers were up with the dawn. Alice had steadied. If only she could remain still, all would be well. Carefully she descended the stairs. Then, on turning a corner, she was charged down by young Tom FitzClifford, headlong and heedless. He caught her as she tumbled, and half-

293

helped, half-carried her to a stool, averting his eyes, mumbling disjointed apologies, fretting about the babe. She'd not observed Hal's approach until he was on one knee before her. He rapped Tom smartly with his knuckles. "What have you done?" The voice was deep and familiar.

Enthralled, Alice seized the chance to inspect the man. Hal and his father must be unusually close in age. And how much easier on the eye would Robert be without that leather patch!

"Must I summon a physician?"

"Don't be absurd, lad." Hal's eyes had not left her face. "The Duchess will live some years yet, despite your carelessness." He held out his hands – identical to his father's – helping her gently to her feet; slow to step back.

"Master Tom, is it? Don't fear," said Alice, "for you have not hurt me. There is nothing amiss."

But the boy was still looking nervously at his brother, and turned towards her with lowered lids. "It is good of you to say so, madam. But…may I beg you not to mention this to our father? Lord Clifford has forbidden us from speaking to you. Or looking at you. Or thinking of you."

Hal winced and closed his eyes, and Alice let out a peal of surprised laughter. One eye cracked open and then the other, and Hal grinned into her face, a smile full of merry amusement.

"Come away, you ridiculous boy, before you shame me further! The Duchess will keep our secret, and our father need never know that we have broken every one of his commandments."

* * *

For some time after Gloucester departed, Edmond examined the visitor in his mind, wondering at himself. He, who evaded strangers and preferred no company to familiar company, had been so beguiled as to try to detain the man. And, he now realised, he'd neglected to ask the fate of the Earl of Devon, which was truly unpardonable.

Sleep never did visit. As the end approached, he awaited the gift of insight; the divining of some higher meaning in the dregs that had been his life, but his thoughts slid about, evading his control, and when he had done with Richard of Gloucester, he could manage only quietude.

There was a quite a crowd gathering as the faithful knights followed their lord out into the beautiful dawn, bowing clumsily with hands bound; sombre and stooped. Edmond was followed by good Humphrey Audley, who couldn't seem to meet his eyes. He went to clap the knight on the back but, as he couldn't, he nudged the fellow awkwardly with his shoulder.

"Play the man!" whispered Edmond, with a little smile. Audley nodded.

When all were assembled in the modest courtroom – rather too crowded for comfort – Richard of Gloucester swept in, magnificent and stern, just as promised. Short as he was in stature, every one of those inches proclaimed him Constable of England, with the promise of further greatness yet to come. The febrile murmuring petered out, those at the back craning for a glimpse of the rising young man. Gloucester's steady gaze touched the prisoners' faces as he passed, slowing only as he drew level with Somerset. He halted. The briefest of pauses, haughty still, and then he had given Edmond a tiny nod, perhaps, a swift wink, perhaps, before turning away, before taking his place and commencing.

The trial was perfunctory and predictable, the proceedings serving no particular use but to illuminate in passing the last wretched moments of the Earl of Devon, a tale of dubious profit to its hearers. Run to ground, defying capture at the bounds of his desperate strength, Devon had been brought down at last by a crowd of churls armed with quarterstaffs. Somerset stared at the scuffed floor, envisaging, against his will, Devon's handsome face smashed beyond recognition, the dark curls sticky and straggled with blood. If he didn't stop, Jonkin's image lay not far behind. Edmond was of a sudden wearied beyond fortitude. His knees were fragile. He longed for the cell.

On went the shrill and grating voice, one phrase or another lapping idly at his mind. The verdict was pronounced, and after the verdict, the sentence. The voice ground to a halt. An eternity of utter silence before Gloucester spoke again, waiving the customary horrors reserved for treason; conferring the mercy of beheading. Many lungs exhaled. Eyeing the expressions along the line of prisoners, Edmond was dazed at his own naivety. For the prospect of the full array: drawing, hanging and disembowelling; it had simply never crossed his mind.

Gloucester's going was attended with as much commotion as his coming, but when the condemned men filed after, their judge was dawdling in an antechamber. He plucked Edmond aside, searching his face with merry expectation.

"I don't expect your thanks, but it could have been worse, Cousin! I've managed to save Gabriel Appledore and little James Delves amongst sundry gentlemen who never took up arms before. The rest of you are beyond redemption, of course. But no grisly indignities to be inflicted upon your body and none upon your corpse. I hate the habit of heads on sticks; yours to lie quietly, atop your neck. And while I can't quite send you home, you shall slumber beside your would-be prince and your friend, the would-be Earl of Devon, in this great West Country abbey. Farewell, Cousin. Farewell. It ends here; here lies Lancaster."

A swift kiss to each cheek, another embryo wink, and he was gone, a short and rapid stride, mantle billowing in his wake, leaving an expensive trace of sandalwood.

* * *

If Clifford struggled to find peace, Blanche too was weary and heartsick. Had she spoken out at the priory, joining her voice to Elizabeth Ullerton's, she might have prevented this disaster. She'd been caught out entirely when Lord Clifford swept in and took charge. Blanche had no one to confide in but Sir Hugh Dacre, and there she had found a ready and prejudiced listener. As they journeyed, she poured the story into his ear to find the sentiment chimed with his own.

Dacre determined, at last, to seize the initiative; to rescue his beloved and return to the King's peace. When next they halted, in a copse by a river, Sir Hugh led Blanche out of the others' view and, encumbered by the great weight that burdened him, he vaulted clumsily into the unknown. It had been so long in coming that the question had assumed a life of its own, mushrooming in the dark of his mind. When she accepted him, calm and brisk, he was surprised that his magical words had not transformed her. But the woman was just as she had always been. Grinning with pride and relief, he confessed his silly fears of Loic Moncler.

Blanche tamed her face. "You had never anything to dread from Sir Loic. His affection is engaged elsewhere; there is no room in his heart for another."

It is himself, divined Sir Hugh. The man loves only himself.

Squeezing his hands, Blanche excused herself to attend to Alice. She found her mistress some way off, curled upon a cloak on the ground, her knees to her chest and her face in her hands, tears seeping through her fingers; tears for Jonkin. Hovering over her, Mitten, Joanna and Constance. Elyn had disappeared.

It will not happen, thought Blanche, grimly. *She won't speak to him, but pass through Goodrich and miss the chance to save herself.* Girt in the armour of her rescuer, Blanche determined to face down the enemy herself. She walked upstream, hoping to find him alone. He was not, of course, alone. There he was, circled by a group of the lesser men, all of whom turned at her approach.

"Mistress Carbery. What can we do for you?" came his deep and carrying voice.

Someone made a quip she didn't catch, and there was laughter.

"May I beg a word in private, my lord?" They drew curious glances as she led him off. "Mistress Elyn, my lady's half-sister, has wandered. I fear she's with your son...I forget his name; the handsome one. She is a naive girl." She ignored the speculative eyebrow. "And I have my hands full with the Duchess in her present condition. Would you warn him off, my lord?"

"I have done so, and will again."

Diverting him thus, she passed to the attack. "My lord, I believe that when we reach Goodrich, we women must remain with Lady Catherine while you go on. If you care for the Duchess's good name, you'll agree that the Countess is the best protector of her reputation. Sir Hugh will remain with us as escort."

He folded his arms. "So you make a match of it with Sir Hugh, at last? Probably wise. Sir Loic quickens your pulse, of course, but he was never so steadfast as you would wish."

He was baiting her, and she said nothing, her thoughts clear upon her face.

Clifford was suddenly curt. "Ah – you're wasting your time, and you know it. But there, you've said your piece and your conscience can rest easy." He raised a finger as she opened her mouth. "I will not relinquish this lady, not ever, not even if I have to throw her over the saddle and cut my way out of Goodrich. Beware, Mistress Carbery, beware! I've witnessed your pleasure in the woods of Angers. I've savoured those intimate reports of the Duchess that you poured so obligingly into Sir Loic's ear. If you play me false, I will destroy you."

He walked away, towards the watching men, and then spun on his heel. "And you *know* that child is not my child. I have laid not a finger on her."

"The damage is done. It makes little difference now!" she cried, furious, heedless of the audience.

"It makes all the difference in the world."

* * *

Clifford watched as Alice was raised, waxen, behind Sir Andrew.

"I've lost my cat, Rollo. He was following, for a time, but no longer. He's a good mouser, though. Rollo must shift for himself, now, I suppose."

She wasn't looking at him; she wasn't looking at anyone, but the words hung, as if demanding his compassion.

Mother of God, thought Clifford.

At the very back of the cavalcade, Blanche was hard pressed to keep from weeping as she was lifted behind Sir Hugh. A tumult of emotions surged, leaving her as breathless and nauseous as her mistress. Dacre was unsurprised at her silence; he was awed, himself, by what had just passed between them, but he was taken aback when it transpired she'd changed her mind utterly on the plan.

"It seems Lady Alice sets no store by her own good name. And that terrible man will not relinquish her, I'm sure of it. We must make our own future, now. As you said before, London is our best hope. George of Clarence, perhaps; we both know the Duchess Isabel well; she was well-disposed to me

298

when we lived at Middleham. King Edward seems to have forgiven his brother for that entanglement with Warwick's treason, and when he confirms Duke George in possession of Warwick's lands, you should be useful to him, with your knowledge of Middleham and its estates. The Duke might even make you his under-steward."

"I'm not so sure about that," whispered Sir Hugh doubtfully. "Warwick's northern estates are entailed in the male line. George of Clarence may never come into them by right of his wife. But I agree with you about the Duchess Isabel; no doubt she'd welcome you, and find us both a place in the household. We should go to London, yes."

"I've heard some talk that Lord Clifford means to secure my mistress in a bolthole close by while he goes on to Chepstow to meet with the Earl of Pembroke. That would be the time to make our escape, when there are few of them around us."

He nodded. Anything that avoided a confrontation must be preferable. In fact, imperative.

She continued, "You're on friendly terms with Patrick Nield: find out from him what place Lord Clifford is thinking of for her. But be discreet! His lordship is already suspicious. Regard these men as his spies."

* * *

Alice had never felt so ill in her life. She thought she might be dying. Somehow, through the afternoon, she managed to cling to Andrew Chowne. All too evident was the muttering among the Wyverns; the dark looks cast in her direction. The party was travelling too slowly by far; she dared not test the men's patience by begging a halt. It took an exhausting effort to master her churning stomach, which continually threatened to overflow and spill down the horse's flanks.

At long last, as the shadows lengthened, the sandstone towers of Goodrich came into distant view. By this time Chowne was leading the column so that Lord Clifford could keep Alice within view. In a dream of weariness, he was soon lulled by the slow rhythm of the girl swaying before him.

As they drew before the great barbican of the castle, Hal rose in the stirrups. "Alice!" he cried, in a low, urgent voice.

Clifford was ripped from his reverie as Hal swung his leg and leapt from the saddle in one fluid motion, hands outstretched for Alice as she began, very slowly, to slip from the horse. As she slid down Hal's body, her teeth collided painfully with the bridge of his nose; by the time she was on her feet and her eyes had focused, a trickle of blood was running in the furrow beside his mouth.

Alice exclaimed and reached up with her handkerchief, dabbing at the scarlet rivulet. Hal was holding her hard against him. The whole party had halted.

"Alice." His lips were far too close.

By now Lord Clifford had flung himself from the saddle. He snatched the Duchess from his son's arms. She was trying to slip the handkerchief away to her sleeve. He threw it to the ground, spinning Alice around to face the gate, reckless hands gripping her shoulders.

Behind his father's back, Hal bent to retrieve the scrap of cloth. His thumb stroked at the de Vere badge embroidered in the linen – the Star of Oxford. A fine chain had tumbled from within his shirt, a bejewelled ring swinging to and fro at its limit in tiny twinkles of azure; a woman's ring. Hal slipped the chain back into seclusion and tucked the handkerchief after, the two tokens nestled side-by-side.

All the while, the Countess of Shrewsbury watched the little scene with frowning interest. The rumours were so rife that she'd been impatient for a glimpse of them together, and now she saw. An unlikely pair, in truth, but something was afoot.

Releasing the girl, Clifford looked round for the Earl, missed him, and his brow blackened. The Countess accepted his ungracious kiss of greeting. Alice smiled wanly and stumbled into her embrace.

"I welcome you to Goodrich," said the Countess. "I'll have you shown straight to your chamber, Lady Alice. You look half-dead with weariness."

When Lady Catherine's steward had guided Clifford to a guestchamber, the door was barely closed before he rounded on Hal for not alerting him to the girl's state.

"For you were surely watching her, as you are always watching her – don't think I haven't noticed."

"How could that be, Father, since you have forbidden it?"

A strange growling noise. "Do not make a joke of this! I have forbidden you to touch her also, but that did not stop you clasping her to you just now." His voice was strained and peevish.

"I saved her from a fall, Father," said Hal smoothly. "It's a good thing one of us was watching."

"You had no call to embrace her like that, before the whole company. Never again let me hear you make free with her name." His face was thrust against his son's so that the scowl filled Hal's field of vision. "Why do you think I've been so particular that none should come near her?"

"Except you, my lord? I assume it's because you want her for yourself."

"How dare you speak to me in that way?" he roared at his intolerable son, and boxed his ears, too, for good measure. This wretched boy: almost his twin in looks, but so much younger than he – just a few years older than Alice – and fully sighted, and unencumbered by a sickening reputation. Just now he was hard to be near. "She is carrying an heir for King Henry, you mawk! I'll risk no scandal attaching to her."

One brow had tilted up as high as it would reach, Hal's face plainly speaking his mind. Loic was peering round Clifford's shoulder, shaking his head – in disapproval, perhaps, or warning. Hal allowed his gaze to drop with insolent slowness. In a violently sullen mood Clifford stalked down to dinner, but the day was to grow dramatically worse.

He started to interrogate the Countess for news of Somerset. She shook her head: there was no certain news of the prisoners from the Abbey, only rumours that they were to be taken to London, to be beheaded on Tower Hill. Clifford had a fleeting vision of himself at the head of a rescue party. They would need hundreds; it could not be done. Edmond was gone from them.

Then she startled Clifford. "You know the Duke of Exeter's in the Tower?"

"Exeter? No, no. I was leading the left flank with him at Barnet. I saw him go down."

301

Lady Catherine was adamant. "He's not in the best of health, they say. But alive for now."

He passed a hand over his face. It seemed impossible. He'd seen the Duke's visor clawed up; the man's face had shivered with blades. And Clifford would have turned aside for him, but it happened in a whirl, and bloody Robbie was wandering around looking for an executioner, and bloody Loic had got himself imperilled, again; ever the damsel in distress. He drained his cup, over and over, and squared himself to ask the question: "The Earl of Devon: what tidings? He was seen crossing the river west from Tewkesbury. By now he'll be heading to find Tudor, I suppose."

Slowly she raised her eyes and he saw, with dawning dread, that they were brimful of a warning pity: there was something more.

"*Not Devon.* Say it's not so!" He choked it out, and then he could actually see the shadows of the dead crowding in on him, and the room upended.

* * *

In the darkness, the spectres resumed their torment. All hope of sleep had flown. Clifford laboured through the night, his frame racked, fitfully, by great, wretched sobs. As the hours crept on, Loic held his master, stroking his hair, dabbing his face as if he were a child.

George's face conveyed his dumb pity – until he lay down, and at once sank to peaceful slumber. Hal slumped on their pallet, eyes closed, widely wakeful. Sharing a room with his father was dire at the best of times; the most restless sleeper he'd ever encountered. How Loic survived it night after night was beyond him. But this was infinitely worse: a horrifying collapse. Englishmen didn't weep. It may be fashionable in continental courts to give vent to one's feelings, but he'd never have anticipated his father, of all men, picking up the distasteful habit. He flung himself on to his back and forced his fingers into his ears.

At length, at last, Hal was soothed by the warmth in Loic's voice as he murmured like a mother, and he slept.

* * *

302

The past night's wide wakefulness was the perfect, if accidental, preparation for Somerset's last hours. The jailer bowed his way into the stale cell on that final balmy evening and asked, with respectful delicacy, if any comfort was wanting. None but a priest, expected at any moment. The confession was dutiful, though he found he'd few sins to offer up. At last Edmond bethought himself of his little wife. With self-conscious gravity he forgave the lady any offence she may or may not have committed. He felt in his hidden heart that there was none, but still he could not bring himself to dwell upon the child growing within her and so he did not.

Tomorrow, at this hour, he would be far away. Edmond lay down and slept easily, lulled by an exquisite melody that had caught in his inward ear. When he awoke before the sun, the song was with him still, soon abetted by his tuneless humming. Long-familiar in the hinterland of his exile, it was born, no doubt, at the lute of that master player, Robert Clifford, but not the less lovely for that. Melancholy and haunting, the music disturbed his cursory prayers. And Edmond, who never troubled to listen to lyrics, found he could recall the verses quite easily, though he didn't sing them aloud – surely inapt, on such an occasion; suggestive rather of insanity than poignant farewell. Stirring him with a winsome love for the England he was forsaking – this stone in the sea – the song accompanied him at early light to the scaffold at the market cross, and there it contrived to drown the final farewells and bathe Edmond's last moments on earth.

* * *

And so Edmond of Somerset had abandoned all mortal care by the time Robert Clifford emerged that morning, blinking against the light. He found Cuthbert Bellingham leaning at the door to his staircase, unsummoned, petrified into a hunch as though he'd lingered through eons.

"Lord Robert?" Upon the knight's face, a stricken look.

Clifford turned on him; turned not his neck but his body, shuffling in small steps redolent of pain. He gazed down upon his marshal's silvery crown. Heavy brows obscured the older man's eyes. At last Sir Cuthbert's touch found his master's neck, and rested. Clifford's fingers brushed the hand, but there were no more tears inside him; none at all.

303

As the Wyverns made their way to the gatehouse every passing man examined Clifford's face for a fraction too long.

The Countess stroked Alice's arm. "They say that morning sickness is a sure sign of a strong son. Go as slowly as you can, Robert." She preferred to be thought overfamiliar than to gamble with his title.

"We have no choice but to make what haste we can to Monmouth, my lady. Remember me to your husband, and pray for a safe outcome."

Their hostess would remember him to her husband; there was never any doubt of that. The Earl of Shrewsbury, who hurried to London last year to free King Henry from the Tower, and now, it was embarrassingly clear, had hurried to Edward of York to plead, to grovel and to repudiate them all. How long, Clifford wondered, before the lady's message reached her husband; how long before they heard the hoofbeats behind them? The capture of Robert Clifford with a pregnant Duchess of Somerset: there was no finer declaration of loyalty.

And so, as soon as the red towers of Goodrich were out of sight, the cavalcade abandoned the Monmouth road and swung east, deep into the woods; slower but more secluded; a risk, but they would never outrun a pursuit, even upon the sounder road. Concealment was the better choice.

The travellers began their descent into the rimpled, swaying forest of the May dawn. Though Loic's heart brimmed with a tender and helpless pity, his mind was soothed with the balm of verdant wonder, and his ears filled with the angelic piping and fluting which attended them on their way. Alice was untouched, her eyes lagging closed. She tried so very hard to remain on the horse, clinging to Andrew Chowne, dizzy and nauseated.

At last even this was beyond her, and they made a halt. Alice was lifted down by Aymer, hot hands colliding roughly with her breasts as he reached for her. He lingered over her hips, pulling her against him with a jerk. Alice was too wretched to think on it, twisting away into Blanche's arms. Leaning into her gentlewoman's tender clasp, she heaved and heaved again, but there was no food in her stomach and it brought her no relief.

At once, the clamour sparked up behind. It was Bertrand Jansen inciting the revolt, railing that the Wyverns were doomed if they kept to this pace; that they'd no choice but to abandon the ailing lady and double their speed south. Clifford, who'd walked into the woods to relieve himself, returned at that moment and was barely restrained from assaulting him. Jolly and one of the Walters intervened, pleading that Jansen was only voicing what everyone thought: that a rider should carry the Duchess back to Goodrich and leave her in Lady Catherine's care. Other voices assented. Aymer volunteered.

Clifford drew himself up and scanned the circle as menacingly as he knew how. In him reposed their devotion, their loyalty; he was sure of it now, bound together in adversity as they were, all other paths being closed to them. But their faith in their lord, in his judgment suffering, of late, some violent buffets: it was faltering. He hissed through his teeth. *"Abandon her?* Understand this – if the lady stays, I stay with her. Under no circumstance will I abandon her. Those who disagree are free to fuck off."

No one moved. Clifford was barely mollified. Their lead was eroding all the time; he didn't need to hear the hooves to know that; everyone knew it. It would take little for mutiny to break out again. Turning his back on the recalcitrant men, Clifford discovered Alice some way off, slumped on a fallen tree, the salt tracks crusting her cheeks. He sank beside her and rubbed his face, grey with exhaustion. Could she continue if she rode before him? She nodded wordlessly. He pushed himself up and called to his groom to swap his saddle for the female style, with its lower pommel, and lengthen the stirrup leathers as far as they would go. Moving behind Alice, he detached the travelling coif, crumpling the wilted linen in his hands. She touched her hair and frowned up at him.

"The ties smell of vomit," he whispered. "I can't have it under my nose."

Blanche began to protest the seemliness of the proceedings: my lady's inappropriate appearance, my lady riding in a man's lap – that lap in particular.

Alice watched Lord Clifford stride away, stalked by the cadaverous priest whose forefinger was jabbing, insistent, at his master's back; a startling impertinence. Another man who wished her ill, no doubt.

When she glanced around the clearing, her heart sank. Some distance from the main party stood Elyn, back against a tree, breast heaving. Guy was leaning in, a hand on the trunk above her shoulder. He bent lower and

305

blocked the view of her face, his toe rhythmically kicking the tree. Then there was a murmur in Alice's ear, making her jump. "You should keep your gentlewomen on a tighter rein, my lady. That one: her morals are loose. She's corrupting Guy." Aymer gave a quiet laugh.

Her response was as haughty as she could manage. "Your brother shall keep his distance! Mistress Elyn is my father's natural daughter. Please tell your twin of my displeasure, at once."

She turned her back on the youth. The effort had drained her. When finally she glanced back, Aymer was audaciously close, heat shimmering off his skin like a fever. Hurriedly she stepped away. She couldn't meet his eyes.

The groom led up the great white horse, and Clifford lifted Alice, sideways, on to the unfamiliar saddle and swung up behind her. Without ceremony, he clasped her hips and shifted her until she was comfortably wedged between his thighs. There was no thought of protest. As they moved off, her head drooped against his chest. Clifford frowned down. There was a shadow before him once more.

Half the pins in her hair had come away with the headdress. Riding beside his father, Hal watched the captivating tresses uncoil with slow languor down her back, butter-pale and butter-smooth, warm beneath and nut-brown against her nape. He looked to his father, whose lips were now buried in her hair. There was a vinegar sting of envy. The younger man had been imagining, and now he saw, it was worse. But Clifford breathed her scent – the softest hint of rosemary – and it soothed him; Somerset receded.

Lifting a hand to rummage for pins, and encountered his bristly chin. She snatched back her hand, surprised by the closeness of his face, and rocked as he sat up and flexed his shoulders.

Reining in between the twins, Clifford turned to Guy, his voice stern and dry: "I have warned you already, my son. One woman in this condition is trouble enough; we cannot manage another. You are not too old for me to take my belt to you, and so I will, if you disobey me again."

She did not mean to look; she meant not to look; but her eyes were drawn, and inevitably she peeped around the encircling arm. Guy was dark red and stormy. Behind them, Aymer was examining Alice's hair, reaching out to rub the locks between finger and thumb. With a steadying hand at her waist, Clifford cantered away to the head of the column.

Across Aymer's palm lay a number of fine strands, a yard long. Letting slip the reins, he wound them around his fingers, hands asunder, until the hairs snapped. He glanced across at Guy. "He speaks as though you were a green boy who didn't know how to avoid the consequences."

Richie broke in with a loud laugh. "But Father doesn't know how to avoid the consequences; never did. Look how many of us there are! Look how many consequences!"

Guy's lashes were clustered with angry tears. "I can't risk a thrashing before the rest of them! I'd never live it down."

"Ah, Guymer," drawled Aymer, " he would not do it. He is testing to see if you're a man or a mouse. Do you think our grandfather never tried to call him to heel?"

Guy was warmed, as always, when his brother made use of the old pet name. He paused a moment and considered. At times Aymer was clever and perceptive; sometimes less reliable.

"Though that whore is in no way interesting," continued Aymer. "Why waste your time?"

Will nodded.

"But then George will try her," burst out Guy, revealing the crux of the matter.

Aymer considered for a moment, then snorted with amusement. "I have it! Tell her you cannot love her until you have proof of her constancy. Then you can pull back, and George will get nowhere with her, and we will watch and enjoy ourselves. With luck, it is George who'll get the thrashing from Father."

Richie laughed so hard he slipped a stirrup, and all but fell. Guy regarded his twin with great pleasure.

* * *

Cobbles diffused the flow into a broad estuary. The chairs had been set too close to the platform and slightly downhill, a rudimentary error. As Constable,

307

the responsibility was Gloucester's, but someone else would bear the blame.

Executions should be tabled in ascending order of rank; the crowd was only interested in Edmond Beaufort, but for an hour or two after his passing, the petty men clambered up and were carried down, anonymous and humdrum. Then came a fellow more particularly projectile, or perhaps the block had slipped. The front row flinched. Fresh hay was carted in – another ineffective dam – while the headsman downed tools and swabbed himself.

Simon Loys drew up his feet in stiff displeasure. Two rows before him King Edward was enthroned, stately and splendid, notwithstanding the wobble of sodden cushions beneath his feet. From Lord Hastings, one soft burp after another; the flood lapped his instep while his head lolled lower. To the King's right, Richard of Gloucester was rippling, slow and sinuous, easing the ache in that serpentine spine.

Sir Simon closed his eyes, absorbed by a matter of sharp interest: the news that had galloped into Tewkesbury with the dawn. At last the ladies of Lancaster were unearthed, not ten miles distant and going nowhere. All except one. For little Lady Alice – that unlikely adventuress – was gone; slipped away from the priory two days previously, bearing a most pernicious cargo: Edmond Beaufort's heir.

Loys was still thinking of her when the ordeal concluded. The nobles rose and the sluicing began.

"My lord of Gloucester – a word in private, if I may? No, I'm afraid it can't wait."

* * *

After a while, when Alice may have dozed, the nausea had subsided. Robert had been humming to himself; she recognised the song, melancholy and haunting. His hand toyed with the reins as though a lute lay beneath the fingers.

"Your voice is so beautiful, my lord. Would you sing *Farewell?*"

"Sing?" His voice was desperately grim. "I'm in no mood for singing."

The man seemed grudging, reluctant, perturbed by her proximity. Helpless as she was, Alice should acknowledge the reprieve. But it was quite the opposite: if he felt himself free, her vulnerability was acute.

"My lord," she ventured at last, "I am truly saddened at this news of the Earl of Devon."

"I doubt that. Devon was no well-wisher of yours."

"And for that too, I am sorry. I do not know why I attracted his hostility."

The voice was emphatic. "Yes you do. Let's have no pretence on that score."

Alice had wished somehow to probe the subject of Eleanor Percy, who must surely be lost to him, but the courage was nowhere to be found. She tried again to engage him, on neutral ground. "I was wondering, my lord: Masters Oliver, and Tom, and Richie – are they your nephews or your sons? I didn't follow at the time."

He sighed. "Tom is my son; Oliver is my nephew. Tom and Richie share a mother. It's thinkable Richie is my brother John's get, but the woman died long since, so we'll never know. I couldn't care less."

She pursed her lips, hopelessly confused. "So many boys, my lord."

His thoughts were far away, with Jean, his little soldier. He would write to Babette Delaurin; warn her to spin out that gold, for there'd be no more. "Ah – I have other sons than these; Waryn is now under-steward at Alnwick in Hal's stead; the rest are too young to ride with me."

Good God. "Which of them is most like you, do you find? Master Hal?" And as she said it, she wished she hadn't, for an array of reasons.

He was silent awhile. "Hal's the living image of me at his age, but he's a different man." *A traitor.*

"Would you tell me of your brother John, my lord?"

So he spoke of John: their devotion and their differences. Robert, taller; noisier; the more notable soldier. John's bleak moods; his interminable silences; his casual cruelty; his mordant humour. Thinking of his brother led Robert back to the dreadful March day, the day of the engagement at Ferrybridge. It was ten years ago; and three months after Wakefield.

He recalled, in a blank voice, John's habit of removing his gorget at the first opportunity; he always complained it was choking him. Earlier that day, he remembered, John had undone the clasp to gulp down some wine, and Robert warned then that an archer would get him in the throat. '*That would be a lucky shot,*' and Robert responded: '*Not for you*'. These small and pointless details that had got stuck.

Moments after, Robert had lifted his visor at the sight of Warwick's approaching men and was himself struck in the eye with a shaft. Somehow he'd been borne away, by a few of their entourage, to their own lines. When he came to, some hours later, it was to learn that his brother was dead. It seemed John had been pulling his men back from Ferrybridge when they took the chance of a brief respite. Removing helmets and gorgets, they were taken unawares in a Neville ambush and cut down almost to a man. John was, indeed, taken by an arrow in the throat, drowning in his own blood.

The story was petering out, Lord Clifford staring away. "But those who lived that day took our father's ring from his hand, and brought it to me. What good a ring, when in him I have lost my right arm?" He lapsed.

Almost whimpering with pity, she cast about, alighting on the subject of his father.

"Ah – we revered our father. We competed to please him. The most intimidating man I ever knew, though he rarely raised his voice. He used to say '*Robert, no one needs to hear what's going on in your head.*' He was sparing with words, and thought I talked too much. My brother John was very like him; and young George here is very much alike, in looks, anyway, to his father and his grandfather both – although he talks far too much. As do you. Rest now."

There were so many things yet to say, but after that snub she could not continue.

And all this time, as she was asking and he was answering, the resentment surged within him. She was so contemptibly easy to read: probing his defences, dragging those sharp little grappling irons over him, searching for a faultline, seeking to provoke an avowal; to make herself safe and cherished.

This from a girl who had seduced him into treachery. From a girl who did not ask, and did not care, whether her husband was quick or dead. But it was only for the child. He knew full well that had it not been for her child, she would have sat tight at Malvern, waiting for Edward of York. What then? York would have given her a good, steady husband, and Robert would have been discarded and forgotten, with his pain and his shame, his betrayal of his leader and the destruction of the last decade's hopes. And still she practised those infant wiles on him, as though he were a green and hopeful boy.

* * *

Alice was tidied and readied by Blanche and riding behind her chamberlain once more as they began the steep descent to Tintern Abbey, nestled in its lush and peaceful vale. As before, she began to recover as soon as she'd dismounted. The women were to lodge with Lord Clifford near to the Abbey church; the others were consigned to the lesser guesthouse, set some way up the hill.

Not so much sick as heartsick now and listless, Alice could not abide her gentlewomen's chatter just at present. She had some idea of going into the church with her supplications for Jonkin's soul and slipped away, wandering across the lane in the direction of the great stone ark. As she approached the lay door at the west end, she spied Lord Clifford, alone for once, stretched back upon a bench in the garden beyond the cloister, asleep in the evening sun. She vacillated for a moment, and then she was drawn to him, wishing to turn back time. She sat quietly at his side.

"I was surprised by Anne Neville."

Startled, she looked across. "You thought her loyalties lay with the house of Lancaster?"

"No, not Warwick's daughter. Not she. You two had grown up together at Middleham? Yet she seemed hostile." He turned his face now.

Alice swallowed and let the bitterness soak her. "So were they all, by the end. Many cruel things were said about me." She wanted to add – *about you, about us.*

He looked away. "I've heard them."

311

He hadn't just heard them; he'd caused them. But no admission was forthcoming, no explanation, no contrition.

Her mouth hardened. "My husband believes I betrayed him. He believes the child is…not his. Did you hear that?"

"Mm."

"But of course, I have never done him any wrong." The emphasis on the 'I' was ringing clear.

He was growing hot; he was growing angry. It would serve the little harpy right if he did abandon her. "Do not pretend with me. There have been too many women blaming me for their own weakness; acting the innocent."

Alice closed her mind to the venomous words, and groped for help. "At least now…"

He shrugged. "Now?" His voice was a razor. "What now?"

Fear and bewilderment were whisking up, heart-scorching, until Alice was beset with the despairing urge to throw her arms about the man and sob against his chest – her rock of granite in a plunging sea.

Safer, perhaps – this once, and once only – to have surrendered to the impulse. Instead, the bitter self-pity swept her away. *I am not a woman grown. I have no protector. How has it come to this?* More than anything she had ever longed for, Alice longed for the Earl of Warwick and his countess to appear beside her in the quiet garden. "You told me once that you were my friend." She whispered it, through tears.

"As you told me, more than once, that you were mine. It seems we've each been disappointed in the other." He leaned back, sighing. "Why must you follow me here, woman? You should not be alone with me. You know it. Better for all if you cared less for your vanity and more for the child on whom all hopes depend."

She stood, chin raised, and turned away with rigid steps and trembling hands. He remained there in the fading light, listening to the monks' exquisite chanting. And then he heaved himself up and walked to the church.

* * *

Within the Abbey guesthouse, Hal knocked at Clifford's chamber and put his head around the door. Loic was sitting alone at the workmanlike table, licking the pads of his fingers, restringing the lute. Hal pulled the door behind him. "A good evening, Sir Loic. Where's my father?"

"Praying, Master Hal."

"Again?"

"Lately…he is sore oppressed."

"Don't I know it? We've none us had much sleep." The thought brought on a yawn. Hal ducked to the window. "If he's praying, he's doing it in the open air, and with the lady at his side. Ah no – she is leaving him. Angry."

Hands on hips, Hal strolled to the table and stood very close, looking down on Loic, who breathed the scent of his body. Familiar, but much less clean.

"What is happening?" asked Hal.

"You're in my light."

Hal's hand dropped, heavy, on to Moncler's shoulder, startling him. The warmth seeped through the fabric to Loic's skin.

"I know how well you love him," said Hal slowly. "I am just the same as he. Don't keep me at arm's length, Loic."

The chamberlain placed the lute carefully on the table and turned in his chair. The hand had come to rest; the hand that was just like Monseigneur's. Loic drank in those familiar features, his mind glazed and empty. Their eyes met and the Englishman's wits were whetted, spindle-sharp. A most inopportune moment for the key to have presented itself – the fabled key – just when Hal's heart was overflowing with helpless passion for the girl, the momentum of which carried him, like a flood, toward the other gate.

"Ah – so what is between them, Sir Loic?"

The chamberlain twitched, began a scowl and with difficulty supressed it.

"…for I had thought my father wished the Lady Alice for himself. But if he doesn't care for her…" Hal gave a small, silly, self-conscious laugh.

Loic sighed, righting himself. "He does. Of course he does. But it has all gone awry. He's done Somerset a grave wrong."

Hal raised his brows "Really? I thought…?"

"No, no. Though not for lack of trying. And now Somerset is to die, it goes hard with him, very hard. And Devon, his friend: he is dead; Exeter and the Prince, who was their hope…and Warwick," he added. "Jack de Vere and Beaumont are gone from him. He's lost his lands, an exile once more…" Loic stared into Hal's eyes. "And she blames him. She isn't here for him, of course, but only for the sake of her child."

Hal gave a questioning shrug.

Loic tried to explain, to separate the strands: "But the child matters to him; Monseigneur is lost and must have someone to follow. He'll not touch her; he fears to sully the child's name."

The same gesture, and Hal said dismissively, "There are always such rumours. They say Edward of York is the son of a Calais archer; they say our Prince was Somerset's son. No one believes these stories, not those that spread them, even."

"Ha! Her own husband believes that babe is not his; the rumours have flown far and wide: all Monseigneur's fault; he took what he could, and set those hares running. I don't doubt it's too late already, but he is desperate." Loic gave Hal a slight, sad smile, and shook his head. "And this is so like him now, to turn on his victim and torment her for his own mistakes." Loic rested his forehead in his palm. "I cannot believe what has befallen us."

Hal saw with surprise, concern, that Loic was close to tears. "We will come through this," he said, pointlessly. He had no feeling for what would happen. Every day he was older than the day before.

Loic had stopped attending and rose, abruptly, as if catching a voice inaudible to others. "Master Hal, Monseigneur has need of my service. Please come away so that I can lock up."

* * *

Clifford was stiff from prayer before any peace had settled in his heart. By then he was tugged away by hunger, and made his way back to the room in the Abbey guesthouse. Awaiting him: a tray of food, a jug of wine and a girl. She was seated on the only chair in the room, gazing through the window, chin in hand. Loic was lying on the bed, tuning the lute, as usual. He'd made hardly a pretence of rising when Clifford waved him down. The girl looked round at him, a surprised expression on her face. Perhaps his size; his daunting appearance; or it may have been surprise at finding herself there at all. He was rather taken aback himself. Abbot Colston was a dour man who looked to be running a tight establishment. Truly, Loic was some kind of wizard.

The girl looked a little rumpled. Clifford wondered if his chamberlain had been sampling the wares, but he saw the water on the floor, on Loic's sleeves, and he knew then his man had been washing her. That was thoughtful.

Clifford drained the wine. Loic had quietly laid aside the lute and rolled towards the wall, one knee drawn to his chest. Clifford looked down on him with a fond smile.

"Ah – but I see you, mon petit! Off you go. Give me an hour and then take her out however you got her in."

Loic collected himself and headed for the door. It was worth a try; occasionally Monseigneur was drunk or distracted enough not to heed his presence. And Loic would prefer not to be wandering in the gathering darkness. Lately, Aymer would shadow his moves with uncanny prescience, coming upon him with silent tread and knowing taunts. He was tempted towards the comfortable warmth of the household men, but they were lodged with the boys some way up the hill. He wondered where Benet had got to. The boy would not stray far, but neither would he offer much protection. Loic walked briskly to the refuge of the Abbey church, into the rear section reserved for the laity. There he found Monseigneur's son, the gentle Edwin, on his knees, and they prayed companionably together, flooded by the last rays of evening sunlight, transmuted gemlike through soaring glass.

When Loic returned to the chamber and paused outside the door he could hear nothing. He slipped inside. It was half-dark within. Monseigneur lay sprawled, magnificently naked, the eyepatch hanging on the bed as usual, his face at peace.

Loic stood over him a moment, breathing with his breathing, and then retrieved the sheet from the floor and smoothed it across his body. The girl was watching, fully clothed, upon the chair, as if she hadn't moved; perhaps she hadn't. Loic beckoned her and she followed him out, hand-in-hand, quickly, quietly, through the dimly lit passage and into the shadows of walls and the dark spaces between buildings until they reached a little woodstore outside the infirmary, and there he pulled her down.

Blanche turned from the chamber window. She was a betrothed woman, and her view of the world had changed. But it had not changed far enough or fast enough to protect her. She watched as Mitten brushed Alice's hair in long, steady strokes.

Blanche opened her mouth, closed it; opened it again. "Who would credit this? I see Loic Moncler has procured a trull for Lord Clifford. Smuggled her here, into a Cistercian house, of all places! Sir Hugh says that when they travelled from the field of Barnet together, Moncler conjured women like a wizard: the master has them first, and then the man. Sir Hugh says they're beasts, with the appetite of beasts."

Silence met her words. Alice – who wished Lord Clifford at the bottom of the sea – folded her arms upon the table, closed her eyes and laid down her head. First Elyn sidled to the window, and, after a moment, Joanna.

Constance gave Blanche a scathing look. "We shall not miss Lady Ullerton, Blanche, with you speaking in her voice. In my experience, men are all alike; all of them, given the chance. Either do as I do, and have no truck with them, or accept their natures."

"You have no experience," said Blanche. "They are not all alike."

Mitten plaited her mistress's hair, wiped her eyes and bundled her in to the bed. With no word more, Blanche slipped from the room, taking a circuitous route to avoid passing the way Loic had gone. Drawing her cloak about her, she started on the long flight of steps leading towards the lesser guesthouse. There seemed to be a number of shadows skulking that evening. These need not concern her, so long as Loic was not among them. She passed his manservant, the pretty Cornish boy, who appeared to be out searching for him, and hurried on. A male figure turned the corner towards her, short and bulky, with long arms, his movements marking him as an older man. On seeing her, he halted and swung back into the shadows. When she drew level, he was gone.

As Blanche approached the lesser guesthouse, there was yet another lonely figure, this one lounging on a wall, scratching a dog's ears and swilling from a tankard.

My God. Everyone is out and about, tonight. She'd been aiming for discretion, to no good purpose now. She lifted the lantern aloft, and the features leapt into life. Dominating his face was a pair of pale eyes fringed with sooty lashes. She looked on the broad cheekbones and the curving lips with their tinge of lilac. It was the handsome one, the nuisance.

"Mistress Elyn is safe abed in the Duchess's chamber," she chided, "where you cannot harm her."

The eyes looked on, expressionless. It was the other twin, she saw now — though it would be hard to say how she told them apart.

"Your pardon, sir. I thought you your brother."

The eyes followed her as she passed, and then Aymer's soft and lazy tones. "Sir Hugh is with Patrick Nield, I believe, still pumping him, ineptly, for information. So: it is Dyffryn Hall, where we are headed; you had but to ask. When you leave us, make for Newport, from there across the Severn to Bristol, and thence to London. Don't try to take Alice; we haven't finished with her."

Her legs continued to move though her body had gone rigid. Reaching the door of the guesthouse, Blanche shrieked at Sir Hugh in her distress, scolding him for a clumsy fool.

"It's a wild guess; he means only to frighten you. And I know we're for Dyffryn Hall," he said sourly. "It's some ten miles west of Chepstow. Two of the pages have already carried a message to Sir Lawrence Welford."

She considered for a moment, trying to steady her breathing. "We'll reach the house tomorrow then. The men will surely pause and rest there the night. But once Lord Clifford and his followers have departed for Chepstow, we must leave directly; for, at ten miles, it's close enough for his lordship to be coming and going between the two."

"Will he though? The household men say that he's not inclined to her now; his spirit is broken and cannot be roused. It would not surprise me if the men start to desert him."

She snorted. "That broken spirit did not stop Loic Moncler smuggling in a woman for him tonight."

"Really?" There was a dazzled appreciation in his voice "In here, even?" He blinked, his eyes unfocused, envisaging.

Her brows snapped at him. "You men are all alike! All of you, given the chance."

"No – it's not so, I promise. But Blanche, listen to me. I shall go to the Abbot. I would sleep easier if we had some help. The Abbot will know what to do."

She did not relish leaving the matter in his hands, but she would have to become accustomed to it now. His arm creeping around her waist, Sir Hugh escorted Blanche back to the primary guesthouse, an even longer way round, evading the mysterious simian rover; avoiding Aymer, should he still be there, waylaying wanderers like a sphinx, and taking the pair directly into the path of the returning Loic, who doffed his bonnet and gave Blanche his most impish smile.

The next morning, Abbot Colston came out to speed them on their way. He had provisioned them; he had offered them a lay brother as guide – eschewed by Lord Clifford, who knew the way to Chepstow. They were not going to Chepstow. The blessing was given in a severe voice, as if they did not deserve it, and without a smile. The Abbot strode away before they had left the gatehouse.

* * *

Every day in those weeks seemed warmer than the day before. And the FitzCliffords, who had never left the North until that year, felt that this country did not resemble any place they had known, and that the weather would hold for ever.

The travellers continued along a heavily-wooded escarpment. In a high hollow, they drew towards a sturdy, timbered cottage. How restful it would be to pause there and shut the door, shutting out the world. The place was secluded enough to risk a halt. Some slumped on the ground and others refreshed themselves with food or drink. Alice leaned against a tree, enjoying the sensation of firm ground beneath her feet and the morning sun on her face.

Dismounting together, Aymer and his little faction strolled away among the trees to relieve themselves. Behind him, Richie could hear Guy regaling the others with a jest and wandered back alone, seeking out that intriguing redhead, as he'd been seeking for some time, since her peppery ways first caught his notice. He slouched on his hip, watching the maiden, until Constance turned full-face and scowled. He pretended to examine the cottage. The Duchess reclaimed her attention, and Richie resumed his inspection.

Then a pair of hands clapped him roughly on the shoulders, and he started violently. George jerked him backwards, hissing in his ear. "Don't stare so crudely, you churl. Bede's had his eye on her from the start."

Bede. Richie felt honour-bound to make the obligatory asinine noise, but George's hands were gripping tightly, so he didn't.

"You surely don't think," continued his captor, "that the girl will trouble to look at you, if she has Bede's interest? You fairly stink, Richie. You're just an ugly child. It's a shame if you hadn't realised, but there it is. You've a nose like…" he fumbled for something witty and disparaging. Only 'eagle' came to mind: too flattering. "Piss off and yank yourself in the wood."

George was a stupid lout, but far too eager with his fists. Richie had shaken himself free and stalked away before he flung, from a safe distance, "You're not doing so well yourself. The dark one with the big dugs? Guy's had her already."

An imprudent shaft. What if it should come to Lord Clifford's ears? But George was unscathed, turning away with a derisive smile. And there, lounging against a trunk, smirking at him, was that overbearing knave. Hal and George sauntered off, their arms about each other's shoulders, the laughter floating back.

The others were nowhere in sight. Richie eased down beneath a dead tree, cradled among its desiccated branches. He closed his eyes, churning and morose. He wasn't the worst of them: Tom's skin was terrible and Robbie was wadded with fat; so young, though, that it didn't matter. But he was a man grown, and no girl had ever come to him. Not willingly. Not free of charge. And yet there was Hal – always before him – a great oaf with coarse and brutish features who had his pick among women, and swaggered with arrogant assurance, the darling of the household.

Suddenly he was surrounded by feet, and looking up, he scanned the faces of the other three. Will tilted his head, inquiring, the sleek hair fanning across his neat brow like a crow's wing.

"Nothing," said Richie, and pulled himself up.

* * *

As soon as the party halted, Blanche took Sir Hugh's arm and led him into seclusion. When she looked up, questioning, he hurried in. She batted him away.

"Sir Hugh! Attend! What passed between you and the abbot?"

"Eh? You mean Abbot Colston?"

"I know you're an intelligent man, Sir Hugh, but sometimes one would be hard put to tell. Quickly, please!"

He settled himself on a fallen log and pulled her down beside him. "I spoke to him; I spoke to the abbot. I told him that Lord Clifford had abducted the Duchess of Somerset from her husband and was keeping her as his mistress."

"Keeping her as his mistress? In a monastery? It was plain she was with her gentlewomen in another part of the house."

"Yes," he agreed. "Abbot Colston pointed that out. So I said that Lord Clifford kept his distance on that occasion so as not to alert him. But, of course, she's a married woman and there are rumours abroad everywhere concerning the two of them. As it happened, the abbot had seen them arguing together that evening, so he was the more ready to believe in their intimacy."

Blanche was looking rather pained. "So what then?"

"The abbot believes, as I do, that we're being hunted by York's men. They must be close behind us now; we've made such slow progress. They'll be heading for Chepstow to capture Jasper Tudor. No doubt they'll seek to secure the lady, too, once they learn that she's carrying Somerset's child. So we talked it through, he and I, and we agreed that at first light this morning Abbot Colston would send a messenger back towards Goodrich, as that's the route our pursuers will most likely follow. By now, our destination may already be known to them."

"So you've shown York's men how to find her?" Blanche was breathless, her toes curling at the edge of a yawning chasm.

"I told the abbot that though Lord Clifford means to rendezvous with Tudor, he'll not go on until he's first secreted the lady at Dyffryn Hall, where Sir Lawrence is expecting us. When Lord Clifford and his men ride away to Chepstow tomorrow, the lady will be left all but undefended. Easy pickings for whomever King Edward has dispatched to fetch her."

Blanche was looking at him uncertainly, running over the outcomes in her mind, but she was defeated by the myriad branching possibilities. And, frankly, something felt wrong. She had loved and cared for Alice since the girl came to Middleham as a little child. A tiny, watchful child, silent and dazed at the loss of her father and Aubrey. Blanche's mistress was inexpressibly dear, despite her recent waywardness. There was no doubt that dividing her from Robert Clifford was a kindness; a mercy, though it felt oddly like a betrayal, just at present. But if King Edward had plans for Alice, as he surely would, might it not be that Sir Hugh and she should form part of those plans, and remain at her side? When Lord Clifford departed on the morrow, they would face a painful choice. Or Blanche would face a painful choice; Sir Hugh, probably, would not.

A thought struck her. "Do you know for sure that Abbot Colston has done as promised, sending those messengers north? Where do his sympathies lie? Perhaps with King Henry and the house of Lancaster. He may already have betrayed us to Lord Clifford."

"I don't know where his loyalties once lay. By now, there is no house of Lancaster." Sir Hugh was smirking a little. "But I do know that he's highly displeased with Lord Clifford. You see, the abbot is angry that he's been lied to, his authority has been mocked and his abbey used as a bawdy house."

She did see. Loic had not served his master a good turn there; he had undone it all.

They could hear Lord Clifford ordering the party to make ready. Hurriedly, Blanche tugged up a clump of wildflowers, dawdling back towards the group with her hand in Sir Hugh's and a fond smile upon her face. She was avoiding Lord Clifford's gaze. He saw too much. He would see the triumph.

At the other side of the clearing, voices approached. A pair of peasant girls appeared around the corner of the little house. Glimpsing the group, they scurried inside and slammed the door.

Heart sinking, Alice turned to the boys. By then, Aymer had tossed the reins to Notch and was striding forward. Richie FitzClifford, poised on one stirrup when Aymer led the way, leapt down, now evading the very eyes he'd sought before. Still ahorse, Guy glanced uncertainly towards his father. Will enfolded them in his enigmatic smile, and George grinned also, easier to read.

But Clifford had already halted, arms folded, chin up, a pose intimately recognisable to those who knew. "In *present company*? Have you *lost your wits*? Get back in the saddle and control yourselves."

The boys were checked, returning chastened and sullen to the horses. The queasy relief was writ large on Alice's face. Richie caught her eye and had the grace to look abashed.

Turning, she sensed the breathless pause across the glade. Every creature had fallen still, linked like chains: Robert gazing at Aymer; Loic at Robert; Benet and Castor at Loic; George and Guy at Elyn; Bede at Constance; Joanna at Bede – and so it went on, around the circle of faces, until Alice reached Hal, and then it was she, herself, who was the object of regard: he held her eyes with a look of fathomless depth; something lurched in her chest and the colour crept up her cheeks.

* * *

By the time the party halted at midday, the heat had become oppressive, armour was scalding and conversation had petered out. Sliding from the horses, the company scattered to find what succour they could. A brief meal, a long drink. Alice could eat nothing and the smell of food was turning her stomach. She dismissed her women, and they vanished gratefully. Near at hand, Mitten was soon dozing, mouth open.

Alice balanced on a fallen log, light-headed, her chin sunk in her hands. With slow surprise she saw that Hal and Loic had settled themselves well apart from the rest of the company, heads bent together. Lord Clifford lay not far from her feet, stretched out in the shade, unbuckled and already asleep, as were many of his men, scattered beneath the trees. She wondered idly why he'd chosen to abide so near, when yesterday he wanted to be apart, and so cruel with it.

The man's undershirt had ridden up a little, rising and falling with slow breaths. She glimpsed the broad, double stripe of dark curls undulating along the muscled ridges. Recollections blossomed unbidden, and she closed her eyes.

Her mind meandered on to the morning's distasteful scene before the little house. She thought, then, of Aymer, and lifted her head. Seated beside her was the man himself, his heavy thigh pinning her skirts. Alice shied back, trembling, and would have risen, but she couldn't feel her legs.

For a long moment he gazed at her profile, his breath scorching her averted cheek. "My father acts quite the reformed character when you are near," he drawled. "We're not to take our pleasure lest it reflect badly on him. A good joke, isn't it?" He leaned in to her neck, quieter yet. "Not quite the same when he's off the leading strings. *Black Clifford*. Or *Long Lankin*, let's say. I've heard him called the most evil man in England."

She gaped at him, dizzy and breathless, as his features twisted with spite, the words like pestilence spewing from his mouth. His hand seemed to be reaching, with fingers improbably, impossibly long – but she never felt it alight.

"Ah – we're all alike. There must be bad blood among the Cliffords. Even Hal is not so honourable as he pretends. Beware: that one has a thirst for the daughters of earls." He nodded at her, his eyes dropping to her belly. "Your son will be the same: tarred with our wickedness. It is a son, of course – my father only breeds boys."

It was becoming difficult to understand, the sounds hastening to a torrent of something almost visible; black and disgusting. Alice no longer knew where she was. Her mouth was filling with water. She tried to raise her hands to cover her ears, and slid, unconscious, into his arms.

* * *

Guy was itching to speak with Elyn, to put her to the trial as Aymer proposed. He had sauntered down to the stream after the women, but spying Nield and Chowne and Sir Hugh Dacre standing sentinel like guard dogs, he wandered disconsolately back up the hill, passing Bellingham and Bertrand Jansen disputing together with low, urgent vehemence. A little further up he uncovered George and Bede lounging on their bellies upon a shaggy outcrop, a hidden vantage above the water. Sending them a sour look, he trudged on through a steep dell on the far side, below the fallen tree where Alice had been sitting. Sweating heavily, Guy stopped to draw breath. He could see no one from where he stood. He could hear nothing. It was difficult to keep the sense of urgency in this heat, but the impromptu nap had gone on too long.

Guy had turned upwards to the clearing, thinking to rouse his father, when he was brought up sharp, the strangest sight before his eyes. Hunched forward on the fallen tree, Leonard Tailboys was gazing in rapt attention at a disturbing tableau arranged before him. Alice lay close by upon the ground, apparently asleep, her dress hitched and disordered, littered with the debris of the forest floor. And stranger yet: there upon her, fastened like an incubus, his tongue in her mouth, was Aymer. His knees were planted among her skirts, one elbow balancing his weight; one hand lost to view. The girl was barely breathing. Guy had drawn closer and stood grimacing down on the pair; a spectacle both fascinating and disturbing. Suppressing a bizarre impulse to cross himself, Guy kicked his twin in the ribs with the toe of his boot. Aymer recoiled, and then came the smile.

"She fainted," he said coolly. "I was trying to rouse her."

The bland delivery of the lie was so reminiscent of their father that Guy was almost surprised into laughter.

"Ah – I can't halt now, Brother; stand guard."

"Christ, no! Have you lost your wits?" Guy thrust out a hand and heaved his twin to his feet.

Catching sight of his spellbound audience, Aymer clapped Tailboys on the back, conspiratorial. Across the dell, Will stretched, shrugged himself up from the trunk on which he'd been leaning and faded away.

Alice twitched and coughed. Swiftly, before Aymer could compound his wretched folly, Guy had her in his arms. A dart of his eyes drew Aymer's attention downward to the tell-tale disorder in his apparel. The repair was insolently unhurried.

Guy stood, a moment, considering the evident nearness of the catastrophe; considering the most necessary rescue of his twin. And then, with an almost imperceptible tweak to the planes of his face; a slight, well-practised shudder, he *became* Aymer. There was something chilling in the metamorphosis, for an onlooker – but there was no onlooker.

So slight she all but floated before him, her ribs were twigs beneath his hand. A strand of saliva trembled from the girl's lip like cobweb and Guy flicked his fingers at it. She smelled sharply of Aymer; the fresh and salty tang. Alice was stirring and her eyes opened, looking up at her saviour without interest. He carried her to Mitten, who jolted awake, flustered and spouting. The commotion roused the others. Clifford sprang to his feet, shouting for the women. Guy turned his back, and turned back into himself.

Aymer had swaggered over, exaggerating the expression of concern, hamming it up like a mummer, strumming at Guy's taut nerves. He was amusing only himself. Clifford glared round at his sons; at the twins and at Hal, who'd appeared, vigilant, at their side. Instinct told Clifford that something untoward was happening, but the scene that Guy had chanced upon was, fortunately, beyond their father's imagining. Alice remained drowsy and confused and when Clifford remounted, she was before him once more, silent in the crook of his arm. The collapse had shaken him. She was increasingly frail, and his conscience smote him heavily – a feeling all too tiresomely familiar.

As the grooms readied the horses, Guy elbowed past a smirking Aymer to seize the arm of Leonard Tailboys. "My brother was trying to wake the lady, Tailboys. Pay it no heed."

325

"Oh aye," he leered.

Which wasn't sufficient, and Guy changed tack. "Lord Clifford would cut you into collops for watching that. Mind you keep your mouth shut."

"Aye, I know it."

Nudging Aymer away to the side, he muttered in a low, frantic voice, "What in God's name are you playing at?" Already he knew that it was futile. Aymer would do what he would do. He was ignoring Guy now, staring straight ahead, brows raised in mockery. The insouciance was breath-taking; a heedless rush toward the cliff edge.

Then Guy knocked a finger in Aymer's back. His eyes sent a warning, and the twins turned as one to confront Hal who was standing directly behind them, arms folded, head back.

"What have you done?" snarled their elder brother. An honest question; Hal had no very clear idea what Aymer had done. Something Guy didn't wish Tailboys to speak of, evidently. Some silly prank, perhaps; or something horrific.

The culprit yawned. "You're no Robert Clifford, no matter how slavishly you copy him. Run along now."

"What have you done, you little shit? I'll break every bone in your body." The threat was conspicuously idle.

"Get you gone, Hal!" hissed Guy, so vexed that he actually stamped his foot. He was pulsing with tension already; this additional provocation was too much to bear. "I know you saw nothing."

Hal was sorely tempted to summon help, but that would never do. Whatever malice had been practised, the girl seemed blessedly oblivious. But draw down his father's wrath upon Aymer and she would be destroyed in the storm. He raised a warning finger, also in unconscious imitation of Robert Clifford: "*I'm watching you,*" concentrating all possible menace into the words.

"Really?" drawled Aymer. "You and Tailboys both, then. I seem to be doing all the work around here. Not that I mind, but I will be charging onlookers, next time."

Guy ground his teeth. After that appalling exhibition of recklessness, the fool should at least have the sense to keep his mouth shut. If it wasn't Hal, of all men, standing before them, Guy would have knocked his twin down by now. Then he noticed Richie, smiling, malevolent, at their elder brother's back.

Hal only got one good punch in, and they were on him like wolves.

* * *

As soon as George beheld the carnage, he steered Hal off to the side of the column, full of virtuous excitement. "Who has done this? Was it those pricks?"

Hal gave a slow nod, grateful for the plural; the assumption that one man alone could not have inflicted the damage.

"I thought Aymer was looking queasy. Seems you got him square in the mouth."

"Nmm," said the hideous creature at his side.

"You've broken Richie's nose and, from the way he's moving, I'd say also cracked a rib or two, and Guy's holding the reins one-handed."

Dear George, doing his best. Guy always held the reins one-handed, and was in fact all but unscathed, contributing nothing beyond an obliging armlock while the other two wreaked their worst.

"Did they jump you before you had time to shout?"

Hal stared at George until he had his full attention. "I started it. Listen – I don't want you speaking of this and I don't want retaliation from you, you understand?" His voice sounded like he had a mouthful of wool. "Aymer will certainly regret his actions when he learns the result." He sat up, paused, and recited thickly and self-consciously, 'Raro antecedentem scelestum deseruit pede Poena claudo'." He'd been waiting all his life to declaim his only words of Horace – though not necessarily to George, who was gazing at him vacantly. "It means something like 'Rarely does Vengeance, though lame, fail to catch the guilty man, though far in front.'"

George shook his head in wonderment. Hal was, after all, so very much cleverer than he, and this slow-burning retribution could safely be left in his hands. "I will always be there for you, Hal."

* * *

327

Unable to settle, Guy was beleaguering Aymer again. But his twin was adamant: when Guy had disturbed him, he'd been trying – vigorously – to rouse the girl. At last, Guy understood. Aymer's conduct was not surreptitious, only opportunist. He'd fully intended Alice to wake, to be terrified, to be shamed, and to struggle to keep the secret. He meant to watch and enjoy that struggle. The enormous risk added the spice; the girl's connection with their father had not deterred him; quite the contrary. What Tailboys – and even Guy, who knew his brother so well – had read as lust was, in fact, an impulse altogether less manifest. Darker compulsions were mastering Aymer.

* * *

When Hal passed to his accustomed place by the head of the column, Clifford gaped at his eldest. "How could you let this happen? Were you attacked in your sleep?"

"There were a number of the boys, my lord. And I began it."

"Mother of God!" His father shook his head, deeply offended. "You know I designated you the master. I have done what I can to support you in the rule of them: singling you out to accompany me to Lord John's tomb…" He tailed off. That was all he'd done, actually. "Do not expect me to step in. Baseborn as you are, if you wish for command you must earn it."

Hal would be magenta by now, had not most of his face been magenta already. He treasured Loic's look of indignant sympathy.

While Clifford was holding forth, the shades of Somerset and Devon waited patiently for him to conclude. Clifford dismissed Hal's trouble from his mind and they swamped him.

* * *

With Alice slumbering in his arms, Clifford rode on in silence, warding off his dreadful, and by now thoroughly tedious agonies with a fantasy of himself as stepfather to the heir of Lancaster; leading a French army to England; slaying Edward of York in some archaic and improbable bout of single combat. This particular mental path was already worn to a rut, as dear and familiar as the approach to Skipton.

While he rode, and dreamed, his tender fingers touched her face, her lips, her throat; after some time drifting downwards; over, and eventually into, her gown. Hal had turned, distracted by the movement. With slow menace, Clifford's head swivelled to meet his gaze, repelling his son with truculent hostility, until the onlooker's mashed face slunk back to the road. Hal found he couldn't master his sliding and spellbound eyes, gave up the struggle, and focused on mastering his breathing instead. The girl stirred and straightened, and Clifford's right hand was tranquil upon the reins.

She'd awoken some long minutes before. Fleeing a suffocating dream, Alice was rescued by the familiar scent of Robert's body – so much stronger now, after a day half-armoured in the sweltering sun – and the robust and leathery tang of his sweat beneath. At first the caressing hand belonged, ominously, to the nightmare. Then the bewilderment cleared: it was her protector himself, hot and tangible behind her. And so distressing was his earlier coldness that her response was not offence or dismay but shameful relief, that her power was yet holding sway. She lay in his arms and mastered her breathing. Moments passed beneath his touch. In flooded the memory of the preceding evening; his words and his cruelty dawned on Alice anew, and she would not have it, and twisted and sat up.

Then she lifted her eyes to Hal, riding at her side. The youth was almost unrecognisable: one cheekbone monstrously swelled; one eye flaunting its rainbow promise. A bloated hand lay palm-up upon his knee, curled in a claw. He gave a faint, deprecating shake of the head, and winced.

Hal had been untouched when she came round from her faint, she was certain of that; standing at his father's side, but sparing her not a glance, instead sending clear and vindictive looks in Aymer's direction. He must have assaulted the boy directly. It was perplexing; it was distasteful – particularly when Aymer had shown himself so concerned for her welfare; so unexpectedly gentle.

With brooding fingers, Alice traced the hollow of her throat; the place where Lord Clifford's hand had lain. The skin was smooth and naked. The emerald – Edmond's betrothal gift – was gone.

* * *

The horses were labouring as they drew up to the sharp ridge overhanging Dyffryn Hall. Far below nestled a plain and sturdy house. As the party made the steep descent towards the gatehouse – festooned with cobwebs – its master could be seen, hunched on a milking stool, one leg thrust stiffly before him. Clifford dismounted and lifted Alice carefully to the ground. Up limped Sir Lawrence Welford and embraced his old comrade. The knight was creased and ruddy, with a strong, stubbly jaw and hair that was tow-coloured and sparse.

The man's first words were spoken not in gracious greeting or measured empathy, but blurted out in an agony of doubt. Had they any news of his son, Edward? Sir Lawrence knew only that after the combat at Tewkesbury, his heir had sought refuge in the Abbey and been brought out by Richard of Gloucester at swordpoint.

Clifford knew nothing, either, of Edward Welford; wouldn't recognise him if he saw him, and didn't give much for his chances. With Welford leaning on his arm, Clifford moved slowly to Alice and the others, watching the man's kindly blue eyes slide away, distracted, from the forest of faces. There was no Lady Welford living, and the knight pushed forward his only daughter, Cecily, a slim girl with eyes of clear blue and hair of flowing honey. Her gown was rather threadbare, the sleeves perceptibly too short. She looked bewildered and pleased, her shy and supple gravity at once commending her to the Duchess.

Clifford helped Welford up the stairs to his chamber, and the two of them drank cider together, raspingly strong, exchanging what little Clifford knew of the battle with what little Welford knew of Jasper Tudor's movements, falling back on reminiscences of campaigns long past and men long lost, when all the present news was so quickly exhausted. In witnessing the knight's anguish over his lost son, Clifford came to some sense of perspective. For the first time, it crossed his mind to count his blessings.

When the party was washed and refreshed, Cecily led the Duchess and her ladies over the garden and the orchard and they stood together on the rickety bridge, admiring the wide stream stuffed with fishes.

A gaggle of youths trailed the women like goslings. Hal was following not the Duchess, but Aymer, holding him always within view, just as he'd promised. The quarry would keep making little forays away from the group, his face set and purposeful, all for the fun of seeing Hal swerve after him.

As Aymer had directed, Guy made his little by-play for Elyn's benefit – rather late in the day, for the men would be gone at first light. But if he would not profit from it on that occasion, at least George would not either, which was the greater part of the objective gained. The girl was entranced at the drama: his thrilling jealousy of Master George; the whispered indictment of her constancy; his demand for evidence. Anything; she would go through any trial to prove her love. Guy bowed his noble head, and left her.

Bede had made no headway whatever with Constance. At length he concluded that honey-coloured tresses were more appealing than copper curls, and turned his attentions to Cecily, but he was too late. Within so short a timespan, a vision of handsome and jaunty grace had presented itself among the crowd of young men, and her heart was claimed. This one had seized the chance to speak quietly with her among the trees, and before it was time to part, she had kissed him.

After dinner – early and plain – the warm shadows and drifting scents of the gardens were calling. The company turned out into the evening light and sat, in cursory deference to Sir Lawrence's shredded nerves, intermittently hushed, talking together and laughing only when they forgot themselves. To their relief, the knight excused his wretched manner and took himself off to bed, unable to bear young and lively company at such a time, promising to be up with the dawn to see them off.

Once Guy had abandoned the field, Elyn was promptly besieged by the reliable George. Mindful of her sweetheart's cool appraisal, the girl passed the test with aplomb, serving George a withering sneer. When she presented her back to the surprised youth, Guy rubbed his hands, chortling aloud, turning about in the hope that his father was watching. Aymer glanced across at Will and smirked, though that was a mistake; just now, smiling caused Aymer a stab of pain; he'd lost one tooth, and another was in peril.

With the irrepressibility of youth, Bede thought again of Constance, but the pervasive and frantic flirting had proved too much, and she was gone. His eyes lighted on Joanna – whose cheeks flushed at his notice – and flew off again.

Hal lounged on his side, talking with a number of the household, now and again flicking a glance to Alice. The girl seemed untouched by the day's mysterious ordeal. Recollecting a question that had caught his interest some time back, Hal began in his accustomed vein. "Ah – I know what I wished to ask you, gentlemen: who was my father's chamberlain before Sir Loic?"

Arthur Castor shook his head. "You will always be wishing to ask something, will you not, Master Hal?"

Walter Findern was more obliging. "Dormer. Osbert Dormer. We lost Osbert at Montlhéry, fighting for Duke Charles against the French. You can guess how shocked we all were when Lord Robert named Loic as his chamberlain! For he was a mere boy – too young for the position, in truth, and there were senior men – Englishmen – who'd shown Lord Robert great loyalty; he passed them over, and that caused a right bellyaching, for a time. But it has fallen out well. Loic's a clever fellow and a firm friend, if you stay on the right side of him."

Another Walter, Sir Reginald's inferior sibling, was nodding at Findern's words. "I didn't like Loic overmuch, at first." Walter Grey looked around quickly; Moncler was nowhere to be seen. "He's so stupidly possessive of Lord Robert; worse than any wife. High-handed. Manipulative. And prickly! With my brother, even: never prudent."

The others were laughing.

"No one else would dare," agreed Castor.

"I love him now, though," added Grey defensively.

Hal pressed them: "But Osbert Dormer was acting in post, was he not? What of the true chamberlain?"

"Sir Miles?" Findern's voice was suddenly cautious, and so quiet Hal had to lean in. "Randall had vanished when we escaped into Scotland after the defeats of '64." Here Findern held up a warning hand, for Grey had opened his mouth again. "We waited for him, and waited. But he never returned; he simply disappeared. That's all."

"My father sent him off?"

Walter Findern stared down his fellow knight, who shut his mouth again. "Miles went away; perhaps your father knew where."

Walter Grey rushed in. "But Randall was surely expected back, for Lord Robert was heartbroken when he did not appear."

"It's not a happy subject. Let us leave it now," finished Castor repressively.

Hal raised his head, and saw with a pang that Guy and Aymer had taken themselves off while his attention was diverted. He rose to his knees, casting around for Alice.

A number of the company had pushed themselves to their feet, obscuring his view, and were wandering; some to take a last turn in the perfect evening; some to their beds. There was Richie, lying on his back, his great bloody beak poking up, bent and hooked now, worse than before, as tentative fingers explored his chest. George was right: ribs.

The Duchess was still among the group, talking quietly with Joanna, but her eyes were lingering on Lord Clifford, and she looked more than usually troubled. Clifford had remarked it and, rising, he touched her shoulder and gestured her to follow him into the large and rampant herb garden that lay in plain and punctilious view.

Watching Alice move tamely after his father, Hal choked down the hopeless desire to follow, to distract, to intrude himself between them. Then he rose to his feet and set off in the direction of the house.

As the couple walked together, there was the usual silence for a while, beneath the drone of the thronging bees, and then Alice halted. Her manner was direct, with none of the usual struggle to meet his gaze. "I cannot remain here while you go to Chepstow. It is not safe."

"Nowhere is safe. Someone – some greedy man – is bound to be searching for me and for the Earl of Pembroke. And not only for us, but for Pembroke's nephew, Henry Tudor. The lad's a Beaufort on his mother's side, and, as such, a threat to Edward of York, now that the others are dead."

The Prince, he meant. And her husband. "If I bear a son, my child will have the better claim to be King Henry's heir." Her voice was peremptory, the tone reminding him forcibly of Queen Margaret.

"True, your son would be a Beaufort and the heir male, and Henry Tudor is not. But Tudor is nearing manhood; he must be around fourteen or fifteen years now. York will fear him more, believe me. If you bear a daughter, though, the two should marry, and join their claims."

Alice considered that, nodding. But in truth, her child was a son; the heir of Lancaster. She knew it already. "Yet you go on there, heading into danger?"

"Ah – I fear nothing. And Jasper Tudor is all we have left." When her face darkened he added, "Until we find your brother."

There was silence again, for a moment, while she regarded him through narrowed eyes. "Do you even mean to return?"

His shoulders dropped. "After everything, Alice – you ask me that?"

But still the sullen and watchful look, which sat oddly on her sweet face. She was withdrawing from him. "What should I do, if the worst happens?"

He bit his lip. "If you're discovered here? Get a message to me; play for time. Of course I will come for you."

She looked beyond him, retreating all the while, slipping away.

He continued, "And if you refuse to leave, there's little anyone can do. York is no monster, in truth. He would not sanction violence against you." He smiled, and leaned in a little. "And, contrary to popular belief, it's not so easy to carry off a lady who does not wish to be carried off!"

She had stopped listening. "That wasn't what I meant. There could be a siege. If you are captured…?"

"Then I'll be dead. You must do as seems best to you."

She stared at him.

"Alice – this belongs with you." Once more, he twisted off the ruby. As he closed her fingers around the ring, he could send her no surer sign. She did not give it a glance. Clifford tried again; a pleading smile. "You'll need to find your own leash to bind it with; the last time, my purse collapsed and all my coin fell out and rolled about."

Still no answering warmth. By now, there was a faint prickle of sweat across his palms. Wordless, she turned and walked away. He paused and he followed, kicking the billows of sage leaves that tumbled over the path, releasing their savoury aroma. Before them, at one window, Sir Hugh, Andrew Chowne and Blanche, looking shifty; at another, Nield, Bellingham and Bertrand Jansen, arrested mid-quarrel; in the garden beneath the house, a crowd of others. All watching. He turned to her, and tried one last time: a sly and private smile. This time, there was a small, reluctant laugh.

* * *

As Hal approached the house, he marked a number of the party gathered at the downstairs windows, but no sign of his quarry. He skirted the rose-strewn, flaking walls and entered the yard to the side. As he passed the stable, his notice was caught by a tiny glancing flash, sparkling from glass or metal. He ducked under the lintel. In the shift from warm low sun to hot, rich-scented gloom, the youth was briefly unbalanced and unsighted. Drifting dust and chaff filled his nostrils and festooned his brows and hair. He would have backed out again, but an inchoate guttural moan, quite different from the passive stirrings of the horses, alerted him to a presence within. Across his path lay a great tumbling pile of hay anchored by a pitchfork. In the shadows beyond he glimpsed two pairs of legs, scraping and sliding against each other. He moved a few steps closer. But no spellbound onlooker, he; with disgust he beheld a struggling Constance trapped beneath the hunkering weight of Sir Leonard Tailboys. Her mouth was stopped with a rough rag, her wrists pinioned above her head. At her throat, a knife.

"Close your eyes," the assailant ordered. "Lie like you're sleeping."

Just as the girl's wide eyes betrayed him, Hal swung back and kicked Tailboys tremendously hard between the legs. There was a voluble thwack and an agonised gurgle. Collapsing on his victim, the knight rolled heavily into the straw. The knife slipped from his fingers. Reaching for the pitchfork, Hal planted its prongs on the man's sweating face. Constance was quickly on her knees behind her rescuer, picking at the knots of the gag, calmly alert.

"Listen, Tailboys." Hal's voice was quietly reasonable. "You'll want to make a run for it, now. Answer me one question, and away you go. What did Aymer do?"

Now shaking violently, the man didn't seem to be attending. His eyes were jerking around in blank panic as the points softly sank.

Hal tried again. "You saw something in the woods; Guy warned you to keep your mouth shut. What did Aymer do?" He withdrew the fork a little, and resettled it on a plane of undamaged flesh.

The man panted, and worried, feebly, at the points in his face.

"No, no," cautioned Hal.

Sir Leonard groaned; he sounded drunk. "Aymer's kissing the…Duchess when I come up; hand…hand in her skirts; I'm trying to see but he's…on her, he's blocking my view."

He groaned again, and would have lapsed, but Hal motioned with his free hand, drawing it out of the man.

"And then?"

A tiny shrug. "He's readying himself when Guy spoils it and takes her away. Aymer says, '*I'm just trying to wake her*'. They're arguing after – I hear 'em." The shaking had slowed to a steady rhythm. "It didn't hurt her any. The bitch was out cold."

"Ah – so no harm done."

Tailboys blinked at him, clammy and uncertain, both palms guarding his mangled crotch.

Hal reached behind with his left hand, feeling for the girl's unruly curls. Grasping with his fingers, he twisted her away from the supine man, holding her cheek against his thigh. Then Hal braced his grip and leaned in. Perfectly spaced, the fork's outer prongs cleared the face as the inner ones skewered the eyes. As Hal withdrew, some of the right orb came away, which was ugly, but the obedient Constance was pressed against him and did not see.

"Stay just as you are," said Hal, and leaned the fork in a corner. Heaving the body, he piled hay upon the man until he was gone. Then Hal sank to his knee before her. "You're very brave, and deserve better, but I'm going to ask something difficult of you. It would harm Alice greatly if anything were said of these events. Can you keep all this to yourself, do you think?"

She rolled her eyes, exasperated, and Hal reached to slice the gag with his knife. Rubbing her jaw, she looked up at him, spiky as ever. "There was no need to ask me that. I care more for the Duchess than you do, believe me."

He lifted Constance to her feet and helped to pluck the straw from her curls. Then her hand was on his wrist, and when he turned, it was to see Bede's head peering around the stable door. Hal lifted his hands from the girl's hair and wiped his forehead. This day had lasted three times longer than any day of his remembering; it had aged him.

Bede's face fell, miserable and meek, and then he retreated.

Gesturing at his own battered face, Hal gave a rueful laugh. "He must think you're blind." He half-hoped for some kindly reassurance; it was mortifying that Alice should see him like this.

Constance examined him. "Aymer, was it?"

He nodded. "With Guy, and Richie."

"I see. You're right – no one must hear of this. The shame would kill her. I'll go after Master Bedivere now." The girl sighed. "I'll tell him I've resolved to take a vow of chastity. That ought to shut him up."

"Oh – I didn't know it." Hal was momentarily diverted. "That's a loss to mankind."

"As of today."

When he and Leonard Tailboys were alone, Hal lowered himself to the floor, back against the wooden stall. A great bluebottle blundered in on the last slant of sunlight and slipped, prurient, into the hay; soon there would be more, rejoicing in the grisly find. It was too warm.

He concentrated hard upon Constance. While the girl had shown deplorable manners, she was faultlessly calm and perfectly trustworthy; he knew it. Hal savoured his moment of pure and chivalrous pride, for he knew what was lurking just beyond: a sentiment significantly less gallant. Inexorable, inevitable, the door in his mind cracked open, and in crept Sir Leonard's tale. He rested and allowed it. Coarse and vivid, the image took shape before him, but Hal found himself no spellbound audience; he was not Tailboys. He was Aymer.

* * *

Another beautiful morning at the breaking of dawn. Despite the resolve to keep to her room, it was hard to remain upstairs. Alice drew on the reserves of her resentment, and, thus fortified, shucked off any desire to speak with Robert. Some of the men were already ahorse below her window, eating in the saddle. She watched Lord Clifford striding in and out, issuing orders. Each time he turned towards the house, she hung back beneath the shadows. He was in a filthy temper.

All was ready at last, except that now Leonard Tailboys was missing. Someone swore he'd been about only a moment before. "Has anyone checked the kennels?" There was a flurry of coarse banter. After a time, ribaldry turned to irritation.

A further hour was lost in searching and calling. Lord Clifford declared with an oath that Tailboys had turned coward and concealed himself somewhere about the house. He didn't believe Tailboys was concealed anywhere about the house; he thought him long gone, fled, who knows where, or why. The man wasn't popular and wouldn't be much missed, but it diminished their small force and it wasn't good for morale.

Robert Clifford was, of course, quite wrong about Sir Leonard, who was indeed concealed at Dyffryn Hall – not very well concealed, beneath a token layer of straw. The pitchfork that had pierced his eyes was propped neatly between his feet. Walter Grey and Edwin FitzClifford had rummaged the outbuildings during that morning's hurried search and done a singularly poor job of it, Edwin even treading on Tailboys' hand at one point.

While Alice watched, Hal strode out to his horse, accompanied – inexplicably – by Constance. As the man mounted, the gentlewoman swung her skirts, hands clasped behind her back. Her lips were moving. Hal gave a brief answering nod; not of assent, Alice thought, but of acknowledgement. And there was Aymer, adjusting his bridle, observing the pair closely.

The men began to move off. As the horses tilted up the hill, Alice opened the window. Lord Clifford had twisted in the saddle to scan the house. She flinched back and closed the casement, shrouding herself in the gloom of the chamber, watching until he turned away; until the little figures gained the brow of the hill and vanished into the rising sun.

* * *

Once the men had settled into their pace, there grew a general sense of relief that the women were behind them. They may have been pleasant to look upon, but few in the household had reaped any reward, and several were suffering.

Loic remarked, in French, on the pointed lack of a leave-taking. The lady had chosen to absent herself for a reason; Monseigneur would have work to do on his return.

Clifford shot him an aggrieved look.

"In your grief, you have pushed her too far, Monseigneur. You took too much for granted."

"*Loic*. That will do."

Hal, whose French was improving rapidly under Loic's accidental tuition, picked up the gist of the exchange – and wondered. He, alone, had been watching Alice's face as the group approached Dyffryn Hall. Wide awake, eyes deceitfully closed, making no protest at Lord Clifford's illicit touch. Hal could choose to reassure his father, and decided, for a host of reasons, that he would not. There were conundrums revolving within his breast. Not for the first or for the last time, he missed his brother Waryn's sober counsel.

* * *

Aymer's party rode a little apart, voices low. Richie had been left behind by the events of the day before and was shy of asking; of being snubbed by his fascinating, terrifying leader.

"He attacked me, unprovoked, and I've lost a tooth. He will regret it."

"Enough!" Guy's tone was sharp; unusually so.

His twin was probing the cavity with his tongue. It was filled with a bloody jelly that tasted of rust. A back tooth, thank God; his looks were unmarred, once that lip subsided. It felt hugely fat and blubbery. The blow had compromised his dignity. "Enough?" Aymer's voice was quietly incredulous. "Not so. I tell you, Guy – I cannot live with him and I *will* not. I'll not stay."

Richie clamoured in agreement. "He has broken my nose and my ribs, the great knave. He deserves everything Aymer and me dished out."

Guy turned on him, ill-tempered and unjust. "Your ribs are not broken, you fool. If they were broken, the ends would be sticking out. But listen to me, Aymer: Hal could have fetched the others running. He didn't, even when you were kicking him, and he's still not said anything. Father just thinks we've had a row. After what you've done, do you really want to put questions in Father's mind?"

Aymer was shaking his head. "Hal won't tell our father. He saw nothing and, in any case, Father has mistrusted him since our second visit to Alnwick – and with good reason, as Will has related."

Ignoring his own gasp of pain, Richie swivelled to Will, querulous and aggrieved, but the younger lad only yawned.

"Tailboys?" Richie offered up, wishing fervently to be part of the mystery; entirely lost. He suspected Leonard Tailboys was involved in some way – the name kept coming up. And now he was gone, which seemed sinister.

All of them turned and eyed him for a moment.

"Tailboys might have told Hal," agreed Guy reluctantly.

Aymer waved an airy hand, and headed off, apparently at a tangent. "Do you remember the other day, when we were approaching Goodrich: the Queen of Heaven ended up in Hal's arms, did she not? He wouldn't let her go."

Richie frowned, calling the memory to mind. "I thought it was she who would not let him go? She was clutching that blood-stained handkerchief like a holy relic. And Father was angry with her, quite rough."

Aymer raised his brows at that, wincing. "Better yet! I heard Moncler telling Patrick Nield that he was in the chamber with our father at Goodrich, when Father was beside himself with rage. Not with her – with Hal. He accused Hal of wanting the lass for himself, watching her always. After that, I looked for myself – and Father is right."

Will nodded.

"So? Where are you going with this?" said Guy, crossly. Their father's relations with that quiet, sickly girl were of scant interest.

"But Guy! Consider! Father was jealous and wrathful with Hal even before our brother set eyes on the Queen of Heaven, but now…now Hal is truly playing with fire, and I have made it hotter for him."

* * *

The boys soon commenced their racing again, gone in clouds of dust and distant shouting. The party made such good time, unencumbered as they were, that they reached Chepstow by mid-morning, and surprised Tudor's men.

The Earl of Pembroke was overjoyed to see them. What a strange man was Jasper Tudor; as spirited as though ten years' toil and planning had not ended in abrupt disaster, in the deaths of their Prince and their friends. And his household was just as jovial and just as staunch. Clifford cast a sideways look at his own senior men. Patrick Nield was nowhere to be seen.

Jasper made smug haste to display his prize: the nephew he shared with the King; the young Henry Tudor, Earl of Richmond, a quiet boy with a shrewd face. But Pembroke had expected to welcome the Queen amongst their company and her absence was a source of bemusement. Particularly as Clifford had seen fit to carry off Edmond of Somerset's wife – a woman of no importance to anybody – while abandoning the Queen of England, the one who could best have given approval, acclamation, to young Henry Tudor, the new heir of Lancaster.

"I tried," said Clifford, shortly. On the subject of his own heir of Lancaster, he kept his silence. A duel may come upon them, one distant day, but at present such rivalry was a needless distraction. Unquestionably, life would be simpler if Alice gave birth to a daughter.

When the meal was served, Clifford, Pembroke and the young Tudor sat apart. Taking up again with relief the comfortable mantle of soldiery, the other men sat together to eat, with little rank and less ceremony. Time and again Hal's eyes wandered to Aymer. The youth was in a high humour; unusually boisterous; Guy looking grim and Richie looking sour, possibly not for the same reason.

After they'd eaten, Hal was gratified, and relieved, and by now a little surprised, to be included with George in conference with his father and the two Tudors. They had barely begun, however, when they were interrupted by a commotion. A force of several hundred had been sighted a mile or two to the north, drawing closer. Clifford and Jasper Tudor rose together.

Hal laid a hand on his father's arm. "It could be survivors of the field at Tewkesbury, my lord."

Clifford wore a wolfish smile. "Ah – no. This lot have been close behind us all the way south, and now they come on. I look forward to it."

They made a tour of the battlements; or the others did, Clifford choosing not to leave the shadow of the doorway. He scanned the horizon, careful not to look down, his hand printing a glitter of sweat on the lintel; he squinted at the moving column but couldn't read the banners.

The small army was mostly on foot, giving off a somewhat weary and dishevelled air, even from a distance. Eventually the force drew up beyond the range of the garrison's bows and pitched camp below the town in disorderly clumps. There were not enough of them adequately to besiege the landward side of the castle, and the river-facing side was, in any case, unassailable. A few men crossed the Wye in a coracle and lounged on the far bank, keeping watch. There was not one cannon among them.

Talk within the castle turned at once to the identity of their foes, and their next move. They had not long to await the first answer. A messenger begged admittance, nervous – and little wonder. The gist of the message: in the name of King Edward, if the rebel force holding Chepstow would surrender, there would be pardons and safe conducts for all. All, that is, save Jasper and Henry Tudor and Robert Clifford, who were to be delivered up to the King's envoy, Sir Roger Vaughan.

"Vaughan!" spat Jasper. "He has come deliberately to taunt me!"

Clifford turned with a frown. "Vaughan?"

"Roger Vaughan; faced him at Mortimer's Cross in '61. He captured my father and beheaded him in the market square. You were there, Robert!"

"Not I – we were hammering Warwick on the other side of the country." Clifford rubbed his hands. "God has sent him into your path for a reason. Let us leave them a few days to grow careless, then we sally out and kill them."

Pembroke summoned the messenger and dispatched the man straight back to Vaughan. He was to bear no direct response to the insolent challenge, but to carry presents of wine, cheese and ham for his commander.

"Tell Vaughan to settle in and make himself easy," directed the Earl. "We're over-provisioned, and he will have a long wait."

* * *

So now Blanche had reached the fork in the road. She sat with her mistress awhile, framing the words, but reluctant to begin.

Alice was listless, kicking her feet on the bed. "He gave me no idea when to expect him back. We should have gone with him; I said so, but he wouldn't have it. What are Jasper and Henry Tudor compared with the safety of my son?" And then, as if refuting her listener, "He gave me the Clifford ring. He would not part with it if he meant to abandon me."

"Your *son*?"

"Oh, the child is a son, indeed."

Blanche wore a sceptical look. This foolish notion was surely prompted by Lady Catherine; Blanche recalled her remark on the subject of morning sickness. The Countess should have known better than to raise hopes with an old wives' tale. No one ever predicted a girl, she noticed.

Alice stared through the casement, perplexed by her own words. She knew with certainty that the child was male, as though someone had enlightened her, though she could not place or even imagine such a communication. Suddenly it came to her: Aymer. Aymer had told her, in the woods before she fainted. Alice was left with a disquieting impression of the conversation, but only that singular conviction remained, for his words had come and gone without forming a memory. She had revived in Aymer's arms, as he bore her carefully into Mitten's lap. And his expression of helpless alarm, wringing his hands in anxiety: she had seen it. He was a strange and troubled boy, but she believed in him, gifted with visions as he was, as his father was. It was kindly of Aymer to care for her when she fainted, and kindly to share with her his insight concerning the child. And last night, in the gardens, she knew that he was watching over her, and when she'd met his eyes, the smile – that wicked smile, which so troubled her before – was gone. In the pained intensity of his gaze, he conveyed all his concern.

Blanche was staring at the broad floorboards. It may be that a change of scene would clear the snarl in her mind and free the words. She took Alice's hand. "Come with me into the garden for some air." She turned to the others and motioned with her palm: *stay here.*

Hand-in-hand the pair strolled down to the broad, shallow stream teeming with watery life. Standing upon the bridge they stared into the brook, each lost in their contrasting thoughts. Blanche stole a sideways look. The events that Sir Hugh had set in train would play out, come what may. Alice must be persuaded to conform herself or it would go badly for her, and badly for them. And yet the words would not come.

And then Blanche turned a little, catching a movement on the ridge, and looked up, over Alice's shoulder, through the trees high above them. First one horseman, and then a large number all at once. Silhouetted against the deep blue, they halted, hanging there with their backs to the sky, looking down on the peaceful house. Blanche's grip had tightened and Alice glanced at their joined hands, and then at Blanche's face, and then followed her eyes up the steep hill to the men gazing down on them.

* * *

The small force sat tight within Chepstow's great walls, and the besiegers besieged, after a fashion. Observed from a height, they appeared disconsolate, somehow, in their movements. A couple of Tudor's Welshmen crept through the town and mingled in to ascertain Sir Roger's exact position and the disposition of his men.

The disposition of his men was just as it appeared from a distance: tired and cross. Expecting to be released for home after the engagement at Tewkesbury, instead, they'd been ordered to an unexpected and unwelcome march south, now beholding an impregnable fortress and possibly a very long wait.

Then came a spark of discord over Henry Tudor. Clifford had assumed the youth would take a prominent place in his uncle's force. Not so, it turned out. He was to be left behind, safe and sound, within the walls of Chepstow.

"Mother of God!" protested Clifford. "My Robbie is younger, and this will be his second engagement. You must stiffen the lad, or men will not follow him when the time comes."

"I know that," said Jasper. "But he is too important for our cause, and too slight besides, compared with your boys. It's not safe or prudent to take him out there."

"I was slaughtering Nevilles at fourteen."

"At fourteen, you were probably bigger than I am now," objected Pembroke.

"I was bigger than you at nine."

There stood the young Tudor, his narrow face displaying only a careful neutrality. It was the boy's expression that made Clifford yield. At that age, he recalled, he'd been gagging for bloodshed; the lust for it had leaked from every pore. But if you weren't hungry, you weren't ready, and that was that. A poor omen. If Alice bore a boy, Clifford trusted that her heir of Lancaster – his *stepson* – would show a more warlike spirit when the time came. For sure, he'd raise the boy a soldier first and foremost. They'd name him Henry, after the hero of Agincourt.

Hal – Clifford's real son Henry, rather than the imaginary one – had stood by during this humiliating appraisal of Tudor's merits. At least, Hal assumed it was so; it would have humiliated him to be picked over while he loitered, mute and hopeful. But when Hal commiserated with the lad, Tudor gave him a tight smile.

"My time will come. I'm in no rush."

Hal shrugged. *How odd.*

* * *

On the evening of the second day the glorious weather broke. From the windows of Chepstow's great hall, they watched the slow massing: iron thunderheads shot through with iridescent mauve and green; a peacock sky. Then the storm snarled in. Out went the sun.

That night was rent with brilliant lightning and squalling hail. In a warm circle of their familiars, Clifford and Jasper Tudor had been dicing since dinner. The hour grew late but Clifford was winning and would detain his companion from his bed, come what may. Beside his elbow, a tiny strew of silver and an untidy pile of scribbled warrants, never meant to be cashed.

They'd drunk too much and talk was boisterous and easy. Clifford was beginning to drowse. Later he would want for a woman, but there was none to be had. He gave Alice never a thought.

Ten miles to the west, in the steep valley of Dyffryn, the mild stream sprang and roared. Something of great consequence was unfolding.

* * *

On the third day, Clifford and Pembroke called the senior men together: the attack would be made at sundown. Sir Roger must be captured alive; Pembroke was insistent on that.

"Now is the chance to show your mettle, my son." His father gripped Hal's shoulder and gave it a brisk shake.

"You said I did well at Barnet, my lord." The youth's brows were drooping reproachfully. "I killed thirty-eight."

"Mm. If you must keep a tally, do not admit to it. It makes you sound...pitiful. But yes, you did well enough. And your brother, even better."

346

Which brother? "George, you mean, my lord? Your brother's son?"

"My George, yes. My finest." George had all of John Clifford's cool good looks, his physique, his ability on the field. His wits were somewhat askew, but he, at least, was doggedly loyal.

Hal stared bleakly into his father's face and turned away.

* * *

The hours passed slowly and impatiently.

All day long, steady sheets of rain tumbled over the parched land. By late afternoon, the flood had let up, a cheerful rainbow appeared over the enemy camp like an open gate and the ground steamed gently.

As the last rays of sun disappeared, Reginald Grey led them in prayer. With Clifford fronting his men to the west end of the castle and Pembroke, his to the east, they slipped out of the counterpart doors. Surreptitiously, they descended to the town, making their quiet way through the steep streets and on below. Some in the camp were already abed in their sodden tents, some taking the air for the first time that day in the humid evening, talking or singing. None was harnessed or battle-ready.

Clifford's men had the shorter distance to the camp, and although their advance was as slow as they dared, they were the first to reach the perimeter. They had sliced through quite a number of tent ropes before the uproar of tripping and cursing became a full-blown alarm. As Pembroke's men closed from the East and the camp was pressed from both sides, there was, briefly, complete pandemonium, in the midst of which the Wyverns had the good sense to stand still, backing each other. Within a short space of time, the greater proportion of the besiegers had simply bolted into the near-darkness, running north for the hills of home.

Sir Roger Vaughan was taken by Hal and George together in a well-planned manoeuvre as he leaped from his tent, hurriedly harnessed in a random and unsymmetrical assortment of plate, like a harlequin. He was a practised soldier and commenced with a valiant fight, but he stood no chance at all, and shortly, with a smile, resigned and handed his sword to Hal. Jasper had to be content rounding up the few senior men that he could find. There was very little in the way of plunder, and once the prisoners had been secured, the footsoldiers and archers – those who had not already fled – were bidden to make a run for it, and, leaderless, they did so.

"Good to know York fears us so greatly, he sends his best troops against us," said Clifford sourly. Naturally he was proud of the boys; content that Hal had redeemed himself after that shocking mismatch with Aymer. But still he thirsted to be the man of the hour. This time it was not to be; distracted by some pointlessly enjoyable slaughter while the others made straight for the right place. He'd seen only the surrender. Worse for Jasper, though. His father's killer was seated on a camp stool, joking and drinking by the time he arrived.

And poor Tudor was in rather a bad way. A mace-blow had broken a number of ribs, and he winced back up the hill and off to bed, swallowing a great deal of wine to numb the pain.

Unlike his friend, Clifford had lost not a man, though young Tom flaunted a deep sword thrust to the ankle. Through the dark they'd traced the beacon of his enthused squealing and found him sitting on his backside in the fading quiet. The satisfying injury soon turned putrid and stinking and threatened to cost him the limb. God was on Clifford's side, however, and hot salted water and the prayers of Reginald Grey proved effective in preserving the boy.

* * *

"Were you there, when Vaughan was speaking of Jack de Vere? I don't believe you were. As we brought him up here, he let fall that de Vere is believed in Scotland, with William Beaumont."

"A ruse, perhaps, Monseigneur."

"I think not. He mentioned it in passing, as if I already knew."

"So we go north again?"

Clifford rolled on to his side and jogged Loic's shoulder. "You don't sound pleased! My gold – what there is of it – lies in the North Country, so yes, of

348

course we must. We'll try to hold out in Skipton until Lammas Day, for the rents and dues from my tenants."

"Lammas Day, Monseigneur? The upcoming quarter day, is it?"

"Different quarter days in the North Country. The first day of August." There came a gasp in the darkness; that was fully two and a half months off. Clifford said coolly, heavily, "*I'm much in need of the money, Loic.* And yes, someone will surely come against us. We must prepare for that."

"And the Lady Alice?"

There was a silence and then Clifford murmured, "Tomorrow we ride to Dyffryn, just a few of us. We remain there the night, and return the following day to collect the others. I've kept my distance from her, for the sake of the child's claim."

Loic could hear the ill-disciplined smile in his voice, foreshadowing mischief.

"But she promised she'd be mine and I cannot wait; I cannot. Ah, Loic – I did not speak with her before I left; my girl was sulking and it was not the time to seek her promise." There was a slight catch in his voice. "I gave her the Clifford ruby, and she barely regarded it."

"Speak to her if you must, Monseigneur, but I beg you – do not weaken now; do nothing to put our cause at risk!" The chamberlain so earnest, so alarmed, that his English was slipping. "Our first concern is for Edmond Beaufort's little imp, is it not? You must cause no further doubt as to parentage of his heir, or men will choose instead to pledge their allegiance to that strange old child, Henry Tudor. I wouldn't wager on him against the house of York."

"Jesu – nor I." Clifford rolled on to his back. "Don't fret, mon petit." He ruffled Loic's hair. "No one will ever know."

"Reginald Grey will know, for a start!"

"Grey? Mother of God, you're right there. Ah – the fellow won't leave me be; the only Wyvern who doesn't give a toss for King Henry or Skipton. Thrones and earthly powers mean nothing to the man, when Alice was given by God. He follows me around, ordering me to wed her without delay. Loic!"

He was wheezing with suppressed laughter. "Will you stop gawking at me like that? For sure, this is another case in which I cannot do as he bids, though I'll certainly be seeking her promise for the future." There was another long silence, broken by a sheepish murmur. "Sometimes I wish I'd not told him of the vision."

"I wager you do, Monseigneur! But then, you are a great man in this world; it's your duty to think of thrones and earthly powers – and the fortunes of many depend on you doing so. Which is why you should put aside *all* thoughts of the Lady Alice until she has delivered the heir of Lancaster."

But Clifford was intent upon his own lustful path, one that neither Loic nor Grey could endorse. "Put aside all thoughts of her? Hardly likely. Now: I'll take only Bell and Castor to Dyffryn – and you, of course, to make mischief with Blanche if she obstructs me."

Blanche had gone beyond him now. "And Hal, with us?"

The smile decayed. "Certainly not."

Loic turned away, drawing a knee to his chest. "Hal is a good man, a true man, wounded at the loss of your favour."

Abruptly, Clifford pushed himself up. "*Wounded?* How would you know he's wounded? *Surely* you did not dare to discuss with him the cause of my anger? Did I not instruct you most particularly that Hal must reach his own understanding of his evil behaviour, and so come to his own regret? I'll not have your indiscretion show him a way out!"

"Hal confided his pain to me unasked, Monseigneur. Of course he has no knowledge that his trysts with the Lady Eleanor have come to your attention. *In no way* was I indiscreet with your confidences."

"Ah, well. You surprise me. There is a first time for everything, I suppose," said Clifford nastily. "Mark this: if there's one vice I cannot abide, it is deceit."

"There you surprise me also." Loic's voice was muffled, as though he were gnawing the sheet. "Of all the qualities for which you've been praised in my hearing, I do not recall honesty ever featuring among the tally."

* * *

Sir Roger Vaughan was a big man and tall, with a heavy paunch. By the morning light Hal examined his interesting face; its florid veins and intricately broken nose. He guessed the man was well into his sixth decade. His was a commanding presence as he lounged in the chair, feet resting on the massive and ancient table. Clifford stood at the other end, staring distractedly at the great map spread before him, unnerved by Vaughan's manner. Behind his father, Hal leaned against the wall, frowning at a scene in which the captor and the captive seemed to have exchanged places.

"This your boy, Clifford?" Vaughan signalled Hal with the back of his hand, his Welsh burr slow and heavy.

"*Lord* Clifford, to you"

"Oh – *Lord* Clifford: so you did murder your nephew, then."

Clifford's gaze skipped across the map.

Vaughan nodded towards Hal. "Handy soldier, this one; credit to you. Bit of a mess, though. I say: you're a bit of a mess, boy, eh?" He laughed. "Good to have sons of your own, Clifford. Trueborn ones, even better. Never been married yourself, eh? Of course, we all heard the rumours of you and the little de Vere girl." Vaughan tilted precariously in his chair. "But I never believed it myself. She's carrying Edmond Beaufort's child – no doubt in my mind. That's why you kept her out of King Edward's hands. Fancied yourself as stepfather to a future king, restorer of the house of Lancaster, eh? Don't blame you. Happy daydream." There was a very long pause, Vaughan smiling on Clifford with avuncular warmth.

Clifford studied the map, his finger tracing the Severn into the Bristol Channel. "I've no interest in your opinions." He wanted nothing less than to listen while Vaughan trespassed so accurately on his thoughts, but he'd a strong and uncomfortable sensation that this was meandering towards something significant.

Vaughan continued unabashed. "Ha – but then women are such demanding creatures, eh? I don't think the lady appreciated you deserting her at Dyffryn Hall."

Clifford looked up sharply, face slackening. Vaughan shook his head, delighted, determined not to be hurried. Clifford simply stared. Vaughan folded his hands behind his head and looked about him.

After an unbearable moment, Hal intervened. "Dyffryn Hall, Sir Roger?"

"I'd take a long, hard look at my household, if I were you, Clifford. Someone was sending messages back towards Goodrich, disclosing the lady's destination. Leaving a little trail of breadcrumbs, as it were."

Hugh Dacre. They both knew it. At once.

Vaughan gave Clifford a lengthy smile that encompassed Hal. "You know Edmond Beaufort's dead, eh? Days ago now."

As his father looked incapable of speech, Hal took over. "We didn't know, Sir Roger, as it happens, but it's not unexpected."

"So, now the little lady's a widow, and you seem to have discarded her to shift for herself. Not surprising, is it, that she's found herself a new protector?" A long silence, as though Vaughan had concluded. He swallowed a great gulp of wine and folded his arms.

"Pray continue, Sir Roger." Hal's voice was respectful. "You were telling my father of a new protector for Lady Alice?"

Vaughan jerked his thumb at Hal. "Hark at the pretty manners!"

Clifford passed a hand over his face.

A look of warm sympathy from Vaughan, as if he were exasperating even himself. "Protector: yes. So, I travelled down this way in the company of my good friend, Sir Simon Loys. You may know him, eh? Clever fellow, bit smooth? Member of Warwick's northern council – before the Earl lost his bearings, of course. Friend of Lady Alice back in her Middleham days. *Close* friend."

A broad wink, and he leaned back again, settling himself, luxuriating like a cat. Clifford was still staring blankly. *Simon Loys.* The name was in some way familiar, but he was dredging up nothing at that moment.

"So Loys tells me he's coming all this way just to offer the lady marriage, as he's pretty sure she'll accept him. And, blow me down, if she hasn't done just that!" Sir Roger thumped the table and cast around gleefully at his unappreciative audience. "Wedded and bedded already, so I hear! Quick work!"

Horrified, Hal turned to Clifford, whose jaw had, quite literally, dropped. Swiftly he stepped forward as the man sank, Hal's hands seizing his trembling father. Furious, Clifford shrugged him off.

Vaughan grinned with glittering spite into Clifford's lax face. Tugging a crumpled letter from beneath his shirt, he held it at arm's length. "Where are we?" A laborious finger moved across the parchment. "So Loys writes:

'As you know, Richard of Gloucester himself wished to place this poor widow under my protection, and dispatched me into Monmouthshire for this very purpose. Given the trust his lordship reposed in me, it is gratifying that Lady Alice agreed most readily to the marriage. We wed yesterday at daybreak in the church of Dyffryn. I have taken her to bed, and my bride seems highly satisfied with her new husband.'"

Vaughan brandished the letter with a leer and dropped it on the table. "So, no need to concern yourself any further with the girl. You can get on with – " he gave a little shrug – "conquering Wales. Or whatever it is you're doing. Ha! I'm finished now, I think." He sat back and folded his arms again.

Hal reached over and slipped the letter away.

Clifford took rather a lengthy moment and then rose smoothly from his seat. "My son," said he. "Let us summon the Earl of Pembroke. Sir Roger is tired of life."

THE END

LIST OF CHARACTERS

The main characters, as they appear in relation to each other at the opening of the book in 1470 (fictional characters appear in italics):

ROBERT CLIFFORD'S FAMILY AND CONNECTIONS

Robert, 'Lord' Clifford

Second of the four sons of Lord Thomas Clifford (killed by the Yorkists, 1455) and younger brother of Lord John Clifford (killed by the Yorkists, 1461). Brought up in the household of the Percy Earls of Northumberland. Self-proclaimed baron and successor to his older brother John. Diehard supporter of the house of Lancaster. Ten years an exile, residing in Bruges, Flanders, under the protection of Duke Charles of Burgundy

Lady Clifford[1]

Lord Thomas Clifford's widow. Mother of John, Robert, Roger and Triston Clifford

Margaret Clifford/Threlkeld

Lord John Clifford's widow, mother of the young Henry Clifford. Now married to Lancelot Threlkeld

Sir Lancelot Threlkeld

Formerly of the retinue of Lord John Clifford; now Margaret Clifford's second husband

Henry Clifford

A child, son of Margaret Clifford and, possibly, Lord John Clifford. Missing, presumed dead

---

[1] Lady Clifford had, in reality, died by 1470

Gawain Threlkeld	Lancelot Threlkeld's younger brother
Catherine Pawleyne	Sister to Gawain Threlkeld's wife
Sir Roger Clifford	Third son of Lord Thomas Clifford and younger brother of Robert Clifford
Lady Joan Clifford	Wife of Sir Roger Clifford and sister to John Courtenay, Earl of Devon
Sir Triston Clifford[2]	Fourth son of Lord Thomas Clifford. Robert Clifford's youngest brother. The only Clifford to support the house of York
Janet Prynne	Mother to Hal and Waryn FitzClifford (d.1459)
Master Prynne	Janet Prynne's father. Grandfather to Hal and Waryn FitzClifford (residing in Alnwick)
Babette Delaurin	Robert Clifford's mistress. Mother to Jean, Marguerite and Marie FitzClifford (residing in Bruges)
Dorcas	Hal FitzClifford's mistress. Mother to his sons (residing in Alnwick)

---

[2] Known to history as Sir Robert Clifford

LIST OF CHARACTERS

THE FITZCLIFFORDS – ILLEGITIMATE CHILDREN OF LORD JOHN OR ROBERT CLIFFORD – IN ORDER OF THEIR AGES

George

Acting Master-at-Arms to Harry Percy, Earl of Northumberland. Residing in the Percy household at Alnwick

Henry ('Hal')

Under-steward to Harry Percy, Earl of Northumberland. Residing in the Percy household at Alnwick

Waryn

Gentleman, residing in the Percy household at Alnwick

Aymer

Twin to Guy. Residing in Sir Roger Clifford's household in the North Country

Guy

Twin to Aymer. Residing in Sir Roger Clifford's household

Richie

Residing in Lady Clifford's household in the North Country

Bedivere ('Bede')

Residing in Lady Clifford's household

Edwin

Lay brother at Fountains Abbey in the North Country

Oliver

Residing with his mother's brother (a local esquire in the North Country)

Tom	Residing in Lady Clifford's household
Robbie	Residing in Sir Roger Clifford's household
Peter	Residing in Sir Roger Clifford's household
Jean	Residing with his mother, Babette Delaurin, in Bruges
Marguerite	Residing with her mother, Babette Delaurin, in Bruges
Marie	Residing with her mother, Babette Delaurin, in Bruges

ROBERT CLIFFORD'S HOUSEHOLD MEN (THE 'WYVERNS')

Sir Patrick Nield	Steward
Sir Cuthbert Bellingham ('Bell')	Marshal
Loic Moncler	Chamberlain
Sir Miles Randall	Former chamberlain (missing, presumed dead)
Sir Arthur Castor	Master-at-Arms
Walter Findern	Butler

LIST OF CHARACTERS

Sir Reginald Grey	Chaplain
Walter Grey	Almoner. Sir Reginald Grey's brother
Lewis Jolly	Gentleman
Bertrand Jansen	Dane, former mercenary
Leonard Tailboys	Gentleman
Jem Bodrugan	Robert Clifford's manservant
Benet Penwardine	Loic Moncler's manservant
Notch	Manservant to Aymer and Guy FitzClifford
Pleydell	Manservant to the younger FitzCliffords

ALICE DE VERE'S FAMILY AND INTIMATES

Alice de Vere

Only sister of Jack de Vere, 13th Earl of Oxford, brought up in the household of Richard Neville, Earl of Warwick, at Middleham, in the North Country

John ('Jack') de Vere, 13th Earl of Oxford

Second son of John de Vere, 12th Earl of Oxford (executed by the Yorkists, 1462). Younger brother of Aubrey de Vere (also executed 1462)

359

Margaret de Vere, Countess of Oxford	Wife of Jack de Vere; sister of Richard Neville, Earl of Warwick
William, Viscount Beaumont	Jack de Vere's closest friend
Elizabeth, Lady Ullerton	Senior gentlewoman to Alice de Vere
Blanche Carbery	Senior gentlewoman to Alice de Vere
Joanna Ames	Gentlewoman to Alice de Vere
Elyn	Natural daughter of John de Vere, 12th Earl of Oxford. Gentlewoman (and half-sister) to Alice de Vere
Constance	Natural daughter of Aubrey de Vere. Gentlewoman (and niece) to Alice de Vere
Mitten	Chamberwoman to Alice de Vere

EDMOND BEAUFORT, DUKE OF SOMERSET: FAMILY AND INTIMATES

Edmond Beaufort, 4th Duke of Somerset	Second son of Edmond Beaufort, 2nd Duke of Somerset (killed by the Yorkists, 1455). Leader of the Lancastrian faction; in exile in Bruges

John ('Jonkin') Beaufort, Earl of Dorset	Youngest son of Edmond Beaufort, 2nd Duke of Somerset and younger brother of Edmond Beaufort, 4th Duke of Somerset; in exile in Bruges
Sir Gabriel Appledore	Steward
Sir Andrew Chowne	Chamberlain
Sir Humphrey Audley	Gentleman
James Delves	Gentleman

LANCASTRIANS: NOBLES, SYMPATHISERS AND ADHERENTS

John Courtenay, Earl of Devon	Lancastrian in exile in Bruges. Robert Clifford's closest friend
Laura Courtenay, Countess of Devon	Wife of John Courtenay, Earl of Devon. Daughter of Henry Bourchier, Earl of Essex (Yorkist supporter)
Henry Holland, Duke of Exeter	Lancastrian in exile in Bruges. Married to, but estranged from, Edward of York's sister Anne

King Henry (known to the Yorkists as 'Henry of Lancaster')	Henry VI; Lancastrian king of England overthrown by Edward of York in 1461; a prisoner in the Tower of London
Queen Margaret	Daughter of the Duke of Anjou. Wife of Henry VI; an exile in France
Prince Edward of Lancaster	Only child of Henry VI and Queen Margaret; an exile in France
Jasper Tudor, Earl of Pembroke	Half-brother of Henry VI
Henry Tudor, Earl of Richmond	Young nephew of Jasper Tudor and of Henry VI. Son of Edmond Beaufort's cousin Margaret Beaufort. Residing in Raglan Castle, Monmouthshire
King Louis	Louis XI, King of France. Cousin of Queen Margaret. Lancastrian supporter
Pierre du Chastel	Agent of King Louis
Sir Lawrence Welford	Old friend and companion-in-arms to Robert Clifford, residing at Dyffryn Hall, Monmouthshire
Cecily Welford	Daughter of Lawrence Welford, residing at Dyffryn Hall

LIST OF CHARACTERS

YORKISTS: NOBLES, SYMPATHISERS AND ADHERENTS

Edward of York (recognised by the Yorkists as 'King Edward')	Edward IV; Yorkist King of England. Overthrew the Lancastrian dynasty and seized the throne in 1461 with the help of his cousin, Richard Neville, Earl of Warwick. Elder brother of Edmund, Earl of Rutland (who was killed at Wakefield by Lord John and Robert Clifford, 1460) and of George, Duke of Clarence and Richard, Duke of Gloucester
Margaret, Duchess of Burgundy	Wife of Charles, Duke of Burgundy – the ruler of Flanders - and sister of Edward of York
Richard, Duke of Gloucester	Youngest brother of Edward of York, brought up in the household of the Earl of Warwick at Middleham
Sir Roger Vaughan	Yorkist adherent. Executed Owen Tudor, father of Jasper Tudor and grandfather of Henry Tudor, after the battle of Mortimer's Cross in 1461.

THE CONFLICTED

Richard Neville, Earl of Warwick	Prominent Yorkist who overthrew Henry VI to raise his young cousin Edward of York to the throne in 1461, and subsequently rebelled against Edward in an attempt to restore Henry VI to the throne
The Countess of Warwick	Wife to Richard Neville, Earl of Warwick

Anne Neville	Younger daughter of Richard Neville, Earl of Warwick; friend of Alice de Vere
John Neville	Younger brother of Richard Neville. The Earl of Northumberland, until Harry Percy's recent rehabilitation
George, Duke of Clarence	Younger brother of Edward of York, brought up in the household of the Earl of Warwick at Middleham. Aided Warwick's rebellion; married to Warwick's elder daughter Isabel
Isabel, Duchess of Clarence	Elder daughter of Richard Neville, Earl of Warwick. Recently married to George Duke of Clarence
Sir Hugh Dacre	Household knight of Richard Neville, Earl of Warwick. Suitor of Blanche Carbery (Alice de Vere's gentlewoman)
John, Lord Wenlock	Adherent of Richard Neville, Earl of Warwick
Henry ('Harry') Percy, Earl of Northumberland	Scion of one of the foremost Lancastrian families, whose father and grandfather were killed fighting against the house of York. Spent his youth in captivity; recently restored to his earldom by Edward of York and residing in Alnwick Castle, Northumberland
Lady Eleanor Percy	Sister of Harry Percy, Earl of Northumberland. Residing in Alnwick Castle

Marjorie Verrier	Senior gentlewoman to Eleanor Percy, residing in Alnwick Castle
Kit Loys	Page to Harry Percy, residing in Alnwick Castle. Son of Sir Simon Loys
Sir Simon Loys	North Country knight. Previously an adherent of the Earl of Warwick
Sir James Thwaite	Adherent of Harry Percy, brought up in the Percy household at Alnwick Castle
Anna Murrow (née Thwaite)	Widow. Sister to Sir James Thwaite
Lady Catherine, Countess of Shrewsbury	Daughter of the Duke of Buckingham and wife of John, Earl of Shrewsbury, sometime Lancastrian supporter, residing at Goodrich Castle, Monmouthshire. Lady Catherine's sister Anne Stafford was married to Aubrey de Vere
Charles, Duke of Burgundy	Ruler of Flanders, host to the exiled Lancastrians in Bruges, married to Margaret, the sister of Edward of York
Lord Philippe Woodhuysen	Nobleman of the court of Flanders
Lady Isabeau Woodhuysen	Wife of Philippe Woodhuysen

Acknowledgements

I read very widely in researching this series, but I'm particularly grateful for the work of the wonderful historians Charles Ross, Helen Castor, Susan Rose and James Ross.

I would also like to thank Mark Ecob at Mecob, for his excellent cover and ideas for the rest of the series, Anthony Harvison at Palamedes PR, for his help in promoting the books and Dean Fetzer at GunBoss Books for his great design of the interior.

Sophy Boyle
London, 2016

ABOUT THE AUTHOR

Sophy Boyle studied History at Oxford University and then worked in the City for many years. She gave up her legal career to write the *Wyvern and Star* series. She lives in South London.

Wyvern and Star is the first in a series of novels following the exploits of Robert Clifford, Alice de Vere and their circles. Robert and Alice are fictional characters, and their immediate families have been trimmed and shaped to accommodate them. The historical background has been left, where at all possible, untouched.

The next book, *Jewels Beyond Price*, will follow in 2017.

To keep up to date with the Wyvern and Star series and to be notified when the next book is coming out, visit

www.wyvernandstar.com

19760592R00208

Printed in Great Britain
by Amazon